Ann Oakley

is a sociologist and writer. She directs a London University research unit which carries out educational and health research.

Her other books include *The Sociology of Housework,* which helped to establish housework as a legitimate area of study; *From Here to Maternity,* which charts women's experience of first-time motherhood; *The Captured Womb,* a history of medical care for women; *Taking It Like a Woman,* an auto-biography; and three novels, *The Men's Room,* which was adapted into a major BBC television series, *Matilda's Mistake* and *Scenes Originating in the Garden of Eden.*

Ann Oakley lives in London.

ANN OAKLEY

The Secret Lives
of Eleanor Jenkinson

Flamingo
An Imprint of HarperCollins*Publishers*

Flamingo
An Imprint of HarperCollins*Publishers*
77–85 Fulham Palace Road,
Hammersmith, London W6 8JB

Published by Flamingo 1993

9 8 7 6 5 4 3 2 1

First published in Great Britain by
HarperCollins*Publishers* 1992

Copyright © Ann Oakley 1992

The Author asserts the moral right to be
identified as the author of this work

ISBN 0 00 654550 5

Set in Galliard

Printed and bound in Great Britain by
HarperCollinsManufacturing, Glasgow

IN MEMORY OF EMMA

Contents

ONE

Memoirs of a Prudish Housewife

IN MID-AUGUST 1990, Eleanor Jenkinson and her husband, David, drive in their old sepia Volvo through Normandy on their way to somewhere in the south-east of France. It is a vaporous, slightly frantic morning. Rain clouds bustle in the sky like the swollen bellies of the Caen boats, now emptying themselves nauseously on to the ribbon-like roads. Determined holidaymakers, fatigued from their rakish night of travelling, perform a metallic jostle through the different, respectful order of the battlefields: the lines of gravestones are whiter, calmer than the sky. Inside the tourist cars, querulous conversations about misplaced directions and crushed sandwiches ought to pale into insignificance beside the roadside signs describing this as the location of more important contentions – but do not.

Looking sideways through the open window, Eleanor Jenkinson is struck by the image of an old man loading a bucket of potatoes into his car. A slow rhythm. Impossible to tell if it's the pain of arthritis or simply rural languor. She stretches her legs under the dashboard, feeling cramped from a night in the tiny cabin on the boat. 'All right, darling?' David Jenkinson's sensitivity to Eleanor's changes of mood and position is part of his definition of a holiday. In other words, it's not what normally happens back home in Sussex.

'Yes, fine.' She would have said that anyway. Ahead, two spires dance against the sky; they have holes in them like a garlic jar. 'What's that?'

'Alençon cathedral. Or Sées. No, Sées, we haven't got as far as Alençon yet.' David has the map carefully positioned between them, with the roads they will take highlighted in yellow. 'I thought we'd stop at Château-du-Loir for lunch. There's a two-star there. Speciality:

truite de mer à la crème d'ail.' His accent is irreproachable: Francophile French.

Eleanor nods. David feels rather than sees her acquiescence. After twenty-five years he hardly needs to look.

The Jenkinsons drive on through the fields, past the Peugeots and the Renaults and the BMWs, past the swaying, bulky caravans. David has arranged for a special overtaking mirror to be fixed to the car. He's good at that sort of thing. He's good at overtaking as well; for him it's a sort of athletic feat. Eleanor just lets him get on with it.

As they pause at some traffic lights, David takes one hand off the steering wheel, and pats Eleanor's knee. 'Let's celebrate today, my love. Our first holiday *tous les deux* for – how long? That's worth celebrating, isn't it, whatever else happens?'

Eleanor thinks, excavating the layers of remembered biological, social, domestic time. 'Before Heidi. We went to Tuscany, camping.'

They both recall the camp site, effluent clusters of blue and orange tents planted under the trees, with the river almost stationary in the crisp gold light. But the two of them remember different things. David Jenkinson sees himself with a stomach as straight as a plank and hair luxuriant as the Tuscan foliage – an altogether younger and more virile person, manning their little canvas home as Eleanor, for whom he felt such a suitable but intense passion, stands there like a pubescent elf in her pink bikini, amidst the cooking pots. She was both right and different, all he would ever have hoped for, had he been the least bit conscious of the hopes he had. 'It was the seven hundred and fiftieth anniversary of the Magna Carta,' he says, being a historian. '"*Nullus liber homo capiatur* . . . " I remember there was a thanksgiving service at Saint Paul's the day we left England.'

Eleanor Jenkinson, elflike then and now, also sees the two of them beneath the trees, but, while she remembers the tyranny of the cooking pots and David's passion, she can see something else in the dark orange interior of the tent – her notebooks, looking at her casually from a focused pool of light. 'My Novel,' she murmurs. 'I started it there.'

'So you did.'

'It had a different title, then.'

'Didn't we all?' he jokes.

'I'm not sure that's funny.'

He looks at her for a change. 'I'm sorry.'

She says nothing. But in the coolness of the air-conditioned car steadily pursuing the yellow-highlighted route, allows herself to wander back, directionless, through the years of half-remembered and differently lived time.

How had she been, then? More than half her life ago. Had she been happy? What did she want? She and David – how had they been together? Strange to think that people's bodies stay more or less the same through decades of experience, though of course they don't, as their cells must form and reform countless times, and for women there are the sieges of childbearing, like ice ages eroding the contours of the body's physical continent. Eleanor Jenkinson then and Eleanor Jenkinson now; if you put them side by side, one would wrinkle and droop and carry a pretend wisdom in her eyes and more filled and unfilled cavities in her teeth, but she'd only be a version of the innocent upright dentally intact Eleanor Jenkinson. Who exists not only in her own image, but in others. David has his own memory. There are the photographs her children have seen. Heidi, aged five: 'But where was I then?'/ 'You weren't anywhere. You weren't born.'/ 'But I must have been *somewhere*!' The impossibility of grasping the contingency of one's own existence – dependent on the unreliable modalities of time and parental behaviour. Incredible to think one might simply never have been at all.

There might also be others from the camp site in Tuscany who can remember Eleanor Jenkinson and her family. There *were* two girls from Liverpool over the far side by the pool – what were their names? Eleanor searches her head for clues. One was dark-haired and long-legged and full of energy. Eleanor had caught David looking at her once, stripped to an emerald bikini on a rug beneath the electric globe of the Italian sun. 'Do you fancy her, then?' she'd asked, only half-seriously.

'What?' He'd turned to look at her, and it wasn't her imagination that he flushed slightly.

'Of course not!'

'Don't protest, I don't mind!' She didn't, actually. She'd always thought a man who wasn't attracted to other women couldn't really be interested in women at all.

Patsy, that was it! And her friend, a short plump girl in canvas shorts – Maria. She wore a crucifix; it glinted in the sun. But she never lay half naked for David to lust after the hidden luxuries of her flesh.

The more you think back, the more you remember. Cushioned

within the Volvo's interior somewhere approaching the town David has selected for lunch, Eleanor recalls a distinct feeling of apprehension back there in Tuscany next to Patsy and Maria in 1963. Had marrying David been the right thing to have done? What about her writing?

The notebooks reappear, brighter now in the midday sun. Eleanor has always written in the same sort of notebook, a perfectly ordinary stationers' brand, that says 'Student Notebook Ref. 141. Punched for filing' in a white strip at the bottom of the glossy orange-red cover. And much of her writing, certainly there in Tuscany at the beginning, has been about this woman called Esther Gray.

Esther Gray is strong and brave. Esther Gray is beautiful and together. And as she has materialized over the years, Esther Gray has even spoken to Eleanor of Eleanor's own predicament. Esther has become a commentator, an analyst, Eleanor's harshest critic and best friend rolled into one. A kind of alter ego.

Extract from:

ESTHER'S VIRTUE
BY ELEANOR JENKINSON

Looking back, Esther could see how the whole of her life had been a mistake. Dick had never loved her, she had never been happy with him. There had been no free will, they had only been ciphers in someone else's code. It's wrong to suppose one has a choice. For the construction of one's destiny as a matter over which there is control is the problem at the heart of it all; the responsibility that has to be taken for what happens, but yet is not there to take, as it exists only in the imagination. She would never, of course, have attempted to say this to him. Dick would not have understood what she was trying to say, he would only have felt it as rejection. He couldn't see what she could – that time and place had thrown them together, had given them the superficial appearance of a happy couple, while underneath, at heart, each remained both solitary and different. It was almost as though it wasn't about love at all. The embraces of their marriage were no more about love than the habits of those who walk with their hands in their pockets, or touch wood whenever they say something that frightens them.

'Dick,' she said one day instead, 'have I made you happy?'

When he turned to look at her (they were in the summerhouse with a tray of lemon tea), his face wore a totally bemused look. 'What a strange question, Esther,' he said. 'Whatever made you ask it?'

There you are, she thought to herself, anything in this line of questioning will only get you into trouble. 'But have I?' she insisted. Looking past the open door, she could see the neighbours' white cat behind the cherry tree. It appeared to wink at her conspiratorially. Dick poured himself another cup of tea. He held the cup delicately, like a woman. 'Of course you have. Why else would I have married you? It's a silly question. I suppose you've been talking to Eva again. That woman's a corrupting influence!'

The cat slipped away from behind the tree, and the wood pigeon took off into the copse of oaks beyond the rape field. 'Maybe,' said Esther.

David slips a tape of Mozart piano sonatas into the radio cassette player. Eleanor notices that he doesn't ask her what she'd like. 'This all right?' he queries eventually. 'We can have something else if you want. You might even find John Denver in the glove compartment.' He laughs gently, looks at her quickly. 'You see, my love, I'm trying to think of everything! I want to make you happy, whatever you think!'

Sometimes she wishes she could stop thinking about things the way he evidently does. 'When we stop for lunch I'd like to call Georgie,' she says. The Jenkinsons' eight-year-old son, George, is staying with friends.

'You don't need to, you know, he'll be fine.'

'I know. But I said I'd call. I'll feel better when I have.'

'Don't worry, old girl, of course you can phone.'

In the telephone box Joy Mitchell, George's friend's mother, says the boys are out flying their kites on the heath with her husband Bill. Joy reassures her that George is fine, wondering why Eleanor's not more relaxed about a third child. Eleanor herself wonders that sometimes. Perhaps it's because she knows she hasn't been an easy mother for George to have.

She goes to the *toilette* and washes her face and hands. The face that looks back at her from the enamelled mirror could do with a good night's sleep. Back in the restaurant, David is reading the menu with all the attention he would give a seventeenth-century archive. But Eleanor wants to get the meal over, and be on their way. For her a journey is a journey, it can never be a time of relaxation as well. She's anxious to find the place where they'll be, to set up a temporary identification with it. To be at peace, she must know where she is, what kind of bed she'll lay her head on at night, how to orient herself in the darkness, what can be expected in the way of food and warmth and freedom from insects and undesirable memories.

Her eagerness to be on their way is responsible for a certain tension during the meal. David would put it like that, but Eleanor would blame the tension on his wanting to dawdle over and waste money on the kind of meal they could do without and he certainly should – given the size of his stomach which, unkindly, she sometimes compares to Georgie's water bombs: she'd found one on the fruit dish the day they'd left, a green balloon, shaped like an aubergine with a nipple on it, bloated with water and pushed up against an overripe banana.

The clock on the town hall in Château-du-Loir is striking three when the Jenkinsons get back into their car. They drive for another five hours through the Loire to the house they've rented for the summer in the Cère valley. It's a mile from the nearest hamlet, which is itself composed of nothing more than a small church, a muddle of houses, chickens and geraniums. The inhabitants stare with eyes as blue as their shirts and aprons as the Jenkinsons' Volvo pauses, turns, and turns again up the steep inclement route to the house.

The farmer and his wife are waiting to show them around: the gravelled lap in front of the house, with a view over grazing amber charantais cows; the field of cornflowers to the right stretching to a line of brilliant green trees behind which, imagines Eleanor, there is a dankly oozing river; inside, and most proudly, the old Quercy kitchen with the blackened, disused range in the cavernous fireplace now supplanted by the bottled gas, and the cooker, lacking, as usual, a grill. There is a small fridge. A wire poking out of the wall is not to be touched. The Dupannes repeat this, several times. Madame Dupanne is proud of the washing line and directs Eleanor's attention to the cold water tap in the field. Eleanor, too tired to ask its purpose, is then taken by Madame Dupanne for a manual test of the deep mattress on the double bed, which descends when pressed and only slowly recovers, like punched oedematous flesh. The whole of this recitation is washed down with glasses of wine from a dark unlabelled bottle, the Jenkinsons sitting one side of a wooden kitchen table loose-limbed and fatigued by their travels, the Dupannes ordered and upright on the other side. The two couples exchange pleasantries mixed with snippets of information in a stilted or shouted French. The Dupannes have a grown-up son who runs a machine tool shop in Montpellier. Will he come back to take over the farm? The Dupannes shake their heads sadly: Jean-Pierre likes the town life. But a daughter, Madeleine, is already married to a farmer and the mother of twins.

When the Dupannes have gone, the Jenkinsons unpack and get into the high bed, which creaks – no, clatters – every time one of them moves. Round the wooden shutters, there is a pencil line of full moon light. Eleanor lies for a long time in the dark, too tense from the journey to sleep. She feels that outside the shutters the natural world is alive, there are creatures stepping through the cornflowers and the cowpats in the bright white light. David's breathing is loud in the silence of the old house.

In the morning he says he's going into the town to buy some food, and a supply of maps and train timetables and tourist brochures with which to occupy himself while Eleanor, as usual, writes. But first he must set her up a table in the garden where she will be able to sit with her notebooks, not too much in the shade, nor too unshielded from the sun, being careful of the thorns and prickles in the grass – 'Better keep your shoes on, dear.' He fetches a chair and a blanket to drape on it, and a parasol and a thermos of coffee. Is this the view she would like? Or that one? Finally he goes, and she is alone. Deliberately, she moves the table from where he put it, so that her eyes may find a path through the trees which is not the one he chose for her. She sits, puts her feet on the crumbling stone wall, being careful to avoid crushing the ivy growing among the stones. Cows graze before her eyes. Corn bends to a wind from the east. The wind is warm and refreshing, fanning both her face and her memory.

Eleanor Kendrick's desire to be a writer was almost the first piece of information about herself she gave David Jenkinson when they had their first proper conversation in a smoky wine bar at the back of Regent Street. Eleanor had been twenty-two at the time; with a degree in English behind her, she was working for a publisher's. David had just come back from a trip to India with friends, one of whom was Indian and had undergone an arranged marriage in Kashmir; as a consequence David wore, along with his suntan, a look of determination regarding the arrangement of his own marriage, for which he felt the time had definitely come. Eleanor's pixie-like face, minute and fragile above the very large wine glass – reminiscent in its luminosity of the Bubbles painting – conveyed to him precisely the right mixture of vulnerability and assertiveness. 'I want to be a writer,' she had said – well, what could be plainer than that? David certainly heard it, but what he made of it neither of them was quite sure.

From Eleanor's point of view, to know what she wanted was a great deal easier than understanding why. For this we must go further back, past Eleanor Kendrick's plain speaking about her creative ambition to David Jenkinson in the wine bar, back to the beginning of it all, in fact to the beginning of Eleanor Jenkinson herself.

The time is fifty years before the journey to the Dupannes' French house, the place Tunbridge Wells, where Mrs Bridget Kendrick gave birth to her second daughter in a small, expensive nursing home. Bombs were falling at the time, though not in Tunbridge Wells, which was soon to be occupied with a billeting scandal. The well-to-do, including the Kendricks – Bridget's nerves would never stand it – were balking at taking evacuees into their homes; other infamous local refusniks were the bank manager, the vicar, and the chief billeting officer himself.

Charles Kendrick was at his office in the City when his wife gave birth, being in a reserved occupation – accountancy – which was a good foil for his cowardice concerning the rigours both of war and other kinds. He liked children more than his wife did, but that was all right because the upper classes send their children away to school, thus avoiding the whole problem of what a good mother is anyway. The Kendricks' eldest, another daughter, Celia, was already conjugating Latin verbs on her sister's birthday in a second expensive institution, a convent boarding school in Northamptonshire.

Celia had been a planned child in the sense that the Kendricks had thought they ought to become parents as most people do – parenthood being some vague mark of adulthood. But after Celia, and especially when she went off to the Sisters of Mercy at seven,

Bridget Kendrick's life had settled into a congenially busy pattern of social relations based on the village where they lived, Muddenham, five miles from Tunbridge Wells. The social busyness was combined with charity work for disabled horses and spastic children; she was an avid gardener too. In short, she was taxed to the full, which wasn't very far. In the Kendricks' everyday conjugal life, sexual relations took second place to the social kind, thereby reducing the chances of further children. Naturally Charles Kendrick fucked other women from time to time, but none of it meant very much, except sometimes to them. If ever Charles sensed the imminent engagement of female affections, he cancelled the liaison, usually with a large bouquet of spiked flowers and a note judiciously composed in his fine italic handwriting. For her part, Bridget had the occasional fantasy featuring equine genitals, but was, on the whole, morally disengaged from sex. She thought of it as an odd thing to do; and even odder was the notion her body and mind had once or twice registered that copulation might be as enjoyable as any equestrian activity.

Eleanor's conception had thus come as something of a surprise. Charles had blamed it on the war, which wrenched from him an admission of his own mortality that in turn made connections with others, including his wife, a little more imperative than they seemed in peacetime. For a while Bridget denied the pregnancy, even retiring to a health farm in an effort to lose weight, and get away from Charles' military carnality. But no amount of carrot juice could defeat the embryonic Eleanor's own engagement with life. The day she was born, Charles booked another place for her with the Sisters of Mercy. By the time she went, Celia would have left, for there were twelve years between the sisters. That took care of the schooling. The childrearing was equally easy: Bridget Kendrick's old nanny, who was called Somerset because that was where she originated, had been retained after Celia's departure for general menagerial duties and to cover the long school holidays. So it was Somerset whose role it was to look after the infant Eleanor. It was Somerset who measured out Eleanor's National Dried Milk, spooning it generously out of the large blue and white tins, and Somerset who picked up the bottles of thick, livid orange juice from the clinic. Bridget liked it in her gin, but Somerset was sufficiently devoted to the nursery to keep one a week back.

Aside from this, Somerset's saving grace as a childrearer was that she talked. She talked endlessly to Eleanor, though not always of topics suitable for a child's ear. It would be about the population of Muddenham village that she talked, about how Mr Dixon-Joyce was often seen coming out of Mrs Sabina Morris's cottage at night, about how the new people down Marigold Lane had raucous theatrical parties and statues of nude women and urinating gnomes in their garden; or instead she would regale little Eleanor with stories of her multifarious visits to Dr Leakey, who helped so little with all the mysterious pains that plagued her that Eleanor, in her infant wisdom, quickly grasped that the point of going was not to be cured but to continue to enjoy whatever illness was on the agenda at the time. Somerset was comfortably round, and wore dull, usually apron-covered clothes, as nannies are supposed to. She was always there, and, although she talked, she rarely had anything original to say. This was one of the many ways in which her total predictability caused a restlessness in little Eleanor, who ached inchoately, through what seemed in retrospect the never-ending half-dawn of her childhood, for something to happen.

When Eleanor was three, Bridget Kendrick, who had resumed her normal life after she was born, won a national prize for the huge velvet softness of her crimson Christmas roses, bred in the Muddenham conservatory with rather more care than she could drum up for her daughters. Eleanor had gone with Somerset to the gardening event at which her mother was awarded the prize; the sky had been full of hats, women fussed in the heat, and an escaped dachshund threaded itself like a black oil slick through the nylon-legged crowd, frightening Eleanor with its yapping, treacly look. She remembered the event for impressing on her an abhorrence at its emptiness of meaning – it was a life she definitely didn't want to live.

But in many ways Eleanor thrived under this regime, as most human infants easily defeat the destructive traps parents set for them. (Child psychologists give the opposite impression, but that's their job.) She was a tiny child. Exceptionally small framed, and reluctant to reach the average line on the child development charts coming into vogue among paediatricians at the time. Somerset fed Eleanor cakes and chocolate, every fattening food in sight, but the child gnawed indomitably on bits of apple, carrot and celery, and would eat sparingly from the thickly garnished plates of nursery food presented to her, whatever was on them. Over their own cocktails and canapés, Charles and Bridget would get out the photographs of Celia at the same age and profess a degree of concern, but, with the help of a doctor friend, and Bridget's recalling an aunt of hers who had also been appallingly thin, they quickly turned this into a theory about the quirks of heredity and man's impotence in the face of genetic imprinting. Anorexia hadn't been invented at the time, and in any case Eleanor was too young to have thought of it.

And so Eleanor had grown, though at her own pace. The billeting scandal passed, the war ended, her father continued making money in the City and her mother went on making charity committee meetings and gardening events. Somerset, who was fairly old at the beginning of this saga, grew even older. Eleanor's sister Celia came home for the holidays, but was bossy and usually had a friend with her. Eleanor admired Celia, though from a distance. Celia was tall and well-developed for her age, and was remembered by Eleanor running through the garden in her jodhpurs, adolescent breasts popping up and down in the yellow riding shirt, shouting to her friend Caroline, or Rosemary, or Sophia, something about the horses Banbury and Lettuce, or else about irreligious school liaisons between Sisters of Mercy who were not, later on replaced by ribald accounts of boys glimpsed at bus stops or briefly experienced propping up the postered fabric of Muddenham Village Hall.

When Eleanor was six, Celia went to Paris to do a course at the Sorbonne. She came home even less after that. There were postcards, usually of Paris at night. Celia seemed to forget that Eleanor already had a number of the Eiffel Tower, glossily illuminated.

Although Eleanor did well enough in these early circumstances, she did suffer from their emotional inhospitality. Her soul, inadequately nourished, learnt to set down its roots in another soil – the world of books. By the time Eleanor was four, she could read fluently. The necessity for this was absolute, as no-one had the time or inclination to read to her. How else would she have known that the Eiffel Tower was the Eiffel Tower, or that her sister Celia had inscribed the back of those postcards to her? Apart from postcards, Eleanor read novels, travel books, cookery books, tracts on accountancy and Eastern mysticism, her mother's horticultural compendia, even the mail order catalogues that Somerset pored over in the long winter evenings as she sat in the wooden rocking chair by the fireplace in the nursery sitting room, the red lampshade giving her sparse white hair the unlikely glint of pink champagne.

Among the books available to the young Eleanor Kendrick was a small tract entitled *Home Nursing* that Somerset kept on a shelf in the nursery. This particularly captured Eleanor's attention, as it had some horrible pictures in it of bedpans and things called bed cradles erected over apparently disembodied legs, and of bandages with arrows on indicating the direction in which they were to be wound on to limbs, like a prisoner's uniform, and words like 'sputum' and 'costiveness' and 'enema', and generally rather a lot about something called The Bowels. The attraction of the book was its size – just right for Eleanor's little hands. Somerset would chide her for looking at it, and wouldn't answer any of her questions about The Bowels, which merely incited Eleanor to read on in the hope of being enlightened.

Next to *Home Nursing* was another quite different small book. Somerset was cagey about its origins – she said it'd been given her by a gentleman she'd once known. It was called *The Mysteries of Marseilles* and it was by someone called Emile Zola, whom Eleanor assumed for a long time to be female. A picture at the front of a woman in a long white apron clutching a child, and a man bursting through the door with a gun – the caption was 'Before she had time to shut herself in he sprang upon her' – especially aroused Eleanor's imagination. The notion of the man springing upon the woman sounded a bit like a tiger, and caused Eleanor to wonder about the nature of men. This made her want to clutch at Somerset. The text of *The Mysteries of Marseilles* was less easy to grasp, but Eleanor could manage the first scene, in which someone called Philippe aged about thirty in May 184– (couldn't this Emile person have worked out the year?) met someone called Blanche who despite her name was rosy, and 'yielded herself to the embrace of him she adored'. Eleanor went round repeating the sentence to herself, fascinated by its sound, and trying to make it compatible with the idea of men being tigers.

From the age of five or six, then, Eleanor had formed the habit of picking up any book and studying it with the rapt expectation that it would feed her soul more than her ordinary environment did. The hieroglyphic arrangement of black characters on the white page was simply the most promising emotional lexicon available to her; it was the code she had to break in order to gain that understanding of the world that for other children in ordinarily sociable households comes in a package, along with parent–child or sibling relationships, conversations over breakfast, walks in the park, or summer holidays by the sea. She read books in order to find out about the world, but did, of course, only succeed in finding out about the world of books. She read children's books, too, when they were available to her, but no-one particularly tried to make them so. Somerset once persuaded Bridget to buy a box of second-hand children's books at a village jumble sale for spastic children. Eleanor watched the box being unloaded from the car along with some white azalea seedlings. Her little hands sank hungrily into its depths; her first find, a pink paperback called *The Family from One End Street*, proved to be a romantic caricature of working-class family life, in which Eleanor was soon lost, envying the children their siblingship, even their social deprivation, which seemed to induce in them a direct communication of a kind absent from life in Muddenham. When Peg, helping her mother with other people's laundry, burnt a pink silk petticoat through setting the iron at too high a temperature, Eleanor wept with shame for her, and with pity for herself that in her own existence she was denied such opportunities.

But the boxed treasures contained narratives of social privilege as well; Rudyard Kipling's *Puck of Pook's Hill* (Eleanor considered this a rather rude title) opened with a picnic of hardboiled eggs, Bath Oliver biscuits and salt in an envelope, as the children, Dan, Nick and Una, went down to a local meadow called The Long Slip to rehearse a Shakespeare play. They seemed remarkably free to romp around with knights and lords and centurions and swords and suchlike, and only occasionally did Father or Mother fuss about what they were doing. In fact, Father and Mother seemed a lot less real than Puck. In Eleanor's mind, Somerset and Puck shared a similar authority. But Puck's permissiveness would have shocked Somerset, who took the view that children should be constantly *occupied* to keep the feverish power of their little imaginations at bay. For Somerset, the child's mind was no *tabula rasa*; all sorts of devils and witches dwelt there, it was a breeding ground of black magic, against which the devices of practical common sense and hard work were the only medicine.

Charles and Bridget Kendrick noted their younger daughter's habit of perpetual reading – the fact that her face was usually turned to fiction and away from fact. But they merely congratulated themselves that Eleanor had found her own answer to the problem of her social isolation before the Sisters of Mercy could be asked to do so. Social convention prevented Eleanor from being sent to the village school.

Instead, walking past it with Somerset on their way to purchase items at the village shop, or simply for the daily airing Somerset believed essential to health, Eleanor would see the children in the school playground and envy them, like *The Family from One End Street*, their easy sociability with one another. She wanted to be in there with them, inside the wire netting, enjoying the sense of enclosure, of territory set aside for children's games and noise and roughness, of a place consigned to the business of being a child with other children.

Fed by reading, fertilized by exclusion, the young Eleanor Kendrick's imagination soon demanded another outlet. So it was that Eleanor Kendrick, alias Eleanor Jenkinson, first conceived her desire to be a writer. The village shop hosted a pile of thin grey-blue exercise books carrying the logo of a thick blue crenellated pencil poised mid-word. Eleanor persuaded Somerset to buy her one, but this was only the beginning. She filled the notebooks with uncompleted one-page stories, the main characters permanently caught in the time warp between infant scribble and a future of maturely limitless possibilities. Princesses, naturally, fairies, kings and queens – but most of all secure nuclear families in little houses with little gardens on a scale not quite so forbidding as that of the Kendricks' own. Muddenham Grange, built originally in the sixteenth century, stood on the edge of the village, looking over at it like a bushy dark eyebrow, its beams and mullioned window panes thickly wrapped in medieval oak trees. There were ten bedrooms. Charles had one as his study and one functioned as the nursery sitting room; but otherwise the upper floors were like an art gallery, as Charles Kendrick collected paintings when he had nothing else to do. But literature came to the rescue of life once more for Eleanor, as in the box forested from the jumble sale was Frances Hodgson Burnett's *The Secret Garden*, which was happily able to bestow for her a much more personal meaning on the grounds of Muddenham Grange: there might, with luck, be a part of it somewhere that was walled and locked, in which a prince in the pale misshapen form of Colin lurked pathetically among the other saplings to give her life a purpose by demanding something particular of her. It was this conventional usefulness of which the young Eleanor first repetitively wrote, cancelling her feeling of being different from other children by enclosing it in the formula of the happy marriage, the cosy family, the little house, the is-there-honey-still-for-tea nostalgia of those for whom families are metaphoric havens from everything nasty.

To write was to feel ordinary, to provide oneself with a chosen, comfortable script. But it was also in its very act extraordinary. Words! The magic they held, the entrapment of the formulation on the previously empty page, the willed, idiosyncratic, beautiful occupation of clean, white space. The concrete power of the full stop, the wonderful, fluttering hesitation of the comma, the musical pause of the semi-colon; the extraordinary possibilities of the parenthesis (to read or not to read, that is the question), the exclamation mark like a lamppost shining excitedly at the words behind it lined up there like a row of incontinent dogs! The paragraph break – the exhalation and then inhalation marking the transition from past to future. Quotation marks like curlers in the hair, or incense sticks burning to transform the atmosphere! For someone like Eleanor whose early life has bestowed on them a feeling of incurable impotence, there's simply nothing to equal writing for creating the empowering perception that one is, after all, behind life's great steering wheel.

But back to Eleanor in Muddenham Grange before she went to school. The Kendricks got someone, a part-time schoolteacher called Dr Brackenridge (though why he was called 'Dr' was never explained to Eleanor, who always suspected he was about to feed her nasty medicines as well as education), from the village to come in and train her in elementary maths and geography, and teach her the principles of grammar, spelling and so forth. Dr Brackenridge's greased hair was as black as Dickon's in *The Secret Garden*, or the hide of the escaped dachshund at the gardening event, but had no similar magical lustre to it. He had a mother he looked after, and Eleanor's lessons were planned round Mrs Brackenridge's toilet and culinary needs; indeed, Eleanor's lessons rested in a shopping basket alongside the nice bit of wensleydale, the half a pound of streaky, and the choice Granny Smiths for Mrs Brackenridge's tea. Had Eleanor liked Dr Brackenridge, she would have learnt more than she did, which was enough.

When she went at seven to the convent in Northamptonshire, Somerset took her on the train, with her trunk. Bridget waved goodbye from the conservatory with her hands resting in rows of salvia plants. Earlier Charles, on his way to the City, had pressed into Eleanor's small nervous hand an envelope containing ten pounds, and had told her to be brave, remembering the saltiness of his own childhood tears on the starched white sheets of a preparatory school dormitory.

She was on her own. Seven is, of course, far too early to be sent away to school. But for Eleanor the sense of isolation was really only more of the same, the lump that filled her throat those first nights in Dormitory Mary Magdalene not caused by the loss of her mother, whom she had never really had, but by that precise fact: that she was motherless. Who loved her, really? Somerset did, but the love of a servant, being waged, can hardly be as real as the other kind. To her parents, Eleanor was their child, but more in the technical sense of symbolizing their joint, unexpected fertility, a sort of extra stake in the future of the race. A symbol, that's what Eleanor principally was.

One day when she was nine, and sitting in the library at the Sisters of Mercy convent reading Hans Christian Andersen's *The Shoes of Fortune* in a pool of June sunlight, Sister Mary Rose came to see her and told her gently that she must go home, her father was ill. Looking up from the page in which the watchman goes back to the hospital to find his galoshes, Eleanor saw this serene figure in blue with the marbled face outlined in crisp white, backlit through the library window, making its announcement of doom, and thought perhaps she was having a bad dream, the good and the bad in the fairy story had got themselves mixed up in a kind of satanic fancy dress party.

'What do you mean, ill?'

'He's in hospital, child.' Eleanor sees Charles with the watchman and the galoshes. 'Your mother says you must go and see him. She's coming to fetch you herself at eleven.'

Her mother coming to fetch her? Always before it had been Somerset, hunched in her brown coat like one of the oak trees that fenced Muddenham Grange.

And so Bridget Kendrick came, fussing, confused by suddenly having too much to do and so much in need of consolation herself that she had no spare energy with which to comfort Eleanor. Charles Kendrick was in hospital in Tunbridge Wells, not far from the nursing home in which both Celia and Eleanor had been born. He lay in a long ward of ill people, their faces as white as the sterilized sheets. He had a tumour on his spine that had quite suddenly grown and paralysed him and rendered him incontinent. Even as Eleanor stood there with her mother, there was an explosion beneath the white counterpane and a smell of faeces hit the air. She felt herself go pink with shame.

Eleanor saw her father once more after that. By then he was in a room on his own, lying quite flat with his eyes closed. The blind on the window was down. Was he already dead? She stood silently by the bed, still small and thin, hardly there at all really. Charles opened his eyes and smiled at her, and then he died.

His death changed everything. Being unexpected, he himself had been unprepared for it in more ways than one. Although he'd made a good living in the City, most of his money transpired to be committed elsewhere, that is, in places other than those accessible to his wife. Even the pictures hung in Muddenham Grange turned out to be on loan from others. Charles had been speculating on a new marina in Cyprus. Much of his money had been used for the purchase of a flat in Piccadilly in the name of Susan Barrington, an actress with whom he'd formed a liaison some five years before. Susan Barrington came to the funeral, a stage-like figure as one would expect, slipping in black silk from its car and joining the mourners at the graveside just in time for the lowering of the coffin, in the manner of a Mafia movie. Susan Barrington lowered some tears into the grave as well, for Charles Kendrick had meant more to her than a flat in Piccadilly. He had been kind and sensitive, anchoring her moods with a deftness born of his long practice with Bridget. Who at the funeral saw her husband's mistress's figure flitting to the graveside, but with the inbred composure of the upper classes regarded her as no more than a ghost.

Unfortunately there turned out also to be a large mortgage on Muddenham Grange. The house had to be sold. Eleanor and her mother moved into the two bedroom red-brick gardener's cottage, whose only redeeming feature was horticultural – a tiny well-stocked garden, with a very pretty stream winding its way through it. Most of Eleanor's memories from the autumn of that first year after her father's death were of Bridget sitting on the wooden seat by the stream bemoaning the price of gin, as the foliage above and around switched into red and golden, and mahogany conkers ripened and rolled amongst dead leaves for Eleanor to find and polish and arrange in order of size on strings in her attic window, where they attracted particles of sunshine from time to time.

But Charles Kendrick's death wasn't altogether a negative event. For it confirmed Eleanor's place in the world of fiction by extending to her a status so many of the characters she'd so far encountered seemed to have. Though she – and others – resolutely believed the world to be full of intact, happy families, the message of children's fiction picked up by Eleanor was far from this: there are hardly any at all. Mary Lennox, for example, found the secret garden only because she was an orphan. Little Lord Fauntleroy had only a mother – and only became a Lord because all the men in his family were wiped out by one accident or another. (He had a Nurse, but this isn't really in compensation, for Nurses and Nannies – like Somerset – haunt rich dual parent families too.) Heidi, the little Swiss girl who lived up a mountain with the goats and Alm-Uncle, and drank endless bowls of frothy milk (though Peter, the goatherd, took his directly from the goat – shades of *Home Nursing* here), would have been spared this fate if her father hadn't been hit by a beam and her mother not been hit by hysteria on seeing the results of this. Even Katy and her six brothers and sisters in all the *Katy* books were without a mother, who'd died when the youngest was a baby. Then there was Emil (decidedly male this time) and Mrs Tischbein, who laundered women's hair in her front room, Mr Tischbein, a plumber, having passed on when Emil was five, leaving Emil to help his mother with all that shampooing. The list is endless. And redolent with suggestions, even, that nuclear families might not be havens of comfort but harbours of unrest. Eleanor was quite shocked when she first read *The Water Babies*, whose ranks Tom, the chimney sweep, joined (never having had a father, of course) when the fairies cleaned all that grime off him and shortened him to a length of exactly 3.87902 inches, like thousands of other water babies – all the little children who cruel mothers and fathers bring up as heathens or abuse or neglect or allow to fall into fires or catch measles and scarlatina, and on whom the good fairies lavish their attention, rendering them amphibious as a cure for parental nastiness. Not perhaps the most obvious solution. But at least Charles Kingsley allowed girls to be rescued as well as boys, thought Eleanor, who'd noted this was not the case in *Peter Pan*. Peter's Lost Boys – dropped (again) out of their perambulators by careless Nurses – don't consort with any Lost Girls: perhaps these aren't so easily dropped? Mind you, the Darling children, living in a conventional happy family, aren't treated much better – their nanny is a dog. And the children are allowed to fall out of the window, though Mr and Mrs Darling do seem to mind this, Mr Darling taking his reaction to extremes by living in the dog's kennel and being carried to business in it every morning.

In Eleanor Kendrick's real childhood, Somerset went back to Somerset when Charles died, as there wasn't enough money to keep her on, and this did cause Eleanor pain. She took out the grey-blue notebooks and inscribed a story of a happy family – not her own, nor those of the extraordinary literary representations she'd read – torn apart by death in a more conventional way. It helped to bury her own self-pity in a fictional saga of orphaned children thrown cruelly upon far greater seas of misfortune than Eleanor herself could claim – poverty of the One End Street kind, lives in perpetuity condemned to the laundering of others' petticoats or hair.

Eleanor was sent to the village school, but it was too late for her to redeem her childhood. The other children saw her as an upstart with insufficient physical presence to inspire respect – she remained small for her age, and with the lack of size went a surprising lack of agility: she wasn't even any good at games. She added handicap to handicap by spending much of her time at school mentally composing short psychodramas, later on passionately stylized poetry, which made her look as though she was dreaming, and was summarized in her school reports as displaying an obstinate and worrying lack of attention, the explanation of which in terms of her disturbed family circumstances would do only for a time.

During the said time, Celia came back from France, briefly, but there was nowhere for her to stay in the gardener's cottage, except in the dining room amongst the detritus of the rapidly greying family silver. The sisters, now aged ten and twenty-two, had little to say to one another. Bridget made up for this by having a lot to say to both of them. She was a wounded woman, highly resistant to the notion that through no fault of her own she'd been put at the helm of her own life. Celia, who ought to have helped her work out how to take control of the steering, wouldn't, and Eleanor, the most awkwardly self-contained child – one never had the slightest idea what was going on in her head – couldn't have done so even if she'd wanted to.

TWO

The Pursuit of Happiness

ELEANOR JENKINSON, sitting in her chair in France looking at the cornfield, has two accounts available to her of what has gone before, the one in her head, and the one in her notebooks. This notebook, the one she holds in her hand, has the figure 64 written on it. Opening it, she glances down at a page near the beginning: 'After Dick's death, Esther was unable to think about the meaning of their life together,' she read. 'She was possessed by a sense of relief which weighed on her like a sin. She took her guilt, and a small suitcase of clothes and went to Italy in the vain hope that time and distance would cure what her own inadequacies could not.'

Esther Gray, unlike Eleanor Jenkinson, has killed off her husband in the manner of those schoolgirl stories that can find no satisfactory role for men in families, once the procreating has been done. Eleanor's not aware of any conscious envy of Esther's manoeuvre. On the other hand, since she wrote it, she supposes the impulse must originate in some stray thought or other belonging to her, though it's difficult to feel responsible for all the odd thoughts wandering in one's head.

Esther, alone, has to build a life without Dick. She must unlearn her earlier lessons, which taught her a sufficient deference to male power to render marriage possible. But habits, especially those one struggled to learn, are hard to get rid of. Eleanor contemplates a variety of options. None of the easy answers – a new marriage, affairs, a political conversion – seem plausible, given her knowledge of Esther's character. By a process of elimination, Eleanor realizes Esther must undergo a resocialization. The answer satisfies, but is only half the battle. Next she must decide where and how. But, convinced she's on the right path, the next challenge fills Eleanor with a gentle elation. She will enjoy speculating on the possibilities. She will find pleasure in the imagined experiencing of each, before passing to a contemplation of

28

the next, like a butterfly winging its way from one clump of flowers to another. And then, finally, when she has chosen, she will write. In the writing she'll take great care over the details, as well as the straightforward telling of the story. She'll practise the dialogue in her head before setting it down; she'll test the descriptions of Eleanor's psychological development against her own standard of authenticity, lacking, for the moment, any other. Increasingly these days she feels it's the act of writing that is the essence of authorship, not the claiming of the finished product. It's like parenthood: the process of childrearing is all one has a right to: one has no right to the grown child itself.

Eleanor's eyes flicker from her page of jottings to the horizon. The sky, a curious unbroken silver, looks back at her without expression. In the trees the wind makes a low hissing noise. A flock of birds shadows the cornfield, the whole of which seems turned to face the sun, which is springing on the landscape from somewhere behind her. It begins to feel hot.

Eleanor, like Esther, the one released from marriage, the other not, ponders her misdemeanours. This holiday is a cutting edge, a breaking point, a new beginning, or an end. There are lots of words for it. But both Eleanor and David know it isn't just a holiday. They have agreed to talk about their future together. Whether there should be one – what it should look like; or, if not, what might happen instead. Eleanor fancies that this objective is already getting in the way of her writing. But she laughs inwardly at the thought – just imagine if she were to say this to David, how he would react! It functions as metaphor, though: what is for *us* cannot be for *me*. If it isn't *for* me, how can I *be* me, the writer? Eleanor is an old hand at recognizing the conflicts of convention and creativity; indeed, it's in their gender-specific recesses that she most tends to lose and find herself. Though she's spoken of this to David, mostly she keeps her own counsel. It seems as though the experience of growing older is at one with the experience of loneliness – the older you get, the more you appreciate how difficult it is to explain to anyone else what it's like to be you. This is true of her relationship with David, though it is less true of those she has with her female friends. There's more likely to be an immediate connection there, a sense, even, of not having to complete the sentence. It's the same with her daughters. What does that say about marriage? Or about Esther Gray's own journey out of bereavement?

29

Watching the cornfield with her steady, writing eyes, Eleanor is gripped, suddenly, by a vision of marriage as an extraordinary cultural artefact – man-made in the true sense, bizarre, unbelievable; coming from another planet, how would anyone believe that two people yoked by law could thereby find the resources to communicate with one another for ever? You'd have to be really stupid to believe that! She laughs out loud this time, tips her chair back against a crop of buttercups, and squints at the sun melted into the diamond blue of the French sky. It shines resolutely back at her, challenging her not to squint or blink. But Eleanor Jenkinson, unlike her heroine, Esther Gray, is merely human.

Eleanor and David had been married in the church in Muddenham in 1964, Bridget officiating as The Bride's Mother between spells of advancing senile dementia or Alzheimer's disease, as it would later be known. Uncle Hal, Charles's brother (of whom more later), had come over from France to give Eleanor to David, even though he himself had substantial misgivings about the appropriateness of the gift being made, not to mention of the giver to make it. Celia was in Australia, in a place called Coffs Harbour, from whence she sent a telegram which reached Muddenham the day after the wedding. Bridget bought them a bed as a wedding present, or, rather, two. 'You can tie the legs together with string, my darlings,' she said in a voice reminiscent of instructions to the secretary of one of her charity committees. 'Then you can untie them later.' (She didn't say why they might want to.)

After the wedding, David got a job teaching history in a boys' public school in Hammersmith. Eleanor continued with her job at the publishers in central London, travelling on the underground every day from their little house in Wimbledon, and doing the shopping on the way home in a cramped Cypriot grocer's that stayed open late for deviant women like her. She had a coil placed inside her womb to prevent conception.

The argument about children started a year after the wedding. It was a Saturday morning. David had gone to a colleague's house to set mock O level examination papers. After breakfast, Eleanor had stuffed their dirty clothes and sheets into a large plastic bag and taken it to Mrs Shenkey in the Bendix laundrette on the High Road, to whom she paid an extra 6d for processing the wash. Then she hoovered the sitting room, dragged a wet cloth round the visible parts of the kitchen floor, took some haddock out of the freezer compartment in the fridge for supper, had a bath, made herself some coffee and got back into bed with her notebook. (At least at this point in her life she recognized that the duties of the ménage came before the exertions of real creativity.) But no sooner was she into an encounter between Esther and Clare in the Place St Sulpice concerning the nature of Charles Dickens' view of women, than in bounded David, energized by the reduction of the entire span of English history to ten sentences all beginning, ending or implying the injunction 'Discuss', and having picked up some strange ideas from his colleague's house, which was inhabited by large numbers of small children. Eleanor remembers the scene clearly, even now: David springs into the bedroom, tears off his tie – necessary to the authoritative act of writing exam questions – and is undoing his trousers before she's decided where to put the next full stop.

'What are you doing?'

'It's time for a screw. And it's time you had that bloody thing taken out, my love, there's more to life than scribbling in notebooks.'

The argument raged the whole of that day and most of the next. The haddock was never cooked, and Mrs Shenkey had to hold on to the wet washing until Monday. It was only 1965. Capital punishment was about to be abolished in Britain, and the Race Relations Bill had been published earlier that year. Public policy, attending to death and the blacks, hadn't yet got round to women. Had it been 1924 or 1972 the culture of women's position – what was said about it rather more than what was done – might have enabled Eleanor Jenkinson to throw her husband off and get on with her own life. The problem was that the ideological equipment available at the time was simply inadequate to the task of defeating – even delaying for a year or two – David Jenkinson's plan. His plan triumphed because his wife's was insufficiently formulated. All she could say was what *she* wanted to do, and that wasn't enough, especially as her size, as usual, counted against her getting her own way. Even as she stood there in her nightie flipping the haddock at him, she found it difficult to take seriously her mental image of herself in the act: a dwarf wielding a wet piece of fish at a man who, à la Zola, writing of mysteries in Marseilles, had sprung at her before she had time to shut herself in. Her defence, even from behind the fish, could only invite the easy penetration of David's counter-argument, that what *she* wanted could not possibly have equal status with what *they* had to do. Procreate.

There were two other flaws in Eleanor's response. One, she loved

David. Not adored, like Zola's Blanche, but loved – more or less. It's what she would have said at the time, and even if she didn't know the meaning of the statement, she could have spelt out its implications. For a start, she wanted David near her. She wanted him there in the evenings across the table from her. She liked the sickly notion that in the evening they both wended their ways from their respective jobs, across London, to this little house with its freezer full of haddock, its cracked Victorian oak bureau full of competently paid bills, its bathroom cupboards stocked with pale azure toilet paper and Domestos, its front gate clicking crisply like a full stop behind them. She liked the edifice of intimacy, the territorial enclosure. She liked the fact that David was solicitous of her – her health, her safety, the contents of her purse, if not her mind. She was not allowed to go out for a walk on her own at night and consequently rarely wanted to. All she wanted to do was to write in her notebooks, which ought to have been safe enough.

David knew that Eleanor loved him. The other flaw was articulated by him. Eleanor had been having a moderate amount of trouble recently with Esther's emotional transactions in Paris, and had spoken to David of this, not in any concentrated, systematic fashion, for that was not how she treated her writing, but in odd bursts and staccato murmurs after brushing her teeth, over Sunday lunch, or while scraping the cinders off the toast in the mornings. She had indicated to him the great reluctance she was encountering in Esther to become . . . well, real. But she hadn't quite been able to identify why this was so. David could. 'How can anyone write a novel,' he questioned her (deliberately, she thought, not then, but a long time afterwards, using the genderless 'anyone') 'when they've had as little experience of life as you've had?'

She levelled her inexperienced eyes at him, knowing that one of the moments of truth had come. The procession from the Sisters of Mercy to Manchester University's idea of a degree in English literature, interspersed with spells in Marigold Lane, and followed by a sojourn in a shared all-female flat in Hornsey, did, indeed, add up to a severance from certain critical areas of human experience. What did Eleanor Kendrick/Jenkinson know of great passion, of sordid fantasy, of real squalor? How could she know what went on in the lives and bodies and minds of the truly disadvantaged, the irredeemably troubled? So how could she give to her characters the authenticity of which the world so far had deprived her? Her characters could speak only versions of her own small and unauthoritative voice. Not even the misfortune of her father's early death could make up for the appearance of invulnerable privilege others saw when they looked at Eleanor Jenkinson, an outer shell erected in part by Eleanor's own inner resistance to acknowledge those imperfections in herself which were the origin of her creativity. Why, she even argued to herself that her father's untimely death was a lot less adverse than the alternative of his absolute desertion of them all for the Piccadilly actress. The loss of Somerset at a time when Eleanor's own umbilical connections ought to have been severed anyway hardly counted. Neither David nor Eleanor could see the core of emotional pain inside Eleanor that made her want to write. Eleanor was trying to look outside herself before first looking in, which is always a mistake – for a writer. But facing David across the haddock in Wimbledon in 1965, Eleanor also hesitated to say what she ought to have done, that a career of wifehood and motherhood as planned for her by David would scarcely push back the frontiers of her knowledge of the universe. What of the glorious bloody gamut of human events and emotions would Eleanor experience along with the entrapments of a baby? Or two?

But resistance is often more in the soul than anywhere else. When Eleanor went to have her coil out, she visited a stationers' on the way home and bought herself a new supply of notebooks. She made a pact with herself, and with Esther Gray. The pact was, that if the experiences of the next few years didn't supply enough of the stuff of which novels are made, then she would seek out some of those that did. Secretly. It could all, if necessary, be the slyest of manoeuvres.

Extract from:

MEMOIRS OF A DEAD HOUSEWIFE (short story)
BY ELEANOR JENKINSON

And that was the moment it died in me, the self-sacrificing angel who scrubbed the bottoms of the pans, monitored the heels and toes of other people's socks, and cut the purple heads off the chives in the kitchen window box, caring more for their culinary usefulness than for their aesthetic grace. I knew then that life was not for me. He could have it if he wanted. But he didn't. He only wanted it with me in it – or rather with me suppressed, obsequious, fawning, elegiac in my dependence on him. So he took out the large brown knife there and then and killed me with it. As I was menstruating at the time, he tried to pretend that it wasn't him but my own uterus that had been responsible for my untimely and criminal exsanguination.

At twelve o'clock David comes back from shopping. He makes a lot of noise unpacking the food from the car, along with the other objects he's bought, which include a long length of cable for his loudspeakers. Eleanor can see it snaking its way across the blue sky between the house and the car. If her own emotions are vested in her notebooks (now, then, and for all time), David's tend towards a technological materialization. When the machines in his life work, he's happy. Making them work is, by a process of inverse deduction, therefore his preferred route to happiness.

A red admiral glances off the flat top of a clump of meadowsweet. David, having fixed the cable, strides manfully across the gravel, and tries to take Eleanor's hand. Unfortunately, it's the one with the pen in it. 'How is it then?' he asks, instead. 'I mean, for writing?'

She knows he wants to hear she's been productive, written one thousand or two thousand or five thousand words of elliptical aesthetic description, or better of dialogue, arranged in that wonderful way dialogue has of taking up lines on the page and making you believe you've written a good deal more than you have. Understanding this, Eleanor murmurs something intended to reassure him (and knowing he will listen only to the message and not the content of her answer). Craftily, she then stages another interlude for herself. 'Why don't you go and find out about the local restaurants, darling?' she invites him. 'You know how you like to do that. Later on perhaps we can take a siesta.'

David Jenkinson's own relationship with words is unproblematic. They're easy currency to him; he speaks them readily to students year after year at the University of Sussex, writes them, albeit cryptically, in lecture form, and has five or six what you might call books to his credit. The style of these is itself nothing to write home about, but it's more than adequate to David's purpose. History doesn't have to be well-written; to be written at all is the only requirement.

That's what Eleanor's Uncle Hal had said once. Enter Uncle Hal.

Like most respectable families, the Kendricks had a few skeletons in the cupboard. Eleanor first knew Hal – Henry Kendrick, Charles's brother – when she was very small, and he was an occasional visitor to Muddenham Grange. He was as large as she was tiny – as much above the fiftieth or even fifth centile for male height as she was below the appropriate female one; it seemed to onlookers as though Hal could almost hold this pint-sized niece of his in one large hairy hand. He would burst in, dangle Eleanor in the air, eat dinner, drink, and burst out again. Then, when Charles died, Hal was the one who came from abroad – he lived almost permanently in France conducting various poorly specified businesses from a house in a Provençal lavender field – to sort out their affairs. It was he who forced upon Bridget the full realization of her financial downfall – the move to the gardener's cottage, the dismissal of Somerset. He was the one to tell her clearly that the child Eleanor would have to be removed from the convent and sent to a state school. That Celia, supplied in her continental wanderings with money from the Kendrick estate, would have in future to fend for herself. Bridget, thankfully, would not have to work, provided the remaining money was invested sensibly, and Uncle Hal, for all his own follies, certainly did this for them.

For a long time the nature of Uncle Hal's follies hadn't been at all clear to Eleanor. She didn't find out until she was sixteen, and in that phase of angry disengagement from her mother through which adolescent girls often pass. Bridget had discovered over the years a gnawing anger against Charles for dying when he did, which hid a more justifiable objection to him for living as he had. But, more than Susan Barrington, Bridget ranted against the tragedy of motherhood Charles had inflicted on her – that fact that Eleanor, deprived of boarding school and Somerset, required Bridget to be a mother after all. Eleanor, for her part, was never taken in by the whole construct of Bridget's maternal self-sacrifice. Bridget's fussing about her (was she eating/wearing/sleeping/learning enough) was to Eleanor neuroticism, not maternalism. Eleanor's view of her mother as very ill-acquainted with her as a person was confessed in wrathful prose to a series of diaries, kept under her bed with a serrated knife laid on top as a warning to any literary snooper.

So at this juncture of her life what Eleanor Kendrick wanted to do was something dramatic, but at the same time safe, by way of a gesture to her mother that she was growing up and had become thoroughly unpredictable within the terms of her mother's restricted knowledge of her. One day, when Bridget was out at a meeting of the regional spastics society, Eleanor thumbed through her mother's old green address book, found Uncle Hal's telephone number, lifted up the telephone, dialled the operator and asked for the long string of numbers inscribed there, going on to tell rather than ask Uncle Hal about her intended descent into the lavender field. Though he was very surprised, as he was fond of Eleanor he could not find it in his heart or anywhere else to say no.

The task of getting herself from Tunbridge Wells to Cavaillon was an exciting expedition for someone as young and as inexperienced as Eleanor. At the Gare du Nord, she was propositioned by a garage mechanic who took her train ticket when she refused him her virtue. The school in Tunbridge Wells had been rather good at French, so Eleanor was easily able to persuade the ticket clerk, who remembered her, because she was so small and he'd made the usual mistake of assuming her to be a child, to sell her another.

Uncle Hal was at the station to meet her, quite insolently jaunty with his long grey-orange beard, open white shirt, and heavy silver medallion twinkling in the sunlight. They climbed into a crumbling Citroën Dyane and Hal said, 'I take it you've told your mother where you are?'

Eleanor hadn't.

'We must telephone her,' said Uncle Hal firmly.

'You can if you must,' replied Eleanor, 'but *I* am not going to.'

A quick glance at her face revealed to Uncle Hal the mask of Eleanor's determination. It reminded him of his brother Charles, of whom he had been quite a lot fonder than Charles had been of him.

'This is Thurston,' remarked Uncle Hal at the door of the farmhouse which squeaked like a whole bevy of mice on its hinges. 'My friend, Thurston Blane. Meet Eleanor Kendrick, alias my niece. Who has run away from home. As we all do in our own way!' Hal's medallion and his eyes glinted. Thurston unfolded his frame from the kitchen sofa and rose, extending in Eleanor's direction a hand as skeletal as a dead bat's wing. He squinted at her from a considerable height and a face rendered by the Provençal sun as orange as Hal's beard had once been.

Eleanor said to Hal, with the unthinking impertinence of the truly young, 'Who's Thurston? You didn't tell me you lived with anyone. I thought you lived here on your own.' Disappointment painted her face.

'You didn't ask me with whom I lived, my dear,' replied Hal reasonably. 'But Thurston's quite a nice chap really. I think you'll find him quite congenial. He is house trained, you know. Lots of practice, been here since 1935.'

'Didn't you warn her, Enrico? How very unfair of you.' Thurston uncorked a bottle of wine and poured them all glasses. He didn't even ask Eleanor if she wanted one. 'Well, we might as well drink to it, whatever it is!'

Eleanor, as can be imagined though she hadn't, had rather a good time in Provence with her uncle Hal and his friend Thurston. The two men were very funny together; once Eleanor had relaxed and they could see she was enjoying their company, they played to her like an audience. Both spoke a kind of staccato language with all the frills missing, rather like an interminable ping pong game. The three of them sat on white chairs in the long evenings looking out across the lavender fields drinking the rather sharp rosé Thurston and Hal liked, and eating little meals of artichoke hearts, calves' brains and other bits of things concocted by Thurston with enormous care from a battered copy of Elizabeth David's *French Provincial Cooking*. Thus, Eleanor was given a view of a world beyond that she had known in Kent. The circumstances were congenial enough for her to take Hal and Thurston into her confidence about the ambition to be a writer. It didn't seem to surprise them.

'Thurston used to be a poet,' observed Hal casually.

'In a former life,' recalled Thurston, flushed with the rosé.

'We've got some of them here, haven't we, Thursty?' said Hal.

'Over there somewhere.' Thurston's hand waved at the black recesses of the kitchen. Eleanor walked over and had a look – there were five or six thin volumes with Thurston Blane's name on them. She picked out one and walked back to the door to see it better. The first poem was called 'Christ at the Crossroads', and Eleanor read it:

> I carry my goods like a camel's hump
> garments from a gentleman's shop, words
> threaded ready-made on light steel chains

> ointments and unctions glossed with silk
> an odyssey no stranger than His
> whose pink arms on the cross
> stretch here, where the road turns . . .

Eleanor held the book out in front of her, staring for a long time at the title *Couplets*, and underneath this at Thurston's name; and from this to him, the odd fellow crouched in the summer sunset. It was then that she saw her own work, her own novel-to-be, My Novel as it would henceforth be known through all future vicissitudes and phases and events. She saw it coming eventually to rest sagely and stentoriously between two hard blue covers emblazoned with a title, some title not yet thought of, and the words 'Eleanor Kendrick' large and black and annunciative reposing there for everyone, but most of all for herself, to see.

'Wrote that soon after I landed here,' offered Thurston, referring to the book Eleanor held. 'Rather influenced by A.E. I fancy. George William Russell to you, leader of the Irish revival. Christ popping up everywhere. Died that year, you know. Also perhaps Lawrence. *Seven Pillars* in my rucksack. Heavy.'

'A novel is like history,' suggested Uncle Hal memorably in the ensuing conversation. 'It doesn't have to be well-written, but it *is* far better written than not.'

'Yes, Enrico, but one volume is enough! Writers should think about the reading habits of those for whom they write. That's the great attraction of poetry. A few select words say it all. No lengthy paragraphs or peregrinations. Think what you mean, and then say it. Brevity, economy. The curt completeness of nakedness, like a Roman statue, clean white marbled limbs . . . '

'Don't mind him, Eleanor,' Hal nods good-humouredly in Thurston's direction. 'He goes off on these tangents from time to time.'

'Can't read *The Seven Pillars of Wisdom* on the bog, now can you?' says Thurston, not to be deflected from his tangent. 'Can't hold it, too heavy. A nice slim volume of sonnets, now that's a different matter altogether.'

'There's nothing more constipating than iambic pentameters, Thursty!' says Hal, getting up to refill Eleanor's glass. 'Don't corrupt my niece. She's not aiming for the poetry of bowel movements. She might be a great novelist one day.'

'Take my advice, niece Eleanor,' replied Thurston, 'whatever you do, keep it short.'

'But not life itself, Thursty!' Hal raised his glass. 'May we all live an extremely long time, and may young Eleanor here write as many long or short novels as she wants!'

Eleanor bore these words, and the flavour of those Provençal evenings back to Kent, and a taut reunion with her mother, who had discovered in Eleanor's absence the kind of concern for her daughter's wellbeing that Eleanor had wanted her to have all along. Hal wrote to Bridget, Eleanor saw the letter resting on the letter plate in Marigold Lane one Monday morning. Judging from the bulkiness of the envelope, it was a long letter; Bridget didn't tell her what was in it, but Eleanor supposed from her mother's subsequent response that it was some kind of peroration on her character; she's all right really, a chip off the old block, let her get on with her own life, sort of thing. Which it was. Though Bridget Kendrick also searched the letter for echoes of her own love for Hal, steamily and ineptly confessed one night when, as they both now realized, Charles must have been ensconced with Susan Barrington in Piccadilly.

But this Eleanor would never know. For there are as many things daughters never learn about their mothers as there are secrets kept from mothers by their daughters. Eleanor would, for the same reason, never have told Bridget of the moment in the Provençal doorway; she could not have trusted her mother with the moment's sanctity. Bridget would probably have laughed at her. 'You want to write, then? What *do* you mean? Write what? What for? What kind of a life is that!'

At three o'clock the sun's about to move behind the red-tiled roof of the house. Even in the shade, Eleanor has grown too hot for comfort. Esther Gray has moved on, and is now riding a donkey on a silver-sanded beach in Brazil. She, too, is hot. But at least she has the visual image of the sea to cool her down: blue beyond anyone's imagination, with strips of lacy foam laid over it. The donkey's back is warm and silky. Esther has found a temporary paradise.

Eleanor closes the notebook, and picks up her pencil case and her coffee cup. She walks across the patch of grass between the field and the gravelled yard, thick broad-leaved weeds and thistles inserting themselves through the thongs of her sandals. She goes inside. David sits at the table, his maps spread out on the yellow oilskin cloth. 'I'm going to take a shower.'

He scarcely looks up. She takes her notebook and pencils to the bedroom, and fetches a towel from the walnut wardrobe. In the bathroom – if the rancid space under the stairs can really be dignified by that name – she studies the taps on the shower wall. She fetches her glasses. They're both marked 'froid'.

'It's the one furthest away,' calls David from the kitchen.

The water runs thinly, but it's hot, which she wants, even in this climate.

Later in the bedroom, David says he wants to make love to her. They get into the deep bed, their bodies collapsing together in the pool of the middle. 'It's hot,' she complains again. She has this fear that when he tries to find her vagina it will have sunk right down into the mattress so that it doesn't exist any more; has become a feather.

In her sleep she hears the cows on the hillside, the bells clanging on their necks, their soft heavy hooves making reverberations on the dry white grass. She imagines Esther Gray on her Brazilian donkey among them. The grass becomes sand. Sea and sky merge. Esther and she are suddenly alone in a landscape configured entirely of blue and silver.

Extract from:

A FRENCH FANTASY
BY ELEANOR JENKINSON

Esther would never forget that summer. Martin held her every night in the wide, wide bed, and every morning they woke to the light in each other's eyes and to the flower fields, immaculate and colourful. 'My lobelia' or 'hyacinth' or 'snowdrop' he would whisper to chide her on, as her lungs felt themselves unequal to the ascent he had that day planned for them.

It was a bit like climbing a mountain, as Martin had a lot of energy and even more enthusiasm. He wasn't at all like Dick. Where Dick would ponder for hours, or procrastinate, and generally appear indecisive (though the decision would always be made, Dick could be depended on for that), Martin would throw himself in the deep end, dragging her along with him, completing the whole mission in the time it took Dick to scratch his head and say, 'Well, I'm sure I don't know'.

She did try not to compare them too much, though. Not because it made her feel guilty, but because it might make her want to walk away from her old life altogether. Martin had all sorts of plans for them. He wanted to take her to the Italian lakes, to the Peruvian mountains on the Inca trail, and to this little farm he knew in Wales. He'd learnt sheep-shearing as a boy, and he wanted to demonstrate all his talents to her.

'I want to call her Heidi,' Eleanor had said almost as soon as she saw the black-haired infant in the Wimbledon maternity hospital. Naturally the child, each child, would have to be named after a character in a novel. First Heidi, as Johanna Spyri, Heidi's creator, had led Eleanor Kendrick through the flower fields to a place where a young girl could argue with a man too old to be her father. David Jenkinson, happily, was too enamoured of his own easy transition to fatherhood to mind what the baby was called – within reason. He was getting what he wanted, wasn't he? It would be unreasonable of him to make a fuss.

First Heidi, and then Eliza. After George Bernard Shaw. Another patriarchal cabaret. When Heidi was very little, Eleanor would whip her notebooks out every time the dark blue eyes closed in sleep. Household affairs were done in 'Heidi time', with the infant watching from her little canvas chair, or strapped to her mother's front or back in the fashion debased from its African origins now entering Mothercare. Desperately Eleanor would sweep and dust and launder to fill the time until the notebook could be opened again.

It was 1966. Eleanor's housekeeping efforts and emotional upheavals were dwarfed by the landslide in Aberfan. The thought of all those buried children invoked not only Eleanor's new maternalism, but a defence of her own buried desires. Pushing Heidi back from the shops one day, she called in at the local polytechnic for a brochure. Later, while Heidi slept, and when she ought to have been washing the nappies, she sat down with a cup of tea and a packet of custard creams and the brochure in front of her, imagining all the nondomestic delights waiting for her just around the corner. There were courses in everything from practical jam-making to Bengali for Beginners. She was mildly tempted by 'Twentieth-Century Philosophy' (perhaps it would help sort out Esther Gray in Paris). But in the end, she picked a writing class. 'An Introduction to Creative Writing' it was called.

'But what will you do with Heidi?' David asked, as husbands at the time could be trusted to.

'It's in the evening. You can babysit. You will, won't you?' David was trying to write a book himself, which didn't make it easier. Except that his interest didn't lie in the literary composition angle, but rather in the book's content, which was historical. He wanted to make his reputation with it to drag himself out of schoolteaching and into a university, which would mean a bit more money and considerably more status, but which represented practically the limits of his ambition.

In the evenings David bashed away at his typewriter whether Eleanor was there or not. So before she went to her writing class, Eleanor prepared Heidi's supper and David's. A glass bottle of expressed breast milk for Heidi, and a little apple purée (transferred from a Heinz tin; Eleanor knew David thought she'd prepared it most lovingly herself, but no-one could open a tin more lovingly than she could); for David a plate of stew and rice, or sausages, mashed potatoes and peas, or a piece of plaice in breadcrumbs with a few chipped potatoes and a grilled tomato or two. Nothing fancy. And who consumed which elements of this feast she would, of course, never know. Though most of the time it was true to say that David Jenkinson could be classed as a good father.

The writing class was run by a man in his fifties with a large stomach but only five feet one inch in height. Only a bit taller than Eleanor herself, in fact, though making up for this in width. Tom Sherringham was altogether very full of himself – much fuller than Eleanor was, even when pregnant – and quite convinced that he would always recognize a good piece of writing when he saw one. He himself had published only three scant volumes of stories poorly modelled on Saki's, plus a tedious travelogue on Rutland pubs. Eleanor showed him chapter three of *A Month in Paris* as it was currently called. Tom Sherringham wrote all over it in green ink: 'unbelievable' he put, and 'stilted dialogue' and 'she wouldn't say this, my girl' and 'OTT'. They went over her manuscript in the pub; Eleanor had to ask him what 'OTT' meant. Tom Sherringham drank beer and the rest of the class effete glasses of warm white wine – they were all women except for Michael, who worked for Dolcis and preferred tonic water.

'Have you ever been to Paris?' Tom Sherringham asked Eleanor. And she had to say no, not except for changing trains at the Gare du Nord. She told him the story about the garage mechanic. He laughed. 'I like that. Why don't you write about that? Something real instead of all this airy fairy stuff. You need to get some living done, my girl. Go back to Paris. Find out what a month there is *really* like. That's my advice to you, Mrs Jenkinson.' He leered uncompromisingly at her, the froth of the Heineken coating his lips like a rabid dog. The same useless advice, in other words, as Mr Jenkinson had given her.

'But how am I to do that?' she expostulated. 'What will I do with Heidi?'

'Heidi, sheidi,' enunciated Tom Sherringham from the depths of his Heineken. 'Which comes first, life or art? You want to be a novelist, you must put art first.' He slid his arm disreputably around her small, and shrinking, frame.

There was another young woman in the class, Eva Summers, in a similar situation to Eleanor. Eva had two children, Luke and Belinda, a husband, Christian, who only talked to her after sex, and a parrot who talked to her most of the time, though she usually didn't hear it, as she was deaf and wore a hearing aid. Eleanor wheeled Heidi round to Eva's house one morning for coffee to discuss her (Esther Gray's) dilemma. Eva was lying in a bed packed with towels, bleeding heavily. 'Go and buy me some tampax, Eleanor, Christian won't, he doesn't like to hear the word menstruation, it makes him sick.'

Afterwards Eva told Eleanor what to do. 'You can't go to Paris, that's far too extreme. Anyway, it's rather hackneyed as a solution, don't you think? Change the setting, that's what I say. Make it Leeds or Twickenham instead. If you can't adjust life to the requirements of art, do it the other way around.' Eleanor started to say something, but Eva wasn't looking at her and didn't have her hearing aid switched on. 'Tom Sherringham's quite right,' she continued. 'You must get out of the kitchen. So must I, as a matter of fact.' She wandered distractedly into her own to fetch a clean ashtray. 'I tell you what.' Eva was still locked in her own train of thought. 'I'll have Heidi for you. I'll have Heidi one day a week so you can go off and have some adventures.'

Eva's plot reminded Eleanor of her pact with Esther Gray the day she had her coil taken out: life on the sly. This was how Eva herself appeared to cope; she never told Christian much about what she did, or thought. When challenged by Eleanor about this, she merely said,

'Oh I tried that. It's a waste of time. We just argue, it's the same performance every time. I turn my hearing aid off and he goes to the pub. Then he creeps home in the early hours all contrite. I can't bear him like that. He reminds me of a snail. No, believe me, Ellie, there's no point in openness. If you want your own way, you're far better keeping it all to yourself.'

They planned Eleanor's adventures together, or rather Eva planned the adventures, and Eleanor executed them. Every Tuesday she fed Heidi, pushed the pram packed with clean nappies and Heinz tins round to Eva's and then set off for wherever it was.

The first Tuesday it was Soho.

'Just walk around,' admonished Eva. 'Keep your eyes open. Don't say no.'

'Don't say no to what?'

'Anything.'

A sheet of October drizzle covered Wardour Street and Old Compton Street and Soho Square, which consequently reminded Eleanor of anything but nightingales. The whole area had scarcely woken up after its usual abbreviated night's slumber. Some of the red neon signs were still turned on as Eleanor walked, a sharp little figure in a shiny blue mac and rainhat. She'd pulled the rim of the hat right down over her face against the rain. Then, realizing this defeated the purpose, which was to see and experience rather than stay dry and get there, she pushed it back again. A man stood in front of her, in the middle of a good deal of litter on the pavement. Eleanor's heart thumped. This was it! But no sooner had her heart thumped than the man moved out of the way, lithe as a lizard, with a similar set of darting movements, into a doorway. She paused. The doorway belonged to a shop. The window was full of leather garments, black and thoroughly studded. Eleanor's hands deep in the pockets of her raincoat sweated into the lining. 'Not a lot for you here, I shouldn't think, dearie,' commented an offhand, female voice. Eleanor turned to look at its owner, a busty blonde in an off-the-shoulder red dress.

'I was only looking,' Eleanor defended herself lamely.

'That's what they all say, duckie.'

After that she walked on fast, convinced that numerous curious eyes were watching her. She went into a cafe round the corner in Tottenham Court Road, and had a cup of coffee and an egg sandwich. Then she phoned Eva. 'It's not easy,' she complained.

'What?'

'Put the phone on the other ear, Eva.' The whistling noise of the hearing aid filled the phone box. 'I said it's not easy.'

'Well of course it isn't,' said Eva impatiently. 'I must go now, Heidi wants her dinner. Go and get on with it, for God's sake, I don't want you back before five.'

At the mention of Heidi's name a surge of milk ran into Eleanor's breasts. She asked for the toilet, took her mac off and hung it on the door, pushed her jumper up and her nursing bra down and squirted some milk rather aimlessly against the sides of the wooden cubicle. As she went on doing this (there was quite a lot of it), she heard voices the other side of the wall. Giggling. The rustle of paper, then smoke aromatically rising to the damp ceiling. She hooked up her bra and put her raincoat back on. Outside the cubicle she observed that the door to the next one was open. A girl, about fifteen or sixteen, sat on the toilet, another on the floor. 'Want a whiff?' They giggled again. Eleanor swallowed hard, with a certain amount of discernible resolution. 'Yes, please.' They stopped giggling then and looked her up and down curiously. But they handed her the joint, damp and succulent at the end, and Eleanor smoked it, bravely inhaling, and quickly feeling quite heady with the news she would bring back to Eva, rather than with the effects of the hash, which was of poor quality, having been harvested in a garage in Bradford.

Janice and Michelle, the girls were called, and they found Eleanor enough of a laugh to adopt her for the rest of the day. Eleanor, eventually high, unwisely told them exactly what she was doing – collecting experiences in order to write a novel. They thought this quite exhaustingly funny. They called her Mrs J. 'We could teach you a thing or two about life, Mrs J,' they kept saying. They lived in Archway and should have been at school. Eleanor had the feeling, though they didn't say as much, that they knew themselves headed for a life, or rather two, of unremitting domesticity and poverty, and if they didn't get the giggles in now they never would.

'Well, Mrs J,' said Janice and Michelle at the end of the day, 'Give us your phone number, then.' Eleanor bit her lip, but remembering Eva's instruction never to say no, gave it to them, thinking as she did so, but not quite hoping, that that would be the end of it.

That evening Eleanor told David she was tired and had to go to bed early. 'Why, what did you do today?' he asked, looking up momentarily from the fifth-form history essays he was marking. 'Oh, nothing.' She managed an offhand voice. 'I expect my period's due.'

It was, but that was Eliza.

The Tuesday trips continued for the first half of the pregnancy: Eleanor made it to Wapping, to Cambridge, to Birmingham, to a market in Southall and a cattle show in Market Harborough. She went on a tour of a cosmetics factory and she even went back to Soho, to a sex show all on her own. It was quite boring. But it did turn her mind to sex that evening and David Jenkinson was once more moved to ask where his wife had been that day. 'To the cinema,' she replied, truthfully.

'The cinema? By yourself? What about Heidi?'

'Heidi went to Eva's.'

'What did you see?'

'A film.'

David looked at her, properly this time. 'Are you feeling all right, dear?'

'More or less.'

She got the notebooks out and wrote some of this down in the form of short stories, which she read to the creative writing class when it was her turn to present her work for critical scrutiny. Michael told her she had a livid imagination. 'I think you mean vivid, dear,' said Doris Rochester, a sparrow-like seventy-year-old with forty years as a minor official in the civil service behind her. Doris's short stories featured flowers as the central characters. Tom Sherringham suggested one evening that she aim for a kind of upmarket Bill and Ben television slot, but none of them knew if he was serious or not. After a while Tom Sherringham pronounced the word 'promising' in relation to Eleanor's own work.

The spring of that year, 1967, was late. At the beginning of April it was still icy cold. The boiler needed replacing in the house in Wimbledon, but David's salary as a history teacher was insufficient, so the Jenkinsons froze. Eleanor, insulated by the pregnancy, did better than David. But the chill propelled him into a new consciousness of his accumulating responsibilities as a family man, and he finally finished his book on *Agrarian Technology and Rural Culture in England from 1660 to 1840*. After that, he applied for several university lecturing jobs at a higher salary and with prospects of promotion.

In the middle of all this, Eleanor heard from Janice and Michelle.

'Is that you, Mrs J?' they shouted down the phone from somewhere, though Eleanor imagined them as she had first seen them, smoking hash in a toilet cubicle in Tottenham Court Road. 'It's us, Mrs J,' they screamed.

'How are you, Janice-and-Michelle?'

'Oh we're great, Mrs J. D'you fancy another day out, then?'

With a bad attack of haemorrhoids, Eleanor staggered out to meet Janice and Michelle on Westminster Bridge. When they asked her why she was walking funny she was too embarrassed to tell them. 'You are a nut,' said Eva afterwards. 'Haemorrhoids is the stuff of life. You should have told all – they're bound to get them one day, if not soon.'

This time Janice and Michelle took Eleanor to a dark basement coffee bar in Waterloo. Here they introduced her to some of their mates – Pete, whose incipient beard was giving him as much trouble as the acne it was intended to cover, Fran, a dark and very silent youth, and someone called Ball who was quite a lot older, clearly the leader of whatever it was, and clothed in black leather from head to foot. The atmosphere in the bar was very thick, and it made Eleanor feel faint. 'You all right, Mrs J?' Janice, the more solicitous of the two, told Pete and Fran and Ball that Mrs J was in the club. It was the first time Eleanor had heard this phrase. Her haemorrhoids ached. Pete and Fran and Ball weren't greatly affected by the news. After a while Janice put her on a bus with some aspirin.

When she was six months pregnant with Eliza, Eva asked Eleanor to have her shopping basket – she had a very large one on wheels – one day while she went somewhere on the underground.

'I don't understand.'

'You don't have to, Ellie. I just want to park my shopping basket in your house for a bit.'

'But why don't you leave it at home?'

'I can't. Christian's at home all the time at the moment and I have to tell him I'm going shopping.'

'Why? Where *are* you going?'

'I can't tell you,' she said.

Eleanor took the shopping basket in, and at intervals during the day, between feeding Heidi who was now walking and talking and getting her hands on things (the notebooks had had to be put away), and doing the nappies and practising her breathing exercises and peeling the potatoes for her and David's dinner, and answering the phone to her mother whose confusion about time had peaked at her shrilling insistence down the line from Marigold Lane that Somerset had gone to Debenham's in Tunbridge Wells to choose a new print for the nursery curtains, Eleanor Jenkinson saw the large shopping basket standing there, and mused on what her friend Eva Summers might be doing.

'Screwing Tom Sherringham,' said Eva at the end of the day.

'Shsh!' Eleanor had heard David coming in; he was now in the next room getting himself a whisky. 'You girls want anything?' he called through the hatch.

'Only Tom Sherringham,' murmured Eva, under her breath.

'We're out of sherry, I'm afraid. Have you put it on the list, Eleanor?'

'How do you stand for it?' asked Eva. 'I wouldn't.'

'You do,' retorted Eleanor, thinking of Christian, who was the most uncommunicative man she'd ever met. At least David talked, even if he didn't usually say the right thing.

David took his whisky into the garden with the newspaper.

'Come on Eva, what was it like?' asked Eleanor. 'Why did you do it, anyway?'

'One question at a time. Diversion, I suppose. I'm going crazy, Eleanor, I wasn't cut out to be a Wimbledon housewife. Or any other kind. Luke and Belinda ignore me most of the time. I've taught the parrot all the key phrases and commands. You know, "Don't spill the cornflakes", "Have you got your dinner money?", "If you don't tidy your room, I'll put it all out for the dustman", "No you can't", and "We'll see". I may as well forget the rest. Christian has, as far as I can see. You've no idea how sweet he was at the beginning, Ellie. He sent me a rose every day until I said yes. If I hadn't, I'd still be getting roses. There's a thought!' She lit a cigarette.

'What about Tom Sherringham, then?'

'Nosy, aren't you! Well, I don't mind telling you it was a most peculiar experience. He talks during it, you see. Not like Christian, who, as you know, only talks after. Myself, I prefer silence for the duration. Partly because then I don't have to keep my hearing aid on.'

Some weeks after this, Eva Summers walked out of her house in Wimbledon one day with her shopping basket and never came back. She telephoned Eleanor once from a call box. Eleanor knew it was her because she heard the hearing aid whistle. But nothing was said. Eva could say nothing, for it had all been said, by the very act of her departure with the shopping basket – later found abandoned in a car park in Putney – from ordinary life in pursuit, everyone supposed, either of art or of her own sexual liberation (with or without Tom Sherringham), though the two might be the same thing.

THREE

Lady's Mantle

'I'M TAKING YOU OUT to dinner tonight,' announces David. He's reading his Michelin when Eleanor wakes up. 'Put your best frock on.'

She has another shower, wraps herself in a towel and walks in the garden. The white heat has gone, leaving a crust of warmth and memory on top of the dry grasses and the flowers. I had the oddest dream, she says to herself, about Eva Summers.

David comes up behind her. 'Eva Summers? Wasn't she that woman you met at the writing class?'

'That's right.'

'She was crazy.'

'Oh, I don't think so.' Eleanor turns to face David. A dead oak tree gesticulates between the figure of her husband and the dark green forest carpeting the horizon. 'Why do you say that, David? She only wanted to write. And that's what I dreamed,' she muses quietly. 'I dreamed she became a very successful novelist.'

'Why haven't we heard of her, then?'

'She published her novels under a pseudonym, of course.'

Eleanor puts on a neat black and white sundress with a tight skirt, earrings of white glass, and red sandals with low heels. Her hair's the same colour as the tarnished mirror, streaked with iridescent opal in the early evening light. She dabs musk oil behind her ears. Using the bathroom after Eleanor, David ties his green tie in the same mirror. He puts his pigskin wallet in the inside pocket of his cream linen jacket, and they set off for the restaurant.

The Jenkinsons are shown to a table on the terrace, which is fringed with terracotta window boxes full of white geraniums. The terrace overlooks the village square, on which the main landmarks are a

50

telephone box, a set of scales for weighing cattle and pigs, and a public lavatory.

Soon after they have sat down, and David has ordered *deux champagne cassis* in his best French, a French family arrives at the next table. The woman is very pretty, with short red hair, a black dress and silver bangles. Her son, a handsome lad of about fourteen, sits on her right, and opposite him is his sister, a little girl of about seven or eight with unattractively bulbous eyes and a plait, and wearing an incongruous white lace dress. Next to her, the father, balding, in a bright blue shirt. They don't quite fit together. Something is wrong. It makes Eleanor remember one of the Jenkinson family holidays. The first one, with herself and David and Heidi and Eliza. Soon after they moved to Brighton, wasn't it? She screws her eyes up in an effort to remember, at the same time noting the evanescent pink of the evening sky across the square – pink like the sunsets that never happened that summer.

Extract from:

MEMOIRS OF A DEAD HOUSEWIFE (short story)
BY ELEANOR JENKINSON

I came back from the dead, you see. To avenge him. It was only to be expected, really. I found him having a holiday with his family. They were camping again. The tents had been improved since my time. Otherwise, I don't imagine he would have tried it again a second time. And do you know, he still had my notebooks there! He had them with him in a plastic Intermarche bag, at the back of the tent. He couldn't have me any more, so he was prepared to make do with my jottings instead. One night, when he was asleep, and so was Mrs Alive Housewife, I snuck my hand underneath the back of the tent and took them away with me.

They'd gone to Dorset, to a damp house on the main road which cost £4 a week. Heidi was almost four, Eliza getting on for two. The time since Eliza's birth hadn't been easy. She was a sickly child, catching every possible illness, and lacking her elder sister's appetite for food. She lay truculently in her cradle, watching everything with gimlet eyes in a wan little face. But early on, Eleanor had decided that physically speaking Eliza took after her; there was therefore no point in worrying about the child's apparent refusal to grow at a normal rate. Instead of taking Eliza to the clinic, where they would lecture her about her nonstandard development, she took to keeping her at home, merely in order to avoid trouble.

When Eliza was a few months old, David had got a job at the University of Sussex. These were the years in which universities were seen as valuable commodities irrespective of their financial value. Like a marrow in a fertile summer, higher education bloomed, and all sorts of jumped-up polytechnics and institutes of technology preened themselves, retitled, in its nourishing earth. There was even to be a University of the Air – as though education could be transmitted like oxygen.

The Jenkinsons had moved to a terraced three-floor house behind Brighton station. They couldn't afford anything grander, since Eleanor wasn't earning. David called her the last of the big spenders. She thought this unfair in view of what she was spending it on. They seemed increasingly to fit the picture of the housewife-breadwinner nuclear family, though she couldn't ever remember agreeing on this with David. None of this had been how she'd seen herself. David, yes: that was understandable. But not the total immersion in the domestic round required by the babies, and now by the position of a don's wife. David got very caught up very quickly in the grippingly tedious politics of academia. At least, she found them so. They all seemed to spend a lot of time complaining about each other's intellectual or administrative (usually administrative) inadequacies. He wanted her to listen to it all in the evenings. Properly, which meant he'd keep it all to himself until the children were in bed, and the two of them could sit down together and have supper in a civilized fashion. What was civilized to him wasn't to her – she found it quite savage having to do this, when all she was fit for after a day with the children was a cup of tea in front of the television. She supposed, however, that it was basically her fault, she should have spotted the contradictions.

She fell into a long-drawn-out trance; childrearing on automatic pilot. Not unhappy, exactly, but sedated by the shock.

The notebooks hid themselves in a drawer: there was no writing class any more. Eliza's birth had put a stop to that, and then, when they moved, there was no class nearby anyway. 'I'll have to do something about this,' Eleanor would mutter to herself from time to time as she tripped around the cluttered house behind the station, but she didn't, because it was difficult to see what she *could* do. Every month or so, Eleanor's mother took the train to see her daughter, and every time, without fail, she withdrew from her bag within five minutes of her arrival a parcel containing an apron. The first was a pleasant kitchen green, with the names of herbs informatively printed on it. The second, a cheery red, had various fruits capering across it. The third was a butcher's apron for David, who would never use it. But the fourth took the prize, being of a horrid yellow and edged with frills. Eleanor glowered at her mother with despair and fury mixed like a bad cocktail in her eyes. But Bridget, who'd never been good at noticing what her daughter was feeling, hugged Heidi and Eliza and fed them sweets and said cajolingly to Eleanor, 'Come now, dear, don't look so down in the mouth, no woman with young children can expect to do anything else! Motherhood's a vocation! A career! You're having the time of your life!'

How could Bridget have so conveniently forgotten the oh-so-vacant stage of her own motherhood? Wisely, Eleanor didn't try to remind her. But she resented all the same the fake sagacity of the apron visitations. All of which was worse because these were practically all the social contact Eleanor had. There was no Eva Summers in Anchor Road. On one side lived a retired schoolteacher, Miss Everest, who had very mixed feelings about children, and a roguish tom cat who slipped into the Jenkinsons' house when no-one was looking in order to spray the carpets. On the other side were an infertile couple, Joanna and Peter Glover, who'd taken up sailing instead, and were always asking Eleanor to take in odd-shaped parcels from the postman for them.

Sometimes Eleanor longed for untidy and enormous London, where even the entrapped housewife could kid herself that adventure and salvation lay just over the doorstep – as, indeed, she had shown it did. On an impulse one day in July 1968, soon after she'd got up, when Heidi was throwing toast at Eliza, and Eliza was throwing up on the floor again, and David was packing carefully written lectures on the consciousness of the working classes in early medieval Europe into his new pale leather briefcase, and the milkman was ringing with a tedious persistence at the door, Eleanor went into the kitchen and slid one of the smart change of address cards David had had printed into an envelope with Janice's address on it. She knew as she did so what a tiny rebellion this was, but it was one all the same – the connection of a potentially live wire from the present through to the electric current of Eleanor Kendrick's erstwhile creative personality, shortcircuiting her own apron-decked false consciousness.

Around this time, she started to read books about women and writing. Good old Virginia Woolf, from whom Eleanor derived the comfort that the reason she couldn't write was the lack of appropriate conditions – a room of her own and some financial independence; and harridans such as Harriet Martineau, who singled out the collapse of family fortunes as their very spur to fame. Charlotte Perkins Gilman wrote only when away from her physician-husband, who confined her to bed in an effort to prevent madness, which was the same thing as writing as far as he was concerned. Eleanor concluded that to have money but be dependent works no better than to be poor and dependent. Plans began to germinate in her head. She was found by David in the spare room one day – the room they had put everything in that didn't have an obvious home elsewhere, such as the lawnmower (no lawn here) or for which there was no obvious use (the thirty-six blue crystal goblets one of David's cousins had given them when they got married). Eleanor was eyeing the room with a view to taking it over. But David didn't know this. Her restlessness worried him, and he searched for a suitable interpretation of it. 'I think we could afford a holiday this year,' he'd announced eventually. 'I'll see if I can book something up, shall I?'

For Eleanor the two weeks they spent in Dorset were much like the time she spent at home, except that nothing was in the same place, and the kitchen didn't have a tin opener of the kind she was used to. On the Monday of the first week, David had generously said, 'I'm going to take the girls to the beach.' Looking out of the window, Eleanor could see that it was raining slightly. But Heidi had heard and was jumping up and down talking about buckets and spades. 'So you can get on with your novel,' finished David grandly.

'My Novel?' Eliza was sitting in a corner of the kitchen playing with saucepans. She was at the age of repeating everything, so there was soon a metallic chorus going in which the words 'My Novel' alternated with the collisions of frying pans and saucepan lids.

David bore the children off, and Eleanor sat down in front of the window looking out over the garden. She put her feet up on the window sill and fell asleep. She never got more than six hours' sleep these days – Eliza still woke in the night, and Heidi started her poking and interrogations at six every morning. When David came home that day, frazzled by the shock of spending so much time alone with his daughters, he said, 'Well, you can come with us next time if that's all you're going to do. And by the way, Heidi's wet her knickers and Eliza cut her finger on the rocks, is there some plaster somewhere?'

For want of something better to do, Eleanor sent a postcard to Eva Summers, who, of course, would never receive it, as she'd left home some time before. The postcard said, 'Our first holiday for five years. Wish you were here. Remind me to ask you when we next meet where you bought your parrot.'

She dropped it in the postbox on her way to the local doctor's with Heidi, who had come out in spots. This proved to be chickenpox, and it lasted six weeks by the time Eliza had had it and given it to David, who confused it with mumps and worried about his potency, but didn't say so.

They had gone out for a meal in Dorset once as a family, like the French one sitting next to them in the terraced restaurant now. They went to a country hotel and sat in a dining room smelling of beeswax and old ladies, and Heidi and Eliza had behaved quite appallingly. It was before the chickenpox, but Heidi must have been sickening for it at the time. There was no other explanation for her behaviour. She insisted on sitting under the table, and there was nothing Eleanor could do about it. The waitress, who reminded Eleanor of Miss Everest, because of her severe demeanour and the fact that she had two long hairs growing out of a mole on her chin, brought them their bill at the earliest available opportunity. 'Why do other people's children always behave, when ours don't?' complained David as they left the hotel.

'Don't look at me,' said Eleanor sourly, 'I only gave birth to them, it's not the same thing at all.'

Back in Brighton, speaking to or rather being spoken to by her mother one day, Eleanor heard that her Uncle Hal was in London for a few days. With difficulty she inserted in her mother's complaints about the erratic habits of Mr Cranbury, the gardener they'd had at Muddenham Grange, who'd died twenty years ago, a question about where in London Hal was to be found.

Eleanor telephoned her uncle at the Crusoe Club in Bloomsbury, and they arranged to meet for tea. Eleanor telephoned David at the university and arranged for him to look after his daughters for the afternoon. 'I've got to go to the family planning clinic,' she explained. It did occur to her to tell the truth, but not for long. David would only require a detailed account of what she and Hal had said to each other and Eleanor, tired of living so much of her life under the open gaze of three pairs of eyes, felt protective of the tiny amount of privacy the reunion with Uncle Hal would give her. Uncle Hal came out of a rosy past – that of her own youth. Also, it was fun to be secretive again – the lessons Eva had taught her had been wasted recently.

Hal was older and more vanquished looking than Eleanor remembered. To Hal, Eleanor appeared even slighter than he recalled from the summer fourteen years ago, her physical presence in some way reduced rather than enhanced by reproduction. She was like a mother wolf sucked dry by her young, cut to a ranginess by the effort of so much nurture and no time to ponder in a solitary way on the overall meaning of wolfhood.

Hal and Eleanor ate a plate of cream cakes together. 'Thurston's got cancer,' remarked Hal suddenly.

'How awful,' said Eleanor, inadequately.

'I've come back to sort out his affairs. A mutual friend, Colin Worsley, is with him now in Le Canard. But I mustn't be long, he needs me.'

'Of course.'

He took her little hand, sticky from the cakes, between his large equally sticky ones. 'And, dear Eleanor, how are you? A mother, I hear, twice over. But of human, not literary progeny?'

To her great amazement, Eleanor started to cry. Hal consoled, then cajoled, but in a very different vein from sister-in-law Bridget Kendrick. 'Life's short, Eleanor Jenkinson,' he said, thinking of Thurston on the sofa in the dark kitchen in Cavaillon, with the bad cells multiplying deep inside him, taking him over bit by bit, turning him from the splendid young man he once had been – and still was in Hal's head – into an unorganized lump of useless flesh. 'Life's short, and one mustn't wait for the good things, one must make them happen. Otherwise they won't. One waits for ever, and for nothing. That's the way it is, my child!'

Eleanor Jenkinson was by this time approaching the age of thirty. Her birthday was, indeed, imminent, and her husband, closeted with his daughters in front of 'Blue Peter', was presently engaged in planning its celebration. A few friends, his new colleagues at the university, Eleanor's mother perhaps – though maybe that wasn't such a good idea, she might by now have completely forgotten who Eleanor was.

David was very fond of Eleanor. He wanted to make her happy, but he was permanently mystified by her. Whenever he looked at her, she seemed to be looking the other way. It was like living with a ghost.

'Hal,' said Eleanor suddenly at the Crusoe Club, 'have you got any money?'

He looked hard at her. He understood. 'For you, my dearest, yes. How much would you like?'

'Just a small loan,' she said, sipping her tea a little frenetically, unused to putting herself forward in this way.

Hal wrote her a cheque and she put it in her handbag. When she got home and David asked her what the family planning clinic had recommended in the way of contraception, she pretended the piece of paper was a prescription for Gynovlar. She would take it to the pharmacy presently, and he could rest assured there would be no more children unless she wanted them.

They order the *menu gastronomique*. With a sense of hopelessness, Eleanor knows she will feel hungry afterwards. For Eleanor eats, she eats her way through life almost better than she does anything else. She's one of those annoying people who can eat what they like without it affecting them. Her waistline is completely immune to the ingestion of doughnuts, chocolate bars, buttery pasta and all other unhealthy treats. The carbohydrate and the cholesterol feed her imagination more than her body; that's why she needs them.

On this occasion she'd seen the structure of the plates as they came in; nouvelle cuisine plates, raised in the middle with a mound for whatever little protein-rich delicacy the menu named, and with a hollowed rim for the thin brown, or cream, or green, or pink, sauce.

'Why does everywhere in France do this sort of food now?' she complains suddenly. 'Whatever happened to those wonderful cheap *earthy* menus – you know, bowls of soup with big ladles brought to the table, shiny green salads dressed in walnut oil, plates of pommes frites . . .'

'Eleanor, stop it!' She realizes he's actually annoyed. 'We don't *have* to eat out.'

'No, you could chain me to the kitchen,' she admits, reasonably. 'Or even dish up a course or two yourself.'

'You're very irritable these days.'

'Are these days all that different from all the others we've had together?'

'I could point out we're on our own now.'

'We were then. We always were, really.'

'I give up.'

'Perhaps you should.'

The waiter brings the wine David has ordered, a Sauvignon blanc. He sips it admiringly. 'Come on, Eleanor Jenkinson, stop glowering at me, and make the best of a bad job.'

She goes on glowering at him, and eats her way through the bread basket. Even the rolls are small, shiny and curled like shrimps.

David starts talking about Mayhew in the Department. 'It's not as if he'd ever *published* anything worth reading,' he was saying, 'so why on earth he imagined he'd be eligible for a Readership is beyond me. Of course, I had to tell him so. I had to say, listen Mayhew, it's entirely up to you whether you apply for promotion or not, but if you're looking for my support, you can think again. I don't think he believed me. As a matter of fact, I don't think he was even listening. Are you listening, Eleanor?'

Over David's shoulder Eleanor observes a white sports car entering the square. It parks by the cattle scales, and a woman with short black hair in a purple costume gets out. She locks the car door, unlocks the boot and takes out a small suitcase. Swinging it lightly, as though it contains nothing heavier than flowers, she walks across the square with extraordinary nineteenth-century elegance.

Extract from:

CHANGING TRAINS
BY ELEANOR JENKINSON

'I'm going off for a few weeks,' she said casually.

'Oh, where?'

'Somewhere in France. An hotel.'

'What for?'

'To write.'

'I'll come with you.'

'You won't!'

'But I love you!'

'Precisely,' she said. And then, turning to go: *'Love confines.
Even yours. And in that confinement resides our mesmeriza-
tion. Too much harmony glazes the imagination. In short, my
desire to write is at odds with your desire for me. Goodbye.'*

Eleanor Jenkinson carried Uncle Hal's cheque around with her for
a while, considering what to do with it. It was quite a large one.
Eventually she took it to a bank manager – not the Jenkinsons' own –
that wouldn't have been a good idea – but to a newly opened branch
of Lloyds Bank in the Lanes.

She took the little girls with her, but kept them hidden as
far as possible behind her long skirt (fashionable at the time –
now 1969).

Mr Gleeting, the manager, asked Eleanor if she would like to sit
down, though he rather hoped she wouldn't, as he wasn't sure he'd
be able to see her at all then. 'What can I do you for, Mrs Jenkinson?'
he opened with a slight snigger. If it weren't for the infants, mingled
with her skirt, he'd think she was a schoolgirl.

'I've come into some money, Mr Gleeting,' she said, having already
decided to put it like this, 'and I'd like some advice on what to do
with it.'

'Always happy to oblige,' he remarked professionally, though
somewhat automatically, as his mind was quite occupied with the
recent demonetarization of the halfpenny, of which there were still
an awful lot in the safe behind him.

'You see, Mr Gleeting, I want to be a writer.' At that moment Eliza,
who was in the early stages of toilet training, peed on the carpet in
front of Mr Gleeting's desk. Eleanor put her foot over it hoping he
wouldn't notice. It squelched slightly. She fed Heidi a few Smarties
from her handbag to stop her giving the game away, and then Eliza
some to stop her complaining about what was happening to Heidi.

'Let me get this straight, Mrs Jenkinson,' said Mr Gleeting, vaguely
aware of unsavoury skirmishes behind the desk. 'You have how much
to invest?'

'Twenty thousand pounds,' said Eleanor. Eliza took her wet knickers off and dropped them in Mr Gleeting's wastepaper basket. Heidi's mouth opened, revealing a display of partly masticated Smarties. Eleanor crammed some more in to stop anything coming out.

Mr Gleeting shook his head sadly. 'At our higher rate of interest that would only give you' – he performed some manoeuvres with an electronic calculator – 'two thousand three hundred a year. Hardly enough to support a budding writer, I wouldn't have thought. Your husband . . . ?'

'How much is that a week?' demanded Eleanor, who was still trapped in a different order of calculation.

Mr Gleeting told her. 'What about shares?' he suggested. 'And Mr Jenkinson, now . . .'

'What about them?'

'You could buy some.'

Suddenly, as Mr Gleeting proved himself unequal to the task of arranging her financial security as a writer, Eleanor decided what she would do with her money. She got up, sweeping her damp, over-Smartied brigade behind her, thanked Mr Gleeting for precisely nothing on the way, and quite forgot Eliza's knickers, which the Lloyds Bank cleaning person, who also cleaned Mr and Mrs Gleeting's house, would find later in the day and use as the basis of false speculations for some time to come.

Eleanor's resolution had two parts to it: one, find a room to rent – a room of her own; two, hire someone to look after the girls so that she could be in it.

She decided to tackle the room first. When Heidi was at playgroup in the mornings, she bundled Eliza up in the pushchair and set off for the estate agents. 'A room to rent? A *room* to rent?' It appeared she was asking the impossible. Flats, yes, houses, penthouses, studio apartments, garages, lockup shops, but not a room. 'Try the university,' they said helpfully. Eleanor telephoned the university lodgings bureau, and spoke to a woman called Angela. A list arrived two days later in the post. Eleanor and Eliza set off again. The first one was a small first-floor room with a powder-blue plastic screen round a cracked basin in the corner. It had no view, except of powder-blue plastic. The second was in the attic – the old servants' quarters – of a Regency house not far from their own. From this point of view, it was suitable. But the windows were too high up – servants didn't need views. The third one, just as Eleanor had begun to feel the whole thing was a pointless and unnecessary self-indulgence – she didn't need to write her novel after all, she could do it in the bathroom standing on her head – had promise. It would do, even. It was a corner room with two windows, from one of which the sea could be seen today, a sharp Tuesday in March, stretched a crinkled blue beneath a herringbone sky. The room had a table by the window, and a gas fire with a meter. The landlady, Mrs Crispin, apologized for the size of the bed – not very large. 'It doesn't matter, I don't suppose I'll be using it all that much,' said Eleanor cheerfully, and then, seeing the look of alarm cloud Mrs Crispin's face like the sky outside, hastened to explain that this was principally a room for daytime use, for a would-be writer. Herself.

Mrs Crispin looked both reassured and not. 'But what about your little girl?' (It must be remembered that Eleanor's efforts to establish herself as an independent working woman were taking place at a time when only 7.2 percent of mothers of young children were what was called economically active.)

'I shall find someone to look after her for a few hours a day,' promised Eleanor, 'and her sister, when she's not at playgroup.'

Mrs Crispin's anxiety turned into practical solicitousness, and she offered Eleanor the name of a friend who had a daughter who might take on that kind of work.

Feeling that her life might be falling into place at last, Eleanor bought some flowers on the way home. The same impulse sent her into Mothercare to buy a new outfit for Eliza, a pink denim skirt and a matching jumper with daisies on it. Then she bought a larger size in yellow for Heidi. Feeling guilty, she nipped into Augustus Barnett for a bottle of –? She stood there, realizing she'd never bought wine by herself before. David, or some previous man, or her mother, had always been there to interpret the labels. She chose a pink one with flowers on the label, like the flowers on the clothes she'd just bought the girls. It turned out to be pink champagne, and it cost the earth, £8, but she didn't care.

By the end of the afternoon the babysitting was fixed up as well. Caroline Dixon, the daughter of Mrs Crispin's friend Mary, would come in three days a week from ten until four. She would look after Eliza, fetch Heidi from playgroup at twelve, give the girls a simple lunch and take them to the park, or swimming or make pastry with them or whatever it is that mothers are supposed to do, but normally don't get round to. This would cost Eleanor £27 a week. The rent of the room was £15. Thus the combined price of her freedom to write, the institution of those material conditions so few women have had, without which the muse can't be liberated, was £42 a week. It didn't seem a lot. Eleanor worked out that at that rate the twenty thousand pounds should last 476 weeks, or 9.2 years. However, when she went into the kitchen to prepare supper that evening, she decided she needed to buy a new fridge as well, with a much larger freezing compartment. Come to that, the washing . . . well, a new washing machine and tumble dryer – there would still be a sizeable chunk of the money left, wouldn't there?

As everyone can by now imagine, the bit of the puzzle Eleanor Jenkinson hadn't solved was how to break the news to her husband David. As we have already established, David Jenkinson wasn't any more of a sexist than the next man, which is to say, he was quite a lot of one. In this respect he was merely, as we all are, a product of his times. In his times women were needed in the home as mothers. At least, that was what was *said*, though everyone really knew that when men talked about maternal deprivation what they *really* meant was what on earth would *they* do if women threw off their shackles and ran out of the kitchen?

On this day that augured her own liberation from the mould David Jenkinson had constructed for her, Eleanor laid the table nicely, and chilled the champagne in the old freezer thinking of the new one. She served Heidi and Eliza fish fingers and baked beans, and washed their hairs before David got home so they would smell nice, and he would think what a good job she was doing. (This on reflection might have been a bit of a mistake, as, if she were doing such a good job of it all, surely she shouldn't give it up to write a novel?)

Eleanor had obtained from the butcher a couple of nice steaks, and bought some fresh spinach and new potatoes; she'd organized a cheesecake (made from a packet but with fresh frozen strawberries on top) for dessert. With the girls in front of the weather forecast – normally the television would be off by this time, so they both understood this was a special favour and were happily transfixed by rumours of belts of low pressure over the British Isles – she had a quick bath and looked in the cupboard for some alluring clothes to put on. But anything alluring she'd once had was either not the right size any more or had holes in it. With some lipstick and a dab of perfume – the very last drops of the Chanel No 5 bought on the boat back from Tuscany the year before Heidi was born – the clean black jeans and black embroidered blouse Eleanor put on were the best she could do. David, in any case, probably wouldn't notice. In any case, what did she want to convince him of? It was, naturally, herself she needed to convince. That she was a worthwhile investment. That the only obstacles holding My Novel back *were* spatial and domestic.

'I think it's a very good idea,' said David, and not only because of the champagne.

'You do?'

'Provided that Heidi and Eliza don't suffer, of course.'

'Of course.'

(There is, after all, nothing much wrong with *ideas* of liberation. They're often very attractive, as the open vistas they conjure up are seamless fields with none of the tacky pits sprinkled on real terrain. Many men, or slave-owners, or aristocrats, have thus had no objection in principle to emancipation. There's sometimes even quite a prize to be won by claiming to support it. Only when the women or the slaves or the peasants start getting their act together may a certain churlishness make its appearance, normally veiled as some unanticipated consequence, rather than an objection that was lurking there all the time.)

The Jenkinsons bought the new fridge and washing machine and tumble dryer on the Saturday, and on the Monday at 9.55 Carrie Dixon arrived to start work. Eleanor had stayed up late on Sunday night writing out lists of instructions, which were now taped in place on the shining new fridge. About first-aid – how to give the kiss of life to small children, even if sometimes you feel it's the last thing you want to do; likes and dislikes unevenly shared between her two daughters – milk for Eliza, but Heidi can't abide it, it brings her out in spots anyway, don't expect Eliza to eat carrots but on the other hand she can always be tempted by a nicely cut ring of green pepper. Numbers to call in case of emergency: the doctor, David, the landlady, Mrs Crispin – Carrie's mother's friend – who surely would be prepared to relay messages.

'Don't worry, Mrs Jenkinson,' said Carrie, unzipping her tight denim jacket. She flicked her long hair back over her shoulder and practised a capable expression. But she was capable, wasn't she? Both girls screamed as their mother left the house. Eleanor repeated the name of Esther Gray like a mantra as she fled down Anchor Road, hearing the protests of her abandoned infants long after these had been stopped by the Jelly Tots Carrie had brought as bribery. 'We'll be fine, won't we girls!' Heidi and Eliza looked up at her in the narrow hallway, eyes round and wet with tears, mouths round and full of Jelly Tots. Carrie put the television on, made herself a cup of instant coffee, and sat down with Jackie Collins.

Ensconced in Marine Parade, Eleanor watched the sea for signs of movement capable of stimulating her fallow imagination. The room was simply furnished. She'd moved some of her books in, along with My Novel in a Habitat plastic bag, but had deliberately not taken pains to create a cosy interior. It was for looking out from, this room, not into. A vehicle for thought, not an end in itself.

But Eleanor had made the mistake all unsuccessful writers make of being too hard on themselves. A certain air of indetermination is required – either it happens or it doesn't. Sit back and let the words form, if they will, in your head. If they won't ... They don't at all easily. It had been too long since Eleanor had had uninterrupted time. She could hardly remember who Esther Gray was, let alone where she'd got to in her moral and geographical development. Eleanor sighed a lot, paced the room, and worried from time to time about her children closeted with Carrie Dixon.

By the end of the first day she'd written exactly two paragraphs six times, leaving one final version of one of them. At that rate, each paragraph would cost £14. Like the reluctant patient on the psychoanalyst's couch, the reason Eleanor put a value on her time was because she couldn't get rid of the notion that she might have been wasting it.

After this agony she stormed home, where everyone to her surprise appeared to be well. The children were watching television still, but Eleanor thought it was again.

'Someone phoned, Mrs Jenkinson,' said Carrie a little suspiciously. 'He said his name was Ball. Or that's what it sounded like. How can

Ball be a name? Well, I don't know. I've written the number on the pad in the kitchen, anyway. It might have been an obscene phone call, I suppose. Did you write a lot, Mrs Jenkinson? Is it finished yet, My Novel?'

After Carrie had gone – yes, Eleanor affirmed she had done a *very* good day's work – she racked her brains to try to remember who Ball was. It was a while before she recalled the coffee bar in Waterloo. The pain in her bottom at the time had caused her to put a lid on the episode. Before David came home, and out of curiosity, she telephoned Ball at the number Carrie had written down.

'Oh, Mrs J, how kind of you to call me back!'

'Cut it out, Ball,' Eleanor said, speaking like a man Esther had recently met in Montmartre (a scene written in the Creative Writing Class days, and re-read that day). 'Did you want something? Or, rather, *what* do you want?'

He laughed, a rasping sound like an elevator that needs oiling. 'It's Janice, Mrs J, I think you should look her up one of these days. Could you manage that, d'you think?'

'Well, not this week, Ball,' said Eleanor firmly, 'I've just started a – a job.'

'That's nice, Mrs J.'

'Well, not a job exactly, but I've rented a room so I can get some writing done. Away from the girls, you see. I have two now, you see,' she added clumsily as an afterthought.

'Some of us is lucky to have one home to rent, let alone two,' remarked Ball. 'And I'm not into kids, meself. Anyway, please yourself, Mrs J. I just said I'd pass on the message.'

Eleanor wrote five pages the next day. Then she counted the number of words she'd written – eight hundred and forty-six. At two o'clock she indulged in the luxury of a walk by the sea. But she called it necessity, beginning to learn from her mistakes. She strolled to the pier and back, concentrating on the character of Esther's foil – a young female refugee from a surveyor's office in East Cheam – in chapter four of *Esther's Virtue* as it was now called. Standing by the pier, looking straight out to sea, she saw two girls on the beach, their heads breaking the sea's anodyne pallor in this whatever season, and she remembered Janice and Michelle and through them her friend Eva Summers. She wondered again what had become of Eva, and whether she should telephone Christian Summers to find out. He presumably would have read the postcard she sent Eva from Dorset. Eleanor thought fondly of Eva's hearing aid whistling in a telephone box, and with an unusual charity derived from the newly changed circumstances of her life – a little step for herself, an even smaller one for womankind – she thanked Eva for sending her on those paltry Tuesday adventures. If she was no nearer being a successful novelist now than she was then, at least she was no further away. Perhaps as an act of appreciation, she should take some time to seek Janice out. She couldn't, after all, expect herself to write all the time (the speed at which Eleanor was learning was truly amazing!) or she would write herself out – there'd be no life left to act as a dictionary.

Extract from:

HOW MANY LIGHTBULBS?
BY ESTHER GRAY

The rhythm of the music in the basement, densely packed with bodies, glasses, sweat and laughter, is his as well as theirs, and is communicated to Eleanor in the light conjunction of their shoulders as they sit at the table together watching the others dance. She is content to sit there, hypnotized by the coalescence of heat, light, smoke, flesh touchable but as yet untouched.

After a while he stands up, takes her by the hand and leads her behind the bar and through a door on the left-hand side to a large, unexpectedly white room, beautifully painted in a sheer ivory gloss. There is one window, crossed with white bars. A table in the centre holds a pot of apricot orchids, their damp stamens exposed like torches. There's a bed in the corner of the room. Narrow, only really big enough for one.

They are naked suddenly. And standing beneath a single unclothed lightbulb. His body is as white as hers. But they don't touch. The music from the other room fades. She smells spring flowers. Her cunt is wet. Nothing happens.

The door opens. Janice and Michelle come in, giggling silently.

One each side, they guide her to the bed and lay her down. Janice parts her legs and brushes her pubic hair as lightly as Ball's shoulder had touched hers. Michelle goes over to him beneath the lightbulb. Michelle kneels – Eleanor can see the crescent curve of her buttocks in the stretched denim, the silhouette of the upturned high heels against them – and she takes something of Ball in her mouth. He closes his eyes and rests his hands on Michelle's head, sliding his fingers into the stark yellowed curls. Janice watches, casually taking one of Eleanor's nipples to play with, but without looking at her.

Nobody wears any expression, though two of them still wear clothes. Even so, it is just flesh. The flower smell is cloying, the silence absolute.

Michelle leads Ball over to Eleanor and stands behind him. Janice, her left hand occupied with Eleanor's breast, takes Ball's erect shaft in her other hand. Michelle begins to moan, is rubbing her breasts against Ball's back, her hand clamped between her legs. 'It's time, Mrs J,' croons Janice then.

Ball kneels now; Janice takes his penis, rubbing it very slowly, then faster. Eleanor can see its liquid end, like a tap. Her cunt aches. 'It's all right, darling,' says Michelle, cradling her head. 'It'll be good for you, you'll see, we'll look after you.'

Ball's down on Eleanor now, their genitals are awash together. A wave hits her, then another. But he is nearly, not quite, still. She opens her eyes, and sees Janice and Michelle kissing, and taking off each other's clothes at last, under the lightbulb. Then his eyes, satanically focused, are looking into hers. 'Was that enough, Mrs J? Or shall I move again? What do you think? No, don't answer: this one's on me.' It is, and it goes on and on, tides without end, desire without meaningful object or satiation. And all the while Janice and Michelle grimace like pubertal puppies on the floor under the lightbulb.

'What about you, Ball?'

'What about me, Mrs J?' He pins his mouth on hers so she can't answer. Janice is beside her again. 'Don't you worry, Mrs J, we'll take care of Ball, won't we, Michelle? We're good at that. One for you, one for him.' Abruptly Ball withdraws. 'That's good, Ball,' says Janice, 'don't want any little Mrs Js, do we, not with your record!' Michelle slips her hand into Eleanor's soaking vagina.

Eleanor, shocked, tenses, and her eyes alight, as they are meant to, on Janice's hand, which is wrapped around Ball's organ but only momentarily, as soon it shoots a hot opal jet through the humid atmosphere.

FOUR

She Didn't Do Any of It for Love

ELEANOR ORDERS *salade de canard* to start with, and David
tian St Jacques. When the *salade de canard* arrives, it proves to be
composed of small grey oblong slices of duck cartwheeling out
from a bright vegetable mousse, with cherry-sized bombs of tomato
pulp encircling the whole like a necklace.

'Very pretty,' she says.

David also exclaims at his. After the second mouthful (there are
only four or five to be had) he says gently, that is, in what most
people would regard as the nicest possible way, 'I've been very
patient, Eleanor, a very patient man. Don't you think so? Well,
I do. The reason for my patience is that I've always believed
in you, you see. More than that, I've believed in *us*. That may
come as a surprise to you. Perhaps you haven't realized how
much I've known about what was going on. Not the details –
you kept those from me. Wisely, probably. But I certainly knew
that things weren't right. I didn't probe, because I didn't feel it
would help. I thought it might even make things worse. But
now it's all over, I feel you really should tell me everything that
happened. You owe it to me. I want to know. Besides which, I have
to know if we are to make any kind of sensible decision about the
future.'

David looks directly at her. The face, white with dark eyes, the
heavy eyebrows, the stubborn cleft in the chin, is still the same, but
the expression isn't. She feels he's a stranger. She shifts uneasily in her
seat. The waiter comes out to turn on the white fairy lights strung
round the terrace. 'Very pretty,' she says again.

'Did you hear me, Eleanor?'

'I'm not a child,' she says. 'Don't speak to me like one.'

'I wasn't. But your behaviour . . .'

'Belongs to me,' she says.

'I don't dispute that for a moment,' he says reassuringly, as though to a child. 'But why are you so angry? You're like a porcupine bristling at me. I'm your *husband*, Eleanor.'

His voice is raised, the woman at the next table looks at them.

'Don't shout, David.'

'I'm not shouting.'

'Oh?'

'I just have a louder voice than you.'

'That's the problem, isn't it?'

'I don't understand.'

'Power, David.' The fairy lights shine like proverbial diamonds, and, as if in sympathy, one goes dead, then another. The waiter comes back and fiddles with the bulbs, trying to screw them back into their sockets. The man at the next table says something in very rapid French that Eleanor can't decipher. Perhaps he's an electrician in disguise.

'Is there anything we say to each other we haven't said before?' She sighs, as when trying to write a novel.

'What do you expect after twenty-eight years?'

'I do expect something,' she admits.

'Oh, Ellie!' This wrings a smile from her. She sips her wine. The lights come back on again. 'You always did have unrealistic expectations.'

'So it's my fault again, is it?' She's relapsed into glowering.

'Stop reading things into what I say that aren't there.'

'If I don't, who will?'

'Why does anyone need to?'

'Each of us is more than we seem,' says Eleanor carefully. 'But in order to become that, we must be seen, interpreted, understood by others. Without these mirrors we can't know ourselves, and if we don't know ourselves, how can we spot the distortions other people throw at us?'

'So life is a cracked mirror, is it?'

'I don't know, David.'

'I wish you'd stop struggling so.'

'I could say the same to you.'

*

Extract from:

ORANGES AND LEMONS
BY ELEANOR JENKINSON

They sit in the restaurant in the fading rustic light. It's a perfect vantage point, up there above the square, from which to see everything except that, as usual, Dick's back is turned away from it.

'It's time you told me the truth,' she says suddenly. 'You've palmed me off with lies for long enough.'

His face whitens against the blushing sky. 'What truth? What lies, come to that?'

'I'm not a child.' She bites back the tears. 'Who is she, Dick?'

He lays down his fork. There's a strange silence over everything, as during a daytime eclipse of the sun. All she can hear is her own heart pointlessly pushing the blood round her body.

'A woman called Eleanor,' he says. 'A writer, actually.'

'Carrie will be staying with the girls until seven tomorrow,' announced Eleanor to David. 'I've got to go to London to do some shopping.'

'What's wrong with the shops here?'

'I'm going to meet my mother in Harrods, actually.'

She caught the 10.05 to Victoria by running to the station. On the train she reread the first and second parts of the retitled *A French Fantasy*, which she carried with her in a plastic bag marked 'Arrow Books, Wimbledon'. But she found herself unable to form any proper judgement of the manuscript. It had been part of her life for too long. Seven years since before she met David; indeed, there were sections of the text that had been composed before that, when she was a student at Manchester. A segment of dialogue in chapter two was even based on a conversation that had sprinkled the lavender fields in Provence the summer she was sixteen – her own youthful tones mixed with Hal's ringing colonial baritone, Thurston Blane's assiduously Oxford cadences counterpointing them both. Eleanor wondered if Thurston had died yet. She ought to write to Hal. Perhaps she should take the girls to see him? She had a passing vision of Heidi and Eliza's shining heads amidst the lavender, childish voices rising and falling in the perfumed air.

Eleanor's attention returned to the book. She had lately begun to think of it as a book rather than only a collection of words, or under the acronym 'My Novel'. But she wouldn't have been able easily to summarize what the book was about. There was this young woman, Esther, who on page one is to be found looking for herself in Paris. Esther's search, not unnaturally, given the reductionist heterosexual ethic of the times, was partly composed of amorous adventures with men. It was in the abrasive concatenation of these encounters that Esther identified, more by a methodology of exclusion than by any clear sense of positive identification, what kind of person she was. So far so good. Since Esther was a student of philosophy, she treated the reader to a series of theoretical peregrinations round this more or less hackneyed theme, the making of which Eleanor (on behalf of Esther) supposed would contribute a unique dimension to the novel. In fact, however, most of the text's philosophizing served only to reiterate points that had already been made succinctly enough within the context of Esther's sociosexual encounters. They didn't drive the point home, so much as act as a hammer making a great unnecessary banging noise.

What Eleanor needed to do, she began to see on the train to Victoria, was to solicit someone else's opinion on My Novel. She needed to be taken outside her own view of it, in order to see what it was really about, and whether it was any good or not — by 'good' meaning would anyone else want to read it? Almost anyone would do for this purpose, though someone with a literary consciousness would be better than someone without. Eleanor hankered after her creative writing class in Wimbledon, even after Tom Sherringham's beery stomach and clipped literary insults. She remembered the word 'promising' her efforts had finally wrung out of him. The answer was obvious. But was not on the agenda for today, which had to be occupied with other things.

Eleanor made her way to Janice's new address, given her by the laconic Ball on the telephone. It transpired to be a council estate in Hackney. She walked from the underground, twisting her A to Z this and that way, being the kind of person who must always hold the map in the same direction as the one in which they're walking. Number 35 Austen House was reached via the usual graffiti-strewn staircase. She knocked at the door, which was decked on the inside by a sheet of white nylon hung with wedding bows. Janice – it was Janice, wasn't it? – opened the door. 'Mrs J! What are you doing here?'

Janice looked really pleased to see Eleanor. But she seemed to have aged a lot since they had last met properly, five years ago. Eleanor had worked it out on the train: if Janice had been skipping off her last year of school then, she must be twenty-one now. Of age; but she looked rather worn down by it, in her pale lemon candlewick housecoat buttoned up over breasts that had descended a floor since Eleanor had last been in proximity to them. On her feet were fluffy honey-coloured slippers matching her hair – short and in need of washing. Janice's blue eyes seemed to have lost the piercing brightness of youth, the whites, indeed, being yellowed to a shade almost matching the housecoat.

She took Eleanor into a little crowded sitting room, densely carpeted in a red-brown pattern, with an embossed grey and green paper on the walls. There was a large teak-framed television, a print of horses in a field, a buttoned brown shiny sofa, and on this, between two humps, a tiny baby dressed in white. 'Well, it is nice to see you, Mrs J! I'll make a cup of coffee, shall I? This is Marlon, by the way.' She flicked a finger in the direction of the baby, who watched without much interest, coughing slightly. Janice moved a packet of cigarettes and an electric blue cigarette lighter from the other chair in the room, and flopped down into it. Eleanor sat down next to the baby.

'How old is he, Janice?'

'Seven months. And a half, tomorrow, aren't you, darling?' She got up then, and paused on her way to make the coffee to tickle his chin. 'Milk, no sugar, isn't it?'

As Janice walked out of the room, Eleanor saw on her pasty legs large dark blue bruises. These matched one on the side of Janice's face; perhaps the closed housecoat concealed more? Soon the whole sorry story came out over the Nescafé, served in tinted Pyrex mugs; a plate of circular almond creams eyed them from the coffee table.

Janice and Michelle had both left school – that is, officially – in 1967. Janice had gone to work as a shrink wrapper in a processed meat factory, and Michelle in the local M&S. Janice's mum had produced another baby, making seven in all, and Janice's dad – he wasn't really but she'd always thought of him as such – died suddenly. 'We never knew what it were, Mrs J. Me mum said it were from the asbestos he used to work with – he had an awful time with his lungs latterly

– but the doctor put heart attack. I think that's what they write when they don't know what else to put, meself. What *is* a heart attack, Mrs J? It sounds odd, don't it? Does your heart attack you? Or is it an attack *of* the heart? It's quite worrying, really.' She patted her own, somewhere under the candlewick, and lit a Camel. After that, quite soon afterwards in the chronology of Janice's account, a new man, Sam Bates, a plumber, had moved in with Janice's mum – you could understand it, she'd been desperate, with seven of them and only Janice working; but Sam Bates had soon been loathed by Janice with a virulence that spluttered now like fireworks through the Nescafé, and made her cigarette ash narrowly miss baby Marlon's downy scalp. Because of Sam, Janice had moved out. 'I went back to see me mum when he wasn't there, but I haven't seen Sam Bates since that day I moved me things to Michelle's place,' said Janice proudly. Then Michelle had married her boyfriend Fran (the dark silent youth from the Waterloo coffee bar) and again Janice had been homeless, though she did for a while, she said, stay with Fran and Michelle. 'They've got a little maisonette behind the London Hospital, just two rooms, k and b, I slept on the sofa, but the walls were that thin and it weren't fair, really.' Michelle had a baby girl, Alicia, and there'd really been no alternative for Janice but to follow the same path herself.

'Remember Pete?' interrogated Janice. Eleanor nodded, recalling the early beard, the acne, and the wave of dislike that had hit her along with the acrid atmosphere in the coffee bar. 'Well,' said Janice, pausing for effect and blowing a large smoke ring round herself in self defence, 'that's Pete's, that is.' She nodded in baby Marlon's direction. 'But he weren't me first; I had another little boy first. Beautiful little chap. Born at six months on a Saturday night, died on the Thursday the next week just before dinner time.' She stubbed her cigarette out, and reached down beside the sofa to the lower shelf of a mock walnut coffee table, bringing back up a large red photograph album. She picked herself up, and sat down on the sofa, sliding up towards the innocent, now sleeping, Marlon, then patted the space the other side of her. 'Come and sit here, Mrs J, and look at me snaps.'

And there, captured in a series of square Polaroid photographs which, due to some quirk of the development process, were unduly dominated by red and blue tones, was the gestation, birth and death of baby Lawrence Carew. The child himself could hardly be seen behind the tangle of doctors and nurses and machines, but Janice was obviously there, looking very loving and crying, and a young man holding on to her, who wasn't, Eleanor didn't think, Pete. 'Michelle's brother,' explained Janice. 'He was a mistake really.' It wasn't clear whether she meant the man or the child.

Eventually Janice closed the photograph album and lit another cigarette. Her face was wet. 'I can't forget him, Mrs J, I keep seeing his little face. Every time I close me eyes I see his face. Like a little monkey's, it was. D'you know what got me most, Mrs J? He needed me, poor little scrap. It were the first time anybody did.' She drew heavily on the cigarette, blowing out the smoke so Eleanor could scarcely see her face behind it.

She seemed unaware of the living child beside her. Eleanor reached over Janice and picked the baby up. 'What about Marlon, Janice?'

Janice looked down. 'Yes.'

He seemed well cared for. His clothes were clean. He looked adequately fed.

'He's okay, Marlon is. But I don't feel the same about him, Mrs J. It's not Marlon I want. I want Lawrence.'

'Where's Pete?' asked Eleanor to fill in time while she thought about this.

'In the Scrubs,' said Janice sourly. 'Went there Friday.'

'What did he do, Janice?'

'Nicked some jewellery from a house in Worcester Terrace. Flogged it to pay for the stuff in this place. Said he wanted the baby and me to have a nice home. That's what he *said*, anyway.'

'What do you mean?'

'Turns out none of it belongs to us. It's all on the H.P. So's the car. Great big black thing, can't remember what it's called.' Janice got up and lifted a corner of the curtain, as if expecting the car, somewhere down there, to call out its name. She started to cry, treating herself to staccato puffs of her cigarette between the tears. At one point she held it up and looked at it in the struggling spring light from the window. 'Doctor said this was what did it. Should have packed it in, he said. Criminal, he said. Like Pete. Cigarettes brings them on early. D'you think that's true, Mrs J?'

'I don't know,' said Eleanor truthfully.

'Well, it's not true,' said Janice vehemently. 'I know, 'cos I went to the library and looked it up. They don't know what makes some of 'em come early. Doesn't happen to women like you, though.'

She glanced at Eleanor for a moment almost resentfully. 'Privilege protects.' She stubbed the cigarette out again, 'Excuse me, I'm just going to the toilet.'

Eleanor could hear a lot of sniffing and nose blowing as well as sounds of the lavatory being used. She looked around her with a feeling of futility. At the room with its fussy, clashing colours, the interrupted blue to be glimpsed through the heavily curtained windows, at the white baby unable to contend even in angelic sleep with the Polaroid memoirs stored under the coffee table. She thought of Pete in prison, of Janice's knowledge of the male sex, so different, presumably, from her heroine Esther's in Paris, or her own. Eleanor considered Janice's financial debts, the unmentionable bruises on her pastel limbs. The awful poverty of it all. And as was to be expected of a person of her class, she ran through some conventional strategies: to call a social worker, to consult a Citizens' Advice Bureau, to suggest that Janice's doctor, supposing there was such a person who cared to claim expertise over this bundle of pains, might call round and advise her. Then Eleanor thought, guiltily, of her own little girls in their protected – though by no means problem-free, especially now Carrie was there – environment; why was Janice not able to experience, unlumbered by these dreadful burdens, the exquisitely simple maternal love Eleanor herself believed she felt?

None of this could be put into words, of course. Janice came back into the room, sat down opposite Eleanor, and said, 'What am I to do, Mrs J?'

The two women looked at each other across the yawning divide of their different social circumstances, uncertain as to where, if anywhere, their shared female status fitted in, or what relevance that nonsense of their initial meeting – Eleanor seeking experience with which to create fiction, Janice already living all its seamy factual rottenness – had to any of this. Were they enemies or friends? And if friends, which both of them would have preferred to think, then what could Janice Carew do for Eleanor Jenkinson which would repay any of the gestures of amity Eleanor was about to make towards Janice?

The silence, pregnant with difficulty, hung between them, an impossible gestation. Janice looked at Eleanor, clothed in her grey linen jacket and blue print skirt, her crisp hair curling on the white blouse ironed with an easy middle-class carelessness, at the delicate face implying a concert repertoire of refined emotions, at the small-boned hands drawn together thoughtfully like the spire of a meticulously schemed cathedral – and Janice thought of Eleanor, I should like to be like her. Except then – and this thought followed fast upon the heels of the previous one – except then I wouldn't have had baby Lawrence. The notion that, for all its pain, Lawrence's birth and death had been an experience that *belonged* to her, seemed irrepressibly right. Something she had not considered before. For which she consequently felt grateful to Eleanor.

And Eleanor, viewing Janice from the same distance, saw someone at first pitiable – there but for the grace of God, patrimony, the sibilant nonsense of the British class structure – might go I. But since I don't, Janice's presence and her sorry state will serve as useful *aides-mémoire*. Her poverty is my invigoration. The thought that it might also have a literary purpose crossed and recrossed Eleanor's mind several times, but then exited at the same time as her memory provided her with a flashback, the torn pink cover of *The Family from One End Street*. The world captured therein was not pitiable; indeed, had it not evoked envy in the child Eleanor, so unconnected to the universe of human affection and sociability? The culture wrapped between the pink covers was noble in its own way. Noble and cosy. A defence against dark nights and things that move terrifyingly in them. Eleanor's mind wrenched itself back to Janice and saw her in a different way. Compared with herself, who knew nothing very much at all of what really matters, Janice's wisdom was as redolent as the cigarette smoke that hung about the fibres of her lemon housecoat. The suffering through which Janice had passed, and which no doubt would continue to afflict her, whatever someone like Eleanor might offer to do about it, gave her the moral edge.

Eleanor, comforted, smiled at Janice. Janice smiled back. 'You got any money, Mrs J?'

Eleanor heard herself asking Uncle Hal the same question. She smiled again.

''Cos if you have I thought we might go out to lunch. Take Marlon for a pizza down the Mile End Road. We could see if Ball's in. He's working in a garage round the corner from here. And Michelle – d'you think you'd like to see Michelle again, Mrs J?'

*

In the restaurant overlooking Sousceyrac village square Eleanor and David Jenkinson have finished their first course, which wasn't difficult. Eleanor reaches for the bread basket again. Her appetite seems to her much like Esther, her fictional heroine's, general orientation to life. Both of them are unable properly to benefit from their experiences.

David waits.

Eleanor says, 'I'm not going to tell you anything.'

'Who was he, Eleanor?'

'It's in the past,' she declares. 'And anyway why do you think there was one?'

'Oh yes. You could have fooled me.' He looks, she realizes, injured. 'Was there more than one, then?'

'I didn't ever mean to hurt you.'

'Such clichés aren't worthy of you.'

'It wasn't an admission, you know. And, in any case, what about yours?'

'My what?'

'Your admissions. Of sins committed or only imagined. Which can be worse.' She laughs, as if to herself. Then, recovering, and bringing herself back to the present, she addresses him directly: 'It is to be expected, David, that you erred from the path of conjugal rectitude while I was . . . while all this was going on.' She gives him half a moment to answer, and then closes the subject. 'But I don't really want to know. You see, I find the prospect of having to deal with my emotional reactions to your escapades frankly tiring. I only mentioned it because I didn't want you to think I was blind to your side of things.'

Fortunately at that point their main course arrives. Hers is a slice of salmon trout, overlaid with minuscule strips of creamy bacon. David has something dark in gravy with a moon-shaped potato cake. Eleanor, rearranging the stiff brocade napkin on her knee, thinks to herself of the inordinate comparison between the two tasks awaiting her: one, to demolish the trout, which will take a minute or two at most, though must be spun out to accord with the solemn niceties of the French culinary ritual; two, to account for those parts of her life to her husband, David, which she has always before hidden behind clichés, and the recitation of which might occupy the pages of a reasonably-sized novel.

The woman with the suitcase full of flowers is striding back to her car in the square beneath. Nothing in the way she carries herself or it is different from before. But something must be, or she wouldn't be returning.

Extract from:

A MONTH IN PARIS
BY ELEANOR JENKINSON

Dick?' She could scarcely hear anything, the line was so faint. As there was no light in the phone box, Esther couldn't even be sure she'd dialled correctly.

Then she heard him shouting down the line, 'Esther, is that you?' The tone of his voice reminded her of the way he used to call out for her when he came home in the evening. Slamming the door and stamping round the house shouting like a bull. Sometimes she'd deliberately wait to answer, hoping the short silence would make him realize he shouldn't take it for granted that she'd always be there. But it never seemed to have the desired effect. Dick's face when he found her, sitting with her book in the bedroom, typing, sewing, or peeling onions, would only be a bit redder than usual, and it wouldn't have been worth even the slight effort she'd made to deceive him.

'I'm coming home,' she shouted in return. 'I'll be back tomorrow. Tea-time, I should think.'

The line was too bad for her to discern his reaction to this news. But it must surely have been as unexpected to him as it was to her, when she woke up this morning and knew this was what she had to do next.

Ball didn't seem surprised to see them. He was under a red Ford Anglia. Janice kicked him lightly. He sat up, creased. 'Hallo, Mrs J, glad to see you made it, then.'

They got in the Ford Anglia, Eleanor cradling Marlon in the back. Michelle and Alicia were at home, but Fran was not. Alicia was nearly two now, she had a squint and a mop of pale red hair. They went, as planned, to the Pizza Hut.

After imbibing some nasty Algerian wine, Eleanor said to Ball, while Janice was away enquiring about the heating up of Marlon's bottle, 'Why did you ring me actually, Ball? I mean, what do you think I should or could do for Janice?'

Ball finished his side order of garlic bread and looked at her quizzically. 'A listening ear? Money? Yes, money would help, Pete's no good for her, even though he is my mate. Even though I say it meself, Mrs J, she's better off with him in the Scrubs than anywhere else.'

Eleanor thought about Hal's money tucked away in Lloyds Bank in the Lanes in Brighton. Of Mr Gleeting and her daughter's knickers in his wastepaper basket. She realized she'd got lost in her own train of thought. 'Sorry.'

'You don't fancy a little investment, do you?'

Apart from in Janice? 'In what?'

'A – well, a business. Guaranteed return of twenty percent on your capital within six months. Can't say fairer than that, can I?'

Eleanor had no idea whether he could or not. She tried to remember Mr Gleeting's calculations. Then David's voice entered the Pizza Hut reprimanding her for ever considering such foolishness. 'Okay, Ball, why not? How much do you want?'

'Five grand?' Ball's voice was hopeful. The figure had been calculated carefully as lying somewhere between what he'd like to have and what Mrs J might of her own accord have offered. He had no idea whether she had that kind of money or not, but he had a nose for who had money and who didn't, and Mrs J had the right scent about her. The whole idea was, in fact, based on his accurate sense of Eleanor's own current position sitting on the fence dividing routine from excitement; the known from the unknown; the safe from the outlandishly risky. It was he who was taking the risks, in any case.

Eleanor prised her cheque book from her bag and wrote Ball a cheque for five thousand pounds. She'd written 'Ball' on the cheque before he'd thought to tell her his name was really Stewart Devizes. She'd had to tear it up and start again. (She began to ask the origins of the nickname, then thought better of it.) She wrote another cheque for five hundred pounds for Ball to give to Janice after she'd gone back to Brighton. Actually handing the money over struck her as rather sordid, besides which she wouldn't have known what to say.

Writing these cheques gave Eleanor an odd feeling. Some of it was Lady Bountiful and some was female masochism. For was she not handing over the means of her own liberation, and might she not consequently lapse back into her old sorry state? What would she say to herself then? Well, it must have been the sense of the moment that inspired her. The banality of the Pizza Hut as a setting, the surrealism of her close encounters with this working-class subculture. Time out of time; the very stuff of which fiction, but not fact, is made.

When Ball had gone back underneath the car, the three women, with Alicia and Marlon, went for a walk in Victoria Park. The season was early summer. A green crispness in trees and hedges nearly cancelled out the litter of soft drink cans and crumpled paper. Daisies sprouted; a clump of lemon roses by the gates swayed in a light wind. Alicia in bright red shoes ran everywhere chasing everything: dogs, butterflies, rubbish. Marlon rested in his transparent lie-back pushchair, head a little to one side in a nervous sleep. 'Hasn't he grown, Jan!' exclaimed Michelle. 'Quite the little boy now, isn't he!'

Michelle seemed to Eleanor to have been treated more kindly by life and specifically by Fran than had Janice either by life or Pete. But Michelle, too, had aged. Both women seemed to have adopted the physical and mental posture of middle-aged hausfraus. When it was not about domestic themes, their conversation sparkled not with anticipation of pleasant things to come, but with a nostalgia for events and associations garnered from a storehouse now securely padlocked against the certainty of permanently lean times. Their faces wore a faintly ravaged look, as though the tinted foundations they squeezed from a tube had a chemical sting embedded in them.

When it started to rain just after three o'clock, Eleanor left them, observing to herself that Janice looked more cheerful than she had that morning. 'Did me a world of good, Mrs J,' confirmed Janice brightly. 'Come again, will you?' Eleanor said she would. Michelle touched her arm as they said goodbye, a gesture which recalled for Eleanor the damp edges of the joint shared once in Tottenham Court Road.

She got on a bus and went back towards the centre of London. At Hyde Park she got off and went into the Hilton. She needed the interior of a plush hotel for Esther Gray's meeting with her estranged mother in chapter ten of what she suddenly thought she ought to call *Oranges and Lemons*. The clash of classes – from Hackney to Hyde Park – also interested her, though she wasn't sure what Janice and Michelle would make of it. She found the public phones on the ground floor, complete with telephone books, and looked up Tom Sherringham; she tried the number but there was no answer.

Somewhat later, just before she boarded the train for Brighton, she tried again and this time he answered.

Of course he remembered who she was – how could he forget?

Tremulously, Eleanor explained that she now had a certain amount of, well, text, something resembling, well, about half a book, and she'd lately begun to feel she needed a second opinion on it. Rather like a patient with a long cherished illness.

'I'd be delighted,' said Tom Sherringham. 'Where are you living now?' She explained, also that she was presently at Victoria Station about to catch a train back after a day in town.

'In that case,' he interrupted her before she'd had a chance to suggest that she bring a copy of the novel down with her next time she came (she vaguely thought of combining this with seeing Janice again), 'in that case,' he breezed at her, 'I'll come and pick it up. A day at the seaside wouldn't come amiss.'

He said he'd come on Friday. Eleanor felt sick with anxiety on the train on the way home. What would he think? Supposing the word 'promising' had escaped from his vocabulary? And what would he think of that section in chapter four? She'd better rewrite that tomorrow. But tomorrow Carrie wasn't coming, she'd have to fit it in with the playgroup/'Watch With Mother' routine. And then there was one chapter still to be typed . . . she considered telephoning Tom Sherringham back and putting him off. But she knew she was being cowardly. You'll never make a novelist, Eleanor Kendrick, said Eleanor Jenkinson to herself as sternly as she could manage, if you go on being more inventive with excuses than you are with writing.

When she got home, David made her a cup of tea and enquired about her meeting with her mother in Harrods. 'Isn't it about time you had her down for a day or two?' he asked. David took these responsibilities very seriously.

That night, she slept badly. Eliza woke just as the dawn chorus was starting up, complaining of a sore throat. Eleanor took her back to bed with them; her little head was hot and Eleanor wanted to give her the kind of care she was afraid Janice's Marlon wasn't getting.

David reminded her in the morning that he had invited his first-year students round for a drink that evening. Eleanor, who had forgotten, pretended to have remembered. She took Heidi to playgroup, Eliza to the doctor, and while waiting made a list on a corner of *Woman's Own* of things to be done: (1) buy wine (2) shop for supper and bread and cheese (3) rewrite the day at the beach section in chapter four (4) buy typing paper (5) type chapter six (6) make cuts for T.S. (7) photocopy first six chapters (8) tidy room (9) wash hair (10) ring Carrie re Friday.

The doctor told her Eliza had a sore throat.

'Yes,' she said impatiently, 'I expect it's tonsillitis again. She had it three times last year. Can I have some penicillin? Penicillin always does the trick. Within twenty-four hours,' she said, thinking of Friday, and the time that needed to elapse between feeding Eliza the first dose and the miracle cure.

The doctor, who was new, looked hard at Eleanor. 'It's not your place to make the diagnosis or tell me what to do Mrs – er – Jenkinson,' he said glancing down at her notes. 'As it happens you are right this time. But remember you may not be the next.'

Eleanor grabbed the prescription and fled. She parked the car outside Augustus Barnett – she felt quite like an old customer now – and asked the man behind the counter for half a dozen bottles of a decent dry white and a medium red on account. And four large packets of crisps and two tins of peanuts. She put one of the bottles in the glove compartment of the car and the rest in the back with Eliza, whose blonde head and feverish strawberry cheeks now flopped sideways in an uneasy sleep. Eleanor managed the stationers and the grocery shopping and getting the penicillin all before picking up Heidi. At home, while the cheese on toast was cooking and the amoxil was sneaking its way round Eliza's bloodstream, she telephoned Carrie. Who wasn't in, but her mother said she was sure that would be all right and would pass on the message. 'From eleven to five not ten till four,' said Eleanor clearly. The children fed, she cleared a space on the sofa and sat down with them to rewrite a day at the beach. Eliza was fretful and wanted to sit on top of her. So therefore did Heidi. With a child on each knee, Eleanor held the sheets of paper in the air above her head and could immediately see what needed doing to them, but was physically unable to do it. She put the chapter down, picked the girls up and put them in her bed with one of the jumbo packets of crisps. She moved the television to the end of the bed and found an old Shirley Temple film. 'One hour,' she said giving Heidi the alarm clock. 'When the big hand . . . '

'I know how to tell the time,' said Heidi. 'You are stupid aren't you, Mummy?' As Eleanor left the room she heard her saying to

THE SECRET LIVES OF ELEANOR JENKINSON

Eliza, 'Mummy's writing My Novel again. You'd think she'd have finished the bloody thing by now, wouldn't you?'

Both of them fell asleep, which was wonderful, as Eleanor got the scene rewritten and chapter six typed before five o'clock. When they woke up she gave Eliza some more penicillin and involved them both in the business of putting the wine glasses out and opening the bottles and setting the remaining crisps and peanuts in little dishes. She looked in some despair at the state of the sitting room. But once the toys had been pushed out of sight, and the tartan rug thrown over the collapsing sofa, it didn't look too bad. Then she took the girls upstairs and crammed them into their new Mothercare outfits. Eliza's temperature seemed to have gone down. She had a shower, intending to wash her hair as per the list, but found there wasn't any shampoo in the house. She used soap instead; the effect was odd.

She was crossing items off her *Woman's Own* list with Eliza balanced on one hip when David came in. 'They'll be here in a minute,' he said, in case she'd forgotten again.

'I know,' she said confidently.

They all came together, like a school outing. This event happened every year, and every year Eleanor was amazed to find how nervous and impressionable they all were. Coming to the Professor's house seemed bad enough, but meeting the Professor's wife well nigh impossible. 'This is my wife, Eleanor,' said David (did she imagine proudly?) 'Eleanor, this is Gary, and Julia, and Debbie, and Ranjit, and Jonathan, and Aisha, and Fally and Dorothy, and William, and . . .'

'I'll never remember all of that,' chirped Eleanor brightly, in the best imitation of a don's wife she could manage. 'Do come in, all of you, and help yourselves to a drink.'

'Do you mind if we smoke, Mrs Jenkinson?' asked the second young man David had introduced, a youth tall as a gatepost, with the social manners of a minor public school.

'Go ahead,' invited Eleanor, who detested the habit, and made a mental note to fit in a sentence or two soon to Heidi and Eliza on the dangers of smoking.

Heidi was behind the table on which the wine bottles and glasses had been set, behaving like a barmaid. She handed them all glasses, simpering in an unusual way (copied from an American

TV programme, Eleanor realized later), and when Gary lit up, she said, offhandedly, 'That gives you cancer, you know.'

'My, isn't she advanced for her age!' This came from Fally, who was for some unexplained reason wearing white gloves. 'It must be wonderful to have a child like that, Professor!' she said, eyeing David, who was handing round the stuffed olives Eleanor had found in an old tin at the back of the cupboard under the sink. Where does he find them? thought Eleanor to herself. 'Excuse me, Mrs Jenkinson,' said Ranjit, 'but could you please direct me to the men's room?'

In the passageway showing him the downstairs loo, which was overcome with raincoats and wellingtons and automatic washing machine powder, Eleanor noticed the awful eczema on his rich dark skin. She took the opportunity to slip into the kitchen for a quiet glass of water. She really was feeling very tired and very apprehensive about tomorrow. Also, her period was late, and she could scarcely bear to think about that.

'Mummy, Mummy, that Indian's locked himself in the toilet,' chanted Eliza at her feet.

'There must be something the matter with him, I expect, he's been there an extremely long time,' announced Heidi, coming up behind her sister with some empty plates. 'I brought these out to the kitchen to help you, Mummy, isn't that nice of me? Have we got some more peanuts? That lady with white gloves on has eaten all what we put out.'

Eleanor started a sentence about racial prejudice when Eliza interrupted: 'I think he's being sick now. Ugh, Mummy, are we going to have to clear the sick up?'

She was crouching down outside the lavatory door listening. Eleanor picked her up. 'It's nothing to do with you, young lady.' She sent Heidi to fetch David. 'One of your students needs you,' she said. 'Well, probably they all do, but this one particularly. I'm going upstairs to put these two to bed.'

When she came down, Ranjit was sitting in the corner of the sofa, holding his head. 'I'm terribly sorry, Mrs Jenkinson,' he said, 'I can't think what came over me.' Julia, demure and pink-lipped, was sitting next to him, holding a packet of aspirin. David sat opposite, deep in conversation with the remaining students ranged around him. Eleanor imagined them all at a French impressionist's garden party, half naked with picnic hampers. 'You see, the history of the Industrial Revolution is precisely that the class system as we know it is entirely a product of technology,' he was saying, 'that is, of technology understood in its broadest sense to encompass not only machines themselves but the social relations surrounding their use.'

'I'm sure you're right,' said Eleanor out loud, and unthinkingly.

They all looked at her. 'Well, you are right, aren't you, darling, you always are – that's why you're a Professor!' She tried to giggle lightly.

In the end, she had quite a sensible, though unlikely, conversation with Aisha, a young Afro-Caribbean woman from Hampstead, about imperialism and motherhood. Aisha impressed her with her thoughtfulness. She wondered how David coped with her. Also why Aisha was doing history, given that it would be, as they had both already agreed, of a distinctly partial kind. 'If you want to change something, Mrs Jenkinson,' said Aisha simply, 'you've got to know all about it first. I want to address the issue of racism in the curriculum from a basis of knowledge, not ignorance.'

'You'll go far, won't you!' said Eleanor, meaning it.

'I hope so.'

'Take a tip from me,' she went on, surprising herself. 'Don't allow yourself to be handicapped by motherhood. Imperialistic or otherwise. As I am. Do what you want first. Then have children, if you must. Not the other way around.'

Aisha looked intently at her. 'But you've got everything, Mrs Jenkinson. Position, money, a good marriage . . . What have you to complain about?'

'I can't do what I want,' said Eleanor, sounding petulant even to herself. And then went on to explain to Aisha what she meant, though in hushed tones, lest the others should hear. She didn't criticize David, though, that would never do, that would be too much like letting the side down.

The students departed just after eleven. Judging from their effusive thanks at the door, it had been a successful evening; at least they weren't nervous any more. Ranjit had gone to sleep, but they woke him up to take him home. 'Please accept my most humble apologies, Mrs Jenkinson,' he said, stumbling out of the door.

At midnight, when they got into bed, Eleanor had a headache and David complained when he found himself awash in a sea of potato crisps. 'Who was that Moroccan one?' she asked, to take his mind off the prickly feeling in his pyjamas. 'The one with the great dark eyes and the gloves. Is she in love with you or something?'

'Not Moroccan,' said David, 'Greek-Cypriot. Her family own a carpet factory in Limassol.'

'Oh.'

He liked the thought of his students being in love with him. Eleanor, who knew this, took advantage of his self-absorbed silence casually to mention, just before she herself slipped off into a well-earned slumber peopled with bossy Moroccan doctors with eczema and wine merchants who dispensed penicillin in whisky bottles, that, although it was Friday tomorrow, Carrie was coming for an extra day as Esther had just reached a point in chapter six where . . .

David grunted. She wasn't sure if he was asleep or not.

'I think she's suspicious,' admitted David Jenkinson to Marion Cumberledge. They were sitting in the staff canteen eating shepherd's pie.

Marion looked up with alarm. Grey mince dropped off her fork. Her large glasses reflected the equally grey light which didn't illuminate the room. 'But how could she be? We've been so careful.'

'I don't know.' David searched his memory.

'Perhaps it was that evening we took Gary to *Murder on the Orient Express*. What did you tell her you were doing?'

'Giving a seminar,' he hissed grimly.

'On what?'

'Does it matter? John Ball and the Peasants' Revolt.'

She put her fork down and her hand across to his, then withdrew it, looking nervously around her. 'We don't have to go on, dearest,' she hinted.

'I know, Marion.' He sighed. A man weighed down by the burden of convention and all its accompanying conventional guilt and duplicity.

He cleared his plate. She watched expectantly. 'Is that what you want, then?' she enquired after a while, a note of truculence in her voice.

'Of course not.' He looked at his watch. 'What time is Gary home today?'

'It's an INSET day. Mrs Bradford's got him, but only until three. Anyway I've got an essay to write for you.'

'Pity,' he said. 'What's it on?'

'Does it matter? I do love you, David.'

'I know,' he said, despairingly.

'I must go, if you're to get your essay on time.'

He watched her manoeuvring her way through the plastic tables bearing their forbidden fruit of plastic water jugs and sauce bottles. Her brown skirt was too tight, and it didn't flatter her legs, which the unkind might have compared to tree trunks.

'Want some coffee, Jenkinson?'

'Oh, yes. Thank you.' Mayhew sat down next to him with a tray of coffee. 'You going to the History Today conference this year? It's in Edinburgh, you know. I'm giving a paper.' He paused, for effect. 'I thought I might take in a bit of the Festival as well. Feel like some culture for a change, know what I mean?'

'No. No, I don't know what you mean, and no, I'm not going to the conference.'

'You all right, Jenkinson?'

'I expect so.'

At 11.03 Eleanor was in her room in Marine Parade trying to make it look as seriously literary as possible. She arranged a worn copy – bought in a second-hand shop – of Roget's *Thesaurus* at a much used angle on a table by the window, also Chambers' *Dictionary of Dates* and a small encyclopaedia of wild flowers they'd found with some stuff in the attic when they moved into the Brighton house. The bottle of wine retrieved from the glove compartment of the car stood suggestively on the bookshelf beside two glasses. Too suggestively. Eleanor put the glasses the other side of the room and a copy of *Proust Volume I* in front of the bottle. The photocopied pages of chapters one to six of *A Month in Paris* (the earlier titles were taking precedence again) awaited Tom Sherringham in a green file; she'd made it to the Xerox shop before Carrie came. Eleanor thought she might take Tom Sherringham to the new seafood restaurant next to the Grand Hotel.

He didn't seem to be on the twelve o'clock train, though. Her eyes were scrutinizing the rest of the passengers when a hand on her shoulder made her jump: 'I came on an earlier one.'

Eleanor felt considerably at a disadvantage. The meeting hadn't got off to the kind of start she'd imagined. Which is, she imagined, why he'd caused it to happen like that.

They walked by the sea. It was a windy day, clouds did what other people's novels had taught her to think of as scud across the sky. Seagulls shrieked and dipped; waves foamed. 'Very marine,' pronounced Tom Sherringham. He said it the way she'd heard the word 'promising' all those years ago. 'Where is it then, Eleanor Jenkinson? Where is My Novel?'

She took him to her room. Absurdly proudly. Mrs Crispin heard their voices in the hall, and slipped out to have a discreet look, being rewarded with a sight of Tom Sherringham's corduroy trousers bumping up the stairs. With an unerring sense of where the important things are to be found, Tom Sherringham moved the Proust rather quickly and found the wine. The bottle opener was in Eleanor's handbag which was, she thought, a bit of a giveaway. But of what? They toasted My Novel looking out at the green marbled sea. And went to lunch where she had imagined they might. Since he'd left the manuscript in her room, they had to go back there afterwards. By this time they'd had not only the original bottle of wine to drink but another one, and a couple of amber cognacs too. 'Would you like me to seduce you?' asked Tom Sherringham. His stomach, full of scallops floating in an alcoholic pond, was outlined against the window, and his eye fell on her carefully arranged pile of reference books. 'Remember, my dear, in case it worries you, in Roget's *Thesaurus*, sex is classed under Abstract Relations.'

Eleanor remembered Eva Summers. 'I've got to be home by five,' she said.

She was, and her period started. Eliza's temperature was up again. David phoned to say he'd be late – he had a seminar paper to work on. Eleanor had just got herself and Heidi fed on a tin of tuna and frozen chips, and Eliza on a double dose of Febrilix syrup, and all of them in bed, when her mother rang complaining it was Christmas day and no-one had come to see her. 'You always were a very naughty girl,' she chastised. 'Where you learnt those four letter words I shall never know. Probably from books. I never approved of all that reading, you know. Celia was much healthier with her horses. By the way, have you seen my *Radio Times*? I don't want to miss the Special Christmas Edition of "The Black and White Minstrel Show".'

FIVE

Bad Weather

OVER DAVID'S SHOULDER in Sousceyrac the sun sets. The family at the next table ask for *l'addition*, as the little girl with bulbous eyes is tired. Eleanor Jenkinson lays down her knife and fork, and decides to tell a story.

'It's complicated,' she begins.

'I've no doubt,' says her husband.

'Perhaps I should never have married you, David.'

'That's not a very helpful beginning,' he observes, wiping his plate energetically from side to side with a crescent of bread.

Eleanor interprets his actions thus: if only problems of human relationships could be disposed of as easily as surplus gravy.

'No, I mean,' she insists, 'that perhaps what has been difficult is the combination of your idea of marriage and my idea of myself. I hesitate to use the word ambition.'

There is no doubt in Eleanor's mind that David is the more ambitious of the two; he, not her, is concerned with social prestige, the accolade of peers, ascent from one salary scale to another. Becoming a Reader. Then a Professor. Professor David Jenkinson and his tiny wife, Mrs Jenkinson.

'Why is it,' Eleanor continues, though her train of thought would not be obvious to him, 'that men who aren't grown-up never understand this, while women spend their lives becoming so?'

'You know what I think of statements like that,' says Professor David Jenkinson, as if to a poorly trained student. 'The predicament of the personal can't be slipped out of sideways by engaging in unsubstantiated generalizations.' Idly he recalls Marion Cumberledge and others of similar ilk, but comforts himself with the thought that, whatever else he'd done, he'd never generalized about them.

'Why are you so determined to be confrontational about this?'

'Why are you so reluctant to look at me?'

She could have said, because the pink and violet stripes of the sunset, the horizon against which his face is shadowed, distracts her attention from the matter, as he defines it, in hand. The contrast is unhandleable; between these graceful lines and his graceless face; between nature continuing in her own dignified respectful way, and culture composed of human beings getting themselves into time-wasting and ultimately unresolvable scrapes. All of which would crumble in the end and pass to nothing, lie in the earth with dead lizards and the imprints of a few billion sunsets.

'Eleanor, please! We've come away for our first holiday together alone in how many years?'

'Twenty,' she says automatically, and again. Women are the calendars, she thinks, we *keep* time while men live it. But she's wise enough not to say this.

'We've grown apart over that time. What couple doesn't? It's only natural. We've got some talking to do. I've always been honest with you – my life's an open book to you. You know all about it. There's nothing to say.' David swallows, as though choking on the stray remnants of his darkly gravied potato cake. 'But we both know you've hidden things from me. Tell me about them, Eleanor – you've got to tell me about them now. I don't need the details, but I do need the substance of the . . . whatever it is – was. To imagine is much worse than to know. You must see that. We have to sort it out, Eleanor. Do you want to spend the rest of your life alone? I don't. We're a couple, Eleanor. This is a *marriage*, isn't it, or it could be. Tell me the truth.'

Quite an impassioned speech, really. But what is David Jenkinson trying to get at? Eleanor Jenkinson's infidelities in the writing of My Novel? Or in the getting of the experiences necessary to this act? Or in episodes that occurred from time to time in her life as they do to all of us – and most of which she's forgotten by now, as they really didn't have any lasting importance.

Tom Sherringham that day in Marine Parade.

And after that with Ball and with Jim Maitland and with Jordan. Are these such terrible infidelities? Really? And compared to his?

The family at the next table pay the bill and leave with a scraping of chairs. Eleanor watches them walk across the square. The little girl leans on her mother, heavy with tiredness, the father puts an arm lightly on his wife's shoulder. The son walks a pace or two to the side, kicking a large piece of gravel. David Jenkinson finishes his wine and wipes his linen napkin vigorously across his face.

While Eleanor wonders where to start and even more how it all should end, the waiter takes their plates away and brings them each two round scoops of a pale lime sorbet.

Extract from:

THE LAST SUMMER
BY ELEANOR JENKINSON

The tower of the hotel could be seen for miles in the ironed-out landscape of bulb fields and low brown lace-curtained houses. Esther and Martin had rented bicycles, and on the second day of the conference, when there was a long enough break in the sessions, they unlocked them and sped off to the sand dunes.

Martin said he could smell the sea in the air and it was only a question of following his nose. Esther followed Martin. They pedalled fast along the narrow cycle lanes. Esther felt extraordinarily content to be here doing this with him. It seemed only right.

Eventually they reached a barrier across what had become a sandy path spiked with clumps of gorse. 'This is it,' he said. They propped the bicycles up against the metal barrier and set off the rest of the way on foot.

Over the sand dunes they came quite suddenly to the sea, peaceably, carefully lapping the silver sands. For a while Esther and Martin stood there wordlessly, the sun beating down on their heads, the white sand shifting and settling round their feet. She thought to herself: I will love you for ever. Whatever happens, this moment, the moment of realization of love, and of myself, will stay with me always.

In 1973 a number of things happened to Eleanor Jenkinson: some of them are easier to describe, to pin down, than others. One, Eleanor received news from Coffs Harbour, Australia, that her sister Celia had died in a road accident. Remember Celia? Eleanor never had much to do with her – the age gap was too big, and boarding school didn't help. Later on Celia couldn't take her parents, especially her mother, and so used emigration as a means of repudiating the whole of her class culture. It was a bit of an extreme reaction, not what most of us would do, but then Celia was an extreme person. The middle-of-the-road reasonableness was concentrated in Eleanor, which was unfair, as Eleanor could have used some of Celia's outgoing, renovative *joie de vivre* – perhaps if she'd been more like Celia, she wouldn't have led such a compromising, trapped life, and at least three My Novels would have been published by now.

Celia Kendrick had died at forty-two by driving too fast one wet night in the Coffs Harbour winter. Having paid insufficient attention to the condition of her car, she'd been the victim of failing brakes when another car came, also too fast, round the corner.

Bridget Kendrick wept on the telephone to Eleanor. Although the last ten years of her life had been occupied by a jumble of personages, happenings, places and conversations, such that it had often been impossible for her or anyone else to understand what she was talking about, the central fact of her motherhood had never disappeared from her mind. She wept as much for the daughter she had never had as she did for Celia herself, but then her inability to tell the difference had always been a major part of the problem. Eleanor tried to reassure her mother of her own goodness, and that Celia's life had not been in vain. But neither of them could escape thinking that, whatever Celia had done, she'd done on the other side of the world precisely so her mother and her sister would never know whether it had been in vain or not.

The family solicitor, J.K. Slattersby, went out to Coffs Harbour to wind up any remaining of Celia's affairs. There was no way Bridget could have coped with the journey; she'd probably have forgotten the purpose of it within five minutes. Eleanor herself could hardly go, as this would have meant putting her own daughters to one side. J.K. Slattersby telephoned both Bridget and Eleanor early one morning from Australia to report his discovery of quite a large outstanding piece of untransacted business belonging to Celia's estate: a daughter by the name of Yolande, thirteen and a half at the time of her mother's death. When informed of this extra grandchild, Bridget refused to believe it, as Celia, to her recollection, had never been married. As a matter of fact, she never learnt to see Yolande as her granddaughter.

There was no real reason why she should, except perhaps, as she was about to discover, a slight resemblance in the set of Yolande's eyes to those of her grandfather, Charles. But it had been a long time since Bridget had seen those eyes. Charles, long dead, wasn't even much good as a ghost.

J.K. Slattersby regarded Yolande's existence as tiresome, but wasn't in any doubt about what should be done about it: she must of course be brought to live with her aunt in England. Eleanor, who had never thought of herself as an aunt, was horrified at the news. But she only said so to David, whose own response was much the same as J.K. Slattersby's: come on Eleanor Jenkinson, there's nothing else to be done. You have as usual everything to lose but your chains.

And My Novel, thought Eleanor grimly. Again. She remembered Eva Summers, and how Eva had loosened her own chains. What courage! She'd have liked to talk to Eva now. She'd have liked to find out if it had worked – had the chains gone for ever, or had they merely realigned themselves for a time? Eleanor needed someone to talk to. She went to Marine Parade, and sat in the window, intending to write to Uncle Hal instead.

The sea was a summer blue, though it was February still, but the sky threw a cold bright blue down at it. A resolute crispness covered everything – feelings were to be buried or drowned, it said, life in all its numbing drabness must go on. Eleanor stared, hard, at the horizon – at the line of intersection between the two fields of blue, the one caused by the other. She thought she could see the earth's curve as she moved her eyes along this horizon – the great useless golf ball of the earth, spinning around for a few billion years just biding its time until the sun blows up and puts an end to everything. Life as we know it. But there's nothing else *to* know, is there?

Mrs Crispin knocked at the door. 'Are you all right, dear?'

'What?' Eleanor was startled from this reverie of hers in which she felt she was alone and alone understood the meaning of everything – or rather the fact that nothing *has* a meaning.

'I heard you crying, dear. I just thought I'd pop in to see if there's anything I can do. To help, you know.' She stood there, substantial and ordinary, her cream-coloured cardigan matching the streaks in her hair, the cardigan fastened over an apron. It was in the apron's pockets that Mrs Crispin's hands were resting, in an attitude of domestic rooting that seemed, at this moment, more enduring to

Eleanor than the meeting of sea and sky, the sun's finite flames, or the galactic cartwheels of the earth.

'I'm sorry. I didn't know I was crying. I mean . . . '

Mrs Crispin advanced to the window and brought a bunch of paper handkerchiefs out of her apron pocket. She bent down and looked carefully into Eleanor's face, then pronounced, 'It's the same for all of us, dear. But it passes. Mind you, don't expect the moon, you won't get it. But bide your time. Things'll get better, you'll see.'

Eleanor blew her nose. 'What's the same, Mrs Crispin?'

'The depression, dear. Women's burden. I had it myself. When my Warren was little. I remember it as though it were yesterday. Hardly had the energy to put one foot in front of the other, I did. Of course Warren was very highly strung, he used to buzz around just like a racing car. The doctor said it was either him or me. And Warren's daddy wasn't any help. They aren't, of course.'

She straightened up, looked philosophically beyond Eleanor at the waves curling themselves rhetorically up the beach. 'You see there really isn't anything to be done about it. All this talk of women's lib, it's not for mothers like us.' She shot Eleanor a glance of conspiracy. 'And here you are, trying to be a writer! I didn't say anything when you first came to see the room, but I knew it wouldn't work. It'll only make things worse.'

'I don't understand.'

'Oh you understand it all right, dearie,' said Mrs Crispin in an offhand way. 'You just don't want to believe it, that's all. I'll make us a cup of tea, shall I? And perhaps you'd care to share my lunch? I've got a nice pair of kippers in the fridge. Enough for two, with bread and butter. We could listen to "Woman's Hour", if you like.'

Accepting the tea, but assuring Mrs Crispin that neither the kippers nor 'Woman's Hour' would really help her, Eleanor wrote her letter and then went home.

A hotchpotch of feelings wriggled inside her as she bundled her daughters into their clothes, hauled bags of shopping around or dipped nervously now and then into her notebooks to see if it was all still there. Somewhere inside Eleanor it *had* registered – there was Celia's death. The disappearance, not only from this continent, but from this earth, of one, who, linked to her by blood, had never seemed so, particularly, by any social form of sisterhood. Eleanor dwelt guiltily on memories of Celia – Celia in her jodhpurs in Marigold Lane,

SECRET LIVES OF ELEANOR JENKINSON

Date Ordered: 04/09/93

000654550S

Order Quantity:

Price: 5.99 *

Oakley,A
Flamingo
HARPER COLLINS PUBLISHERS   AF
PBAC

Pub. Date: 13/09/93

Contemporary Fiction

HEATHCOTE
BOOKS

LANGTON'S BOOKSHOP
Sales Order No: F489574

* ACTUAL PRICE MAY DIFFER

A/C No: 94611
Customer Ref: 1309-94611-0

haughty and condescending from the height and breadth of her newly adolescent stature; Celia as the sender of the Eiffel Tower postcards doing – what? A sister, in short, she had never really known. Any grief Eleanor felt – and she did feel some – was more for the loss of a future in which she might have known Celia, than for a ruptured present intimacy. Celia, after all, had made the emotional impact of her death problematic, by enforcing the discovery of Yolande. About whom Eleanor also had mixed feelings. If she'd wanted three daughters, she would have had another of her own! How would Heidi and Eliza react? And thirteen was a difficult age. There were bound to be problems.

When J.K. Slattersby handed Yolande over to Eleanor and David and Heidi and Eliza at Gatwick airport, he had a look in his eyes that said: this one's going to be difficult, but it's for you.

Yolande had spiky hair and was flamboyantly suntanned. She wore pale jeans and a large, not very clean check shirt and plimsolls. She carried a sweater, but no coat. All her possessions were apparently gathered in one canvas bag. When J.K. Slattersby introduced Yolande to her newly found family, she neither held out her hand nor made any other gesture towards them. Her body was stiff, arranged like a windscreen. She nodded briefly only at Eleanor. Eleanor put her arm round Yolande and brushed her cheek with a kiss, but it was, indeed, like making contact with a pane of glass. Seven-year-old Heidi stared with her coal black eyes. She held her hand out after a bit, but Yolande ignored it. Eliza hid behind her sister, sucking her thumb.

Yolande was a vegetarian and was allergic to all food additives, she said, stressing the 'all'. In addition, she was virtually uneducated. She and Celia had lived, it transpired, in a sort of shack by the beach at Coffs Harbour. Where it had been, as Yolande endlessly emphasized, very beautiful. Nothing much had happened but it had been beautiful. A far cry from this household, which was not beautiful and was now even more crowded by Yolande's presence. There wasn't any room for her, she had to sleep in the spare room with the lawn mower. Heidi and Eliza were at first bemused by Yolande, and unusually quiet, then resolutely hostile. They glared at Yolande, and she glared back at them. Eliza put Yolande's toothbrush down the lavatory, Eleanor heard Heidi chiding her on, and went to rescue it just in time. 'I know it's hard,' she told the little girls, 'it's hard for you to take Yolande into your home. But just imagine, had it been *you* left without a home, wouldn't you have wanted your Auntie Celia to have taken you in?'

'No,' said Heidi, 'I'd rather live with Granny, even if she *is* mad. Granny gives us sweets.'

Eliza was still sucking her thumb. 'It'll get better, you'll see,' promised Eleanor with fake jolliness, to herself as much as to them. 'Yolande'll get used to us, and we'll get used to her.'

That evening, when they sat down to eat, Heidi deftly moved Yolande's chair so she hit the ground. 'You little bastard!' screamed Yolande, and ran from the room, slamming the door.

Eliza wept into her soup. David picked his fingernails. 'Aren't you going to say something to her?' demanded Eleanor. 'She shouldn't be allowed to get away with this dreadful behaviour.'

'She knows she shouldn't have done that, don't you, Heidi?' said David, still picking his nails.

Eliza looked at them pinkly. 'I think Yolande should go back to Australia,' she said in a very quiet voice.

'Well, she's not going to. And you two are going up to bed, I'll bring you some food later. If your father can't be bothered to discipline you, then I'll have to.'

None of which helped My Novel, of course. With a mixture of resignation and anger, Eleanor shoved it in a drawer.

In October of that year, the Queen's speech began, as usual, with the famous words, 'My husband and I,' and, anticipating trips to the New Hebrides and Papua New Guinea, talked of legislation to remove sex discrimination and widen the economic and social opportunities available to women. Eleanor sighed, reading this in the newspaper. What opportunities? It had been a while even since her faintly emancipatory meeting with Tom Sherringham. She continued to go to her room in Marine Parade, avoiding Mrs Crispin, hovering with threats of kippers just outside the door, and reading, rather than writing, in it. She sat for hours at the table overlooking the sea with a book on her lap: George Gissing's *The Emancipated*, an embittered revelation of Victorian small-mindedness, using the device of the unfolding, half-credible realizations of a young widow, Miriam Baske. Eleanor vicariously lived out the creation of the novel's form, while watching the ever-changing light on the sea's surface spread out before her – the paradise in which Eleanor Kendrick the novelist would one day live. Somewhere beautiful, where nothing happens except that words flow, melting steadily – though not without that frisson of struggle that gives the whole activity its necessary edge – into congenial, meaningful, melodic, publishable prose. The war between the ravages of creativity and the rules of ordinary life – Reuben, Miriam Baske's blacksheep brother, Mullard, the painter, quietly sketching red scenes of Vesuvius – but alone.

The second thing that happened in 1973 is that Eleanor asked Ball for the money she lent him to be returned to her: the problem of Yolande couldn't be solved, but might become less pressing by the purchase of a larger house with a garden for the lawn mower. Every penny was therefore needed.

Eleanor went to the garage in Hackney. Yolande was at school at last, Heidi too. Eliza sat, as usual, with Carrie on the sofa in front of the television. David, also as usual, was in his redbrick tower at the university reading a doctoral thesis from the University of Southampton on *Class and Culture in Eighteenth-Century Scotland*, and worrying about his relationship with Marion Cumberledge.

This time, Ball was in the office doing the accounts. He had acquired a ring through his nose, Eleanor noticed. 'Hallo, Ball, can I have a word with you?'

'Well, well, if it isn't Mrs J!'

He made her a cup of tea. 'Janice was very pleased with the money you gave her,' he said. 'Quite set her up, it has. And I don't know what you said that day, Mrs J, but she's been a different person since. Pete's still inside, Janice has got a new bloke now. A businessman, like myself. Even if I am the one to say it!' He made a noise which was a cross between a cough and a laugh.

'That's what I came about, Ball,' she said, 'actually. The money I lent you. I wonder, could I have it back? I need it, you see.' She began to explain, but gave up, as she knew that Ball's reaction would hardly be affected by any further information she gave him.

He reached into a drawer, taking out a wad of notes. 'Twenty percent didn't we say, in six months, on £5000? I make that £1000.' He counted it out, in £50 notes. She took the money, wondering where it had come from – was this garage the business in which her money was invested?

'Actually,' she said again, 'it's also the capital I'd like back, I'm afraid.'

'Don't be afraid, Mrs J, it's all quite safe.'

'But I want it back, Ball!' Why, Eleanor wondered, did this very reasonable request seem to have a childlike ring of petulance about it?

'You'll have it back, Mrs J, you will, I promise. I'll bring it down in a couple of weeks or so. That suit you?'

Which was how Ball, alias Stewart Devizes, came to be the second man to enter Eleanor Jenkinson's literary haven.

The first one, Tom Sherringham, telephoned Eleanor soon afterwards. 'You want to know what I think, Eleanor? About *Changing Trains*?' (it's changed its name again). Behind her in the kitchen, Eliza pulled Heidi's hair. Heidi shrieked. Yolande, who was supposed to be doing her homework, slammed the front door. Tom Sherringham, hearing the domestic commotion, plunged on. 'Promising,' he said. 'Though you may have heard that word before. But I'm afraid there's one major problem with the book, Eleanor. You've got to stop being a prudish housewife. There's no sex in it.'

In the silence that followed, Tom Sherringham inserted a paragraph to contextualize his point. 'Yes, I know women writers aren't supposed to write about sex, but that's bullshit. You've got to change the rules, Eleanor Jenkinson. Cut the shackles of convention . . . '

Suffice to say, next, that Tom Sherringham proved to be quite a good teacher. In the course of the teaching, Eleanor was surprised to learn that he made the fifty percent of his income that wasn't derived from running creative writing classes from a regular slot in a monthly magazine called *Mail Fantasy*. She saw the text protruding from his typewriter one day. The machine had a black and red ribbon in it; in a paragraph where the word 'clitoris' appeared rather often, the typing was mostly red. A new light was thus cast on Eva Summers' pastime, separated, thanks to Eleanor, from her shopping basket.

'It's not good enough, David,' pronounced Marion Cumberledge from beneath the polyester duvet in Rosebush Avenue.

David Jenkinson began to sweat slightly. 'I'll open a window, Marion, shall I? It's rather hot under here.'

'Thirteen-point-five tog,' she said, 'twenty-nine ninety-nine in the BHS sale. I don't want the window open, you know how I feel the cold, David.'

Marion had got an upper second degree two months ago, and was now teaching what she learnt to polytechnic students. The transition from student to teacher had done wonders for her self-esteem. The role of a mature student – for this was what Marion had been – is quite difficult, as one is neither one thing nor the other. But Marion hadn't chosen to have an affair with David Jenkinson to solve this dilemma: the two of them had, rather, fallen into each other's lives in search of different kinds of temporary solace. David had wanted someone to talk to. Eleanor never listened to him any longer; he had the distinct impression he merely featured as a character in the novel of her life. He felt he wanted to step out of line, and, by having an affair, play a role she hadn't scripted for him. Perhaps then she'd notice him as a man again. Only recently he'd begun to wonder if Eleanor hadn't, after all, written this part for him, along with all the others. For her part, Marion had wanted a man in her life, not a novel, and her absolute lack of any kind of imagination had recommended her to David. But he was proving to be more of a mistake for her than she was for him, as she'd really have preferred a man with whom she could have had some public liaison – the strain of keeping this one secret had been telling on her, and her nine-year-old son, Gary, had been telling it all anyway at North End Primary, where he had little else to boast about. Marion worried about Gary's emotional condition, but blamed most of it on his father's death. Like Swiss Heidi's dad, Mr Cumberledge had been a carpenter, and had been hit by a large beam in a seventeenth-century mansion he was renovating without a crash helmet.

'I can't help it, Marion,' said David gloomily, throwing off his side of the duvet. 'I mean, I didn't *choose* for Yolande to live with us. Neither did Eleanor. She can't be expected to cope with *everything* on her own.'

The argument was about a meeting between David and Marion the previous week that David had cancelled in order to attend a parents' evening at a school Yolande might move to. It had been Marion's birthday, and even the flowers he'd sent had arrived a day late.

'I don't see why not. Yolande's not *your* child, after all!'

'When you marry someone,' said David Jenkinson fairly pompously, 'you take on their family responsibilities as well as your own.'

'Sod you!' said Marion, blinking back a few mature tears.

He pulled the duvet back on top of him, feeling the chill of her attitude towards him. Turning towards her, he lifted her glasses off her face; they were too steamed up to be much use to her anyway. Her muddy hazel eyes were attractively liquid. 'Marion, please!'

'Please what? I suppose you want sex now,' she said crossly. 'Aren't you getting enough of that with her?'

He ignored this and put a hand on her left breast. It was encased in apricot nylon.

'Gary'll be home in forty-five minutes.'

David took his hand away and sighed. She felt sorry for him, and with her pity came some sort of desire for intimacy, for physical connection.

'Hold me!' she ordered, keeping an eye on the time. Six minutes it took. David Jenkinson, with thirteen-point-five togs on his back, was grateful to Marion Cumberledge for wanting *him*, and said so as he released himself into her waiting spaces.

As the house behind Brighton station was sold and another bought, Eleanor Kendrick fled regularly to Marine Parade to rewrite sections of My Novel, finally retrieved from its drawer, concerning Esther's encounters in Paris. Not all of them, for that would have been OTT. But even the transformation of a third proved difficult. There was the primary technical question of which ones to transform and which not. How to separate the two categories? The one to remain passages written by Eleanor about Esther based on Eleanor's own particular – one hesitates to use the word limited – experiences. The other to be turned into didactic texts transformed under male instruction to become what men think women ought to be writing about. Eleanor thus did have a problem. It seemed self-evident to her that, if women wanted to write about sex, or about cooking, or about doctoring, then they should be able to do so in a manner that seemed right to them. If the matter was settled in this way, then women would write about these things in a variety of ways – as women, looking at women in the way men might, as lesbians, boringly, excitingly, damningly, irritatingly or whatever. But if the paradigm was absolute, and absolutely not women's own, then quite a different kettle of fish would result. There was no question, however – Eleanor never doubted this for a moment – that to write as men believe women should was much more likely to result in that prize called success.

By this juncture, our heroine was naturally becoming quite desperate. She was thirty-four and had forty-two notebooks. Inside which were nine different beginnings of a novel, three middles, but no ends. These novel fragments were interspersed with a few dozen short stories and a number of poems (always written at the back of the notebooks). All of which, with the possible exception of some of the poetry, was quite publishable – leaving aside, for the time being, the meaning of the term 'publishable'.

In addition to the years of age and the notebooks, Eleanor had two children of her own and one of her sister's to look after. An income of a little more than £1200 per annum (Uncle Hal's original £20,000 depleted by the £500 given to Janice and the £5000 lent to Ball, replaced with £1000 interest, minus £485 for the kitchen equipment and a considerable sum for the rent of Marine Parade and many hours of Carrie Dixon's inexpert babysitting time). She owned a largish house in Hove with her husband, David, who was rather tetchy these days, and had a mother who would soon be dotty enough to require constant full-time care. What were Eleanor's prospects, then?

It was clearly time to take stock of things.

Eleanor, in need of a friend, invited Davina White, whom she had known well in her early days in publishing, to lunch. Over smoked fish and salad in the garden of the new house – which also contained fruit trees, a number of golden azaleas, wild roses and a summerhouse – Davina and Eleanor discussed the world of publishing which Eleanor had left to have Heidi seven years ago, and in which Davina, who was quite ambitious, still was. Davina ran through amusing accounts of what so-and-so was doing now, who was having an affair with whom, and of the writer who turned out to be male instead of female and black instead of white or the other way around. The comedy of it all was quite gripping. But was not the only reason Davina stayed in it. She stayed because she had her eye on a top job. Her boss, a controlling type called Phyllida Grossman, would be retiring soon, and Davina fully expected to be Phyllida's inheritor. This expectation was informed by the culture of the current era, which was one of multiple manipulations and power games, as the media carried stories of how wealthy unscrupulous architect John Poulson's financial affairs were being delved into by the Official Receiver, and found to offer quite a few clues to other people's equally culpable corruptions.

Eleanor noted a message for her in all this. For what the media and

Davina told her sounded to her much less of a serious world than her own – the one in which she was ineluctably locked in the effort to produce both the next meal and the next stage of her children's development, but also to create a more superior text than all these, one which would transcend the dragging-down minutiae of everyday life, though unfortunately – the nub of the problem really – by denying their importance. The lesson was that it was only by saying 'yes but' to the family, to the social and manual labours and relations of the household, that Eleanor Jenkinson would be able to liberate herself sufficiently to finish My Novel; but with the process of liberation would come the need to devalue what she did the rest of the time. The road ahead was bifurcated, blocking any unitary march forward. It reminded Eleanor of the old advertisement for Startrite shoes.

'But you do see what I mean, don't you?' said Eleanor Jenkinson in the garden in Hove to Davina White, following this quickly with, 'There's only one thing to be done about it. I must get myself a proper job.' She hesitated to go into the meaning of this term 'a proper job'. It was, however, one that she'd been hearing increasingly often these days. David Jenkinson, for example, said it all the time, ploughing through the bank accounts, or introducing his wife at parties, or coming home to find Carrie on the sofa with his daughters and Jackie Collins. It was certainly one that issued from Yolande's lips in several of the disputes that had developed between her aunt and herself. Apparently Yolande found it impossible to have any respect for work of her aunt's literary kind which so little resembled anything 'proper'. While Eleanor wondered what Yolande's own mother, her sister Celia, had done to pass the time, Yolande told her: Celia may have lived a hippie-like existence down there in Coffs Harbour, but she'd been a rampant local activist, campaigning on behalf of the environment long before anyone else had thought to do so. A sort of one-woman Greenpeace. 'Mum *cared*,' said Yolande again and again, 'she cared *passionately*, and you don't care about anything except your bloody novel!'

Eleanor bit her lip, thinking how unfair this was, and how much an echo of what others, like Yolande benefiting from Eleanor's commitment and Eleanor's labours, had been saying. Why, if she had *really* only cared about My Novel, it would have been finished long ago!

'You're not even doing anything *else* with your life,' continued Yolande remorselessly. 'No wonder your marriage is breaking up!'

These two statements didn't seem to have a lot to do with each other. Eleanor looked hard at Yolande. 'What do you mean?'

'Don't you know? Uncle David's having an affair,' offered Yolande defiantly. 'I saw them together in Carlo's, the coffee shop by the Pavilion. She wears very thick glasses.'

'Probably a student,' said Eleanor absently, remembering Fally and Julia and Ranjit, and all the rest of them. 'Don't jump to conclusions, Yolande. And it's none of your business anyway.' The little girls, Eleanor's own, hummed something of the same response, though more because they were tired of My Novel than because they'd seen David having coffee with Marion Cumberledge. Though they hadn't liked Yolande at first, she had increasingly become a role model for them, which was exactly one of the things Eleanor had feared would happen.

As the rumoured solution of the proper job was everywhere winging its way though the air, so eventually and inevitably it came to rest in Eleanor's own resolve to put a stop to this mindless battle of labours – her own two unrewarded kinds, carried out in Hove and Marine Parade, and those resulting in a pay packet that were the only kind the world in its multiple follies acknowledged. But she knew better than to confess this change of direction to anyone, and especially to Bridget, whose current confusion centred on one of the many ramifications of the Poulson affair – the Tunbridge case. Bridget phoned with the headlines 'Poulson given Cannon Street'. 'One can't even *get* to Tunbridge from Cannon Street,' wailed Bridget down the telephone. 'And he looks such a nice man, too!'

A month after this, Eleanor had her old job back. Most conveniently, the firm had moved to Victoria. Eleanor was attracted to the idea of an hour by herself on the train every day. In this time she planned to reconceive My Novel, which would accompany her in its various editions in a newly purchased leather briefcase with gold locks, and no longer in a series of plastic bags. The briefcase would be just like the ones all the other Brighton to Victoria commuters were using. But while *they* would be doing crosswords, or reading the newspaper, or chatting to their neighbours, or sitting half awake or half asleep envisioning through sticky eyes the misty countryside, *she* would be chiselling away at something much more important. She would be reconceptualizing the characterization of Esther Gray and her foil Amanda Green. She would resketch the cafe and other intimate scenes so they were less prudish, though on her own terms.

For a while Eleanor thought about asking Yolande, who had now, at fifteen, reached babysitting age, if she would mind Heidi and Eliza after school and in the holidays, but she soon saw this wouldn't work. Her sister's child was too fretful still about the disturbances to her life, added to which was now the sulky intractability of an English adolescence. Yolande was barely civil most of the time. Eleanor treated her like an ungrateful but powerful house guest. If she thought of her as a child, she would treat her like one of her own, and never let her behave like this (she thought). It wasn't only the incivility, the utter lack of domestic co-operation, it was the noise and the mess. The mess, above all. Eleanor knew what any foray into Yolande's room would reveal – a posse of dirty mugs, half drunk beverages floating cigarette ends like flattened ducks, used knickers and yoghurt cartons and cake wrappers turning into compost on the floor; the room did, actually, smell. A mother's help was hired for Heidi and Eliza, someone more capable than Carrie Dixon, but a good deal more expensive. David Jenkinson performed the calculations expected of husbands in these circumstances, fearful that the household would be making a net loss by Eleanor's switch to materially rewarded labours; he was, however, pleased to find this wasn't (quite) so.

The mother's help was called Rosemary. She wore John Lennon glasses and shorts, and was on the large side, in fact about four times Eleanor's size, though the children seemed to like this. Rosemary had done nursery nursing and car maintenance, which seemed to Eleanor potentially a very useful combination.

David was now able to introduce his wife at parties as a publisher rather than as Mrs Jenkinson or, worse, a writer. This was an improvement, as saying someone is a writer always meets the response, what have you written then, by which people mean published. This is one of the definitions of publishable (see earlier, p.103). Eleanor herself was also able to refer to 'my job', which naturally she had to, when, reluctantly, she turned in the key to her room on Marine Parade. Casting one last look at the table where she had sat composing, decomposing and recomposing the adventures of Esther Gray, and where, later and discouraged, she had treated herself to Gissing, George Eliot, and translations of Stendhal and George Sand, plus a lingering glance also at the bed wherein – but it was probably better not to spell that out, wasn't it? – she took a deep breath, and said gird up your loins or words to that effect Eleanor Kendrick-Jenkinson, this is your life and it has to go on and you'll get there one day. And so life continued. 1974 moved into 1975 and . . . Heidi and Eliza got bigger and quite a lot bossier, Yolande got five O levels and rather glowed with pleasure and surprise, for no one, least of all herself, had expected this of an uneducated maiden from Coffs Harbour. In the aftermath of academic success Yolande even warmed a little, finally, to Eleanor. She took Heidi and Eliza to the cinema and talked to them almost politely in sororial tones.

Eleanor went to the office every day and David to the university. He was doing the same old thing all this time but the students changed, so no one noticed (and all the other staff were doing the same thing too, anyway). David Jenkinson and Marion Cumberledge had finally been outwitted by Gary, who, like little Lord Fauntleroy, wanted his mother to himself again, and had taken to skiving off school and entering his mother's bedroom in the middle of the day looking for money for fruit machines.

Eleanor now read other people's manuscripts instead of her own, at first dull political tracts, then gardening manuals, and then at last, in fact quite quickly, she was moved to the fiction department, where she whiled the time away reading dozens of My Novels. It would have been useless to pretend that she didn't derive a degree of solace from the awfulness of other people's work, for she did. It was simply wonderful that other people wrote such trash and that she was in a position of power to tell them so. She did so much enjoy refusing to use the word 'promising' unless it had been earned. One arrogant young man said once to Eleanor, after she'd scathingly turned down a monologue (she called it a diatribe) concerning the desecration of Saigon called *And Naked Statues Walked in the Garden*, 'Who are you, anyway?'

'I don't understand the question.'

'I mean you're only a junior assistant, aren't you? You have no real basis for judging the value of what I write. You've no experience of the writer's craft have you?'

'More than you'd think,' she'd replied, 'and a good deal more than you're ever likely to have so long as you carry on in this vein.'

'Which is what?' he'd asked, his curiosity roused slightly.

'If I am, as you said, merely an assistant,' she replied with dignity, 'then I'm hardly in a position to give you advice on how to write, am I? You can't have your cake and eat it too, you know.' She replaced the receiver with a crisp click.

The phrase 'men's lib' had hit the media by then, though there was even less clarity about what this was than there had been about women's. The day of Eleanor's curt exchange with the haughty young man, Princess Anne was fired at in the Mall by an unemployed man of no fixed address called Ball – Ian. Anne's detective had fired back, but his gun had jammed. Eleanor had a drawer in her desk at the office in which she had jammed My Novel. It now had a proper end. The final scene wrote itself between Burgess Hill and Croydon – some days Eleanor chose to take the slow train home to get away from the commuters and have more time for writing. No, it wasn't true to say the final scene wrote itself – the idea that when women finally manage to write it just escapes from them willynilly is just another of those myths. Rephrasing it, then, we would say: Eleanor wrote the final scene on the train with extreme difficulty but some exhilaration.

Esther Gray was fifty, she was reviewing her life from a medieval chateau in the Perigord. It was October, a golden autumn. She stood in the window of one of the chateau's towers one evening as the sun set with luminous beauty on the rich landscape of fields and trees and little villages and fat red foxes and squirrels with tails as pretty as anything in nature. The sun set, and Esther Gray did, too, into a vision of her life, in all its untidiness, as a completed project, sustained, coherent and not unsuccessful in its way. The red disc tipped itself over the edge of the sky, Esther Gray murmured words of wisdom to herself, and her lover, who had only received shadowy mentions recently, came up behind her and tipped her over the edge, too.

When Eleanor got home she told David My Novel had an end now, which was a mistake. Because straightaway he wanted to celebrate – feeling the need to mark the transition out of his own affair with Marion Cumberledge – and Eleanor wasn't sure there was anything to celebrate. It was nice, finishing My Novel – no, it was more than nice, it was a profoundly good feeling – but the end was only another beginning, after all. There was still all the revising, all the rewriting, all the searching and fussing with a publisher to be done. Also David fussed a lot these days himself, or was it the way she saw him, confident now that she was doing a job in a man's world and the woman's one as well? David fussed about the little things that seemed to Eleanor merely things to organize – when to get to the bank, what to have to eat, whether one should take vitamin pills, which newspaper to read. And he was now fussing about how to celebrate. 'I'll ring the Cousins,' he offered, 'and Jon Gordon and Bob Pryor and the Worthingtons, and we'll have champagne. No I won't. Don't you think, Eleanor, that just the Cousins would be nice? We could try that new French restaurant. Where's Yolande? Will she babysit? Or perhaps we should ask her to come as well? What do you think, Eleanor?'

Extract from:

SHADOWS OF SUCCESS
BY ESTHER GRAY

It was a red-gold autumn day; there had been a touch of ground frost in the north. The winner of the Aphra Behn literary prize left home early, while the sun in the south was still gathering its energy to take the chill off the autumn leaves, and certainly before anyone else in the house was up to remind her of her real identity.

The prize was to be awarded at a formal luncheon in the Hilton Hotel in London. Eleanor took a taxi from Victoria. As they sped along Park Lane, she checked her face in the mirror: did it wear an expression appropriate to a lady novelist on her way to receive a literary prize? She combed her hair and practised smiling. Her green velvet skirt had survived the train journey, and her prepared speech, on a sheet out of one of her Ref. 141 notebooks, was in her pocket.

In the hotel foyer, a large notice board indicated the way. You for the literary do, Madam?' asked a porter, as well. Yes, indeed. He pointed a gloved hand. As Eleanor crossed the foyer, she imagined she saw a figure flit behind one of the tall columns: a figure recognizable, but at the same time strange. Puzzled, she resolved to put it out of her mind during the coming ordeal.

Her place, in the middle of one long side of the damask-dressed table, was between Dame Moira Leggatt, who was to award the prize, and Harvey Walker, Chairman of the Society of Novelists, whose prize it was. Harvey was a little man with a pointed beard and a bow tie. Eleanor warmed to him. He started talking to her about his children. Dame Moira, on the other hand, considered herself superior, and was anxious, so she told Eleanor, that the luncheon should be over by 3 p.m., as she had an appointment with her accountant in the City. Her expensive cream wool dress was trimmed with red squirrel fur. A cubed diamond flashed among her fingers. 'I do this for family reasons, you know,' she admitted. 'My mother was a suffragette. She was always very keen on women working and getting to the top, and all that sort of thing.'

Anything less like a suffragette it was hard to imagine. Eleanor drank her Perrier. Dame Moira rose to her feet and everyone clapped. Eleanor felt dizzy, and tried to look as though she wasn't really there. In the process she saw the same figure as she'd glimpsed earlier, sitting on the other side of the table, towards the corner, tucking into a bread roll.

She blanched the colour of the roll when she saw me. I didn't mean to give her such a visible shock. I waved a little at her. I was enjoying myself amongst all those fake people – literary figures, entrepreneurs, dilettantes. I began seriously to wonder about the meaning of the word 'fictional'. You see, I would have said, like Dame Moira, if I'd been able to speak to Eleanor at all, you see, I would have said, I came for family reasons. To keep it in the family, so to speak. You owe it all to me. Not to David Jenkinson. Without me you never would have got My Novel published, or written, come to that. And without me as an excuse for practically everything you've done these past ten years, where would you be? Don't go away with the impression that I mind. On the contrary,

I'm pleased to have been able to help you on your way. I only want my role acknowledged, that's all. And perhaps, in return, you could do me the favour of cutting out that awful scene in chapter four? The sand's still stuck between my toes, not to mention in other unmentionable parts. I don't like the ending, either. Fifty's no age to finish the life of an interesting woman, even if she is fictional, and even if it is during a sunset in the Perigord.

SIX

Confessions

'I'LL BEGIN WITH with Tom Sherringham,' she says, making tiny inroads into her lime sorbet with the heavy silver spoon. 'Yes, that would probably be a good place to begin. You know who Tom Sherringham is, don't you? Yes, I thought you'd remember. He was my first literary advisor. No, not my first — the first was really Uncle Hal.

'It was Uncle Hal in whose presence the desire crystallized in me which has been (as you would say) my/our downfall. I ran to Uncle Hal to get away from home and found myself another one, even more imprisoning. His lover, you know, wrote poetry. He was a kind of latter-day Rupert Brooke. His sonnets of nostalgia for noncarnal love and eighteenth-century moral relations are famous.

'Thurston Blane died twenty-one years ago. I drew the attention of Cambridge University Press to the desirability of reissuing some of his poetry. *Couplets* came out in 1982. I wrote the foreword. I enjoyed doing that.

'But after that, you know the story pretty much. How isolated I was in Wimbledon and then in Brighton with the babies, how completely cut off from any kind of intellectual or aesthetic stimulation. Except for what you brought home in the evenings, which wasn't much, was it David? Be honest. You're not exactly what one might call a stimulating person. You may be as a teacher, of course, I wouldn't know about that. I was joking when I asked if your students were in love with you. But for all I know, they might have been. For the time being I accept your version of your life as regards me — that it's an open book (although this I suspect is a parody on the closed text of my own — book, that is). Yes, I accept that for the sake of argument, or rather in order to avoid it. I won't challenge it. That's an intellectual decision. To

112

be guided by my emotions would produce a different response. I just want to let you know that, so that it's understood between us.

'What you couldn't do for me was partly why I found the writing class. Tom Sherringham was incidental, really. Then. He wasn't even terribly helpful. I'll never forget his green pen, that deciduous handwriting. He screwed Eva Summers. I wonder if she kept her hearing aid on?

'Eva sent me on some adventures. But I won't tell you about them, as you might find them rather silly, and I don't think I could bear that. They weren't silly to me, you see, except in the sense that Milton uses that word in his poem "Character of a Happy Life" where "silly" truth and honest thought are coupled as enviable goals. I met some people, some interesting people, in the course of them. And then when we moved to Brighton my life became more difficult because you were getting what you wanted – well, to be fair not *because* but at the same time as. Eventually I felt a little concerned about my sanity and wellbeing, and also about the progress of My Novel. Eventually I asked Tom Sherringham to read it for me and he obliged. The advice he came up with, though, again wasn't all that useful. He tried to show me what he meant in a practical way. He was well-meaning, though it's probably not what you would call it. I'm not sure I want to go into that, though. Would you mind if I just left it here? I think it would be better, really.'

Extract from:

MEMOIRS OF A PRUDISH HOUSEWIFE (short story)
BY ELEANOR JENKINSON

He slid in and out of her with as much facility as an operative in a nineteenth-century sausage factory.

She lay there thinking of the sea pounding outside the window.

He clasped her buttocks like a piece of cling film, but this did, eventually, make her feel as though something tangible was being done to her. (He intended her to feel this.)

After a while he took his penis out of her cunt and looked at it, rather as a whale might look at a colleague stranded on the shore. It glistened as it struggled for life.

'Breathe on me breath of life,' she murmured solicitously.

He took her hand and put it there and she caressed him vaguely for a few minutes, considering him (it) as some kind of marine animal too, although not a whale, perhaps a small pink sea anemone or a boned herring.

He kissed her nipples sharply (sensing her thinking these thoughts).

'It's not a competition,' she insisted. 'If men want to win competitions against women they'd be better off playing chess.'

He penetrated her again and gave her what he thought, lacking sufficient imagination, she deserved.

The social structure in Eleanor's publishing office was a bit like it was in David's university: there were the few great(ish) men at the top and then the vast body of females in inferior positions beneath – the teaching/editorial assistants, the secretaries, in David's case the students, in Eleanor's the young women editors/secretaries/writers struggling to make their voices heard against the general overpowering clamour of received literary (patriarchal) wisdom. Eleanor was kinder to the women writers than to the lordly young (old) men. She searched for points in their favour, an original theme, a felicitous turn of phrase, a striking angle of vision. For them, the word 'promising' – if at all possible. But not uttered in the patronizing way Tom Sherringham had used it; for, with the tedious wisdom of hindsight, Eleanor Jenkinson had at last begun to understand the nature of Tom Sherringham's project towards her.

History, being partly of ideologies and consciousness, was encouraging Eleanor Jenkinson to a more noble and emancipatory idea of herself; sweeping her along, indeed, in a great tidal wave of self-awareness. But the water, clear and pure in its main aspect, was mixed with an awful lot of junk. Seaweed, discarded bathing suits and old bottles with occult messages in them competed for her attention, reducing the force with which this could be applied to the chief task in hand, which was, as always, My Novel. Still, the prevailing political climate, especially that among the women who worked for Maitland & Ware, the publishing firm, also renamed, in which Eleanor was, was such that Eleanor would now find it harder to push out of the way for any length of time her unpublished work. According to David, the conjunction of the finishing of My Novel and the taking of the Maitland & Ware job was a happy one, as Maitland & Ware might reasonably be expected to publish it. David had himself suggested that Eleanor suggest this. Which she would, in her own time. But it must be her own.

Women's conversations were flavoured by feminism now, in the office and out of it; which is to say that the existence of feminism as a political position in its own right was now the flavour which brought others out – the consciousness women always have of the social structures and devices of their subjugation, of men's veiled animosities towards them. Eleanor was one of three not exactly junior female editors for Maitland & Ware. Araminta Close, one of the two others, had lately begun to call herself a feminist, wear little silver women's sign earrings to work, and had ceased to bleach the fringe of dark hair on her upper lip. Araminta had had a hard time with her father, an over-sensitive paediatrician, who'd picked her as his favourite and kept her close to him while divorcing the rest of the family: Araminta talked about this a lot. A nice woman at the Women's Therapy Bureau was helping her to see the light twice a week. Araminta's new identity was fragile, but she was working at it, deftly keeping her father at arm's length while ensuring he paid the therapist's bills. The third woman, Rowan Carter, was a bit critical to Eleanor of Araminta's new alliances (especially of the newly visible facial hair) but Eleanor sensed this was merely out of Rowan's own fascination for the pull the said alliances also had for her. Unlike Araminta, Rowan's background was boringly unneurotic. The child of two schoolteachers from Letchworth, her grasp of reality had the solidly shiny and comforting shape of a well-rounded white cabbage.

Maitland & Ware belonged to Jim Maitland and Vernon Ware and their shareholders. Jim Maitland, who'd inherited one third of the firm from his father Godfrey, had once been young and dynamic. In the 1950s, he'd driven a second-hand Alfa Romeo, and worn a pale pink cord suit over a black shirt and black underwear to the office. But age and the salacious living fanned by expense accounts, especially those one has control over, had swapped a bawdy stupor for the earlier impression of a keen young man of whom the phrase 'the driving force behind the firm' was often used. At fifty-three it had lately occurred to Jim that his days in publishing were numbered, as were, indeed, all his days anywhere.

He hardly remembered Eleanor Kendrick from when she'd first worked for the firm in the Regent Street office. Insofar as he was able to resuscitate any knowledge of her, she was merely a slip of a girl who vanished, as they all did, to have babies, having first given birth to a few semi-witty memos. Now, twelve years on, Eleanor appeared to possess an altogether different presence. One which suggested to Jim Maitland there was more to her than met the (his) eye. All of which provided a promising beginning for Eleanor's own approach to Jim Maitland, in November 1978, concerning My Novel.

She sent him one of her memos:

> FROM: Eleanor Jenkinson
> TO: Jim Maitland
> Could I make an appointment to see you about an unpublished manuscript of mine? It's a novel on which I've been working for some time. I'd value your opinion of it.

Which wasn't true, of course. She wouldn't *value* his opinion, but she might have to pay some attention to it. Jim Maitland scribbled on the bottom of Eleanor's memo, 'Delighted. Lunch on Friday? J.M.' and returned it to her via his secretary.

Eleanor took My Novel to lunch with her in a white plastic bag marked 'Gateway for Value'. The new briefcase seemed pretentious, or likely to draw people's attention to the fact that she was. Besides, she'd grown used to the plastic bags. She put 'Gateway for Value' under the table. Jim Maitland thought it must be her shopping. He also thought, now he had the opportunity to study Eleanor Jenkinson closely and away from the distractions of the office, that she had an extremely appealing Modigliani air about her. At close quarters, her assertiveness was dissolved by her size. She was also too thin, pale, exhausted and generally in need of feeding up. This latter was partly a projection of his own needs, but permitted him to order a Chateaubriand accompanied by a bottle of Chateauneuf du Pape – he was always childishly pleased by alliteration.

'Tell me about it,' he invited.

She did. To some extent, that is. She told him how hard My Novel had been to write, though without going on too much about the domestic distractions that had beset its path, as these she knew he'd find boring and insufficient explanation as to why it had taken so long. Another danger was that, once Jim Maitland had read it, he'd be overcome by the meanness of the project for which she had struggled against so many trivial odds.

Ellen Moers' *Literary Women* had just been published, and was doing the rounds of the office. Araminta, whose eyes effused an unusual brilliance which quite took Rowan's own off the moustache beneath, had become fond of quoting one of Moers' revelations about Elizabeth Barrett Browning – the lines, 'A curse from the depths of womanhood/Is very salt, and bitter and good'. When the women in the office talked about the book, they all agreed that the new picture of Elizabeth Barrett Browning was a lot better than the old one, in which she is chiefly to be remembered for the droopy love poetry she wrote regarding her much more famous husband, whom she regarded adoringly from her position invalided on the sofa with some kind of dog. Araminta had even cited EBB's words to her father on the telephone, when he'd last rung from the neonatal intensive care unit to try to get her out to dinner; she'd enlisted EBB's help in the effort to explain how healthy for both of them her rejection of him was.

Concerning Elizabeth Barrett Browning and *Literary Women*, Eleanor herself had been much impressed by Browning's pronounce-ment that on her tombstone should be written 'Ci-gît the greatest novel reader in the world.' Eleanor remained uncertain about the relationship between reading and writing with respect to the novel, including My Novel; on the one hand, it seemed to her that the motive for reading could only be to write oneself – as it had been in Elizabeth Barrett Browning's own case, even if all she'd managed was *Aurora Leigh*. Possibly, if Mr Browning hadn't been around, *Sonnets from the Portuguese* would have been franker fiction. As it was, her work echoed the tendency women have to need convincing that they *do* have something to write about, unlike men who are a lot more likely to be born with that conviction. Other people's (men's) novels are for women a source of tidbits, prods to the imagination, or the stuff of what, around the same time, Eleanor learnt from retrieving from Hove library a volume of Mary Ellman's *Thinking about Women*, referred to by the said Ellen Moers, was called 'phallic criticism'. Eleanor enjoyed the phrase and repeated it to herself silently on the train, looking at the commuters with their briefcases so like her own, but containing such different substances. 'Phallic criticism,' she said with closed lips to the man from Wildwood computers who tried to show her his brochure passing Lewes; and to he who, from a vantage point straphanging at Three Bridges, ventured the opinion, trying to look directly into Eleanor's eyes, that such commuting was for idiots and he really envied his wife at home. Was Eleanor not, or had she not been, a wife at home? She was certainly not willing to be classed as anything else (a man).

But if women read in order to gather the strength to write, there was also the danger that the process could backfire. The result could be lowered, not enhanced, self-esteem. That was why books such as Ellen Moers' or Mary Ellman's or later Elaine Showalter's *A Literature of Their Own* were so much of a tonic for Eleanor and her friends; they provided splendid, utterly convincing explanations of their own lack of success, but without showing their efforts in a paltry light, being as much about why women are said not to have written – and are often also stopped from doing so, which isn't at all the same thing – as they were revealing of the culture of what women write about.

Eleanor Jenkinson, at lunch with Jim Maitland in Les Fleurs du Mal, a stone's throw from where Princess Anne's detective had had trouble with his gun, realized Jim Maitland's understanding of women didn't really embrace the kind Ellen Moers had written about. But that he would in all probability have assented to the overplayed truth of Stendhal's remark that all women's works should be posthumous ones – a statement that was later to resonate with Andrea Dworkin's decree that the only really good women were the dead ones. The formula underscoring Eleanor's side of the dialogue she was having with Maitland was her own knowledge that a first novel by a woman was as hard to publish as – well, salt-encrusted tablets in a foreign language lying at the bottom or even floating on the top of the Dead Sea.

Jim Maitland took the Gateway plastic bag home with him; that is, to the attic flat to which his second wife Diana had recently consigned him, due to her discovery of his infidelity with the Maitland & Ware crime writer, Stella Reeves. (He *thought* of Diana as having consigned him to this uncosy bachelor existence, but of course everyone knew it was his own fault. On the other hand, as it was evident it wasn't what he wanted, there had to be some deep confusion of motives in there somewhere.) On that same Tuesday evening at seven o'clock, Jim Maitland opened a tin of artichoke hearts and one of duck in gelée, made himself some strong French coffee and began *The Last Summer* (a title inspired by Esther Gray's new untimely end). By midnight he was through with it, and so impressed – his own word – that on impulse he obtained Eleanor Jenkinson's phone number from Directory Enquiries (where it was of course filed under David Jenkinson) and gave her a ring.

The Jenkinsons were in bed. David was asleep. Eleanor was listening to Yolande banging around in the kitchen, and had a boorish headache derived from the Chateauneuf du Pape at lunchtime. As she listened to the sounds below, she despaired of Heidi's being about to embark on the phase out of which Yolande, though admittedly still noisy, was now showing signs of coming. David picked up the phone – for some reason it was on his side of the bed. He grunted and passed it to Eleanor, who sat up in her creased flowery nightdress, and was naturally surprised to hear Jim Maitland congratulating her for having achieved something truly remarkable. 'Such a *modern* novel,' he murmured, 'so *European* in its conception' (from which Eleanor gathered it was good both to be modern and European, though she wouldn't necessarily have thought so herself). 'And the dialogue,' continued Maitland, now getting truly stuck into his theme, having, as we have seen, nothing else to do at this time of night, 'do you know, my dear, I don't think I've *ever* encountered any with the same sort of utterly *naïve* profundity – or should I say profound *naïvety*?' He himself didn't know which, as he wasn't altogether sure he knew what he was talking about. 'And of course you manage the *animalistic* aspects of Esther's conversion to femininity' (what conversion?) 'so well – the urges are so *primitive*, so *inchoate*, and at the same time so *contained*, so civilized . . . ' He was talking, Eleanor gathered, about the one third of the sex scenes she'd remodelled on Tom Sherringham's instruction. 'However,' Maitland broke his own stream of consciousness with a little of the lexicon for which he'd been famous in the old days, and Eleanor, hearing the implied hesitation of the word 'however', sat up straighter in bed in order to attend better, 'however, I do find the dialectics at the centre of the novel somewhat unconvincing. Perhaps not in themselves, you understand, but in their *technical* aspects. There's too much mythologizing, I fancy. Not quite enough *confrontation* with the underlying *grim reality*.' He stressed these words to drive his point home, despite the fact that he hadn't much idea what he meant (the phrase 'phallic criticism' rang in Eleanor's ears).

She was conscious throughout Maitland's unexpected review of My Novel of David very much awake and restless beside her. He'd got up and had a pee to while away the time, but was now back in bed with his hands behind his head staring indicatively at the ceiling. 'It's really nice of you to call, Mr Maitland,' said Eleanor, then, 'and I'm really glad you liked it. Perhaps we could talk about it a bit more tomorrow?'

'Of course, of course,' said Jim Maitland, getting a faint inkling of what Eleanor was on about. 'It's late, I'm probably disturbing you.' She didn't contradict him, instead repeating – she wasn't silly and knew full well on which side her bread was buttered – how essentially overjoyed she was that after all this time My Novel was receiving such a wholehearted literary reception from someone who was as much of an authority as he was.

She replaced the receiver and turned off the light. 'Sorry,' she said to David. 'That was Jim Maitland. I've no idea what made him phone so late.'

'Is this going to happen again?' demanded David, in his slumped irritation beside her. 'The man's timing is awful. You do know I've got an important paper to give tomorrow, don't you? On working-class culture in pre-Reformation Europe. At the Historical Institute in West Berlin. I need my sleep.'

'Yes, dear. So do I.'

'What was he ringing about, anyway?'

'Oh, only My Novel. He likes it.'

'Oh. That's good, isn't it, Eleanor!'

Jim Maitland wasn't at the office when Eleanor got there, nor did he appear throughout the whole of the rest of that day. When she enquired of his secretary where he was, Belle shook her head a little mournfully and said, 'I'm not his keeper, Eleanor' (the tone of voice suggesting that she might like to be).

'Okay, then,' said Araminta, who was feeling quite on top of things after a good session with the nice therapist, 'what's going on, Ellie?' Eleanor confessed the handing over of My Novel to Jim Maitland and his maritally disturbing midnight call, but was completely unprepared for Araminta's reaction.

'Probably the last you'll see of it,' she said, almost casually. 'Mine disappeared into the black hole five years ago.' It had been a bad time, that. The beginning of the trips to the Therapy Bureau, in fact.

'Your what, Minty?'

'My My Novel,' she said. 'A good yarn about a Marxist monk in Assisi who fell for a visiting Sardinian lady. I worked in Rome for four years as an au pair girl/person,' she added, as though this explained everything.

'What happened to it?'

'Maitland said he liked it. It was entitled *Might on a Rare Mountain*.'

'Don't be ridiculous!'

'Well it might have been. I can't remember what it *was* called now. Though I have got a copy somewhere.'

'Where?'

'In my bottom drawer, of course,' said Araminta, 'where yours was, no doubt. Hey Bonnie,' she called across the room to Rowan, whose office alias was Bonnie Clyde, and whose head was down over Stella Reeves' latest effort, the chronicle of an evil horticulturist who buried his wives in a garden centre and was only found out when the compost orders changed.

'This woman can't spell,' said Rowan irritably, these being the days before novel writing got mechanized and spellchecks were available on software packages. Not for nothing had Rowan's childhood been riddled with expletives concerning spelling from her schoolteacher parents.

'I said, Hey, Bonnie,' Araminta reminded her. 'Tell Ellie here what happened to yours.'

Rowan lifted her eyes from the telltale compost orders. 'It looks very odd with two "N"s in it,' she remarked. 'Gave it to Maitland, he offered me a pittance for it. Friend here, Araminta whatsit, advised me to try Castle Books with it. Reasonable offer, went out of business soon after.'

'But was it published?' insisted Eleanor.

'Oh yes.'

Eleanor was stunned rather than impressed.

Araminta, seeing this, said, 'It wasn't a novel, though, was it, Bonnie?'

'Not on your life,' said Rowan. 'A biog. Much easier stuff, really. Didn't think it at the time, though. Had lotsa trouble finding her at home. Annie Oakley,' she explained. 'Died alone and penniless, after experiencing the glamour of world fame.'

Jim Maitland reappeared two days later with no explanation of any kind for his absence. In fact he'd been down to see Stella Reeves, but she'd said she never wanted to see him again, so he'd holed up in a Suffolk pub. 'About My Novel,' ventured Eleanor, spying him in the corridor, ' . . . '

'Your what?'

'My Novel.'

'Did I read it?' He stared at her for a minute or two. 'Oh yes, of course I did. Very fine piece of writing. European, wasn't it? Looking forward to reading the next one.' He went into his room and shut the door. Eleanor stood there stunned again.

'Don't worry, my dear,' advised Belle, who'd overheard this. 'He's in a funny mood today. It'd be a mistake to take it personally.'

But Eleanor did. She brooded and moped and worried. 'Ask for it back,' counselled Araminta, 'or you'll never see it again.' Reflecting on her own new assertiveness, she added generously, 'I'll give you the phone number of my therapist, if you like.'

'Ye Gods, what an offer! But I don't hold with it myself,' observed Rowan. 'Women must be able to claim their rights without behaving like puppets and getting someone else to work their mouths.' She looked at Araminta gently. 'No offence, Minty, but you know what I think. No,' she turned back to Eleanor, 'my advice would be more practical. Try Fontana or Hutchinson instead.'

'Get yourself an agent, Mrs Jenkinson,' said Tom Sherringham, whom Eleanor still saw from time to time.

She'd had a very odd meeting with him a while ago. This time it had been Janice who'd called her. 'It's me, Mrs J!' She'd got Eleanor's office phone number from Yolande, who was often at home hovering over the telephone these days in case one of her young men phoned. 'Janice Carew, remember?'

'Oh yes, how are you, Janice?'

'Not too bad. And yourself?'

'Fine, thank you Janice.'

'Long time no see,' continued Janice unmemorably.

Eleanor began to explain how busy she'd been.

'None of us gets any younger, does we, Mrs J? Met a friend of yours the other day,' she added. 'Writer chap. Fat belly. Raunchy type. Said he knew you *very* well, Mrs J!'

Eleanor gulped.

'Anyway, the reason I'm phoning is I'm having a little party Saturday, wondered if you'd like to come. Maybe bring hubbie? If hubbie's still around, that is?'

Needless to say, Eleanor didn't tell David of the invitation. She attended Janice's party with the normal excuse of all such experiences being potentially the subject matter of fiction. And there he was, Tom Sherringham, in Hackney, in Janice Carew's council maisonette with Janice's new-old bloke, Drake, and Michelle and Fran and Ball, who at first tried to evade Eleanor's penetrating where's-my-money look and then decided to come out with it (of which more anon), and Ball's girlfriend, a Marilyn Monroe lookalike called Sheila. Numerous others too, of course, but as most novels are overstuffed with minor characters, we won't bother with those.

They all drank some pungent mixture Janice's man had prepared containing neat alcohol purloined from the London Hospital's pathology department – 'don't ask me how, you wouldn't like the answer' – and were given canapés on plastic trays prepared from a recipe in *She*. Tom Sherringham told Eleanor that *Mail Fantasy* had foundered – too much competition from Scandinavia. 'They did full cunts there in 1968, you know.'

Ball, standing next to Eleanor and Tom, took the opportunity to say, 'I'm glad you didn't ask where your money was going, Mrs J. You'll get it back. I'm working on it.'

To get back to the point – one of the points – of this deviation, Tom Sherringham was still in Eleanor Jenkinson's life as a veritable source of help in times of trouble, even if he had less money than he'd had before and was missing the stimulation of his monthly column about clitorises.

'Have you got one, then?' she enquired by way of return, when he suggested that what she needed now was the help of a good literary agent.

'No. Did have once. He fell off a cliff. They're worth their weight in gold or rather ten percent sometimes. Particularly for the young starting out.' Which she wasn't, really. But he gave her the names of two literary agents anyway. These Eleanor attached to a long list she already knew about via her labours in Maitland & Ware. She'd never much liked the sound of any of these, they'd always been too much on her side and too little on the author's to convince her that Eleanor Kendrick *qua* author rather than Eleanor Jenkinson *qua* publisher could benefit from their attention.

The first name Tom Sherringham gave her, Gordon Blount, was always on the other line when she called. Since she knew the real meaning of the phrase 'on the other line', she dropped him. The second, Chrissie Parkes, was an extremely well-known name: the 'best' literary agent in London according to various reports, and whatever that meant. So off Eleanor trotted one day with My Novel in an 'Our Price Records' plastic bag – though the black briefcase would have been better – to inter-view/be interviewed by Chrissie Parkes. Who inhabited a showy office in Chelsea. Eleanor took the boat from the Embankment. It would have been a splendid journey, had it not been pouring with rain. Eleanor was standing in the hall of the suite of offices occupied by Chrissie Parkes' literary agency, dripping inconsider-ately into the pink Wilton floor, when Chrissie Parkes herself came out to greet her, dressed in a thin petrol suede skirt, cream silk blouse, and suede waistcoat. Her hair, immaculately henna-ed, was held high with tortoiseshell combs to give an air of authority. She led Eleanor to a showcase office, and sat one side of a gargantuan pine desk, while Eleanor sat the other, like a patient, and counselled her about all the things Eleanor already knew – the inherent unkindness of the publishing world, the long time it takes for anyone to make their mind up about any-thing, the distaste we all feel for confessional writing, etc. Eleanor wondered why Chrissie Parkes thought My Novel was confes-sional. What was confessional anyway? (We will come to that later, in about 1983.) Throughout her soliloquy, Eleanor did wonder why Chrissie Parkes was being so nasty to her. Surely agents needed authors, they couldn't afford to treat them like maggots? Chrissie Parkes wanted to know why Eleanor hadn't written any-thing before.

'Before what?'

'Well, when you were younger.'

'I have actually been writing this book for quite some time,' explained Eleanor uneasily. 'And I have been doing a few other things as well.' Like having children, she would have added, had she thought Ms Parkes would have been able to comprehend what she meant by this.

The end of their encounter was marked, not by Eleanor's feeling it to be concluded, but by a transatlantic phone call. Chrissie Parkes asked the caller to hold for a moment while she shepherded Eleanor out. She shook her hand, and while Eleanor found her wet umbrella, Chrissie flounced back into her office again, her suede skirt swaying expensively across the carpeted hallway.

Chrissie Parkes read My Novel and rang Eleanor a week later. 'Well, I liked it,' she confessed, 'but I have to tell you I wouldn't go to the stake for it.'

But I don't want you to *go to the stake for it*, thought Eleanor. All I require is someone who will help me push My Novel out of the bottom drawer into the limelight, which is quite a different matter.

So much for literary agents. Eleanor decided they would add rather than subtract problems from the path of My Novel. Back to Mr Maitland. I will bait him, determined Eleanor, liking the alliteration, as he did.

It was a few days before Christmas 1979. Outside the office, it was raining and people were trudging the streets, considering the approaching dramas of who to eat Christmas lunch with, whether to have duck or turkey, what about Mother-in-law and those unfortunate enough to lack such choices, and where is the back entrance to Hamley's anyway?

Eleanor stayed late knowing that Mr Maitland would (information passed on by Belle: he was waiting for a delivery from his wine merchants).

She knocked and entered without waiting. He had his feet up on the desk, on a rejected account of a Norwegian scholar's search for his ancestors among the geysers of Iceland. 'Too cold for comfort,' he'd noted in his memo. To warm himself up he'd started to read a copy of a Mediterranean cookbook belonging to Stella Reeves, which he'd determined never to give back, and was in the middle of a lush description of how exactly to make *pommes dauphinoises* when Eleanor said, 'Excuse me, Mr Maitland, I wonder if you could just tell me, are you going to publish My Novel or not?'

'What a waste of cream.' He put the book down and took his glasses off. 'Or not, did you say? Let me see, who are you, and what are you talking about? Ah yes, it's Eleanor Jenkinson again. Well come in, Eleanor Jenkinson, I was just not thinking about you!' Hysterical with his own sense of occasion, he shifted his feet on to the floor and stood up, adjusting the waist of his trousers. 'Oh yes, that would be a sad fate indeed, wouldn't it, for such a dynamic European piece of confessional existentialism?'

Eleanor pondered on the word 'existentialist'. She pondered. He staggered. Round to her side of the room. Put his furry hands on her elfin shoulders and breathed alcohol and cigarette fumes at an angle of forty-five degrees down into her small appealing face. 'Tell you what, Eleanor Jenkinson, have dinner with me tonight and I'll give you your answer.'

Expecting this, Eleanor had already armed herself with excuses – a cocktail party for Stella Reeves' new book, don't expect me home till late – and with an iron reserve to do whatever was necessary to get My Novel published. And by whatever, she meant whatever. But come what may and almost certainly he would and she wouldn't, Eleanor Jenkinson wanted to beat Mr Maitland at his own game. Less honourably, she also wouldn't have minded proving to her co-soeurs in the office that she could succeed where they couldn't.

She made sure he drank most of the wine this time and towards the latter third of the meal said, not unlike one of Tom Sherringham's erstwhile female harlots, 'I'll sleep with you, Mr Maitland, if you'll sign this first.' And produced from her handbag one of the Maitland & Ware standard contracts with herself named as author of a text of some 95,000 words entitled My Novel, delivery date one month hence, to allow commuting time for the alterations she knew she might still want to make.

Jim Maitland, who'd never met anything of the kind before, was so taken aback and so drunk that he tried to sign his own contract with the prickly stem of the rose in the centre of the table. Eleanor offered him her pen and then, mindful of the legal niceties, summoned the waiter, whose name transpired to be Paul

Goodfellow, as witness. She folded the contract up and put it back in her handbag and got into a taxi with Mr Maitland and went to his attic flat, conjugating briefly with him before catching the 11.05 back to Brighton.

SEVEN

Shadows of Success

'YES, THERE WAS JIM MAITLAND,' continues Eleanor Jenkinson in the darkening rose light, 'but I expect you remember him chiefly from the phone call he made one night when you were in such a bad temper about being woken up before going to a conference in East Berlin.'

'West.'

'He was a dreadful man. But I cornered him. The physical contact was momentary and repugnant to me but not so much as having My Novel languish year after year out of sight, gathering dust, becoming some kind of historical memento.

'It was about that time that I discovered what men did to women. I mean in a purely literary sense. What amazed me is that I could have spent all those years filling all those notebooks and reading all those novels other women had written and not have noticed. I mean for a while I swallowed hook, line and sinker – though I naturally disassociate myself from the inhumane sporty metaphor – the one about there being no great female writers/artists/people. You know, if Wilhelm had been Wilhelmina, he/she never would have written her/his fifth? Genes write the score. Beethoven was a crabby old syphilitic incontinent anyway; the social workers would have institutionalized music out of him if he'd been alive today. Did you know Alma Mahler was a composer before she married Gustav? After that, he didn't allow her to compose any more. She had to help him write out his scores instead. And have you heard the one about Sophia, Countess Tolstoy and *The Kreutzer Sonata*? How his criminal attack on womanhood had to be bowdlerized and transcribed by her? I don't suppose you have – it's not your period is it – but I can't be bothered to repeat it all, you can read it for yourself if you're interested.

'Of course, even when women did achieve, history teaches us – or rather historians do, and you are one of them, aren't you, David? – that they didn't really. How many people realize that the words on the Statue of Liberty – "Give me your tired, your poor/Your huddled masses yearning to breathe free . . . /I lift my lamp beside the golden door" were written by a Marxist-Jewish scholar, one Emma Lazarus, for example? As Virginia Woolf so ably said, if Shakespeare had had a sister, she'd have killed herself and been buried where the omnibuses wait at the Elephant and Castle.

'It was in that mood of cynical reappraisal of my own and My Novel's possibilities that my determination to get Mr Maitland to produce the goods was born. (By the way, Aphra Behn wrote a poem about premature ejaculation, but it's not in *Palgrave's Golden Treasury*. I have it if you'd like a copy.)

'You know what happened next, don't you, David? Would you like to put it in your own words, or shall I do it for you? Mine would be the more literary effort of the two. But it wouldn't be the more sanitary one.'

David Jenkinson asks for the bill. The waiter brings it curled up delicately on a Limoges plate, with a couple of tiny wrapped chocolate éclairs on top.

Extract from:

SHE DIDN'T DO ANY OF IT FOR LOVE
BY ESTHER GRAY

Oh, Eleanor Jenkinson, what are you doing, in this your prime of life? Where is your sagacity, your dignified composure, have you quite forgotten the moral code of the class from which you came? It can hardly be right to debase yourself thus.

And while I'm on the subject I have another set of questions to ask you. They concern your familial obligations. I want to know when you last considered, seriously, as women ought, the welfare of your children unborn as well as live, in a manner of speaking, indeed now probably out on the streets up to god knows what kinds of mischief? Remember Heidi and Eliza? Heidi is menstruating now and needs advice on how to deal with dysmenorrhoea and other potential diseases. Little Eliza does have headlice – her manner of scratching that fresh blonde hair of hers isn't simply touching affectation, but you haven't noticed, as it's two and a half years since you last looked. The mother's help, Rosemary, may be a sap to your conscience, and a drain on your bank balance, but she's not really been doing her job for quite some time now. The whole situation needs your attention. Your sister's child Yolande is ready to talk to you as an equal, but finds this impulse incompatible with your absence. The time will soon have passed; you will have failed again.

Husbands, I suppose, can look after themselves, but I think you ought to attend to yours. There is also the matter of the son to contend with. He is on the agenda, as by now you are beginning to realize.

In 1980 Eleanor Jenkinson rewrote the middle sections of My Novel so as to render their dialectics more confrontational with grim reality as prescribed by Jim Maitland. Before this rewriting, much of the necessary work had been done by Esther Gray in dreams, or as she roamed the streets of Paris. This was what Maitland had objected to, requiring the substitution of more basic interactions for the meditations of the dreamy mind. Esther's conversion to the kind of person who does more and dreams less would have been harder for Eleanor to accomplish five years before than it was in 1980, when her own fantasies had been substantially reduced in scale, intensity and frequency by the dire weight of pragmatism – what Jim Maitland would have called grim reality.

And out in the grim real world, the backlash had started to bite. Social pundits argued about the meaning of poverty while people increasingly had to live in it. A definite tiredness had begun to creep over the faces of campaigning women, who did not regard the birth of the world's first test-tube baby as being necessarily what the battle had been all about.

David's colleagues recommended a new play for the Jenkinsons' edification, *The Suicide*, by Nikolai Erdman. It proved to be a play in which a man denied the right to work wants to blow his brains out. His wife eggs him on, wanting an excuse (his funeral) to buy a new hat. But there he is sitting up in his coffin – draped in a red flag – complaining about a revolution that wasn't one.

'I know how he feels,' muttered Eleanor with feeling on the way home.

'Reminiscent of Kafka, wasn't it?' commented David, thoughtfully. 'The little man against the vast bureaucratic machine.'

'Or the little woman,' she whispered.

The previous week, she'd come home early and discovered Rosemary eating a box of truffle chocolates Davina had given her for her birthday, and reading My Novel. A half empty vodka bottle was also part of this scene. Something clicked at last. 'You've been filling up that bottle with water ever since you came here, haven't you, Rosemary? No wonder my evening pick-me-ups haven't.'

'It's my childhood, Mrs Jenkinson,' pleaded Rosemary. 'I was the victim of abuse.'

'Well, you should have told me sooner if you expected me to believe you,' said Eleanor firmly, 'and you're likely to be again if you stay around here much longer.' If My Novel hadn't been published yet, at least Eleanor had learnt to say what she meant and mean what she said. Sometimes she even wondered whether My Novel had somehow been published inside her, and that this was the reason she'd become different: the text had converted her experience, she had become the object of her text's manipulations, rather than the more normal way round.

Rosemary went. 'We don't need anyone now,' Eleanor told David. 'The girls are thirteen and fourteen. We'll have a rota for the housework.'

He lifted an eyebrow, but said, 'Whatever you think is right, Eleanor.'

Eleanor's life had settled down to a rhythm of its own – not of her – choosing. There was the early morning weekday rise, skirmishes in the kitchen concerning dinner money, the state of children's clothes, what to have for supper, and, following Rosemary's tearful departure, pointed references to the red, green, blue, yellow and purple rota system pinned to the kitchen notice board (Eleanor was purple, the dominant colour). The bumpy sojourn on the train came next – a corner seat, and the retrieval of My Novel from the lookalike briefcase, the sharp trot to the office; greeting Araminta, Rowan, Belle, et al. Maitland's hours continued to be erratic, as he was now engaged in a fruitless attempt to persuade Diana to return to him.

The day rolled on: manuscripts, meetings, wearying conversations with dispirited or angry authors and agents. Four times a year there was the *raison d'être* of it all: Eleanor had a book personally to supervise through the entire production process. Hers was the dubious (grim?) joy of chasing each manuscript from author to copy-editor to author to copy-editor to printer . . . and so forth. To hold the finished product in your hand was nonetheless, like the delivery of any child, delightful. But the rewards of publishing must be nothing compared to the rewards of writing; Eleanor remained firmly convinced of this – publishers after all are only second-hand merchants, vicarious exploiters of others' talents.

Weekdays at six Eleanor left the office and after the reconstruction of a little more Parisian dialogue (she had by now become a practised hand at defraying the leering asides of her fellow commuters) she was home – how conveniently – just in time to cook supper. To be fair, these days, niece Yolande, if she was in, had peeled the vegetables and made the salad and laid the table. Yolande was the only one of them to have the domestic rota memorized; she'd become a thoroughly nice young woman, twenty, with a frank expression and a direct way of speaking to match, almost the only remnant of Coffs Harbour. A photograph of her mother remained on the dresser in her room; Celia Kendrick, athletic and golden brown, outside their habitation on the beach. Yolande looked very like Celia, but here in Hove the outdoor Australian ranginess had nearly become an urban beauty. Yolande carried herself well, in the nineteenth-century meaning of that term – she walked with her head held high, as though a library were perched on top. She'd now totally stopped wearing tatty, ill-fitting jumble sale clothes and was fastidiously and fashionably, though cheaply, dressed, and attending Brighton School of Art for a course in graphic design.

So Eleanor Jenkinson cooked the supper with her niece's help, and David Jenkinson came home in time to eat it. What *he* had been doing with his day was never entirely clear. Eleanor supposed that his time was spent in a mixture of teaching, administration, research and writing, with a fair amount of idle intellectual argy-bargy built in. She wasn't wrong, but she wasn't as interested in the content of David's days as David would have liked her to be. It was for this reason that Eleanor had never found out about Marion Cumberledge. She hadn't even been suspicious as David had thought – this had been only one among various misreadings on his part of her self-absorption. She simply hadn't had the slightest interest in his doings. And so hadn't noticed his latest – Patsy Drew, a virginal horse-riding administrative assistant from the university offices – with whom David found a solace of admiration – hers for him – that was lacking in his Hove establishment.

Across the dinner table in Hove, David and Eleanor sat in a silence usually described as comfortable – they had, after all, eaten and been together some sixteen years now. But neither, to be honest, would have used the word 'comfortable'. Eleanor was bored by her marriage. David would have spoken of his wife's sad reduction to a domestic automat because of the strains of commuting and a full-time job, and would have liked her to give it all up to become less of one. Sometimes David thought he could remember the days long ago when Eleanor had called out to him when he came home in the evening, and they had had a drink together (in fact a cup of tea; David's salary couldn't at the time run to anything else, but his impulse to nostalgia was so strong he'd forgotten this). Even further back he fancied he could recall some rather delicious meals Eleanor used to cook – a long way further back actually, before the children: lamb casserole and treacle tart; chicken and mushroom risotto; apple snow. It was all this that he had replaced with his friend Patsy Drew, whom he plied with cookery books in an effort to bring back the past. (It was no accident that the two men currently in a position of power as regards the fate of My Novel – David Jenkinson and Jim Maitland – both spent a lot of their time imagining meals they wanted women to cook.)

Between David and Eleanor at the dinner table sat Heidi – flowering, insouciant and only a little rebellious (though all of it reserved for Eleanor, David being seen as the soft option), and Eliza, carefree in a determined sort of way. Eliza's line was that there wasn't much point getting worked up about things, as this was uncomfortable and tended to be wasted energy – life proceeded, governed in some way by laws over which individuals, particularly children, could expect to have little control. She, with her large grey eyes and small figure like her mother's, was the family peacemaker, jumping into the domestic fray whenever she sensed a moment of tension and smoothing it out – pricking the bubble silently and dissipating the toxin before real trouble erupted. Heidi regarded her sister as a bit of a wet. She liked to think of herself engaging in the full range of human emotion, and wanted to be an actress.

Like most women, Eleanor's weekends were a frenetic mix of all the things there wasn't time for the rest of the week. The purchase of food and lavatory paper; arguing with the girls to tidy their rooms; concentrated conversations about their academic progress; the management of the household's external social relations. Eleanor and David usually went out for a meal on Saturday night. Yolande and her boyfriend, a trainee stage designer, baby-sat. On Sunday the whole family walked on the cliffs by the sea. Eleanor insisted on this, whatever the weather, for reasons she had long since forgotten. And then it was Monday again. For three weeks in the summer the family holiday was taken, usually in France. A weekend at Easter might be spent in a rented cottage in the English countryside – Dorset and Yorkshire being favourites.

It didn't sound very exciting, did it? When you added in Eleanor's exhaustion, you really began to wonder if it was all worth it.

Early in January, Eleanor received a telephone call from her daughters' school. The head would like to see her about Heidi.

'What have you been up to, Heidi?' she asked.

Heidi, cool-eyed as usual, denied all knowledge of anything relevant. But looked a little paler at the question, so Eleanor thought.

Mr Chapman handed her a sheet of paper. 'I think you ought to see this, Mrs Jenkinson. It's a record of your daughter, Heidi's, absences from school last term.'

'She had flu,' commented Eleanor defensively. 'And a piano exam.'

'Those don't explain thirty-seven days' absence,' pointed out Mr Chapman, 'they explain two or three. Where was she, Mrs Jenkinson?'

'How should I know?' asked Eleanor. 'I'm only her mother.'

'Where were you, then?' she asked Heidi later. 'I hope you've got a sensible explanation that doesn't make me too cross.'

'Nowhere much, Mum.'

'So how did you go nowhere for thirty-seven days? You must have been *somewhere*, Heidi!'

'Well, different places. Some days I went to listen to records with Simon. Sometimes I just came home again. There wasn't anyone here. School's boring.' She hung her head and bit her lip and waited.

'Where was Rosemary?'

'Asleep, usually.'

'Why didn't you tell me?'

'You had enough to worry about, Mum, what with My Novel and My Job.'

Eleanor weakened, as Heidi had intended her to. 'You'll have to go and apologize to Mr Chapman.'

'Why? I'm not sorry. You wouldn't want me to lie, would you?'

'Heidi, that's not the point.'

'Okay, Mum, I get the message. If I do it again, you'll write me a note. Yes?'

'Stop manipulating me. You can't wheedle your way out of this one.'

'We'll see,' said Heidi, under her breath.

In January, people believed a new era was being born in Britain when the Council for Social Democracy was formed. From his Limehouse residence, Dr David Owen and friends spoke endearingly of an 'open, classless and more equal society' in which all ugly prejudices would be banished. Eleanor, a fairly random voter, thought about her own, as she reworked marred passages of My Novel, while husband David was tied to the news, speculating boringly on the historicity of Britain's two-party system, and the fact that there was no such animal as a new ideology; idly Eleanor wondered if the same was true of novels.

When the amendments to My Novel had been made, not in a month but by the springtime, Eleanor gave it back to Jim Maitland. She had now begun to visualize it in the windows of bookshops, a large handsome hardback with a glossy cover, mostly in yellow and greens, she fancied, with her name in black lettering, and a small black and white photograph and concise biography on the inside of the back cover. But wait: what name? Eleanor Kendrick? Eleanor Jenkinson? What title? My Novel was hardly sufficient. Aside from that, there was a long string of names, each of which captured an element of the text but none its historical development or its whole. How was the product to be packaged? Or before that blessed and sent on its way? Had David Jenkinson, for example, read it? If not, should he have?

'David,' said Eleanor one Saturday morning, when the two of them were in the kitchen, she using Dabitoff to scrub at some oil stains on one of Eliza's skirts, he examining the liquidizer at her request to see why it would no longer liquidize (this being entitled a division of labour); 'David,' said Eleanor, 'you know My Novel?'

'How could I forget it?' he jested, peering up into the insides of the Moulinex as though searching for a star in a very black night.

Perhaps he should buy Patsy one of these? It might help her on her way through the rather amazing Californian cookbook he'd bought her for Christmas.

'Well,' Eleanor rubbed the Dabitoff furiously back and forth, 'well, I wondered if you'd like to read it?'

She'd told him about the contract of course – about its signing, that is. He'd only half-listened. For David Jenkinson, as for us, My Novel had become something of a saga. It had dogged many of his waking hours for fifteen years now, had perpetually followed the Jenkinsons on home moves and on holidays in its ever-changing plastic apparel. David had become novel-fodder, anything he said or did being likely to be taken down and used in evidence against him. Only his dreams were sacrosanct, but even there, he thought, My Novel had developed a habit of following, forever interpolating its yet-to-be filled pages, and roving his head in sleep looking for odd bits of dialogue, a wandering thought or two, an unguarded reaction or half-formed promise.

But despite this intense and protracted relationship with My Novel, David Jenkinson hadn't actually read more than a few pages of it. This was because he'd never been given it to read. Though Eleanor had occasionally said to him, 'Sit down, David, and listen to this.' And had read to him from one of her notebooks in a rapid, almost toneless voice. To keep himself on the alert for something he ought to comment on, David had learnt to engage in various devices, such as picking his fingernails or removing wax from his ear, and these Eleanor had always chided him for, refusing to read him her undying prose while he scraped detritus from one orifice or another. The ear picking appeared particularly to outrage her; she claimed it produced a nasty squelching noise. He couldn't hear it himself, but then he'd got his finger in it.

David found what he was looking for in the abdomen of the Moulinex and said, 'If you like.'

'What does that mean?'

'It means I'm very happy to read it if you'd like me to. But I shan't insist on it as some kind of conjugal right. Novels aren't my forte, anyway, as you know.'

Eleanor straightened herself from her labours over the skirt at the table and looked out of the window. Across the street the big cherry tree was blossoming, and the feathery pink flowers danced with feathery white clouds, both opposing the blueness of the sky. She was possessed by a distinct feeling of unease. Would she, in David's place, have wanted to read My Novel for the first time at the same time as everyone else? Shouldn't there have been, as it were, a private view first?

'I think you ought to,' she said. Rephrase that, Eleanor Jenkinson: 'I'd like you to read it, David, if you would.'

David Jenkinson took My Novel to a conference on 'Consensus and Conflict in European History' which was being held in Strasbourg. He expected to have some spare time in the evenings. Indeed, he even joked about it: 'No I can't, old chap, I'm afraid I have to read my wife's novel.' They didn't believe him, of course. But he did go to his room and he did read My Novel, though after phoning Patsy Drew first. At least Patsy gave him the impression that her life revolved around the contact he made with her, rather than making inroads on his professional time, and adding considerably to the weight of his cabin baggage, as Eleanor did. But if the truth were known, David Jenkinson resented the role he'd adopted of illicit lover of tightlipped students and administrators – mature or not. He'd rather have had a happy marriage. Which was what he'd got, if another truth were known. For the Jenkinsons' marriage was not unhappy. Not their *marriage* – only themselves. But David was gripped by the common fiction, promoted more by journalists and politicians and sociologists than by novelists themselves, that marriages could have a condition all their own independently of the condition their participants were in.

While David struggled with conflict in Strasbourg, Eleanor in Hove found she was pregnant. They both therefore had their own reasons for feeling appalled when they next met which, with the astonishing/re-assuring tedium of conjugal life, was in the kitchen again.

She was puréeing the last of the previous summer's redcurrants. He needed a stiff drink (the aeroplane developed a fault in its landing gear and circled Heathrow four times before finally making it), and was peering in the refrigerator to see if there was a bottle of tonic in there somewhere.

'I've got something to tell you, David,' said Eleanor to his back, which was easier. 'I went to the doctor while you were away, and she says I'm two months pregnant.'

The vodka (neat, no tonic to be found, but at least it was real vodka now) and the news effectively blanched David's face. 'How?' he asked fatuously.

'The usual way.'

'But the coil . . . ?'

'Still in there somewhere, the doctor said.' She remembered Araminta telling her once of a friend of hers who conceived 'on the coil' as they say (which always makes it sound as though the coil itself did the trick) and whose child was born holding it like a passport, or identity card, or torch of freedom, except that it wasn't, though that is what contraception was supposed to be.

'Bloody hell! What are we going to do about it?'

Somewhat unkindly, and scraping the redcurrant mush unnecessarily hard with the back of the spoon against the metal sieve, Eleanor said, '*You* don't need to do anything. It's "I" not "we".'

'But I love you, Eleanor Jenkinson!' The words surprised them both. David certainly hadn't formed them in his head. Yet he meant them. This other business of the book could wait. That with Patsy Drew could easily be suspended. Life suddenly became delightfully urgent; he found, though he wouldn't have admitted it, the reminder of the biological imperative curiously stimulating. His adrenalin, and, he fancied, his androgens, started to flow like rivers in flood. Of course he'd known he was still capable of fatherhood, but a reiteration of this power didn't come amiss, particularly at the stage of life and career he was at. He saw himself referring to it in the common room: 'No, the little bugger wasn't planned, but what can you do?' Faced with such enormous fecundity what *could* you do? 'What will we do?' he said again, annoyingly discounting her last remark.

'Did you read My Novel in Strasbourg?' She was rinsing the sieve now, pushing mangled redcurrant stalks down the sink with her back turned to him.

Why was she changing the subject? 'I don't think we should talk about that now.'

'You mean it's not important, now you think you can turn me into a mother again!' Eleanor was surprised at the venom in her voice and the tears in her eyes.

He stood in the kitchen drinking his vodka.

Come on, David Jenkinson, you've given the game away already, haven't you? Why don't you just eulogize like Jim Maitland did when he unfairly woke you from your thick academic slumber? What could be simpler? Which is the more important – life or art?

'You didn't like it!' It was another accusation, a worse one. Eleanor turned to face David.

He imagined he could see a slight bulge below her waistline, reminiscent of the old days in Wimbledon. He sighed. 'No, it's more complicated than that. If you really want to talk about it, I suppose we'll have to. I *did* like it. I thought it was very clever, in fact; I was impressed. It surprised me. I didn't think you could write as well as that. No, don't interrupt. The point is, Eleanor, I think you need to think quite carefully about the implications of publishing it.'

'Which are?'

How could a fetus survive the anger in Eleanor's body? It must be like living in a volcano, thought David. The poor little thing would be burnt out. 'It might upset the children,' he observed frankly, and, he considered, dispassionately. 'People will think the novel's autobiographical. Some of the scenes . . . are, well, they are a bit *crude* aren't they? In fact, I'd go so far as to say it's unpublishable, Eleanor. You must have known that when you wrote it. It's private stuff – it belongs in your head. Not on paper, or in a bookshop. You can't publish it, Eleanor. You mustn't.'

Grim reality, she thought. Tom Sherringham: you've got to stop being a prudish housewife, Eleanor. The requirements of the novelist's craft being different from those attached to the art of being a woman. Eleanor Jenkinson didn't often get angry, but she was angry now. 'Sod you!' she said to her husband, and 'You'll have a lot to answer for from now on.' Various other unwomanly expletives also issued from her lips, and then, with no further attempt to draw out his meaning or provide an explanation of hers, she left the kitchen and David Jenkinson in a flurry of redcurrant purée.

Extract from:

A LITTLE WITCHCRAFT
BY ESTHER GRAY

Inside the little room, incense burned, and musty glass cases displayed historic wares. Powders in jars were for sale by the ounce, and some were already tied up in coloured linen pouches with labels indicating their content and effect. They promised fortune, or love; fertility and death. Manuals spelt out the details, but were costly, as there wasn't much call for them these days.

Eleanor Kendrick, on her world tour, stops off to appear on television in New Orleans. After a night in a luxurious suite in the Hotel Windsor, she fits in a morning's sightseeing. No-one told her about the witchcraft shop, but she's not surprised to find it there. She is surprised to find herself in it, though.

The woman behind the counter, dressed in black like a ripe olive, offers to tell her fortune. From behind the cash register, she extends a hand brown and pockmarked like the surface of a stale digestive biscuit, to take one of Eleanor's own, the one without the pen in it. 'Gee, what an amazing lifeline!' she exclaims throatily. 'D'you know, honey, you're practically indestructible!'

Eleanor's sensible British breath is quite taken away by this performance. I sidle up behind her, just to keep her company. The result is, she looks nervously over her shoulder.

'What about your friend, honey?' intones the fruity voice. 'Maybe she'd like a session?'

I push Eleanor behind the curtain. Anything to get away from me. While I'm waiting, I look around the shop. It seems to me we could all use a little witchcraft.

Eleanor talked to Araminta and to Rowan, even to Jim Maitland. They were all – even the latter – quite unsympathetic with David's point of view. 'Leave him,' advised Araminta and Rowan. 'What do you need him for, anyway?'

Eleanor didn't tell them about the pregnancy. One thing at a time. 'I'd be proud of you,' said Jim Maitland, 'if you were my wife.' Knowing perfectly well that he wouldn't have been.

Eleanor telephoned Janice Carew. 'Will you read it for me, Janice?'

'Course I will, Mrs J,' she said, responding to the tone of distress in Eleanor's voice. 'What is it?'

'My Novel.'

'My, what a privilege!' acclaimed Janice, having heard about it for almost as long as David Jenkinson.

Eleanor explained why.

'Rotten bastard,' said Janice. 'Why do you stay with him, Mrs J?'

'I wish people would stop saying that,' said Eleanor mournfully.

'Know what you mean. I'm not the leaving sort either. Hang on in there being abused, that's me. Pete came out of the Scrubs, you know, Mrs J. Went back in three weeks later. GBH in the chip shop. Marlon thinks Drake's his Daddy. Why not pretend? There's lies and lies, that's what I say.'

The new maisonette had the same small squares of blue peeking out of the concrete walls of the staircase. Janice was worried about how much time she'd have – the soft porn business she'd got into with Drake and Ball and Tom Sherringham was taking a lot of her time, and baby Marlon, now five, had a younger brother, Eliot, with an enzyme deficiency that called for a special diet.

'I'm pregnant, Janice.'

'Are you now, well that's nice, isn't it, Eliot?' Eliot sat on the floor eating a matchbox car, which wasn't part of his diet. 'Can I take it this infant wasn't intended, Mrs J?'

'You can.'

'Right old mess you're in, aren't you, Mrs J?' reflected Janice.

'I am, I am.' Swamped by misery, Eleanor cried into the crevices of Janice's leatherette sofa.

'Leave it with me, Mrs J.'

Janice Carew's inveterate bounciness was quite the inverse of the put-upon melancholia of yesteryear. She was up now, and Eleanor Jenkinson was down. This shift in positions was merely relative, however. Eleanor, dragging herself with the nausea of early pregnancy and the threat of My Novel's non-publication round town, found it hard to remember this. She felt more put-upon than any other woman had ever been. Quite the most oppressed female in history, in fact.

Janice Carew, understanding the conceit of this, contemplated telling Eleanor so. But to draw Eleanor's attention in her present state to the very singular and extra oppression of class would not have been fair, Janice judged. Consulting Drake and Ball, she decided that of the two murders currently on Eleanor's horizon – one of My Novel, the other of My Baby – neither was to be preferred but, equally, the commission of one was not to be redeemed by the other's omission.

'Mrs J?' she telephoned Eleanor at the office. 'How are you feeling?'

'The same, Janice, the same,' replied Eleanor wearily.

'Well, we've decided,' said Janice. 'You're to have the baby and publish the novel. *Courage, mon brave!* (Ball told her to say this.) 'Come round one evening and we'll go to the Pizza Hut and celebrate. And when the crisis is over, you and I must have a talk, Mrs J.'

'Must we? About what, Janice?'

'About women's lib and all that, Mrs J,' said Janice mysteriously.

At work Araminta, Rowan and Belle tried to cheer Eleanor up. Belle bought her primroses for her desk.

'It's not the first time, Ellie, history is simply *studded* with examples of men who've tried to stop women publishing,' said Araminta. 'Look at what happened to Annie Besant and Frances Hodgson Burnett, amongst others.'

'Though mostly it was more subtle than that,' added Rowan helpfully. 'As in John Middleton Murry's call to Katherine Mansfield, "Tig, isn't there going to be tea?" Tea-making should not be a gendered activity. Belle,' she called, 'how about some of that new orange herbal stuff? The stuff with "female harmony" on the label?'

'Do you think that makes me feel any better?' replied Eleanor remorselessly. 'To know I'm only one of a class?'

'Or think of all those who avoided the issue by pretending to be men. Currer, Ellis and Acton Bell, George Sand, George Eliot . . . ' observed Rowan, still helpfully. 'Not to mention Eliot George, F.G. Trafford, Vernon Lee, Michael Fairless, George Egerton, Ralph Iron and Isak Dinesen – all women, every one of them.'

'I hope you're not suggesting *I* should do that!'

'No, of course she isn't,' said Araminta, hastily. 'Anyway, adopting male names hasn't stopped women being accused of disguising themselves. Take Charlotte Brontë. When revealed to be a woman, she was said to have a brother who really did it. Brother Branwell though . . . '

'Shut up, Minty! I don't know myself if you should,' said Rowan, being herself possessed of what she liked to think of as an androgynous name.

'Of course,' went on Araminta, who wasn't so easily put off, 'there *are* other reasons for choosing pseudonyms. Kierkegaard now, he wrote some of his books under a false name so he could have an argument with himself.' Her last boyfriend, before the therapist, had told her that in the middle of their last row. It had actually been a criticism of her, but that point had receded. 'Sounds very far-fetched to me. Kind of like masturbation. Yuk! Anyway, you know what Eleanor Cady Stanton said about pantaloons. You could say the same about pseudonyms.'

'What did she say about pantaloons?'

'We have no reason to hope that pantaloons will do more for us than they have done for man himself.'

'There are too many women around pretending to be men,' said Eleanor sharply, 'for me to be one of them.'

Davina White called on Eleanor one Thursday afternoon. It was raining, and Davina's hair and black shiny raincoat dripped all over the office. 'Fucking cow!' she said, and again, 'Fucking cow!'

Eleanor, Rowan and Araminta all looked up sharply from their desks. 'Which one of us did you want?' enquired Rowan.

'Eleanor. Listen, Eleanor,' Davina slid wetly into the chair positioned for visiting authors in front of Eleanor's desk, 'I have to talk to you, I have to talk to someone!'

'We'll go out for a cup of tea,' suggested Eleanor quickly, 'shall we?'

It transpired that Phyllida Grossman had not appointed Davina as her successor after all. Instead, she had fastened on a man. The post had been given to Saul Richards, a 32-year-old editor from the States who was, according to Davina, very much her junior in terms of experience and expertise. 'I'll get her for this,' hissed Davina through gritted white teeth.

'But are you sure Phyllida had anything to do with it? Surely as the departing person, as it were, she wouldn't have done?'

'Don't you believe it. No formal control, but a fuck of a lot of the other sort.' The language wasn't at all typical of Davina. 'You know, Eleanor, it simply didn't *occur* to me that this would happen! I wasn't even nervous in the interview! Phyllida had said so often I'd take over from her. I was really confident. Besides which, I *know* I'm the best qualified person of those who applied. I mean, I know we've had some problems recently, but . . . '

'What sort of problems?'

'Oh you know, disagreements about how to run the office. About some manuscripts, too. And then there was the matter of Gilbert, that didn't help.'

'Gilbert?'

'Phyllida's nephew. He worked with us for a while. Gilbert and I had, well, a relationship.'

'I don't see why that has anything to do with it,' remarked Eleanor fairly.

'Neither do I. It certainly shouldn't have. But I think the old cow was jealous. She's never had much success with men, you see. She's a repressed old hag, she is.' Davina stirred her tea punitively.

'Who's this Saul Richards then? What's he like?'

'Really creepy.' Davina put four cubes of sugar in her tea and whacked them round the cup.

'Did you mean to do that?'

'What?'

'Put all that sugar in.'

'Couldn't care what I do,' said Davina. 'This is the end. It's the end of everything I've worked for. I'm not working with Mr Creepy Richards, I can tell you.'

'He might be all right,' offered Eleanor helpfully.

'You know what it is,' said Davina suddenly. 'It's sex discrimination, that's what it is. I'll get them under the Sex Discrimination Act. What do you think of that, Eleanor?'

'I'm not sure,' said Eleanor, feeling tired and not undiscriminated against herself.

Indeed, over the ensuing days she looked more and more tired. A mixture of the nausea plus intractable constipation confined her to the lavatory at Maitland & Ware for most of the day. Unlikely as it sounds, Araminta, Rowan, Belle and Jim Maitland put their heads together. A change of air, they decided, would help Eleanor to get things in perspective. They proposed a holiday, but the thought of having to make all the arrangements merely added to Eleanor's fatigue. So Jim Maitland kindly plotted to have her sent as the firm's representative to a conference of medical sociology shortly to be held in Holland. Maitland & Ware were taking over the publication of an academic journal called *Health and Society* and needed to spy out the land. It was a long cry from fiction – or perhaps not, as things turned out.

Too tired to argue, Eleanor packed her suitcase with Yolande's help and went to Holland in early June. She was to be away a whole week. Full of a compost heap of emotions, she kissed Heidi and Eliza goodbye. With David she was, as she had been for the past few weeks, distant and uncommunicative, wrapped up in the symptomatology of her own body and thoughts. David had tried to broach the subject of My Baby several times, but couldn't get past Eleanor's insistence that it was nothing to do with him. The air round Eleanor in the house in Hove bristled with Keep Away signs. David, noting she had put up some kind of electric fence, had no wish to give himself any further shocks.

He'd given himself a few with Patsy Drew, who hadn't been as easy to suspend as he had thought.

Patsy Drew met Marion Cumberledge one day rather in the nature of consequences. The two of them found each other at a protest against the rerouteing of heavy traffic through the small complex of little brown houses in which they both, quite accidentally, lived. Patsy was alerted by Marion's first name, which she knew belonged to David Jenkinson's previous liaison, and as she was deeply upset by, and on Valium because of, the news of Eleanor Jenkinson's pregnancy, she didn't even try to swallow the question 'Do you know David Jenkinson?' along with her next Valium tablet.

Marion Cumberledge felt sorry for Patsy Drew. 'You'll be happier without him,' she advised. 'He'll never leave his wife. She's got some sort of hold over him. I think because she doesn't do what he wants. Which I did,' she reflected sadly, 'for a while until I saw the light. Though I did insist on keeping the windows closed.'

At Schiphol airport, while waiting for the coach to the conference centre, which was out in the countryside amongst the bulb fields, Eleanor got into conversation with a GP from Hammersmith. They had an interesting dialogue about home confinement. The GP seemed pleased to be talking to someone who wasn't either a GP or a sociologist or a sick person. Eleanor carried her twin secrets in her heart and her uterus respectively. It was difficult for her to deny that the change of air was already doing her some good.

There were two hundred of them from forty-three countries out there in the bulb fields. Some of them wore turbans and African headdresses, others nose rings and tight black pants. The conference papers were unintelligible, being loaded with words like 'dysfunction', 'syndrome', 'epidemiological' and 'motivational'. But Eleanor went dutifully to some, tried hard to be attentive, fell asleep, and was kindly woken at the close of the session by whoever was sitting next to her. She went to her room, which was located in a tower at the corner of the building (the conference centre used to be a monastery) and slept peacefully in the pleasing pastel Dutch interior, with the window open slightly so that voices outside contending the merits of Foucault's version of the evolution of the clinic, versus Illich's potent but less trustworthy metaphors of medicalization, or different desiderata for studying youth drug subcultures, or lay ideologies of health and illness with particular reference to dissonances of class and gender, mingled and floated in the vegetal air, insinuating themselves into her sleep. Like Esther Gray, Eleanor was tempted to dream her crises all away, to pack the hours of unconsciousness with such material as would never, consequently, need to see the light of day, but, like Esther Gray, she'd learnt that if you do this you have to do it all again when you're awake anyway. In grim reality.

There was a swimming bath in the conference centre. Large with palms. Eleanor swam or lay, eyes closed, comfortably floating, hoping herself cured. She said hello nicely to people in the swimming bath and at meals in the communal dining room, or during cocktails in the garden. But all her conversations were superficial ones. Except for one.

She saw him watching her, a figure in white against the concrete grey of the building, the dark green trees, and the pots full of lobelia, around which a hungry marmalade cat recurrently sniffed. He had dark blue eyes, hair pulled back with an elastic band, and an odd pinkness to his complexion, like dried roses. 'Jordan Herriot,' he extended his hand genially to her. She took it, looked into his marine eyes and felt a sense of apprehension as diffuse as the faded pinkness of his skin. 'And where do you fit in here, Mrs Jenkinson?' he was asking.

She heard the question, finally. 'I work for Maitland & Ware, the publishers who've just taken over the journal.'

'I didn't think you looked like a sociologist.' He folded his arms and smiled at her. 'Two of a kind. Or rather not.' He explained he worked for Microsoft Inc., the world's largest software company. Run by Bill Gates, one of the top twenty richest men in the United States. Jordan was here to sort out the computerization of the conference facilities. The installation had been done, but was full of bugs.

Soon Eleanor was telling him about My Novel. Jordan wasn't as interested in the substance as he was in technical aspects of the writing process. 'You don't mean to say you write by hand?' he expostulated incredulously. 'If you don't mind me saying so, that's rather prehistoric.'

It simply hadn't occurred to Eleanor to do anything else. Indeed, there was such a symbiotic connection between the mental construction of the text and its dispersal on to the page – the rhythm of the flow from one to another – that for Eleanor any other system would have been unthinkable. Perhaps, though, after filling the notebooks . . . 'You *must* have a computer,' declared Jordan.

'But I wouldn't know what to buy, or how to use it.' Eleanor's protestation was both feminine and true.

Because they were looking out over bulb fields with glasses of Dutch punch in their hands, he offered to help her. And she suddenly had this extraordinary vision of going with Jordan Herriot, still dressed in white, into Wildwood Computers or whatever on Tottenham Court Road, and purchasing with her Visa card a stylish little machine with an electric green screen and taking it home to her – where? To the corner of the bedroom she shared with David Jenkinson? To the shelf where the liquidizer and the coffee machine were kept? Alongside the lawnmower? She would have to burrow around and find some space of her own again. Oh, Marine Parade, with your view of the sea matching the newly discovered blue of Jordan Herriot's eyes, where are you?

'What are you thinking about?' he looked at her curiously. At this tiny woman with the pretty pale face, somewhat lined now with age, better known as experience, and the slight frame hung with a decorous, cheerful red-print dress. She wore a wedding ring, he noticed. Her mind was a long way away.

They went into dinner and sat opposite one another. Eleanor ate sparingly, Jordan untidily, his jaw clicking in a manner a number of women had told him about but which he couldn't himself hear (though he didn't have his finger in it). As she helped herself to a small portion of salad, Eleanor asked suddenly, 'How old are you, Jordan?'

'Twenty-seven. And you?'

'Forty-one.'

It was difficult to know what to say after this.

'Have you rented a bicycle?' he enquired, eventually.

'No, can one?'

'One can. How would you like ... ' he picked his way more delicately through this sentence than ever through any meal, 'I wonder if you would care to come for a bicycle ride with me after supper? We could go to the sand dunes. I know the way. It won't be dark until ten. Unless of course you want to go to the evening session?'

Which was on sociological imperialism and ideologies of professionalization. 'Oh no, thanks,' she said hastily. 'I mean, yes, that would be very nice.'

It was (see p 93).

Afterwards, when the sun had gone down, and the moon was up, and when Eleanor and Jordan had locked their bicycles in the bicycle shed, they bought two glasses of wine (actually he bought them but this ought to have been a triumphantly nonsexist relationship), and sat at one of the tables outside amidst the lobelias. Medical sociologists came and went, boring each other.

'So full of themselves, aren't they?' he remarked. 'Mind you, they're slightly better than the last lot. Last week we had the annual meeting of the European birdwatchers' association.'

She laughed.

'You've got a pretty laugh, Eleanor.'

'Flattery will get you nowhere,' she said. But didn't mean it for a moment.

'I'd like to kiss you.'

'Go ahead, then.'

'Not here, the sociologists are watching!'

At first Eleanor Jenkinson thought the entry of Jordan Herriot into her life made it better. For she'd fallen in love, to coin a phrase, with this pink computing creature who wore his hair in an elastic band. The pleasurable anticipation of things to come, which is a feature of the nascent-in-love state, at least replaced the feeling of dread Eleanor had grown used to waking up with in the mornings. Towards the end of that week in Holland it was Jordan she woke to instead – Jordan's pink skin and his caresses and his philosophy of life, which was so unlike her own you would have thought they had practically nothing in common. Whenever she asked a question about his past, Jordan was likely to say 'I really can't remember,' and, when they got on to the subject of the future, he said instead, 'I don't really care. What happens is going to happen, I have no control over it.' He made it abundantly clear that his concern was only for the present: whatever he wanted he wanted now, and that included Eleanor Jenkinson.

Eleanor had explained about David and about the menage in Hove – Yolande, Heidi, Eliza. She mentioned her mother, newly diagnosed as having Alzheimer's disease. 'It's the aluminium in saucepans,' pronounced Jordan, instantly. 'What have you got in your kitchen, Eleanor?' When she admitted she might have some of the tainted culinary ware, Jordan said, 'In that case I will buy you some new ones.'

The next day when Eleanor came back from a lengthy session on the costs and benefits of the pharmaceutical industry in the Third World, she found that Jordan had bicycled into Amsterdam and bought her a whole new set of saucepans. They were lined up on her bed flashing in the slanting afternoon sunlight. 'But how am I to get them home?' she objected, laughing.

'Pack your dresses in them,' advised Jordan, 'or maybe carry them on your back like a camel. But you won't, in that case, get through the metal detector at the airport. I wanted to buy you a computer,' he added compassionately, 'but I'm afraid I don't have enough money for that at the moment. My family cut me off without a penny.'

She didn't know what he meant, assuming that's what families normally do. Jordan explained his father was a rich businessman, he made a lot of money out of a new kind of spectacularly hardwearing tennis ball. He, Jordan, had been expected to follow suit. But due to some odd quirk of biology or fate, he had proved to be an inordinately lazy child, and had grown up to be an even lazier adult. If he could do nothing he did, and if he had to do something he did as little of it as possible. Computing, which he did entirely untrained and out of necessity, having first tried hairdressing and found it made him tired to stand up all day, only really interested him when he could play around with computer programmes *ad nauseam* without thought of gain or profit. Jordan himself didn't really believe in genes, but he preferred to blame them for the way he'd turned out rather than assume any responsibility for it himself.

Eleanor Jenkinson, however, fell into the one category of things or rather people Jordan wasn't striving to avoid the expenditure of energy on – women. Jordan believed, despite what any good (or bad) Marxist knows, that sex and capitalism had nothing to do with one another. Marx was one of the many authors Jordan had never read. He carried on his travels Richard Feynman's *Lectures on Physics* and the *World Book of Film and Television*. Apart from that, he'd read Jack Kerouac, *On the Road*, *Lady Chatterley's Lover*, *Zen and the Art of Motorcycle Maintenance* and *Silas Marner*. Why *Silas Marner*? asked Eleanor, approving of his choice. But it turned out it had been no choice at all; Jordan had once had a bad attack of dysentery in Turkey and in the place where he was staying at the time, a house belonging to a French archaeologist, the only books in English were *Middlemarch* and *Silas Marner*. *Middlemarch* was too long.

The belief was enough, though. Jordan played with Eleanor under the light Dutch counterpane with an extraordinary elegance – extraordinary, that is, given his general clumsiness and lethargy.

But I expect everyone is wondering what has become of Eleanor's child. What has she decided to do? Has Jordan noticed? She was, after all, eighteen weeks pregnant by now, her lower abdomen must really bulge, her breasts be burgeoning, the nipples a spreading chocolate brown. The nausea and fatigue must have passed. Vitality, abetted by love, had set in. It had been a long time since Eleanor Jenkinson had felt or looked like this. She said so casually to Jordan on their last evening in Holland, when on the agenda are all sorts of things like, are we going to see each other again, do you love me as much as I love you, what about your husband/girlfriend, how can I possibly get the saucepans home, and do we have a future together – most of which, in any case, Jordan refused to talk about – as casually as she could manage, 'Oh, by the way, I'm having a baby. That's why I said we needn't bother with contraception.'

'I wondered when you were going to mention it,' said Jordan, tracking the sunlight on the wall opposite the bed, his vigour temporarily spent.

'But if you noticed, why didn't you say anything?'

'Not my business,' he observed. 'Well, it isn't, is it, love?' He rolled over and licked her little face affectionately. Her stomach heaved when he called her 'love' like that.

'I was going to have an abortion,' commented Eleanor. 'But it's too late now.'

Jordan didn't say anything.

That was that one out of the way, then.

But if she wasn't going to kill David's child, was she going to let him kill hers?

EIGHT

To Eleanor with Love

DAVID AND ELEANOR JENKINSON drive back from Sousceyrac in their beige Volvo over the winding roads to the farmhouse. David, as usual, concentrates on the driving, so is silent. Eleanor wraps her arms around herself against the heaving of the car over the dark hills, as if to keep the lean cuisine in.

They sit outside in the garden. The moon is nearly full. It slips and slides among the ivory clouds, teasing the Jenkinsons with its light, which is quite enough for them to study each other's faces by. But the moon has a way of depriving them of its illumination at those very moments they most need it. Country noises surround them: cows calling, crickets singing, bats winging their carbon shapes across the moon's whimsical face. Aside from all these diversions, the Jenkinsons are alone with each other; with each other's ghosts and reparations, meditations, moments of exaltation and anguish: all crowd in the shadows cast by the house in the moonlight.

'We can talk about this in different ways,' reflects Eleanor, continuing where she left off in the restaurant, anxious to resume the discussion before David asks her to: it's important that she experience her own interest in the delineation of an area of honesty between them.

'There's your account and there's mine. But that's not all: there's your account of my motives and mine of yours. But that's not all, either. Here I cannot speak for you, but speaking for myself, it's only recently I've begun to be able to tell the difference between my own narrative of my life and the one bestowed on me by you.' She pauses. The moon looks at her with, she fancies, almost a sisterly female glance.

'I've had enough of sexism,' says David Jenkinson involuntarily. He thinks the moon grimaces with hostility at him.

'I didn't mention the word.'

'You know what I mean.'

'David.' She turns to look at him in the dark garden, to look him squarely in the face, at his tendentious eyes instead of the moon's allusive oysters. 'David, I told you when you tried to stop me publishing My Novel that from then on you'd have a lot to answer for. I warned you.'

'You were very angry at the time,' he remarks.

'What did you expect?'

'I thought you'd settle down and be reasonable about it. I thought you'd see what effect publishing the book in that form would have on the children, and on me. I thought you'd see that it would be damaging. That Heidi would be upset and angry at a difficult stage in her life, and that Eliza probably would in her turn as well. It didn't seem to me that you'd thought about that. You hadn't thought about the light it'd show me in either, how the Department would react, the things people would say. Now, I know that's not very important – the children are one thing, but I'm an adult, I can take care of myself, you'd say. I agree up to a point. But we were – are – *married*, Eleanor, we believed, we always said to one another we have to be *honest* about our feelings. That's what I was doing, telling you how I felt, that's all.'

David's monologue rings with all the self-important conviction of his undergraduate history lectures. He's quite taken in by it himself. Marion Cumberledge and Patsy Drew have conveniently faded. As ghosts, they flit in and out of his conscience ringing bells occasionally, but that's all – they've made hardly a dent on his image of himself as a moral family man. And the fact that Eleanor is used to David's style doesn't enable her to penetrate it, lay bare its political nuances, decode its symbolic meaning, any better than someone who, encountering it anew, might initially take it all as intended at face value.

'It's not all. It's *your* account. You know that perfectly well. You're an intelligent man, not insensitive. In your way. How could you live with me all that time, see what a struggle it was for me to write, then at the very moment of my potential success give me the bitter taste of a set of superficial reasons not to publish My Novel, all of which were to do with my family obligations, or with *your* social position, and none of which were to do with me?'

'This is the conversation we ought to have had long ago,' comments David sadly.

Eleanor doesn't reply.

'And if we'd had it, then none of these things would have happened?'

She only recognizes the unspoken question mark at the end of that sentence because she knows the tenor of his voice so well. 'No.'

'What do you mean, no?'

'They'd already happened. Don't you see, David, My Novel and My Life early on established a kind of intimate relationship with one another. Writing demanded living but living, to be more than merely survived, required writing. I learnt how to put it into "my" words. Then, whatever "really" happened to me, it became impossible to tell the difference between the two.'

David Jenkinson can't find anything in his own experience to confirm the truth of what his wife says. But at least he has sufficient intelligence and sensitivity (her words) to let it stand as authentic – as much as the great dipping circles of the bats' wings in the starlit darkness.

Extract from:

SCENE FROM AN ENCYCLOPAEDIA
BY ELEANOR JENKINSON

They're sitting at the table in the kitchen. He's studying train timetables, and has various maps spread out in front of him, propped up against the vinegar bottle (with the stem of tarragon growing in it as on the bed of the sea) and next to the radio, which has just been broadcasting Bruckner's Te Deum, *and the half finished carton of long-life milk. A domestic scene, in short. With a man in it planning extraterrestrial expeditions. She envisages him setting off in the morning with his maps and his water bottle in his haversack, and the look of being an inveterate explorer written all over him, like a boy scout going off to camp, or Hillary's last ascent of Everest.*

And what is she doing?

He would say, she's sitting there with him, reading. One of the books she usually reads: feminist literary criticism, novels, biography, science fiction. That sort of thing.

She isn't, though. She's reading a very old French phrase book.

She had pounced upon it with a certain amount of feminist glee (if this phrase isn't too much of a contradiction in terms – look up the meaning of the word 'glee'). 'Let's see what sexism we have here!' she'd said. Unwisely. Without intending to signify much of anything out of the ordinary. (Esther, we were – are – married, and we'd always believed . . .)

He, looking up from his search, not for devices of oppression but for Rocamadour ('it's on the left', she'd even said helpfully) pronounces then the memorable, but at the same time oh so ordinary words, 'I'm fed up with sexism'.

To which she can only reply, 'I noticed in the Encyclopaedia you brought with you that if you look up Eve, it says "see under Adam".'

Back in Hove, Eleanor Jenkinson had three matters to consider: one, the conception of the third child in the runaway wife; two the conception of a veto on My Novel by the stay-at-home husband; and three, her amazingly distracting ardour for Jordan Herriot of Microsoft Inc. It was the strength of this ardour that carried her through the red goods-to-declare channel in the airport customs, holding the aluminium-free saucepans before her like a shield, for how could she possibly have left this gift behind?

'Saucepans, did you say?' The customs man has heard a lot of funny things in his time, but not, before now, saucepans.

'They were given to me,' said Eleanor, defensively.

The customs man took them out of the bag and turned them over. 'Made in Korea,' he pointed out on the bottom. 'Where have you been, did you say, Madam?' It was late, and he was tired. A colleague opposite raised his eyebrows. 'I should go home if I were you, Madam,' he advised. The two men watched Eleanor go, a little figure with glowing cheeks and some intimate link that even they sensed between the colour of her cheeks and the Korean saucepans.

'I'm going to have the baby,' Eleanor said to her husband David, when she got home. David, like Jordan Herriot, had come to the same conclusion himself. 'It will be born on or around 13 December.' She had at least done the necessary calculation, and considered this practically all the information she needed to give him.

She went back to work, no longer looking thin and exhausted, and wearing, to make the point, though quite gratuitously early, a blue linen maternity dress she found in the attic. It was far too short and lacked any sense of style, but spoke, predicatively, volumes.

'My God!' said Araminta and Rowan. 'How well you look! And a baby, too! Why didn't you tell us, Ellie!'

'Good gracious me!' said Belle. 'I see you had a good rest, Eleanor.'

Jim Maitland, passing Eleanor in the corridor, beckoned her into his room, and said two things: one, 'Where is the catalogue blurb for My Novel, Eleanor Jenkinson?' and two, 'You can have three months' paid maternity leave, not a day more, and at the end of it I expect you back here, promptly at ten every day, with no silly business about blocked milk ducts or nannies who can't cope. The life of a working mother, Eleanor Jenkinson, is a hard one, and you'd better not forget it.' He had dreadful memories himself of his wife Diana's maternities, remembered waking up in a bed full of milk, dropping his electric razor in the nappy bin and other similar awfulnesses.

Eleanor retreated to her office, patting her unborn protectively. The phone rang: it was Davina.

'Section seventy-four,' she said. 'I've sent the bastards a section seventy-four questionnaire!'

'Oh?'

'The Sex Discrimination Act, you know. Obliges them to tell me *why* they appointed Creepy Richards. Since they won't have a good reason, I'll be able to take them to a tribunal.'

'And then what?'

'Compensation, of course!'

'Oh.'

'Are you all right, Eleanor?'

'Fine. Yes, fine.' Eleanor thought vaguely about Jim Maitland's threats just now. Was that sex discrimination too? 'Well, fine, apart from a few problems.'

'We all have those.' Davina wasn't interested. 'Listen, Ellie, if I do that, will you give evidence?'

'Of what?' Her brain felt like cauliflower. Was it the pregnancy? It wasn't at all clear to her what Davina was on about.

'Well, the day I didn't get the job, I came to see you, remember?'

'Oh yes.'

'You could give evidence about the things I said.'

'I'm not sure that would help,' reflected Eleanor, recalling all the four letter words. She added, 'Of course I'll help you, Davina, but don't you think you ought to consider very carefully what you are doing?'

'Do you think I haven't already?'

'No. Yes.'

'You're a fine friend, you are!' Davina rang off.

Eleanor took her notebook and went to Hyde Park at lunchtime the next day to do the first thing Jim Maitland asked. 'This first novel by writer Eleanor Jenkinson,' she wrote, hesitatingly, then crossing out Jenkinson and putting Kendrick, and watching the little boys with their coping nannies and remote-control boats in the round pond, 'charts the growing up of a young woman, Esther Gray, through the radical political consciousness of the late sixties, to a realization of the myth of integrated identity perpetrated by the culture, and specifically by its male psychoanalyst anti-heroes. Painfully Esther learns . . . '

Jordan Herriot, a lurking extravagant spectre, sidled distractingly into Eleanor's mind. Dreaming, she relived, took apart, reconstructed, all her and Jordan's Dutch interactions, examining, like a careful housewife, the spaces and the silences as well as the conjunctions and the communications. Jordan cycling ahead of her through the bulb fields, his pink shirt blooming against the dark furrows; Jordan in the shower, lean and pink (yes, again), soapy and inviting. The slant of light in his navy eyes . . .

The point is that Jordan Herriot had become, despite himself – and it *was* the last fate the poor man would have chosen – a kind of saviour in Eleanor Jenkinson's life. For he had awakened in her (no, rephrase that, she had used him to remind herself of) a sense of her own power. He had saved her (she had used him to save her) from the swamps and bogs of powerlessness. It was an interesting question – and one that was quite germane to the point – as to why this was what had happened. It could be put thus: for a woman in Eleanor Jenkinson's position, what other options were available, either in grim reality or as literary devices, to jerk her out of the morass of self pity – her black mood of put-uponness – apart from this, the love, the sexual admiration of a good man? The love of a good woman, which someone is bound to suggest, *is* one answer, but it was not an answer for Eleanor Jenkinson, because Eleanor regarded herself as incurably heterosexual. This may be plain cultural conceit, but the point about culture is that some bits of it embed themselves so firmly in your soul (body, heart etc.) that no amount of repoliticizing can succeed in ejecting them. They are just sores to be lived with.

The advent of a new political awareness into Eleanor's life might also have brought about the desired effect. But she'd had her conversion; it wasn't a moment, rather a process. And here again her character came into it, for she was a bit of a stumbler, not a particularly rapid thinker, albeit with occasional episodes of extraordinary plunging in with her eyes closed, as into the affair of Tom Sherringham and the creative writing class, the Hackney soft porn business investment, and now the liaison with a representative of the computer software industry.

Head down again into the notebook. 'Painfully Esther/Eleanor learns . . . ' What? That to be a woman is to lead a permanently bifurcated existence? Every woman was supposed to have the same set of motives or else be a monster, said the mother in George Eliot's *Daniel Deronda*. Or, when a woman's strength was the same as a man's, half of hers (but none of his) must inhere in concealment. Or that the moving finger, having writ, moves on, and the lines, though not cancellable, would never see the light of day. Or perhaps the light of day was itself a conspiracy? What was the point of publishing anyway?

Eleanor picked up her notebook and visited Janice in Hackney. She telephoned the office first, to defer a meeting with Jonathan Withers, London's newest rapacious literary agent.

'What did you think really, though, Janice?' asked Eleanor.

'Glad to see you're having the baby,' said Janice, eyes flickering over the blue form of Eleanor's maternity dress.

'The novel, Janice!'

'The novel, Mrs J. Well I have to say I was impressed. Had no idea you were writing about things like that!'

'Like what, Janice?'

'Well, like, like . . . ' Janice searched for words and then alighted with relief on a group of them, 'like all them French café scenes.'

'Would you buy it if you saw it in a bookshop, Janice?'

'Can't say I would, Mrs J. But then don't judge others by me. Don't read much. No time.' She thought of how her time *was* occupied. 'No, that's not right, I don't read books at all. Now, if it was on the telly – I can see it on the telly, Mrs J, four or five episodes. BBC2, 9.30 Thursdays. Or maybe 10.30. What about a video, Mrs J?'

Eleanor wondered only why both David and Janice used the word 'impressed' of their reaction to My Novel, and then went on to make a few less than positive points about it.

On her way home to Brighton that evening, she felt the third child move. Time was getting on. She should, as any good obstetrician knows, have felt it before, but her consciousness must have been blocking it out. It was having enough trouble resuscitating its own life, let alone being expected to take on board someone else's.

She telephoned Jordan Herriot in Holland from a phone box in Brighton station.

'Hallo, my love,' he said, and her heart heaved (or lurched – or was it her stomach?). He told her he'd found a new bug in the Apple in the office at the conference centre. She imagined him cradling it in his arms, or attacking it with his tools – both images seemed appropriate, for Jordan Herriot was androgynous to Eleanor in fantasy, if not in grim reality. 'And how is it with you?' he asked.

'The baby moved. I'm at Brighton station. What do you think of a pseudonym, Jordan?' Time was running out on the telephone call; she only had 50p left. Eleanor and Jordan would soon be into the time-wasting, nerve-wrecking business of ringing each other back in telephone boxes – standing there pretending to be doing something relevant, as people line up in the street outside, hammering on the glass, anxious to get through to their unloved ones, and there one is waiting for the shrill call from the metal box, electronic responses having to thrill in place of the other sort.

Before the money ran out, Jordan said, 'Does it matter what you call yourself? We aren't our labels, anyway.' On the way to Hove, Eleanor completed the conversation in her head. 'It's easier for you, you don't want to *claim* what you do. It just *happens* to you. But I want to claim – what? Esther Gray. Credit for all those years of fighting to get it on paper. To cross it out and do it again. To have the experiences which became mine. But Esther Gray's not me. I'm not her. Did I really write My Novel? Perhaps it wrote itself, it's nothing to do with me really.'

'Come, come,' said Esther Gray, who seemed to be listening in to this conversation, 'you know that won't do. You can't wriggle out of it like that.'

'Okay, Esther Gray, you're my invention. But how do you like that?'

'It'll do,' said Esther Gray. 'We all have our place on this earth and I know mine when I see it. It isn't lives we model ourselves on anyway, it's stories. You made up a story, a better, stronger narrative than your own life. That's what you want to claim.'

'Thank you for telling me,' said Eleanor Jenkinson.

And went home, said hello to Heidi and Eliza and David and Yolande, took Yolande on one side and said, 'Be a dear and do the supper, I've got something I simply must finish – it'll only take me half an hour but it has to be done now.' And Yolande, who was one, did, and Eleanor went into her bedroom and closed the door and completed the catalogue copy for My Novel.

When she came out, she went to find David, who was watching 'Newsnight' on television. Yolande and boyfriend were sitting companionably there drinking tea and looking at some large tracings of hats. 'Can I have a word with you, please David?' asked Eleanor, sounding like a schoolteacher.

Yolande, who had become, as we have seen, a sensitive young person, got up and dragged Mick with her. 'Let's go for a walk round the garden, shall we?'

'What for? I'm quite happy here.'

'Come *on*!' Yolande winked at Eleanor.

David turned the television off. 'Yes?' he barked, like a guard dog or a university teacher.

'About My Novel,' she began. 'I wondered how you'd feel if I reverted to my maiden name. For publication, I mean.'

He seemed completely unprepared for this. After a short silence, he asked, 'You think that'll solve the problem do you, Eleanor?'

'Well, won't it? No-one will connect you or the children with the book. You won't have to worry about the reactions of people in the Department. But it's still my name, so I'll be happy.'

David narrowed his eyes at her.

'Think of it as a pseudonym, if you like.' She herself wondered which was the real pseudonym – Kendrick or Jenkinson. Also whether there wasn't something inherently contradictory about the concept of a real false name.

'There's something you haven't thought of,' he said.

'I'm sure,' she replied wearily. 'What is it?'

'My feelings about your rejecting *my* name!'

'David, you're impossible! You don't want me to be me with your name, and then you say you'll be hurt if I do what I want to without it! What's the *real* problem, David?'

He looked a bit hopeless. 'As I said, it's the book. It's those, well . . . *scenes*.'

She didn't say anything.

'But I suppose you think the real problem is *me*.'

Again she didn't say anything.

'I've got to go to bed, Eleanor. I've got a difficult day tomorrow. We're voting for a new Head of Department, and I don't want Mayhew to get it.'

'You can't do this!' said Jim Maitland, seeking out Eleanor Jenkinson in the office the next day. He held the catalogue copy in his hand, waved it rag-like as the faces of Araminta, Rowan, and Eleanor looked back, startled, at him.

'Why can't she?' demanded Araminta.

'I'm not talking to you, Miss Close.'

'Why can't I?' asked Eleanor, 'It's *my* name. I've got a right to change it if I want to.'

'Don't be daft, woman, I thought you were a feminist!'

'She is,' said Rowan.

'And I'm not talking to you either, *Ms* Carter!'

'I am, though, Mr Maitland,' said Eleanor, 'I am a feminist. Aren't I?' She appealed to the faces of the other women for confirmation. 'But it's a harsh world we live in, isn't it, Mr Maitland? As you reminded me the other day in relation to My Baby. But in relation to My Novel, I choose to remain mistress of my own fate!'

Araminta and Rowan would have applauded, had the atmosphere not been quite so conducive to the alternative of an appalled silence. Jim Maitland staggered backwards clutching the catalogue copy of Esther Gray's first novel with one hand and his heart with the other. Araminta, Rowan and Eleanor watched dispassionately for a moment or two, thinking Jim Maitland's seizure another act of male histrionics. But it wasn't. 'Call a doctor!' ordered Rowan then, straddling Jim Maitland's unconscious body manfully (her mother once made her do a St John's Ambulance First Aid course).

Jim Maitland was fetched by an ambulance and taken to St Mary's Paddington, where he was pronounced the victim of a major myocardial infarction. 'If he lives through the next few days,' Dr Sandani told a weeping Diana (who, as was normally the case, never realized until now what her husband meant to her), 'then he's a candidate for coronary bypass surgery. Does he smoke at all, Mrs Maitland?'

'Oh yes,' said Diana.

'Well, I won't do it then,' said the doctor. 'Do you know how much cigarette smoking costs the NHS, Mrs Maitland?'

The two of them continued with this somewhat pointless conversation while Jim Maitland fought for his life, unaware of the intense health promotion campaign awaiting him should he make it. His threatening demise summoned his partner, Vernon Ware, from the Orkneys, where he'd taken early retirement to write his autobiography, an uninteresting rampage through the minor literary personages of the 1930s. Vernon examined the state of Maitland & Ware in Victoria, and of Jim Maitland in St Mary's and pronounced both of them lost causes. 'I'm afraid you're all fired,' he told Araminta, Rowan, Eleanor, Belle and several others whom it hasn't been necessary to mention. Vernon was wearing tweed knickerbockers – his life of parsimonious introspection had made him a bit of an eccentric. It was hot in London, too hot for tweed. Vernon Ware perspired. 'I had no idea Jimmy had let things slip so much. One gets so out of touch up there in Oban. I'm so sorry, but there's nothing else to say. We are bankrupt.'

'Financially, not morally,' said Araminta and Rowan to Eleanor, who would never be able to erase from her mind the image of Jim Maitland in the doorway having a myocardial infarction because of Esther Gray. What power that woman had!

Araminta and Rowan, who were living together in World's End by now, took Eleanor home with them that fateful afternoon. Rowan's parents were, surprisingly, more shocked than Araminta's father by the new arrangement. Araminta's therapist said this was because her father dreaded losing Araminta to another man, by comparison with which her holing up with Rowan in World's End was perfectly okay.

'I'm a *lesbian*,' father,' she'd even said, just so he was clear about it. 'You can still have children, you know, darling,' said Dr Close, undeterred, his eye on the future and ever mindful of his occupation. 'I know a chap who'll be able to help you with the plumbing. Just tell me when.'

That afternoon Araminta and Rowan installed Eleanor on their little roof terrace with a cup of Earl Grey, a packet of sponge fingers and a copy of *Madame Bovary*, the latter chosen with only a little suspicion that covert resistance rather than outright rebellion had become Eleanor Jenkinson's chosen format in more ways than one.

While Eleanor read, her unborn infant was awoken to overt resistance by her sedation, and Araminta and Rowan talked down below in the tiny kitchen about What Was To Be Done. It was, of course, only to be expected that the idea would strike them (this was by now 1981) that they could take matters into their own hands by setting up their own publishing firm. 'Nothing grand,' asserted Araminta, 'quite a modest venture in fact.'

'Don't be daft, woman,' responded Rowan, echoing Jim Maitland's pre-infarct style. 'Think big. We're as good as the next man – woman. If you don't fly high, you don't fly at all.' Not for the first time, she was puzzled by her own choice of metaphors.

Self-sufficiency was in the air; the rhetoric of women's liberation had made lots of things possible for the white middle-class sisterhood that weren't before (as Janice Carew would one day observe to Eleanor Jenkinson). Araminta and Rowan conceived of themselves as a latter-day Patience and Sarah. In the evenings they sat rerunning old videos – *Rebecca*, *Woodstock*, *Song of Bernadette*, *How Green is My Valley* – and stitching a patchwork quilt in the feminist colours of green, purple and white, with little silver discs purchased from a feminist embroidery shop in New England. They hadn't quite built their own house, as Isobel Miller described in her evocative novel of that name, but the Eden Press, as it was to be called, would do instead.

Eleanor was asleep dreaming of Jordan. This time he'd brought her a diamond ring. He went back to Silicon Valley to fetch a piece of software he left behind, and came back with a diamond ring which he found one day, like a pig smelling a truffle, thickly encrusted with dirt and history, and cleaned, rinsing it in the sparkling Californian sunlight, especially for her. Araminta and Rowan, though, were anxious to tell Eleanor their plans. Moving *Madame Bovary* from her lap, they caused her to stir and see them ranged against the low Chelsea skyline. 'Sssh, Ellie, it's only us.' They sat either side of her on the terrace. A cabbage white hovered in the steamy stillness. 'Tell us what you think of this one, Ellie,' they said, and she did.

NINE

One Day in the Meadow

T HEY SIT IN SILENCE, wrapped in the darkness. It should have been a perfect evening – the peace, the sunset, the good food and wine, the opportunity to let go. But they can't let go of themselves, Eleanor and David Jenkinson, because then the facades they've been inhabiting for so long would crumble and fall back into the earth. They would have to look at one another, stripped of these, which would be like going back to the beginning of it all, to the beginning of themselves.

Instead, they sit separately, thinking. David thinks of the upright nature of his life – upright except for Marion Cumberledge and Patsy Drew and one or two others along the way. These in his reckoning were incidental to his union with Eleanor, because they were necessitated by it; there's no doubt in his mind that Eleanor has been difficult, that she's been more than many men would have put up with, and that he has been tolerant. Nor that, for all these clichés that hop and skip a pattern in his own version of their past together, he in some sense still loves her. His view of this trip to France is that it must establish, confirm, the fact that they have a future together. Though a more accurate rendering of this might be that he's frightened of what would happen if he didn't have Eleanor any more; David's ability to be honest with himself is no greater than his desire to be so. For him, none of this is about honesty, it's about making sure that everything's all right, that he can go on counting on his marriage as the structure around which everything else falls into place.

Of course he knows on one level that, had he wanted Eleanor to be happy, he would have encouraged her to become a successful author. He's proud of the fact that he's always encouraged her to write – but that's a different thing altogether. David thinks of his wife's writing as a domestic activity like needlework or the baking of delicate Madeira cakes. Feminine, almost. He has liked to think of her having the outlet of scribbling in her notebooks – she might, after all, be getting rid of emotions there with which he otherwise would be required to tangle. But publication would have threatened the intimacy of the act, its function as a safety valve.

The other consideration, buried somewhere in his head, is that if Eleanor had become a successful author, she might not have wanted to go on living with him. All the time she was struggling to write My Novel, he felt she was also struggling with herself. As the pages mounted, a butterfly emerged from the chrysalis. She was ready to take off, wings spread to the balmy air. He'd had to do something to clip them, in order to keep the beautiful velvety creature for himself. This, of course, can also be put in the future tense. If Eleanor were to become a successful writer, *then* she would have no need of him any more.

Eleanor knows what David is thinking – not the details, of course, but the substance of the thing. But she is not sure she's ready to consider the future yet – either alone or with him. She closes her eyes and wills herself into a reverie of time past. It's in the past that she's happiest – strolling among the fictitious characters of My Novel and My Life. She meets Janice there, and Ball, and the swaggering Tom Sherringham with a pint in his hand. She sees Eva Summers, and hears her parrot's chorus counterpointed with the whistle of her hearing aid. And Araminta and Rowan with keen young faces and wits as sharp as knives. 'Come on, Eleanor Jenkinson, there's a lot of life still to live.' They urge her on, minor characters all of them – none of them history-makers in David Jenkinson's sense, but it's *her* history, *her* story.

She remembers real meetings and conversations, and imagines many others. That's one of the main delights – to feel free to blur the edges between what really happened and what might have done. Long ago, she herself ceased to be much interested in the difference, though she knows other people are usually preoccupied by it. But does it matter if something that happened was only imagined, or something that was imagined did? It seems to Eleanor now, looking back on it all, that the most culpable human folly of all is to live through something without giving it the benefit of one's imagination. What marks us out from the animals is our ability to construct a mental world, to interpret, to create. What goes on in most people's heads is much more interesting than what goes on in their lives. Fantasy is the stuff of life – without it, you might as well be dead. That's why sexual fantasies are so powerful a cipher: to dream is to live for ever, to fuck is to remind oneself of the living flesh. A double promise of immortality.

Jordan Herriot comes out of the shadows, takes Eleanor's hand and leads her back to the sand dunes where it is always summer, and there is always the chance of something different in the air.

'We had a lot of good times together,' says husband David beside her. 'Do you remember when Heidi was born, and I came to take you both home, and we put her in her cradle and stood there looking at her? She was like a star, a flower. I can see her now pressed against your breast. The two of you were like a sixteenth-century icon. Madonna and child.'

'Nonsense,' retorts Eleanor. 'Well, yes, I remember the occasion, and it was good. But I was no Madonna, and she certainly wasn't sent to save anyone. Rather the opposite, in fact. You've forgotten the broken nights and the dirty nappies.'

'A mere detail.' David waves his hand at the dark night, banishing it. 'Or little Eliza – how tiny she was. The two of them playing together in the garden.'

'We didn't have a garden.'

'The park, then. We hung a bell round Eliza's neck so we'd always be able to hear where she was. Her hair was blonde like moonshine.'

'You should have been the novelist, David. I expect you've forgotten the epidemic of head lice in 1972. Or the threadworms in the snowstorm in 1976.'

'What are you trying to do to my memories, Eleanor?'

'Superimpose a few of my own on them.'

Once Jim Maitland's heart had given way, Eleanor Jenkinson had nowhere to go to any more – she'd lost her status as a career woman (insofar as Maitland & Ware had ever allowed her to be one). She couldn't even complain about sex discrimination like her friend Davina White. She'd lapsed back again into the old package of writer-and-mother; thinking herself cured, she'd found instead that the disease had merely gone into remission; it had come back to afflict her again. No office; no salary; no literary lunches. No independent life. No solitude, courtesy of British Rail. No Marine Parade, either.

But Eleanor Jenkinson was determined not to let it get the better of her this time. How could she, with Jordan Herriot and Esther Gray to remind her of how she did have the power to turn everything to her own advantage? Where there's a will, there's a way. Rowan Carter's repertoire of banalities contained one for every occasion.

For a week, Eleanor took the train to London as usual, telling no one at home what had happened. On the Monday, she cleared her desk at Maitland & Ware, packing it all into one cardboard box to be collected later. Belle wept at her desk like Diana at the hospital, but not for the same reason. 'What will I do, Eleanor?' she wailed. 'Mr Ware says Mr Maitland hadn't even been paying into the pension fund properly. I won't even have a pension!'

Eleanor, to whom the word pension hadn't yet occurred, was solicitous and comforting. She made Belle a cup of coffee and wiped her eyes and told her there was more to life than a pension, and the world was full of better jobs anyway. 'By the way,' she said, 'where did Mr Maitland keep the edited copy of My Novel, do you know?' Belle, sniffing, led her to it. Eleanor consigned it to the cardboard box, along with the cough sweets, the tampons, the packets of instant soups and the squashed crisps and Mars bars that had long exceeded their 'best by' dates.

On Tuesday morning, Eleanor called the GP in Hammersmith she had met in Holland, and in the afternoon she went to see him for advice about her pregnancy. So far, aside from the initial diagnosis, she'd neglected (rephrase that: had chosen not) to seek any medical attention. He pronounced her fit and healthy, despite being in the midst of all sorts of crises and forty-one. 'If you were my patient, I'd deliver you at home,' he decided. 'Of course, you're a bit small, but height and pelvic capacity don't always go together. But you're not my patient, and Hove is an awfully long way from Hammersmith.' Eleanor agreed, thinking all the same how nice it would be to be delivered by Derek Freeden's large capable hands – a judgement made on behalf of her fetus as much as herself. She was beginning to sense the onset of the usual self-effacing maternal altruism, and was both relieved and on guard lest it get the better of her this time. Dr Freeden recommended the Royal Sussex Maternity Hospital, but for only six hours, and with a midwife overseeing Eleanor's entry and her child's and her own exit – a procedure called the Domino System. Eleanor thanked him warmly and he invited her out for a drink. This she declined, muttering something about having a lot to do, especially as she was going on holiday the following week. She did cast a fluttering eye over Derek Freeden's body, thinking of it almost automatically as grist for My Novel's mill. But pressure of time, and the baby, interceded.

She was actually on her way to meet Davina for a trip to the National Film Theatre to see *Limelight*. They'd seen *Limelight* together sixteen times over the years: they always cried in the same places. Afterwards, since it was a fine June evening, they walked by the river. Davina enquired after the welfare of My Novel. Eleanor told her the sad story of Jim Maitland's near demise, and the practical collapse of Maitland & Ware just at the point of My Novel's materialization (though under whose authorship remained a closed question).

'You sound quite philosophical about it,' commented Davina.

'I've got my eye on a solution. This won't go on for ever, believe me.'

'What does David think?'

'Why do you ask? It's my My Novel.'

'Yes, but . . . '

'No yes buts,' said Eleanor firmly. She changed the subject: 'How are you getting on with your Sex Discrimination case?'

'The tribunal hearing's next week. *This* I'm nervous about, I can tell you.'

Eleanor was glad she hadn't been roped in on it. 'Will you win?'

'Probably. But I don't want to count on it. Not as I did with the job.'

'And how's Creepy Richards?'

Davina looked a little embarrassed. 'Well, he, he's quite nice actually.'

'Davina, you haven't . . . !'.

'No, of course not.' She looked down at her shoes and then over to the railings and down the river where a barge was sailing, decked with coloured fairy lights.

'I haven't told you my secret, have I?'

Davina looked back again. 'What secret?'

'I'm having an affair,' said Eleanor proudly.

'Well, that's quite shocking, Ellie, that is,' said Davina curtly.

'Why?'

'Well, what about David? What about the baby?'

'David's a grown man,' said Eleanor, wondering whether this was true or relevant. 'The baby's all right. You mean how can pregnant women enjoy sex, don't you? Why don't you say so, then?'

'How can pregnant women enjoy sex, Ellie?' Davina laughed. Eleanor was quite right, but she hadn't even framed the question in her own head.

'We aren't supposed to, of course,' continued Eleanor. 'As a matter of fact pregnant women aren't supposed to do anything that's at all nice, let alone *enjoy* it. Sex, work, smoking, drinking . . . let's go and have a drink, Davina, then I'd better go home to Hove.'

On Wednesday, Eleanor drove to London instead of taking the train. David, complaining, was shown My Bicycle instead. 'I've even mended the puncture for you,' she added, 'and bought you this,' handing him one of those glaring yellow bands cyclists wear to prevent drunken motorists mistaking them for trees.

She telephoned Jordan Herriot from Maitland & Ware, when she returned to collect the box, also to use the telephone, which was still connected, for this and other purposes. 'It's Black Women's Studies this week,' he told her, 'I can hardly move for fear of being attacked. They're out to get me, I swear they are.' Then he laughed. 'I'm only joking. It's nuclear physics, really.'

Eleanor said: 'I do love you, Jordan! Will you come away with me to France?'

'Why not?' he replied. 'Anywhere in particular? I'll look it up, if so.'

She knew he had the Thomas Cook *World Railway Timetable* in his room. 'Cavaillon. Near Avignon. Next Wednesday.'

'Done. Where are we staying, anywhere in particular? I'll look it up . . . '

'With my Uncle Hal.'

She rang Hal next. He was by now getting on a bit (he was seventy-eight) and when she called had just come back from beyond the lavender fields treading his own grapes with Monsieur Marroufin, who'd loaned Hal his winemaking equipment in return for some English lessons. Mr Marroufin, who had himself seen better days, wanted to take Madame Marroufin to London before infirmity consigned them both to a bucolic old age.

'Dearest child,' spluttered Hal down the phone, 'where have you been? And how is your dear mother? And those little girls of yours?

And that dreadfully boring man you married, Fred, or John or someone?'

'David.'

'Of course. Very limp handshake, I seem to remember. Always judge a man by the strength of his handshake.'

'I'm coming down to see you, Hal. On Sunday,' said Eleanor, 'for a week or so. Will that be all right?'

Uncle Hal thought briefly of the state of the guest room, which hadn't been entered for five years, and when last seen had bats' droppings on the floor, and was full of the suitcases Thurston brought with him when he first came to live with Hal more than fifty years before – suitcases crammed with velvet jackets and silk shirts quite unsuitable for the Provençal climate. 'Don't worry,' he said, 'I'll get Madame Marroufin to make up the bed for you. I expect she'll be glad to do it. Are you coming by train? There's a good one I seem to remember gets into Cavaillon at 6.23.'

Eleanor told Uncle Hal not to bother with incorrectly remembered disused rail timetables (or politer words to that effect). She rang British Airways, booking herself on a Sunday afternoon flight to Marseilles.

Next she drove her cardboard box out to World's End where she lodged it in Araminta and Rowan's sitting room. They were sprawled on the floor designing themselves a logo. 'Got to create the right image from the word go,' explained Rowan, who had ink on her nose.

'Something *definite*, not too *suggestive*, but *meaningful*,' added Araminta.

'A serpent?'

'Don't be daft, woman!'

'A tree. The tree of life.'

They looked at her.

'Well, I'll leave this with you for a while, if you don't mind.' Eleanor put the box on the floor. 'Eat the soup, by all means. And use the Tampax, I won't have much use for it for a while, not in my condition. I'm going on holiday with my lover who works for Microsoft Inc. When I come back, fully computerized I imagine, I'll consider loaning you, that is the Eden Press, my services, in return for a small fee – as small as you like at the beginning, but rapidly mounting to a sum appropriate to a woman of my maturity and experience.'

They pushed her out of the door, laughing, and got back to the logo, finding her suggestion of a tree quite useful.

Thursday's task was to locate Ball and tackle him about the money. After driving round Hackney making enquiries (David had the bicycle again, Eleanor was making heavy weather of the pregnancy, well, why not, he wanted her to behave conventionally, didn't he?) she ran him to ground in Soho. Of all places. Well, not entirely of all places.

Ball had just sold 'A Thousand Blue Knights' to an MP masquerading in dark glasses as an ordinary Member of the Public. Ball had a notebook in which he listed the identity of such buyers in case it should ever come in useful, and was just jotting this one down when the door jangled again and in walked Mrs J. The same small, determined, but confused and childlike figure as he remembered, but swollen with pregnancy and with something else – happiness?

'Ah, Mrs J! Did we manage it, then? Did we get My Novel published at last? Hit the quality Sundays has it? Don't read them myself, I'm afraid to say.'

'Not quite, Ball,' said Eleanor severely.

'Ah, we didn't?'

'No, we – I mean I – am unemployed, Ball. I need my money back *now*. That's why I've come.'

'Of course you do, Mrs J. No problem! Why didn't you ask me before?'

'I did, Ball.'

'Ah. You did. Sorry about that, Mrs J. I remember now. Can you hang on in there a sec? Just got to make a phone call. Sit yourself down. Look around. See if there's anything you fancy.'

The door behind the counter creaked and closed. Eleanor sat on the only chair. One side of the shop was lined with shelves of videos, the other with magazines. Flesh stared her in the face. Pink, grey, dark brown, yellow. Curiously she took a video off the shelf in front of her. It was called, rather relentlessly, 'Punishment'. The photograph depicted a woman who looked uncannily like Janice Carew, black stockinged and black gloved, pointing a small pistol at an erect penis. Eleanor was still looking at it when Ball returned. 'That's one of the new batch, Mrs J. Not bad, though I do say it myself.' He snorted slightly.

Eleanor hastily swallowed the question that was hovering on her lips. 'About the money, Ball . . . '

'I could manage two now, the rest in a month. That do you?'

'Well, it'll have to, won't it?'

'Can't liberate capital that easy, Mrs J.' Eleanor remembered Mr Gleeting all those years ago. Why did he and Ball appear to speak with the same voice?

Well, at least the money would cover the holiday. And a few other things.

On Friday at breakfast, Eleanor told David she was going away for a couple of weeks to see Hal in Provence. David considered this potentially therapeutic for her and therefore a good idea for him, but didn't realize at first that she wasn't planning to take their daughters with her. This put a somewhat different complexion on the whole matter. But Eleanor, good little housewife Eleanor Jenkinson, had anticipated this: 'Eliza's going to stay with Fiona, Fiona's mother wants to take them camping in the Lake District. Heidi, as you know, is going on a school trip to Italy. Yolande will be here to keep you company. I shall clear out the fridge today, and you can go to Sainsbury's tomorrow and stock up with whatever the two of you will most enjoy eating in my absence.'

There wasn't a lot David Jenkinson could say to this, though there was quite a lot he would have liked to, had Eleanor not made it impossible for him to speak his mind. The trouble was, she knew his mind too well, it was almost as though she'd been personally responsible for furnishing it. 'Flying's quite safe at this stage of pregnancy,' she went on to declare, anticipating one objection after another. 'I shall take a large bottle of mineral water with me in order not to become dehydrated. I have booked to have the baby in the Royal Sussex Maternity Hospital, by the way. And I shall tape Hal's telephone number to the fridge in case of emergency.'

My Novel had ceased to be part of the discourse between them. David would not ask what she had decided to do with it, as he only wanted to hear the right answer. His guilt about the stance he'd taken in relation to it could be judged by his willingness not to object too much to all these other plans of Eleanor's. Also relevant was his dragging relationship with Patsy Drew, who'd developed a painful gastric ulcer to command his sympathy. She was constantly chewing liquorice tablets now, and telephoning him with reports of symptoms, and had quite given up on Gourmet Californian Cookery.

She ate only small meals herself, bland concoctions containing horrific amounts of tapioca. She'd sold her horse, as well. David wondered about his effect on women. Was there something about him that stopped them doing what they wanted? Was this what *he* wanted? Eleanor hadn't yet told David about the foreclosure of Maitland & Ware. But there was no reason why David needed to be told about this at the moment.

Extract from:

THE PURSUIT OF HAPPINESS
BY ESTHER GRAY

When the girls have gone to school, Eleanor takes My Novel into the little paved yard outside the kitchen, where crisp late January sunlight heats up a corner sufficiently for her to sit there muffled in coat and scarf with a keen tingling in the hands and toes.

She turns the pages carefully, wearing brown fingerless gloves. She's trying to track down a passage about the pursuit of happiness that's been worrying her. She thought it was in chapter three, but it isn't. Does this mean that chapter three is where the passage ought to be? The mind plays fanciful tricks with itself. Sometimes it can even substitute a solution for a mistake. Ah, she's found it, but just then a shaft of wind zooms through the frosty stillness of the garden, and lifts a few pages of My Novel niftily from Eleanor's woolly hands.

Miss Everest next door finds a page later describing Esther's conjugation with a mesmeric East European philosopher. It takes place in a railway carriage. Not knowing what to make of this, she uses the other side of the page for a shopping list: three pounds of potatoes, two pounds of carrots, an angel cake, a bar of Camay, half a pound of pork sausages, and a solution of Sybol for an infestation of chafer beetles on the front lawn.

Actually, you don't get chafer beetles in the wintertime. It was I who took the pages from Eleanor's hand, I didn't want her to find out I'd stolen the offending paragraph.

*

Le Canard quivered in the late afternoon heat, a little more tumbledown than when Eleanor had last seen it, but a reminder of the solidity of the past, nonetheless. Not just Uncle Hal's and Thurston Blane's, but her own, her family's. Seeing Hal's house now, Eleanor felt herself in the presence of roots which anchored her into something safe, and which stretched securely beyond her present dilemmas.

Hal, at first nowhere to be found, was asleep on the sofa. Eleanor stood there for a moment before waking him. It was years since they had last met. He'd shrunk into himself, at least in shape; his beard and hair had lost their flecks of orange and were now a creamy clotted white. His face, like old leather, had history charted on it. Touchingly, he was wearing a jacket over his shirt in this heat, presumably to mark her arrival.

She bent and kissed him lightly. 'Ah, dear child,' he was awake instantly, 'and how was the train journey? Did you sleep? I'm so sorry I wasn't there to meet you, but I don't go further than the village these days.'

'I came by air, Uncle,' she reminded him gently, sitting down opposite him. 'And then I took the train to Cavaillon.'

He rubbed his eyes, studied her. '*Enceinte? Encore?*'

'Yes,' she said, 'it wasn't planned, and I am rather old for it now.'

'Mere scrap of a girl!' said Hal, rising stiffly and going into the kitchen. 'Got a bottle of Marroufin's best somewhere.' He dug around behind the dark velvet curtain she remembered at the back of the kitchen, and produced one of his unlabelled bottles. 'Not quite *frais* enough, yet,' he said, 'I'll put it on ice while you unpack. You have got some unpacking to do, haven't you?' He looked round the room for her bag. 'Madame fumigated your room, or whatever.' Madame Marroufin had, indeed, used a fair number of expletives when she'd seen the state of it. 'Made me buy some new sheets too.' Actually, he'd told her to buy them and she'd brought back some perfectly frightful ones splattered with purple gladioli from the Omniprix in Apt.

Eleanor rested there amid the gladioli, sleeping better that night than for a long time – though not yet dreamlessly, as in Holland. The night was spent in extreme busyness, sorting out all her affairs. She awoke with a feeling of resolution.

Hal and she talked about the past – about Bridget and about Charles and about Charles and Hal together as little boys in Northumberland.

'We were close, then,' recalled Hal, with liquid eyes. 'Though I was always fonder of Charles than he was of me. He was easier to like, you see – everyone liked him. Whereas I was more awkward, more ill at ease, rougher, like an unmade bed. Or the rocks that lined the coastal walks we used to take, to watch the cormorants and the gulls and find, I'm ashamed to say, the occasional egg. Do you know the poetry of Kathleen Raine, dear girl?'

She didn't. He fetched a book from the dresser, and read her some from 'The Year One':

In my love's house
There are hills and pastures carpeted with flowers
His roof is the blue sky, his lamp the evening star,
The doors of his house are the winds, and the rain his curtain.
In his house are many mountains, each alone,
And islands where the sea-birds home.

'That's about Northumberland, she loved it too. I might live there now if it weren't for Thurston.'

'The memories, you mean?'

'Yes, and those. But I meant,' Hal gesticulated out into the bright distance beyond the lavender, 'that this is Thurston's last resting place. I had a piece of marble carved. Sentimental fool, aren't I? Would you like to see it, dearest child?'

The old man and the tiny pregnant woman walked across the gold and green and purple, hearing church bells ringing in the village, and children's voices. The heat of the day was rising. Thurston Blane lay in the earth, above him the words: 'Thurston Peter Cunningham Blane/born 1901 London died 1969 Cavaillon/Poet and Lover/"an odyssey no stranger than His"'.

Hal's eyes were wet, even now. 'Miss him,' he said gruffly. Eleanor threw her arms around him. 'I love you, Uncle Hal,' she said, 'you're a good man.'

On the way back to Le Canard she told him about Jordan Herriot. 'That must be nice for you, dear girl,' said Hal, and meant it. 'A change from Frank, or George, or whatever he's called.' Back in the house, Hal immediately started making plans for Jordan's visit. Most of these concerned food and wine, but he also expressed some concern about the width of the bed on which the gladioli-sprinkled sheets lay. 'But you're so little, my dear,' he said, reminding himself of her height by looking down at her walking beside him, 'and I suppose this chap wraps you in his arms like a bear, doesn't he?'

The bear arrived, with a briefcase containing computer brochures and a soggy parcel of Dutch ginger cake. For a moment, watching Hal and Jordan shake hands (and remembering Hal's view of handshaking), it crossed Eleanor's mind to wonder whether Jordan was the sort of man whom in his youth Hal would have fancied. Over the ensuing days she saw this was possibly true, but that it was in part responsible for the excellent ambiance that existed between the three of them. She couldn't remember enjoying herself, feeling as pleased with life, as relaxed, for a very long time. Sometimes she felt Thurston Blane's shadow blessing them, reminding them of how it had been twenty-five years ago – she and Hal and Thurston sitting in the pungent twilight, watching shadows cover over the fields in front of the house, doing what human beings do best though rarely – simply enjoying one another's company.

Each day Eleanor awoke amidst gladioli, Jordan Herriot's patterned breathing and sunlight peeking through the shutters. As she lay in that delightful somnolent but anticipatory state, she heard Hal lumbering about downstairs; he woke early, as many old people do, having no further need for sleep's compound restorations. Jordan would eventually stir, and without being too articulate about what he was doing, would make love to her slowly, with the same infinite care as he devoted to the search for bugs in an Apple. The baby was beginning to come between them, but Jordan appeared to find her pregnant body interesting and sensuous, and had no feeling of the fetus, often stimulated by the flutter of his hands across its mother's abdomen, being another man's child. He was very matter-of-fact about it. She had been pregnant when he met her and she supposed he merely saw it as part of her identity. It did occur to her to wonder what the conclusion of the pregnancy would mean – but here she recalled another of Rowan Carter's sayings, which she'd seen inscribed on a kind of Patience and Sarah blue and cream jug in the World's End parlour: 'Never burden today's strength with tomorrow's loads.'

After coffee brewed by Hal on the terrace, Eleanor would take a shower and lie in the sun reading. She read mostly poetry from the enormous stock in the house. Thurston Blane, of course, and Emily

Dickinson and Kathleen Raine, John Donne, and Christina Rossetti, a catholic nosegay. She was surprised by the seeming newness of some very old refrains, for example Wordsworth: 'Our birth is but a sleep and a forgetting', and Gray's 'Elegy Written in a Country Church-yard': ' . . . the paths of glory lead but to the grave'. Thus she was enabled to put her own lack of success in perspective. Literary, or any sort of, fame, became redundant at the moment of death. And afterwards, how was it that one would like to live on? As a name in library catalogues? Or as a warm memory in people's heads?

Hal's poetry collection was extraordinarily up to date. He explained that it was something he did in Thurston's memory. He had various literary magazines mailed to Le Canard regularly, and also mail order lists from English and American bookstores. 'You might like this, dear child,' he said one morning, handing her the Finnish-speaking Swedish poet Edith Södergran's *Love and Solitude*. 'You may find it difficult enough to write in *one* language, but this woman wrote in *four*. German, French, Russian and Swedish. People laughed at what she wrote, of course, but after her death, as is often the case, it was recognized as full of lyrical power. An altogether new direction in Scandinavian literature. Read it, my child.'

Södergran's full Swedish face, piled blonde hair and liquid eyes looked at Eleanor from a sepia photograph on the book's back cover. One poem, *Instinkt*, she found particularly beautiful. It was about the mystery of the body, and the power that comes just from being alive; power without fear, as Södergran put it. Her courage and resolution and love of life were an inspiration to Eleanor, especially as she'd recently been reading a lot of feminist literary criticism that enumerated all the suicides occurring among women writers and artists. The nasty taste this had left in Eleanor's mouth was now replaced by Södergran's will to triumph over adversity, a mode of response which was far more in tune with Eleanor's own present circumstances: the growing child; Jordan's playful, loving, adventurous companionship; Hal's genial, stumbling, affectionate avuncularity, rooting her in a past which, through the cloud of years, no longer seemed itself so unfriendly. Bridget Kendrick's emotional distance as a mother, Somerset's dispassionate conviction that children are like plants – if you water them, they grow on their own – Dr Brackenridge's nervous attempts to plant algebra in her head, her father's sudden death; the transplantation to the mean little cottage, the sense of not quite ever fitting in, the need to guard the inner world – all of it began to seem not nearly as awful as it once did. The impulse to blame began to lose its fire, and to be replaced by a dawning affection for everyone's intense and human, but thereby acceptably culpable, follies. 'There but for the grace of God . . . ' Yet, since it was so evidently the grace of God that the world lacked, this was how, where, we all go: lost, confused, afraid, condemned, but in our very humanity redeemed. Breathing, loving, we make our fragile reparations to one another, join hands and stumble on.

And to what did Eleanor Jenkinson owe this discovery of wisdom? To the beneficence of the sunlight, the blue skies, the long evenings which could be depended on; to the treasury of literature hidden behind the velvet curtain in the kitchen, or perhaps, dare it be said, her hormones? No, of course not; what a ridiculous and ideologically unsound idea! Some explanation would seem to be required, though, of the facility with which Eleanor in Provence was able to push away the knowledge of her own adversities. It was, after all, because there *were* some in her life that Edith Södergran's call to triumph reached Eleanor Kendrick. Her life hadn't gone as she would have wanted it to. By now she should have been an acclaimed writer; and she certainly shouldn't have been having another baby. But about the rest of it her vision had always been less clear. This helped to explain why she could push the implications of her relationship with Jordan from her mind.

Hal and Jordan played draughts under the chestnut tree. The tree's spiky lime-green fruit dangled like Christmas ornaments in the morning air, reminding Eleanor of the one in the childhood cottage garden under which the gin-drinking Bridget had sat in the early months of her bereavement. Later on in the day, Eleanor and Jordan would study his computer brochures together, in an attempt to find one that would suit her purse and her literary purposes. There was the Commodore, grey and severe, something called the Pet, which didn't look at all user-friendly, the Ohio Superboard, described in the language of a baseball game, and the Tandys, which Jordan seemed particularly to favour. Then, while Hal slept in the afternoon, Jordan and Eleanor would retire to the purple gladioli and make love again. The evening was the time for talking. To Hal and Jordan, Eleanor dropped passing remarks about the mounting, apparently insurmountable, complications of My Novel.

They were both counsels of patience, not of despair, though neither advised simply steaming ahead. But neither, remember, had read the offending text. Possibilities were discussed: rewriting again; putting another My Novel together and springing that one on the world first. 'Time solves most things,' sighed Hal under the slightly swaying conker tree. 'People grow up, and die. The text is the only memorial. That and ghosts in old men's heads. I'm no model for you,' he advised her with a sudden sharpness like the prickle of the conker spikes as they are fetched from the ground by childish hands. 'I ran away rather than face the music. Thurston, too.'

'It's easier now, Uncle Hal,' observed Eleanor simply.

'Yes? But Britain's a profoundly prurient culture, my girl. Liberalism may force it underground, but the British don't like deviation in any form.'

'Including in women,' she ventured.

'Of course.'

Jordan listened, an outsider, but in his own way something of a deviator too.

It was into this peaceable progressive discourse that Uncle Hal's telephone jangled the distressing news from David Jenkinson that Eleanor's mother had arrived in, or rather been delivered to, the house in Hove, having been found in a card shop in Tunbridge Wells naked except for wellingtons and gardening gloves. Doctors, police, and social workers – professionals, in short, of all kinds – had pronounced her incapable of looking after herself for a minute longer. That she had been so all her life, and especially over the last few years, was something they conveniently overlooked. Bridget's neighbours in Marigold Lane long ago got used to discovering Bridget in odd locations, querulously discussing the past with herself in a glazed monologue. Finding her thus, in a field, at the station, at midnight grunting down the lane, they had merely guided her gently home and sat her in front of the television, which, alone of all features of her contemporary environment, had the ability to remind her that time has passed on. It was the neighbours who told the social workers of Eleanor's existence – the only relative, but female and able-bodied and a daughter, to boot: the perfect person to take her in. Mrs Warwick, Bridget's left-hand neighbour, had even mentioned accusingly Eleanor's habit of neglecting her mother. 'Never came here, sent for her mother once a year. Mrs Kendrick was always complaining about her.' Mrs Philpott, the neighbour on the right, had a different line: 'Ungrateful bitch, she was. I'm not surprised the daughter kept away. I'd have done the same myself. In self-defence,' she added. 'The daughter is a writer, you know.'

All of this was by the by, however. Down the telephone from Hove to Cavaillon, David Jenkinson shouted, believing in the need to cancel distance with volume, to his wife Eleanor that she must come home, her mother needed her.

'What about Yolande?'

'You can't shift your responsibility on to Yolande!' bellowed David. There was a certain amount of protestation going on in the background, but Eleanor wasn't quite able to make it out. In fact it was Yolande, who was perfectly willing to help out pro tem while Aunt Eleanor recuperated (or whatever, and Yolande didn't even mind the whatever) in France.

But that wasn't the message David Jenkinson wished Eleanor to take away from this telephone call.

'Always was a bloody nuisance, your mother,' commiserated Hal, remembering the evening long ago when Bridget had importuned him in the kitchen. 'Inconstant, inconsiderate and silly. Yes, silly.' He didn't mean it in the Miltonian sense.

'She can't help being old,' said Eleanor, already torn between duty to the family and duty to herself, as David had meant her to be.

'Look at me, I'm old,' invited Hal. 'In fact, I'm a good deal older than Bridget, if I remember correctly,' he sauntered on. 'And I don't wander round shops with nothing on. I'm quite *compos mentis* really,' he reflected in self-congratulatory tones.

'But you probably didn't eat aluminium saucepans,' contributed Jordan not very helpfully, but thinking proudly of the immense technological good he had done, and would do, Eleanor Jenkinson: after the saucepans, a microwave, even an Amstrad! Jordan's mind returned to the safely unemotional recesses of the microcomputer industry. His avoidance was not of complexity *per se* – the insides of computers are fairly complex things – but of anything complex that was likely to be at all painful on a human level. He was beginning to be aware, though, of the challenge to his position posed by his affair with Eleanor. There was a possibility it might wound him deeply.

For the time being, however, Jordan Herriot's role was as Eleanor Jenkinson's helpmate. It was Jordan who telephoned the airport and changed the date of Eleanor's flight for her, who packed her bag and tore her tearfully away from the comfy embraces of Uncle Hal.

'Dear child!' Hal looked wetly at her. 'Have courage. Whatever it is, remember it won't last. Give the old girl my – my love. Write with news of that, and of My Baby and My Novel. Come again next year. In the spring would be nice, when the leaves turn and the Marroufins manure their grapes. Bring little whatsit,' he patted her stomach like a farmer, 'and little whatsit's siblings if you like. The whole coterie. But not John or Bill, or whatever he's called, I've got no time for him. Bring the young man from Silicon Valley back instead – his moves on the draught board are quite astounding!' As a parting gesture, Uncle Hal pressed into Eleanor's already nostalgic palm his copy of Edith Södergran's *Love and Solitude*, inscribed on the fly leaf in Hal's wiry writing, 'For my dearest niece Eleanor. Hoping you find both in the future. With fond memories, your Uncle Henry.'

Extract from:

A CHAIN AT HER THROAT
BY ESTHER GRAY

There was a woman I couldn't abide in red silk pants at the party. She had a chain at her throat it wouldn't have been too difficult to tighten. But I restrained myself, and continued eating my beansprout salad, which took some masticating, I can tell you.

I came here about fifty years ago, it seems, to get away from everyone who was telling me what to do. I lie in bed at night and watch a video of goldfish I have projected on the ceiling. Their flashy scales are oddly calming, I think maybe they set off some semi-epileptic fit in my brain, which pushes it down into unconsciousness.

There's no number on the door, so it's hard for people to find me here. The egg lady comes once a fortnight. She brings me eighteen eggs, but she calls them a dozen. I've never worked out if she can't count, or she has over-fertile hens. Like the woman at the party, she's a breeder. Her butt was enormous in those

*shiny pants. It was hard to imagine anything creative happening
down there.*

Bridget was in the sitting room watching Dr Kildare on television.
'Oh, hullo, darling!' she glanced up briefly as Eleanor walked in. 'Do
you know,' she reminisced, 'he reminds me so much of dear Dr Perry.
Do you remember Dr Perry, dear?'

'No, mother.'

'He delivered you. In that nice nursing home. You were a sweet
baby. Dr Perry said that, not I.' For someone afflicted with disability,
Bridget's speech was curiously elegant – as though it, too, was a
disorder she couldn't rid herself of if she tried.

Eleanor took her suitcase upstairs. Through the half open door, she
saw Eliza, sitting on her bed crying. 'Is she going to be here for ever,
Mum? She keeps calling me Celia.'

Eleanor sat down and took Eliza's hand. 'I don't know what we're
going to do, darling. But don't cry, it'll be all right.'

She herself wasn't quite sure. But as this was what Eliza wanted
to hear, it cheered both of them up considerably. 'Did you finish My
Novel at last?' ventured Eliza brightly.

'I'll tell you about that later. Why aren't you camping with
Fiona?'

'It rained. Fiona's mother got terribly cross. Fiona says she's having
her menopause.' Eliza thought for a moment. 'I hope I never have one
of those.'

'Where's your father?'

'He went shopping, there wasn't any food for supper.'

When David was back and the carrier bags had been unloaded,
Eleanor made a cup of coffee and the Jenkinsons sat in the kitchen
looking at each other. Again. Dr Kildare's blonde tones skimmed
through the air like tailored butterflies.

'I'm sorry I had to cut short your holiday. But it looks as though
the time you did have has done you good.'

Eleanor thought of *Love and Solitude*, the long summer evenings,
the Apple brochures and Jordan sprawled on the purple flowered
sheets. 'It has.'

'It was awful, Eleanor. Simply awful. I mean, she was in an awful
state when she arrived. Terribly confused. They gave me some pills to

give her, but I'm not sure they help.' He was beginning to feel himself an expert on women's pains, as Patsy Drew was still keeping him tied to her with narratives of her ulcer symptomatology.

'Can she look after herself – physically?'

'Who?'

Eleanor looked at David. 'Bridget, of course.'

'Oh yes. So far.'

'I hope it doesn't happen to me,' she brooded, like Eliza and the menopause. 'Perhaps it's genetic?'

'I don't think so. But we must discuss what we're going to do. I have a plan. I want to put it to you. Please hear me to the end, then you can tell me what you think.'

Eleanor was struck by David's use of the pronoun 'we'. He really *is* a proper family man, isn't he? Despite his deviations. Which were also normal. One might think he was doing all this to curry favour with Eleanor, who remained aloof and disenchanted because of his response to My Novel, or because of his continued attentions to the ulcerated Patsy Drew. But it was a good deal simpler than that. It wouldn't have occurred to David that Eleanor would not use the pronoun 'we' of a similar crisis arising in relation to one of his own parents (who were still quite sprightly and living near his sister in York). Moreover, he was not, as we have seen, an unkind man, and it didn't take an immense amount of charity to see how absurdly lumbered Eleanor was becoming, what with this new child, the difficulty over her future as writer, Heidi's adolescent rages, and his own upcoming sabbatical year which he planned to spend in New Zealand, though he hadn't told Eleanor this yet, in much the same way as she hadn't told him she'd been given the sack. These and other secrets hovered much more threateningly than Dr Kildare in the air between them. And also in the thick black air between himself and Patsy Drew.

David's plan for the Jenkinson-Kendrick family was that they build an extension to the house in Hove – an airy ground-floor bedsitting room, a bathroom and a tiny kitchen – for Bridget, to be financed by selling her house in Marigold Lane. Investing the rest of the money would produce an income with which various nursing and domestic services could be bought. Thus, they would be able to shoulder the responsibility properly without, it was to be hoped, being too worn down by it. 'I had thought, too,' he continued, 'that, as Yolande will be moving out in September, you might like to use her room as a study.

For your writing.' (Wisely he didn't refer to My Novel directly.) 'The baby' (see how the good man had thought of everything) 'can have the guest room. If you think it's a problem having no guest room – I suppose Yolande will want to come home sometimes – then we could turn the dining room into one. We don't, after all, use it very much.'

So, Eleanor Jenkinson, what did you think of these fine plans?

The bit she'd latched on to, remembering her recent experience of love and solitude, was David's offer of a room for her writing. She could have had that before. But instead she had found other solutions – Marine Parade, Maitland & Ware – more fitting, and certainly more emancipatory at the time. The architectural plan for the containment of her mother almost escaped Eleanor's attention. Bridget's perpetual presence from now on in her life was something Eleanor found it almost impossible to get her mind round: ever since she could remember – well, for twenty-two years – she and her mother had lived in different places. Eleanor had been able to say the words 'my mother' as if referring to a species, as it were, inhabiting another planet – presiding over the galaxy in a fairly overweening way, certainly, but in a manner against which the shutters could be firmly closed at night. She simply didn't know how it would feel to have her close at hand. But equally saw that not to do what David had suggested would require some fairly strong counter-arguments and amount to a response which others, of all sorts, from Yolande to Heidi, from Janice to Ball to Araminta and Rowan and even to Tom Sherringham, were likely to hold against her. To be seen, herself, as unkind, was not the last thing she would want to be, but she did feel dreadfully tired at the thought of having to deal with the allegation.

The music marking the end of Dr Kildare presaged Bridget's somewhat fumbling arrival in the kitchen. 'Such a nice house, Celia, have you lived here long?' She opened the broom cupboard. 'You've run out of milk, dear. Is Somerset back yet? She takes for ever to do anything these days. But then she *is* getting on, I suppose.'

Eleanor got up and steered her mother to the table. 'I've already made the tea.'

'That's right, dear.' She looked at Eleanor, which she hadn't for a long time. Patted the front of her dress. 'Better call Dr Perry soon, dear. Have you got a name chosen? Now, if I'd had a boy – of course Charles always wanted one, but he was *devoted* to his daughters – if I'd had a boy I would have called him – now what was I saying?'

'Have you told her?' Eleanor asked David.

'No, of course not. I wanted to hear what you thought first.'

'Naughty children!' exclaimed Bridget, imperiously waving a finger at them. 'If you've got something to say, say it for everyone to hear!'

TEN

A Chain at Her Throat

'I THINK IT'S TIME FOR BED,' says David Jenkinson in the farmhouse on the hill above Sousceyrac. 'We're both tired. I don't think this conversation is going anywhere, is it?'

He stalks off into the lit interior, and Eleanor sits for a while, her hands composed in her lap giving her a fake impression of serenity. Yet not quite false; for the stillness of the air and the rural aspect remind her of how it was with Hal and Jordan in France the summer before the awful winter when George was born, and the house was a building site, and Jordan went back to Silicon Valley and Araminta and Rowan waged a most surprising war against her maternity; before all that there had been peace, as now, afterwards. The *Sturm und Drang* – at least some of it – had passed. Eleanor had learnt from these happenings; they were written into her character, if nowhere else.

David calls to her, 'Aren't you coming to bed, Eleanor?' She goes in. Undresses, sinks into the deeply recessed bed, beside him. 'Oh Ellie,' he says, using an old name, a name from when they were young, 'you cannot know what I feel. There's so much I want to say and so much I can't.' A compelling admission from a man such as David Jenkinson, even in the darkness, where no-one can see his face. But the only one who's there doesn't need to see it to know that his eyes and cheeks are moistened with lamentations. David Jenkinson weeps for being a man, and for being unable to avoid the pitfalls, errors, and injuries of his class. This is true whether it is the literary imagination or grim reality one is talking about.

*

187

Extract from:

CONFESSIONS
BY ESTHER GRAY

Charles looked at himself in the mirror. In fact in three mirrors at once, as there was one on each side set at angles and reflecting the third in the middle. His mother's dressing table. Anyone who's ever had anything to do with these objects knows how essentially bent on distortion they are. Charles could see the back of his head in this one; it was only, as a matter of fact, sitting here that he ever saw the back of his head. Looking in the mirror to one side gave him an anomalous view of his left ear, which had a mole like a brown Smartie trapped in the skin beneath it. He scratched it, thinking as he did from time to time that perhaps at his age he should go to a doctor and have it removed.

He sat up straighter, disliking the sloped appearance of his shoulders when he looked in the mirrors sideways. His green and white cheesecloth shirt (Bridget had bought it in Naples) parted at the eighth button to expose a coffee V of chest mounted with greying hair. It struck him as incongruous, as showy, suddenly. He buttoned the shirt up at the neck and at the same time checked his flies. Yes: done up. All done up. Buttoned, zipped, guarded against prying eyes, insects, troubadours, mechanics, wives, aviators of all kinds.

Enclosed, Charles should feel strong. Instead a wave of weakness gripped him in its cloudy depths. What had he done? How would he ever know the extent of the sins committed or omitted, the actions conceived in lust and with malevolent intent, the promises ripped into two? Melancholy, thy name is Man!

'Charles!' Bridget's voice reached him from the hall. 'Are you coming? We're ready!'

Eleanor Jenkinson's third child was born on 12 December, twenty minutes after her arrival in the Royal Sussex Maternity Hospital. He came out feet first, the midwife had to do some skilful manoeuvring of the child's head through the birth canal (otherwise known as the vagina).

Eleanor took the child gratefully – that is, grateful to be relieved of the pressure of the pregnancy which had come to feel interminable; grateful, too, that the baby was 'all there' as they put it. Even more all there than the other two – a boy! But that she had expected. And had decided with David's agreement to call him George. George Henry, the latter after Uncle Hal, the former after a number of literary Georges who adopted the personages of men in order to further their chances of being accepted as a writer. (Few people know that one of the most famous of these transformations relating to Aurore Dupin, alias George Sand, came originally from her mother, who was much on the side of her progeny's untrammelled happiness as the world in its cloying prurience was against it.)

George Henry Jenkinson squinted at Eleanor from the blood and shit into which we are all born, or *inter faeces et urinam*, as Saint Augustine nobly put it. Eleanor moved her finger across the infant's inviolate mucousy face, and his mouth opened sideways like a flower hunting for the gift of life. She offered him her nipple as the next best thing, and with a tailored precision he clamped his jaws around it in that arrangement which renders babies undetachable from their mothers, and so much a source of physical pleasure to them that detachment isn't even on the agenda.

David was there with one red rose. The same as he'd brought her twelve and fourteen years ago. Now as then, he was fussing about domestic arrangements. Should he make Eliza eat school lunches, where are Heidi's jeans? So occupied with the details was David that he quite forgot to mention that the builders had left the back wall of the house open to the elements, which were now about to be inconveniently composed of ice and snow. Bridget Kendrick had temporarily gone into a nursing home, where she was causing the staff a certain amount of alarm with her secateurs. Fortunately, Patsy Drew had gone to stay with her sister Deidre in Leicestershire. The gastroenterologist had referred her to a psychiatrist who had diagnosed stress, which wasn't particularly imaginative or helpful of him. Indeed, it had mostly helped David, who, blamed as the cause of it, was thus temporarily relieved from the opportunity to cause more.

George Henry Jenkinson had bruised his mother so much on his way out of her that she couldn't walk, and so stayed in hospital for two days. On the second day Jordan Herriot slipped in to see her, carrying a large box, behind which she could, indeed, hardly see that it *was* him. Laying the baby on one side (she didn't want Jordan to think it would compete with him for her attention) she joked that she didn't deserve such a large box of chocolates. 'It's not chocolates, my love,' said Jordan, 'but fruit. Forbidden fruit! An Apple 2E!' He rested it proudly on Eleanor's feet in the narrow white hospital bed. 'I got it with a very good discount in Silicon Valley. I thought you'd need something to do, now that you've got . . . ' he looked around then, saw George Henry eyeing him suspiciously from beneath the sheet, a surprising presence considering his size, ' . . . My Baby at last,' he finished.

When Eleanor went home with George, she couldn't take the Apple 2E as well without some convincing explanation of how her short sojourn in a maternity hospital had resulted in the acquisition of a computer as well as a baby. Jordan, therefore, was asked to deliver it to Araminta and Rowan's abode in London. He didn't in the least mind such subterfuges, as a life dedicated to the avoidance of conflict must mean the concealment of his and Eleanor's liaison from David Jenkinson.

In case anyone is wondering about Jordan's part in this, it needs to be made clear that Jordan's feelings about David were that he was welcome to his role of serious family man; it wasn't one that Jordan would ever wish to emulate. The very idea of mortgages and pension funds and senile mother-in-laws and the supervision of building works filled him with horror. On the other hand, on the few occasions he managed to see Eleanor in the weeks following George's birth, Jordan did feel for the first time a passing *frisson* of envy in relation to fatherhood. The baby seemed so amiable and untouched; so unsocialized and irresponsible, lying there attached to one of Eleanor's nipples, or on her lap, or in his little Moses basket. Jordan held him, surprised at his weight, and the calm way he was willing to lie there in these hands that so often dropped things. This thought would resensitize Jordan to avoidance of the leaden weight of responsibility which so dominated his life, and he would hand the baby back to Eleanor, who had been watching this transaction with what Jordan imagined to be a Madonna-like smile.

The scene took place in Hove shortly before Christmas. David Jenkinson was at the university, on the telephone to Patsy Drew in Leicestershire, his daughters were up in London with friends attending a pantomime in Camden Town Hall, *Jack and the Beanstalk*, starring Norman Vaughan. Only the builders cohabited with Eleanor that day. Jordan walked through the snow the builders had shovelled away from the back of the house in order to install Bridget Kendrick's back door. He'd never been there before and was startled by its ordinariness. He'd always seen Eleanor as extraordinary – she had been so, after all, when he'd met her among the Dutch sand dunes, an elfin-sized pregnant publisher. He was amazed to find she lived in a place with Habitat sofas, Moulinex liquidizers, and tea- and urine-stained carpets, with a pinboard in the kitchen summarizing the chief characteristics of this life style – times of piano lessons, recipes for lentil lasagne, a calendar that already stretched well into 1982 with assignations chronicled under headings such as 'Heidi dentist 4.30' or 'end of school term', 'David to the States' and 'Yolande's birthday'. Jordan didn't even own a diary. Or a watch. Time was marked for him by other people's doings, or by machines whose screens invariably gave him all sorts of half-wanted information.

When he asked if they might go upstairs – presuming that it *was* the upstairs in such a habitation which was reserved for screwing – Eleanor declined, citing the builders, whose voices and general commotion could be heard from the back of the house, and as an afterthought the fact that she supposed it wouldn't feel right. She was, in fact, appalled at the thought of her taking Jordan, of Jordan taking her, in the marital bed, though not in the least bit willing at this juncture to work out why. Jordan sat there with a blank pinkish expression on his face. It was the expression he put on when discomforted about something. It was against his religion to get into a rage, so he pulled the curtain down instead. 'What future is there for us, Eleanor, my love?' he wailed from under the pinboard as baby George snuffled and the builders banged and Eleanor Jenkinson's telephone rang. 'It's always going to be like this!'

Eleanor, having not seen before that histrionics were part of Jordan's repertoire, attributed his mood to the displacement he felt from the centre of her life. She cradled his head in her arms, hoping this would make him feel more nourished by her. She smelt milky, her swollen breasts pushed out against her jumper, leaking full cream substances into its fibres and Jordan's long silky hair, even as she attempted to soothe him with the words, 'Don't be silly, Jordan, I'm going back to work at the Eden Press after Christmas. And you're going to be in London, we'll be able to meet there. We've just got to be patient for a few weeks, that's all.'

During these few weeks, Eleanor Jenkinson's own patience was sorely tested. There were too many people in the house. David, her own three children, Yolande and her boyfriend Mick, a homeless Afro-Caribbean friend of Mick's, Bridget Kendrick, and the builders. Due to the latter's usual incompetence, the boiler wasn't working over Christmas, so the only heat in the house was provided by electric fires or by the real one in the sitting room, whose attendance made Eleanor feel like a Victorian housemaid. Since the extension wasn't finished (though it ought to have been), Bridget was in the spare room. Yolande's boyfriend shared with Yolande, and his friend Lem (short for something much more complicated) was on the sitting room floor. George Henry was shifted round the place in his basket like unpacked shopping.

On Christmas Eve, Heidi came home with a young lad on a motorbike who didn't look more than about thirteen, and took him up to her room where it could be assumed they huddled together on her bed, if only in order to keep warm. It grew later and later. Eleanor and David were wrapping presents in their bedroom, the rest of the household was watching television. 'Well, are you going to tell her, or am I?' David Jenkinson asked.

'You are,' said Eleanor. George was waking up, on cue, as it were. 'The baby needs feeding.'

Heidi was outraged, but that was normal these days, and followed her lad into the snow. David Jenkinson wrested her away and back into the house, locking the door behind him, and putting the key down his vest. Heidi beat her fists against her father's chest, her black eyes even blacker with rage, and took her screams upstairs to her mother. George Henry came off the breast with alarm – but he would have to get used to it, it was called family life; it was what he had been born into. Later on he'd have the option exercised by his mother's lover of leaving it all behind him, but for the present he would simply have to make do.

Christmas Day was even worse than Christmas Eve, with Bridget mistaking all of them for somebody else and perpetually describing Christmases past, like Dickens. Lem turned out to have quite a way with her, though she did call him the chimney sweep, as he took her out of cupboards and handed her things and periodically guided her to the television and to improved recall of the current time period. Yolande and Mick drank Heineken, and Heidi languished until motorbike lad turned up after the Queen's speech, which Bridget and Lem were watching, making approving noises concerning the Queen's upright posture and diction. David Jenkinson, passing through the sitting room in search of glasses to wash, heard Bridget turning sharply to Lem at one point, saying, 'What do you think of the Empire, then?' and was glad to be able to interrupt, feeling that we all have our limits and this might be his.

David was enjoying himself. A houseful of family and friends was just his idea of a good Christmas. As it was the idea in this case that overwhelmed grim reality, so the annoyances that impinged constantly on Eleanor's attention were merely exhilarating details to David. But his good mood came in particularly useful later on as Jordan telephoned to wish Eleanor a merry Christmas. Eleanor answered the phone, being more or less permanently in the kitchen, where there was one hung over the proverbial pinboard, and expecting the call to be from her friend Davina, whose case against her Thatcherite boss had been lost on a technical point, causing a long-drawn-out and testing melancholia. Davina rang often to bemoan her illegal fate. When the phone rang, David had feared Patsy, and was relieved when it wasn't. (Though later he would have a passing concern for her welfare, and even later than this she would make an awful fuss about him not ringing her on Christmas Day. ('I couldn't, dear, we had an absolute houseful, and Eleanor was there all the time.'/ 'Doesn't she ever go to the loo? You could have rung me quickly then. Or gone out for a walk. Haven't you got a dog to walk? Why don't you get one? All I wanted was to hear that you love me!')

'Can you get out for a few minutes?' requested Jordan of Eleanor, once he was sure it *was* Eleanor to whom he was speaking.

'Yes. No. Probably. Where are you?'

'You know the off-licence round the corner? I'm in the phone box outside it. I'll wait for you there.'

It was easy enough for Eleanor to say she was going out for a breath of fresh air (Patsy was right), and hand George Henry to someone else – in this case Lem, who had surprisingly maternal hands (it came of having six younger siblings, not back in Africa, but in Doncaster). As everyone will appreciate, David's own guilt about Patsy prevented him from nourishing any perception that Eleanor might have had a Patsy of her own.

Jordan was still inside the phone box. He was wearing a red coat with fur on it, and a red hat and a beard. He looked quite nice, framed in the red telephone box. As he saw Eleanor's minuscule figure approaching, head down against the snow, he opened the door of the phone box and handed her a largish parcel. 'I brought you this,' he said thoughtfully. 'You did say the boiler was broken, didn't you?'

It was a small red electric fire. But, like the Apple 2E, how was Eleanor to explain it to her Hove household? She goes out for a breath of fresh air and comes back with an electric fire?

She lugged it back to the house after kissing Father Christmas, telling him how dear he was to her really, and all that kind of stuff, and claimed she had borrowed it from her next door neighbour. 'But it's got no plug on it!' pointed out David.

How observant of you, David Jenkinson! But the screwdriver's in the kitchen in the cupboard next to the pinboard, remember?

In the midst of all this, Eleanor Jenkinson could be forgiven (by some) for foreclosing on My Novel – treating it as a past episode, dream, nightmare, prize, hallucination. Motherhood and domesticity, by making adjustment out of what is often called neuroticism, restore womanhood to women, that is, they deprive them of the very conditions required for other forms of creativity. As Anaïs Nin's psychoanalyst, Otto Rank, once told her, but as none of the therapists at the Women's Therapy Bureau would dream of doing, a man, on the other hand, who begins by being neurotic, but is cured of it, is released to be a great artist. It is put, often, in terms of choice. Another psychoanalyst, given Thomas Mann's daughter, Elizabeth Mann Borghese, to rehabilitate following an amorous disappointment of hers, advised her that she must choose between family life and her desire to be a musician. But no-one, as Elizabeth says, told her father this – or others such as Bach and Toscanini. No choice, you see, at all: an absolute moral injunction, rather, imposed by the culture. Behave as a woman; it's only if you can't, or when you've done it all, that you have a degree of freedom to arrange your life as you wish.

Eleanor was given Adrienne Rich's *Of Woman Born* for Christmas. It was Yolande who gave it to her. The cover was red, like Jordan's electric fire (or, come to that, David's red rose). Both warmed, and were capable of shocking. Eleanor found much in Rich to admire. But particularly this: that the power of motherhood – its propensity to be felt by women as something which is important, though it is because of this that it's a socially derogated status – may often precede, be a condition for, the attainment of other creative ends. These contradictions and conflicts Eleanor herself was experiencing – the unplanned son, the growing up of daughters, the mad mother, the entire domestic edifice, including marriage – may thus be seen in the light of an ideological apprenticeship. It was how she would have to choose to see them. For how else was she able to live with her own disappointment – Eleanor Kendrick or Esther Gray or whomever, the writer buried beneath a great mound of domestic debris? It was the contradiction that was both the heart of the matter and the creative hubris: the power to feed the baby and the powerlessness to walk free.

'I thought you'd like it,' said Yolande. 'You're a good woman, Aunt Eleanor, it'll all come right in the end.' It was what Eleanor wanted to hear, and she didn't much mind who said it to her, as long as someone did.

In mid-January the builders gathered up their tools and left and Bridget Kendrick moved in permanently. The gutters in the extension leaked, the floorboards creaked threateningly, and the builders would have to come back, but this, too, was par for the course. As Bridget moved in, Yolande moved out; she was going to live with Mick on the Caledonian Road. Eleanor moved her books into Yolande's room, and My Novel, and Jordan's fire to warm her ankles while she worked. All these removals over, the house settled down to a new rhythm, presided over ultimately, of course, still by Eleanor, but between her and chaos stood the new mother's help, Myra Heston.

Myra was pure dynamite. She came via an advertisement in the local paper and on a Lambretta wearing a cerise crash helmet. From the start she called Eleanor Eleanor, and decided that Bridget was someone to be subjugated by being shouted at. 'Nice morning, isn't it?' bellowed Myra, or 'Thought I'd tackle the back steps today!' and Bridget retired to her quarters with her fingers in her ears. It was Myra who found her wandering again, and who purchased a padlock for the back gate. In between her whirlwind scouring and hoovering, she dangled George Henry on her knee, recounting her own adventures with babies (two of her own), and when she sat smoking and drinking tea, having done the nappies and the potatoes, treated Eleanor to a soliloquy on her husband Ken's failure to satisfy her sexually. According to Myra, the problem stemmed from an episode in her second pregnancy when

Ken, upon entering her, imagined making contact with an unborn head. The head, fully born years ago, still haunted his psychology and his potency. He only made it every couple of months or so, and, one imagined, in the dark with a face mask and protective clothing on. Myra arrived flushed and happy at the Jenkinsons' home on these occasions, full of her (his) success, and with some gigantic plan to scrub the Jenkinsons' attic or renovate the covers on the sitting room chairs.

Myra would make some things possible for Eleanor that wouldn't otherwise be, but not My Novel. The more things change, as the phrase goes, the more they stay the same. Corporal punishment in British schools was ruled illegal by the European Court of Human Rights, and shortly afterwards Argentina invaded the Falklands. Eleanor found the militarism and the massacre so much at odds with the experience of gazing into baby George's rosy face that she shut off from it completely. She'd now formed the habit of sitting in her study in the early morning after the five o'clock feed, writing in her notebooks. They were formless jottings at first, but then became a sequence in which Eleanor recognized the life of Esther Gray volume two.

The Apple 2E sat, out of its box now, but with a blank screen like Jordan Herriot's injured face, in World's End. The problem was breast-feeding. Eleanor couldn't get away for long enough to receive proper instruction.

One day Myra arrived with a little cotton drawstring bag, a present for Eleanor. 'That's very kind of you, Myra. But it's not my birthday. What is it?'

'Pump for your tits, Eleanor. Stick it in the freezer and leave the baby with me, he'll be fine.'

Why did everyone keep giving Eleanor technological solutions? Maybe it was because there weren't any of the other kind around. When Eleanor obeyed Myra's instructions, Bridget Kendrick, staggering out of her domain in gardening boots, looking for some roses or clematis to prune, spied Myra Heston giving George Henry frozen breast milk and threatened to call the police, but Myra, unperturbed and safely ensconced in any case in front of Mavis Nicholson's *Good Afternoon*, just yelled, 'Go away, you fucking bitch!' and Bridget did.

Eleanor's first day out was to have lunch with Jordan in the studio flat he'd rented in Earls Court. He cooked her vegetarian paella. They cast an eye over the tree tops and then four over each other. Eleanor hadn't had intercourse since George Henry came out of her (David Jenkinson felt his wife's body was given over to other things, and was quite right). Jordan had to be more careful than usual and was.

'We must work out what to do about the Apple,' Eleanor said firmly afterwards. 'Shall I move it here, or will you come to the office?'

Everything, it occurred to her, was in the wrong place. The Apple was in World's End, whereas it ought to be with Jordan, My Novel was in manuscript form only, instead of in the bookshops. Eleanor's job was with Araminta and Rowan in London, which wasn't where Eleanor lived. My Baby was at home with Myra, though his place was with Eleanor. And Eleanor's mother was in her house, whereas she ought not to be. Jordan himself was at least no longer in Holland, though how long he would stay in Earls Court was anybody's guess, and it was arguable in any case whether he ought to have been in Eleanor's life in the first place. Oh dear, these complications were too much for her! At least Heidi and Eliza were at school, which was where they should be, except that Heidi wasn't, she was defaulting with the motorbike lad and was, at this very moment, listening to Pink Floyd's latest in Dixons. Through all this, David was, however, teaching pre-Reformation history to the second years as he always did: history is the same, even as it's being written. Patsy Drew was back in Sussex, chewing strips of white cabbage, the newest remedy for her affliction. Her affair with David Jenkinson dragged on and on, also not unlike history.

Araminta and Rowan had leased a shop front in the Fulham Road and painted 'The Eden Press' and a green and purple tree of life over the window. They'd hung a white Victorian lace curtain up there as well, to prevent themselves being mistaken for women who sit in shop windows in red light districts. Araminta's mother, who bred goats, had loaned them some capital. They wanted Eleanor to work with them three days a week, soliciting manuscripts and designing promotional material. The office consisted of one very large room, into which they had put three desks, and behind this there was a very small kitchen and a lavatory and shower. 'You can even be a Managing Director with us if you'd like!' they said invitingly. 'Only in that case, you must put some capital in.'

Wearily, Eleanor telephoned Ball in Soho. 'Money!' she said grimly.

'Think nothing of it, Mrs J,' he said airily. 'Be with you right away. Little hitch, but solved now, where are you, by the way?'

They arranged to meet at Victoria station for the handover. She emphasized she needed to catch the 5.35 to Brighton, as George would have run out of freezer milk by then, and in any case Myra was expected back in the caravan where the Heston household lived. Eleanor waited under the clock with half a box of Kleenex in her jumper, but no Ball.

Circumstances continued to defeat her. (Rephrase that: all sentences beginning society, circumstances, social conditions and so forth, are eminently suspect, as these nouns cannot be actors. Counter-argument: oh yes, they can. What is the reality for people (rephrase that: women) like Eleanor Jenkinson, who at every corner find their real aims in life defeated? Society is against women like her, and I don't care if it's unepistemological to say so; that's how it is.)

'I'm fed up with this,' said Eleanor suddenly at dinner. The spaghetti bolognese tasted awful, the mince was overcooked and rubbery. She hadn't been concentrating when she made it or the salad, which was as vinegary as a newspaper full of chips on Brighton pier. They all sat there, chewing the grey meat, and looking at her: Heidi, Eliza, David and Bridget (George Henry couldn't, he was in his shopping basket again), all with a different interpretation of what she meant. Eliza thought: it's the baby, she's got postnatal depression. This was what Myra had said to her confidingly one day over tea: 'Of course your Mum's a bit depressed just now, it's one of the things that happens to women. After having a baby, you know.' It increasingly seemed to Eliza that only unpleasant things happened to women. Babies that came out feet first, and then depression, closely followed by the menopause. Eliza looked at her mother sideways over the spaghetti bolognese and wondered if you could have both (all) at the same time.

Heidi considered her mother beyond the pale anyway, hiding all kinds of sins behind that phrase My Novel for years – there was undoubtedly no such thing. If there had been, it would have been published by now. Heidi had answered the telephone to Jordan a couple of times, which didn't help. He was terribly circumspect on the phone, not even leaving his name, but this very fact was sufficient to embroider a suspicious adolescent's imagination. Eleanor used to complain to Heidi about the vicissitudes of her life (usually as a way of trying to get her to do more in the house), but she'd given that up recently, which confirmed Heidi's suspicions. And Bridget regarded her daughter's disclosure at the dinner table as a purely taken-for-granted and common sense utterance: naturally one gets fed up from time to time, she would have said, had she not instantly been transplanted back into a moment in her own past when she'd said as much to Somerset in the big kitchen of Muddenham Grange, so much nicer than this one with its lovely portscullion windows opening on to the sloping lawn with the quince and the willow trees . . .

David Jenkinson thought for one awful moment that Eleanor had found out about Patsy Drew, back in Brighton with her ulcer (or before that Marion Cumberledge, who had moved on to better things – a senior lectureship, and a chartered surveyor, who treated Gary – sensibly, as the one with the real power in the situation – with more respect than David had). After that, David thought about his year in New Zealand, about the upheaval it would mean for Eleanor and the girls. He still hadn't told her yet, coward that he was. Only today he'd spoken to Cuthbert Sloane, the man in the History Department at Otago, who made it all possible. David was due to be going in August. At least it should mark the end of Patsy, and therefore of her ulcer as well, assuming for the sake of argument that the psychiatrist was right. 'Should be looking for a house to rent,' Sloane had remarked, 'want me to have a preliminary look around for you? How many children did you say you've got, Jenkinson?' It was as though David's own life was developing in one direction but it was, well, largely a direction in which, well, he'd have to travel on his own. Probably.

'What are you fed up with, dear?' He was the only one who had the temerity (lack of sensitivity, stupidity) to ask.

'Everything's in the wrong place,' moaned Eleanor, breaking down all over her spaghetti.

'Overwrought,' said Bridget, pulled into the present by the sight of her daughter crying. 'Go to bed, Eleanor. I'll bring you some hot milk.'

And with amazing efficiency culled from some distant historical garden, Bridget cleared the table, loaded the dishwasher, packed Eliza off to do her homework and took Eleanor up some hot milk.

*

Extract from:

LADY'S MANTLE
BY ESTHER GRAY

At this time of year, the tree outside the window gets too big for its boots, and taps against the glass all the time. I don't know what kind of tree it is, but it has black seed pods on it. Slightly furry. Weird. I dislike having to touch them.

Ned, the gardener in the video man's house, wears a woolly hat in all weathers. It protects him from the falling apples, and from the power of too much sunshine. Maybe without it the rain would cause seeds to sprout on his head.

'You're a mad old woman, d'you know that?'

He said this to me the other day, when he was cutting down the dead spiky heuchera shoots in the border the other side of my wall.

'So what?' I said.

'You can have some of my lady's mantle,' he told me. 'I've got a surfeit of it growing by the compost heap.'

'It's no use crying over spilt milk,' said Eleanor when she woke up in the morning, soaked in her own, baby George having decided to start sleeping through the night. She woke David. 'I'm going to take George to London,' she told him. 'I've got to get back to work. Or something. I'd prefer to get back to writing, but I'll never write a word of anything here. Except shopping lists.' She sounded terribly ruthless – especially to herself. 'Myra can manage the household perfectly well for you Monday to Friday. What do you think, David?'

He rubbed his eyes. When would it ever end? He'd have to ring Cuthbert Sloane. 'You can't have the car,' he pointed out, 'I've got a load of books to take in for the departmental book sale. Anyway, where will you stay in London?' He looked at her in the hard morning light, though not terribly accusingly.

'With Araminta and Rowan in Chelsea. Or they mentioned that a friend of theirs has a flat in Earls Court that's vacant at the moment.'

'A kind of Marine Parade, you mean?' David ventured vaguely.

'You could say so.'

'How much would it cost?'

'Oh nothing.' (Be careful, Eleanor Jenkinson, you haven't prepared this part of the script properly.) 'I mean, I think she just wants someone to look after it and water the plants for a bit. It'd only be a temporary arrangement. She's in – er – New Zealand,' finished Eleanor.

Telepathy? No. There was a letter from Otago for David yesterday. Eleanor had seen the postmark. But David hadn't seen Eleanor see the postmark, and was consequently led to wonder what tricks his wife was up to now (but he was going down the wrong path as usual and fortunately). 'I'll take you to the university, first,' said Eleanor before David had a chance to query any of this. 'With the books. We can put the bicycle in the back. I must have the car, you see,' she went on, 'to drive My Baby and My Novel to London.' And to fetch My Apple from World's End, she added quietly to herself.

Jordan was asleep when she got there. His hours at the Microsoft office in Bayswater were largely of his own choosing, as he was actually quite a brilliant young man, and it wasn't in the firm's best interests to deplete the small amount of energy Jordan Herriot had by making him abide by silly rules. He'd been up until two transferring the latest Berkeley Unix enhancements to the PDP11. Unhappily the computer hadn't wanted to be enhanced, and defeating its multiple objections had taken a lot out of him.

Eleanor staggered upstairs with George under one arm and the Apple 2E, reboxed, under the other. 'We're moving in,' she announced. 'At least that way I get to be able to learn how to use this damn thing, and I can make a start with my career at Eden Press which is, as you know, only down the road from here.'

Jordan, seeing Eleanor there like a miniature camel with two humps, couldn't say he was enormously pleased at the news, but then he wasn't displeased, either. Life (or society or culture) was always dealing him these sorts of blows. He considered himself a member of an oppressed minority group, just like her.

It was a bit cramped in the studio flat for the five of them: Jordan, Eleanor, George, Jordan's BBC and Eleanor's Apple. 'It'll have to be mostly take-aways from now on,' reflected Jordan, siting Eleanor's Apple on the kitchen surface above the fridge.

'We must *plan* our time,' she decreed, stowing George's nappies with Jordan's underwear.

He watched her. 'I can just see me going to work in a Tufty Tail.'

'What I mean is, we need a plan for the week. I want to computerize My Novel. I can't make head or tail of this thing, though I have put a plug on it. And I'm going to have to tell Araminta and Rowan when to expect me in.'

They sat down and wrote out a little timetable. An Apple lesson twice a day from 8 to 9 a.m. and p.m. Eleanor would go to the Eden Press from ten to four Monday to Thursday. Friday a.m. they would keep for each other. Friday p.m. she'd take the train to Hove, returning either Sunday night or early Monday morning.

There were a number of hitches in this plan, as anyone could see, but for the time being it satisfied Eleanor, which was the most important consideration. Time would reveal the hiccups, the holes, the false assumptions, all the 'what if's' with which life was liberally sprinkled. For example in this case, what if baby George was ill? What if daughter Eliza was ill? What if Heidi was caught truanting? What if My Novel didn't want to be computerized? What if husband David telephoned Eleanor in Earls Court and got Jordan? What if, under the strain of all this, David got the ulcer instead of Patsy and Patsy got David instead?

The next day Eleanor drove from Earls Court to Fulham, parked her car on a yellow line, finding nothing of any other colour available, and went into the Eden Press with a flourish and baby George in his shopping basket. Araminta and Rowan looked up from their desks much as they did in the old days at Maitland & Ware, only it was their territory now. 'What have you got in that basket?' asked Rowan suspiciously.

'Why, My Baby of course.'

'I didn't know you were going to bring My Baby to work!' protested Araminta.

'No, we didn't know that was part of the plan,' echoed Rowan.

Well, what else did you expect me to do with him, you stupid unsisterly women?

'He's no bother,' said Eleanor in his defence. 'Well, not usually.'

'I suppose you can put him in the kitchen,' said Araminta doubtfully.

'But won't he cry?' asked Rowan.

'Only sometimes, I expect,' reassured Araminta.

George, like most babies, knew when he wasn't wanted, and wailed from his basket in the kitchen most of that day. Eleanor attended to his needs, and then shut the door on him, but it didn't work, as his most important need was to be in there with the three women having fun. Once this was acknowledged and he was propped up against some cushions, he entertained them all with plenty of smiles and hand waving. This wasn't a lot better, though, as it was distracting in a different way. Moreover, when the telephone rang, and it was a printer or an author or the all-important Jonathan Withers or someone similar, George was likely to blow a raspberry at the wrong moment. Eleanor hardly liked to ask in view of this what plans Araminta and Rowan had for My Novel, whose passage into the limelight had been so rudely interrupted by Jim Maitland's myocardial infarction. She noted that it was on the list, though, of 'probable' projects.

'I'm prepared to use some of my capital,' she told them to ease the atmosphere. 'Will £3,000 do? For a start?' Out of the money Ball owed her, plus what she'd still got left of Uncle Hal's original gift, Eleanor needed to keep some back to buy a car. She couldn't be forever quibbling with David about that. And she also needed to buy a printer for her Apple 2E. Technology breeds technology . . . Talking of which, 'Don't you think we need a computer?' she asked.

'Whatever for?'

'She could be right, you know,' said Araminta back to Rowan. 'You're the one that's always going on about thinking big. We might as well start as we mean to go on.'

Both women watched as Eleanor changed George's nappy. His penis rose from a cotton wool sea of ammonia like a stuffed worm.

'Is it usually like that?' inquired Araminta, curious.

'Is what usually like what?'

'His – his thing.'

'Pity he isn't a girl,' observed Rowan. 'That wouldn't be nearly so difficult.'

Eleanor enclosed George's offending organ in another Tufty Tail. 'Why would a girl be easier? A baby's a baby. A novel's a novel. The only difference it makes is in the mind.'

After the Chinese take-away that evening, and when George was bathed and fed, Eleanor and Jordan sat down with the instruction manual. 'The word processor is called Applewriter.'

'What's a word processor, Jordan?' asked Eleanor. 'I thought I was one.'

'No, you're only the writer, Eleanor. And your Apple isn't a word processor, it's a computer. In order to turn it into a word processor, you have to use a programme . . . '

By eleven o'clock, Eleanor had reached page three of the instruction manual and had a severe headache. Shortly after that David phoned. Eleanor had warned Jordan that when she was there she ought to answer the phone (what to do when she wasn't wasn't quite so easy to determine).

'How did your first day in the Garden of Eden go?'

Eleanor told David about the anti-male and anti-baby atmosphere prevailing there. She managed to make it sound quite funny. While she talked, Jordan played with the keys of the Apple, trying to bring a portion of old deleted text back on to the screen.

'What's that noise? That clicking noise I can hear?' David asked sharply.

'The central heating,' said Eleanor with surprising deftness. 'Very noisy, it is.'

The explanation satisfied him. 'Eliza's lost her library books,' he went on, 'and my third-year Renaissance lecture notes are in the glove compartment of the car, I need them on Friday, you'll have to send them by messenger or something. The Renfrews want us to go to dinner on Saturday. And someone called Ball phoned. He said he'd got something for you. He'll meet you in Brighton, in front of the Aquarium on Sunday morning. Who is Ball, Eleanor?'

ELEVEN

A Little Witchcraft

E LEANOR OPENS THE SHUTTERS and sees a sparkling new
day. Across the sweep of dark green forest to her left falls a
diamond sun out of a toneless blue sky. The hedge of ivy in
front of the house pokes its curled leaves upwards to catch the sun
in their gloss. In the middle distance a white horse flicks its tail at
flies; and Eleanor hears David coming back from somewhere, singing.
'Milk,' he says. 'We forgot to buy any.'

Always the provident one, David Jenkinson, aren't you? Provision-
ing, planning, arranging. Living a man's life while your wife Eleanor
tries to write a woman's one. But the truth is that living such a life
is hard enough; writing about it is nearly impossible. And when
accomplished, much the worst sin of the two. To live it is bad
enough. To write about it unforgivable.

'I think we should do some sightseeing,' says David. 'How about
taking the train up the escarpment to Capdenac? It's the only way to
see it. There's no road. I understand it's quite dramatic.'

At Bretenoux-Biars station, a small building in a deep vanilla decor,
sited where the single tracks become two for a kilometre or so, Eleanor
sits one side of the line in the sunshine tanning her legs, while David,
who can't abide heat, sits the other side in the shade, studying the
map. The arrangement sums up their respective positions in the
relationship – different, and not equal. They are early. He has
bought her a chocolate ice cream, wishing to indulge the easier
of her fancies. Mindlessly, she eats it, drowning in the smell of
creosote (newly painted on the sleepers), the heat and her study
of French railway bureaucracy. The station master, if that is what
he's called, is a young man in his twenties with turbulent dark hair,
a ruddy complexion (it reminds her of Jordan Herriot's), wearing a
surprising deep turquoise shirt. He can't be told apart from the other

205

station staff until the arrival of a train is imminent, when he comes out of the office behind the ticket counter, wearing his hat which sits on the filing cabinet between trains, crosses the track and moves a large metal box hosting a square red and white sign so that the red and white face the supposedly oncoming train. Then he recrosses the track and turns his attention to the points, pulling two long handles towards him, in a gesture indicative of both effort and authority. That done, he stands for a moment to see if the train is melting out of the heat haze in the distance. But it's late, so he goes back into the dark interior of the office.

Eleanor takes a bite out of her ice cream, which is very sweet, and has nuts in it, and a chocolate pole down the centre where one imagines the stick should be. She studies it in the quivering orange light. Then bites into it, only to discover the stick is there after all, half way down, masquerading as chocolate. Dangerous, she thinks; how many tourists have been thus duped, receiving a mouthful of splinters?

But now the station master reemerges. He's holding a rectangular piece of wood painted green and white. The train to Brive (not theirs) comes, obscuring David on the opposite platform, but, being two carriages only, it stops half-way along. The driver, also hatted, climbs down. Much energetic handshaking ensues. There are now about seven or eight SNCF men on the platform, all adopting busy official postures, though clearly lacking very much to do. A large woman in a blue overall comes out, with a cigarette. More handshaking. Laughter. The train waits. Not more than two or three passengers have got off. Eleanor looks at her watch. The train to Capdenac is a good fifteen minutes late. Then there's a sudden influx of people, including David, across the tracks, and Eleanor, getting up to find a litter bin for the wrapping of her ice cream and the stick which she's fortunately not eaten, sees the Capdenac train making its way slowly along the line. It reminds her of Thomas the Tank Engine, dutifully read to George Henry in his early years.

The view from the train labouring its way through the steep-sided ravine is, indeed, dramatic. Eleanor fastens the maroon linen SNCF curtains back with the little rectangles of velcro that glint like cobwebs in the light, and is then able to see the full sweep of the vegetation climbing in a mix of rich green hues up the hillside. Every few minutes the train passes through a short length of tunnel or a large boulder remaining after the railway was cut through the rock. Looking down there is the dribble, sometimes sweep, of the Cère river edged with silver rocks and pebbles, and providing sufficient reason for the siting of a hydroelectric station at an otherwise deserted place called Lamativie.

'Enjoying it, dear?' asks David. He wants to show her on the map on his knee the route they are taking, but she can see it for herself.

They have a late lunch at Laroquebrou which proves to be an undistinguished small town. From the café in which they consume their plates of pâté and vegetables they watch, in a silence that is for once companionable, the life of the town come and go. People parking in the square opposite to buy bread or visit the pharmacy. A young man (reminding Eleanor of Heidi's motorbike lad) who cruises past incessantly in a loud purple T-shirt. A party of young mothers and children, the mothers all looking a little more matronly than Eleanor suspects their age warrants, with an officiousness not unlike that of the SNCF men, and the babies all wrapped in protective clothing – a blue sailor's cap, a strawberry dotted sun hat – against the damaging heat.

After lunch, David says they must visit the Château which claims it has an exhibition of modern art. But, in grim reality, all that awaits the Jenkinsons after the heart-stopping climb to the summit, whence they can see the layered red and grey rooftops of the town spread out like Lego bricks beneath, and the railway to their left, snaking along beside the capricious Cère, winking from its muddy sunlit shallows, is row upon row of truly appalling etchings and paintings – a mix of styles from the simple representational to the crudely cubist – and among which there are pink and blue plywood butterflies affixed to dead branches of trees. David climbs the edifice next to the Château which leads to an elevated ivory statue of the Virgin, arms outspread before what looks like a portable television, but is in fact a light to shine on her face and keep her awake at night. Eleanor crouches in the shade of the Château and watches David, imagining his vertigo. The lens of his camera is pointed either at Mary or at herself, she's not sure which.

On the train back David says, 'Well, that was a pleasant interlude, wasn't it, Ellie?'

*

Extract from:

ONE DAY IN THE MEADOW
BY ESTHER GRAY

I was sitting there drinking my coffee later than usual (it was Saturday, Monsieur Marroufin had kept me up with his stupid prattle the night before, but what could I do, it'd be heartless to turn him away in his hour of need?) and thinking about what I should get my great nephew George for his birthday — the little chap was two in a week — and my eye was caught by a thin band of glistening pink, some extremely delicate substance or thing that appeared to dance on the meadow between the house and the cornfields. The more closely I looked at it, trying to place its nature, the more it eluded me. At first I considered it might be a spider's washing line, strung out between two crab apple trees, but when I got up to test this idea, breaking the space between the two trees with my hand, there was nothing. When I sat down again it was still there. It couldn't be of a spider's making, because, although it formed a straight diagonal against the horizon of the cornfield with the sky, yet a central frond of it detached itself and danced at different latitudes all the time. Now to the right of landmarks such as the group of cows under the oak, now to the left — up and down and all over the place. I must admit, I began to feel quite frightened. I thought of summoning someone to help me to identify it. Not Monsieur Marroufin (the price of relieving my fear would be another of his dreadful monologues) but maybe Pierre, the son. Whom I could hear turning the hay off the tractor behind the house. But what would I say? Come quickly, Pierre, there's a strange pink line out there on the meadow and it frightens me! What would he think? That I'm an old man, grown crazier with age and solitude, put finally out of my mind by a fairy's filament!

Every time I think I've dealt with it by altering my attention to something else, it's still there when I look back at it. You know what I think it is? I think it's something from another planet.

I remember my old friend Rupert once saying, of course there's life somewhere else in the universe. We were sitting outside one evening at the time, a time when we were both young men and quite unsure of our real natures still, and we sat there beneath

*that twinkling sky, and he said, there must be life out or up or
down there, and do you know, it visits us from time to time? Only
we don't recognize it because it's clever and different and it takes
forms unfamiliar to us. It comes in the shape of rocks or white
elderberry trees or of lizards with two tails, or somesuch. And
that's why we can't see it for what it is – we never get past the
disguise, you see.*

Eleanor phoned Ball. 'Not Sunday,' she said, 'Saturday. And don't
leave messages with my husband again, please.'

'Put a spanner in the works, Mrs J, did it?' retorted Ball impenitently.
'Thought your old man sounded a bit put out.'

'Saturday. At eleven. By the pancake stall on the end of the pier.
You can park outside the aquarium,' she added peremptorily. 'And *be*
there this time.'

If it was Saturday, Eleanor could pretend it was part of the shopping
trip which she always did on her own these days. To David she could
therefore say: 'Ball's someone I once knew. In the past. He's a bit odd.
I don't know what he was talking about. I should forget it if I were
you.' David, who wasn't sure he believed her, wished to, especially
as he had enough on his hands concerning Cuthbert Sloane and the
Otago trip.

The car packed with white and orange carrier bags, Eleanor
stood in the February drizzle next to the closed pancake stall.
She scrutinized the mostly domestic traffic passing the pier's end
for Ball's materialization, but did not expect the silver Rolls Royce
in which he eventually arrived, some ten minutes past the hour. He
wore a white waterproof jacket, a white silk polo neck and Lois jeans,
and dangled the car keys ostentatiously as he sauntered towards her.
'Like the Roller, do you, Mrs J? Nice piece of metal, though I do say
it myself.'

'I'm getting wet, Ball,' she said severely.

'Have no fear, Mrs J, we are about to deliver the goods.' He
unzipped the pocket of his jacket and withdrew a couple of sealed,
bulky airmail envelopes. 'There you are, that's all of it. Three thou
plus another three hundred interest. Ten per cent for half a year.
Apologize most sincerely for the delay, Mrs J. But grateful for
the loan – most grateful. Made all sorts of things possible. Not

a bad investment for you, either. If I may be so bold as to say so.'

Eleanor took the money and slipped it into her raincoat pocket. As she did so, there was a commotion of shrieking brakes in the road ahead and two policemen more than sauntered towards them. 'Hallo again, Mr Devizes,' said one to Ball, while the other, approaching Eleanor, said, 'Excuse me, Madam, I wonder if you would mind letting us have a look at what this gentleman's just given you?'

Eleanor's hand gripped the packages in her pocket. 'Why? Why do you want to see it? What's the matter?'

'We have reason to believe that Mr Devizes is making money out of things he shouldn't, not to put too fine a point on it.'

'Well, this is quite above board,' said Eleanor clearly. 'I lent Ball – Mr Devizes – a sum of money some years ago. This is the rest of the repayment he owes me. That's all.'

'Can you prove it, Madam?'

'Why should I have to? I've told you the truth.'

'I can vouch for that,' added Ball. 'Mrs Jenkinson here's purer than the driven. Well, nearly.' He grinned conspiratorially at her. 'Lent me, as she says, a bit of capital when she had some and I didn't. Now it's the other way around, I'm giving it back.'

'Could we have a look, please, Mrs Jenkinson?'

Eleanor handed over the packages. As the policeman opened the first envelope, Ball made a sudden move away from them across the wet pavement, but slipped and fell, streaking his white garments with unsavoury brown and grey matter.

'Guilty are we?' The first policeman yanked him up by his collar.

The second, holding a fifty pound note up to the struggling February light, said to Eleanor, 'I'm not sure I like the look of these, Mrs Jenkinson. I'd like to take the whole batch to the station and have them checked, if you don't mind.'

'Oh Ball, how could you!'

'I haven't, Mrs J, I haven't!' he protested as they took him and the airmail envelopes off in the police car.

Eleanor said to the police something that sounded like a line out of a very different kind of story: 'Don't phone me, I'll phone you.' When she did, later that afternoon, David having gone in to the university to compose an express letter to Cuthbert Sloane, she heard to her relief that Ball hadn't. There was nothing wrong with the airmail envelope money. The next item in this saga, though, was that Ball was asking Eleanor to stand bail for him to the tune of considerably more than that. Before deciding what to do about this one, Eleanor phoned Janice, who wasn't there, as she was in hospital with Marlon who was being circumcized. Somewhere in the conversation with Drake concerning anxiety over the welfare of Marlon's genitals, Eleanor established that he couldn't say Ball's dealings weren't shady, as he and Janice were almost certainly involved in them too. Torn, as usual, between one set of duties and another, Eleanor fitted a quick walk to the police station in between tea with her mother and taking the girls to the cinema. Retrieving her money, she said she'd stand bail for precisely that amount but not for any more. As to the rest, Ball would have to think of someone else. For which – among other purposes – some of you may remember the notebook he kept, which was by now reasonably full of well-known wealthy and suitably guilty names.

'"Alas, a woman who attempts the pen,"' quoted Araminta to Eleanor and Rowan in the park in World's End, '"such a presumptuous creature is esteemed/ That fault can by no virtue be redeemed." Anne Finch, Countess of Winchelsea, 1661. And that includes the device of using a pseudonym,' she concluded. 'Sorry, Ellie, but we've thought about it very carefully, and we don't feel it would be right for the Eden Press to publish feminist fiction pseudonymously.'

It was now the era, the early 1980s, in which ideological orthodoxy had replaced the plastic reflexivity of earlier forms of feminist consciousness. What different women differently laid claim to in the way of beliefs about women's position had become what every woman must. The feminist presses, originating in the desire to circumvent male gatekeeping of the publishing process, had erected gates of their own which only squeaked open when flags of the right colour were waved at them.

Was My Novel feminist fiction? pondered Eleanor. Because it was about a woman, did that make it feminist? She struggled to remember the nature of Esther Gray's own interminable evolution to a definable consciousness and nameable political position. Certainly any conception of My Novel as a whole that she'd once had had slipped into the past; it had become to her as much of a forbidden fruit as the landing by Jordan of the Apple itself on her feet in the Royal Sussex Maternity Hospital.

Only the first three chapters so far were on the Apple. Jordan had shown Eleanor how to transpose sections, how to replace words with others, either for every occurrence or only for selected ones, how to split texts into useful dualities so that one may be tampered with while the other is retained as a standard against which the judiciousness of change may be measured. But while all these stratagems which so pleased Jordan also impressed Eleanor with their potential relevance to the writing process, she was not as yet at all convinced that My Novel was enriched by them.

'I don't suppose you found it very easy to tell me that,' commented Eleanor charitably, though she felt far from that. 'That must be why you invited me and my baby to dinner.'

Araminta and Rowan were surprised. They looked at each other.

'What are you – we – going to publish instead, then?' required Eleanor.

'We thought an autobiography would be a good idea,' confided Araminta. 'We've been sent rather a good one. It's called *Blocked Drains and Other Territorial Objections* and it's by a black Canadian called Bea Purson.'

'What did you say about pseudonyms?'

'It's not a pseudonym. She changed her name officially. That's her *real* name.'

'I think you're both nuts,' offered Eleanor, 'but as I'm fond of you, I'm prepared to try to understand why.' What else could she do? The wall of feminist ideological purity was not likely to be breached by her insubstantial persona (even as she realized this, she recalled the flapping haddock and male procreative insistence of another era). 'I'm even prepared to go along with it, that is, to find ways round it. For this is surely yet another cataclysmic but ultimately surmountable obstacle in the path of My Novel. Isn't it?'

Araminta and Rowan didn't know what to say.

'Would you like me to offer the novel elsewhere?' Eleanor thought back, not fondly, to an old pile of rejection letters. 'Or even to abandon it utterly?'

Her co-Managing Directors made reassuring noises.

'Yes, I thought so. Well, here's my response: one, I am in the process of reconstructing yet again parts of My Novel so that the archaic anti-libertarian device of pseudonymity will no longer be necessary. In this I am being helped by my computing friend, who is, unfortunately, a man, but we'll leave that out of it for the moment, and hindered by my other friend here' – she throws a glance at the shopping basket – 'who is also, as you have commented, not of the right sex. Or even gender. (Though I am working on that, insofar as a mere mother can.) As a consequence of these wholly superhuman efforts of mine and theirs, we may only anticipate with the usual fears, or joyless abandon, the normal anonymity that attends the publication of a first novel. And two, as a result of this enormous moral compromise you have cornered me into, I expect you – us – also to publish my second which will be called, for the sake of argument, *Sleeping Beauty* or, *Put to Sleep by a Prick*. This is a continuation of My (First) Novel. Which is what you would expect it to be. For this reason it can't be published first, which would be another way round the problem. In any case, if things go on like this, all the potentially offended people who don't appear in My Novel but think they might (or should, which is different) will be dead. So will I. Stendhal's triumph after all! And I won't even need to lose my lover, as is his direly punitive proclamation.'

At the suggested title of My (second) Novel Araminta and Rowan started to laugh, but noticing Eleanor's restrained expression, wondered if they should. 'Go ahead,' Eleanor told them, 'most laughter is a nervous response anyway. Have fun at my expense. Or invitation. You're the victims, not I. Personally, I'm off to expunge this scene in a display of what *you* would call inveterate heterosexism.'

She wasn't able to, however, as Jordan was working late at Microsoft. He crept in, waking George Henry, at three a.m. 'Where have you been?' she demanded above George Henry's squawks, and in what sounded like the start of an awfully sexist piece of dialogue.

'Writing a programme for co-ordinating train timetables,' said he, releasing his hair from the same rubber band as he had had when she met him. 'Cup of tea, my love?'

'Tea-making will get you nowhere,' she said but it did. In the morning, though, he said: 'On the subject of who's doing what with whom when they shouldn't be, what do *you* do, Eleanor Jenkinson, alias my love, at weekends in Hove when you go home to your family?'

Eleanor was startled. Jordan's enquiry at least took her mind off the Eden Press's rejection of My Novel, which, despite her measured response to Araminta and Rowan, did seem a bit like the last straw. 'I didn't think jealousy was part of your makeup,' she said.

'You thought it was a piece of software I slipped in only when convenient, did you? Come on, Eleanor, you know what I mean. Do you and Professor Jenkinson still Do It?'

She coloured (thereby becoming the same shade as he was anyway). 'We never agreed to be faithful to one another, Jordan. Only once or twice since George was born. It's not important.'

'It would be to you if *I* was Doing It with someone else!'

'Do you?'

'I could taunt you with memories of the monstrous blonde who captains the reception area in the Keelam conference centre,' he replied. 'Her face as clear as the moon's gaze, and handy with the keyboard also. Women in suits always turn me on. And then in Silicon Valley there was this doll called Barbara . . . '

Eleanor hit him unsuccessfully with a packet of George's nappies. 'It's time for my Apple lesson,' she determined, and thinking, I must at least get on with *something* that can count as an advance.

'Subject not dropped but deferred,' he parried. 'There *is* a problem, Eleanor. We have a problem. The situation can't go on like this. Instability is everywhere. Besides which, my flat's too small. My dislike of domestic responsibility doesn't mean I enjoy not having the space to boil an egg in, or finding babygros dripping into my dental floss.'

Eleanor went out to buy one of those fold-up clothes airers to hang over the bath with which to solve the problem of the dripping babygros. Her current line was that, since she couldn't solve the big problems, she might as well tackle the little ones. She was pushing George in his buggy down the Earls Court Road, thinking about what kind of car she ought to buy (another little problem), when she saw a woman slip into the florists' on the corner some way ahead. Something about her way of walking was very familiar. Also her hair, long and straight and fine. The colour of teak. Eleanor hurried on, bumping George over the ill-laid pavements. Before she could get there, the woman came out again, clutching a large bunch of pink flowers. It was quite unmistakably Eva Summers. She looked left and right, and began to cross the road. Eleanor started running, 'Eva!' but tripped over the pavement, dropping her bag and its contents, though not, fortunately, damaging George. By the time she'd picked herself up, Eva had disappeared.

Eleanor went into the florist. 'Excuse me,' she said to the man behind the counter, 'there was a woman in here just now, she bought some pink flowers, I wonder if you could tell me whether she lives round here?'

The man behind the counter had large navy tattoos on his arm. He regarded Eleanor suspiciously. George, ignored and hungry, cried. The man peered over the counter at him. 'First carnations of the season. Three quid a dozen. She took two. Little chap wants his dinner, does he?'

'But do you know where she lives?'

'Haven't got a clue. Never seen the lady before,' he replied firmly, after a short pause.

Later that day, Jordan accompanied Eleanor and George to the Eden Press. At least Araminta and Rowan had established a *modus vivendi* with George by now: they ignored him. Having ranted for ages to one another in World's End about the practical and ideological impossibility of it all, they'd decided to lay it all to rest to the end of breast-feeding. Araminta had been to HMSO in Chancery Lane and bought a copy of *Present Day Practice in Infant Feeding*, in order to find out how long breast-feeding was supposed to go on. 'Nine months,' she told Rowan, 'Ideally. Give or take a month or two.'

'You're confusing it with pregnancy, Minty,' said Rowan, who was currying lentils and listening to Leonard Cohen's 'One of Us Cannot Be Wrong'.

'I am not, and that gives her until September. We must put up with it/him until then.'

Rowan didn't formulate the thought which had begun to fester somewhere inside her in response to George Henry's distracting gurgles and hand waving, which was that it might be quite nice if she and Araminta had one of those (suitably feminized of course) one day. Araminta's Dad would be delighted if he knew, though less happy if he realized his daughter was destined to be one too.

'This is Jordan Herriot from Microsoft Inc,' said Eleanor, determined not to stand any nonsense with this one. 'Alias My Lover. And I know he's a man, but there aren't a lot of women in computing as yet. Though it *was* all invented by one as it happens, Ada Lovelace. In 1841. Commonly described as Lord Byron's daughter. Though actually the daughter of Lady Byron too. We should commission a biography on her sometime, don't you think?'

Both phones started to ring, so Jordan went into the kitchen and made them all some tea. They only had Typhoo, so he slipped out and obtained some lapsang souchong.

'If you have to have a man around at all,' confided Rowan to Araminta later that day, 'you might as well have one who has good taste in tea.'

'Do you think we could employ him somehow? In a junior capacity? For the lightbulbs and so on?'

But after Jordan had advised them which machine to buy, he was unhappily recalled by Microsoft to California (who anyway paid him a great deal more than the Eden Press could). This precipitated another crisis in Eleanor's life, which included the disappearance of the flat in Earls Court.

'I'm home again,' she said to David Jenkinson. 'I mean Araminta and Rowan's friend's come back, so I've lost my *pied-à-terre* in London.'

'Good,' he said.

To console herself, Eleanor bought a car. It was a red Peugeot, two years old. The first car she'd ever personally owned. She had a seat fitted for George in it.

'But it's not big enough for all of us,' pointed out Heidi.

'It's not supposed to be,' said Eleanor. 'Your father's got the family estate.'

'Don't call him "Your Father",' complained Heidi. 'His name is David.'

'Yes, well,' said Eleanor. She drove herself and George in the new Peugeot up for a day's work in London, and to show Araminta and Rowan her new possession.

'Very nice, Ellie,' they said. 'Can we have one, too? Where's your young man?'

'Gone, but not forgotten.' Eleanor was thinking of Jordan with more than fondness now, as his expertise in various areas had become necessary to her. But he'd be back, he'd promised, like a bad penny. As the weeks passed, the fond thoughts turned into a definite ache. In order to cover it up, she busied herself with moving things around. She packed the car full of work to do over the holidays, and drove home again, parking the car outside the house. The next morning, when she went to look for it, it wasn't there any more. She spent a while searching the streets for it – perhaps she'd parked it somewhere else, and she'd forgotten? But yes she had parked it there. She phoned the police to report it. They asked her to take her Vehicle Ownership Certificate to the police station.

The policeman behind the desk was the same one who had apprehended Ball by the pancake stall. 'It's you again, is it, Madam? Quite a coincidence, isn't it? What can I do for you this time?'

She explained. He asked her a lot of questions, including what was in the car? It was then that she remembered it had been stuffed with manuscripts, including her own. She felt sick, and had to sit down, Of course some of it was on the Apple, but not enough. What would she do? How would she ever be able face Esther Gray again, not to mention Araminta and Rowan? 'Don't worry, Madam,' said the policeman, 'most stolen cars turn up in a day or so. Did you leave anything valuable in it, then?'

'Only a few My Novels,' she admitted weakly.

'A few what?'

'I'm a publisher,' she explained, trying to recover her composure. 'I was taking some work home, for the holidays. Manuscripts, you know.'

'I know,' confirmed the police sergeant. 'My auntie's a writer. Do you know that magazine *Family Circle* you buy in supermarkets? She writes for that, she does. Nice little stories about middle-aged women battling against all sorts of odds to discover their True Identity. Apparently there's a big market for that sort of thing.'

'Yes, there would be.'

'We'll ring you if the car turns up.'

A few days later, Eleanor was at home watching children's television with George, who was too young for it, when the phone rang. She thought perhaps it was the policeman reporting that they'd found her car. She picked it up, there was a silence. 'Hallo,' she shouted. 'Is anyone there?'

'Eleanor?'

'Yes.'

'It's Eva. Eva Summers.'

'Eva, I saw you the other day! Going into a flower shop.'

'Yes, I know,' she said. 'That's why I'm ringing. I saw you, too. I just wanted to get in touch. How are you, Eleanor?'

'I'm fine.'

'How's Esther?'

'She's fine too. Well, sort of.'

'And all the rest of them?'

Eleanor wouldn't have known where to begin to fill Eva in on all the things that had happened since she absconded with her shopping basket. 'But what about you, Eva?'

'Oh, I'm okay. It was hard at first. But it's good now. I'm writing. It's the only way to do it. Please, Eleanor . . . ' Eva's voice accelerated as she thought Eleanor was about to interrupt her, 'Please, Eleanor, don't ask me where I'm living. We can't meet. You see, I've decided I can't have anything to do with my old life. It's too dangerous. I might get sucked back into it. But don't take it personally. I just wanted to say hallo. I think of you often. All the best, Eleanor!' She rang off.

Well I never! Eleanor sat on the floor with the phone in front of her. George crawled over and dumped a piece of rotten apple on her lap. 'Where did you find that, Georgie?'

He squeaked at her, climbed into her lap and reached for her breast. 'Not now, Georgie.' But he wasn't listening, and the phone rang again, so she was glad he'd got something in his mouth that would keep him quiet.

'Mrs Jenkinson? It's Constable Turner here. About your car.'

'Yes?'

'Do you want the bad news first, or the good news?'

'The good news.'

'The good news is that we've found the car. It's up by the university.'

'What's it doing there?'

'A lot of them turn up there, it's the students, they do it for a laugh.'

'Very funny. And the bad news?'

'Is that it hasn't got a steering wheel any more. So there's no point in going to fetch it.'

'You're joking!'

'Indeed I'm not. Wouldn't joke about a thing like that. Most serious matter.'

'What about the My Novels?' she asked.

'The what?' he said again.

'The manuscripts.'

'Oh, I don't know about those. We were only looking for the car. You must go and check that for yourself, Mrs Jenkinson.'

Eleanor phoned David at the university. He was in the middle of a class. One of his students answered. She imagined it was Fally, of the white gloves.

'They've found my car, David,' she began.

'Well, I'm sure that's very good news, but couldn't it keep till I've finished this?'

'I want you to meet me at the police station,' she persisted. 'You see, I've got to check whether anything's been stolen apart from the steering wheel.'

David sighed. 'Give me half an hour.'

The Peugeot lay savaged on a service road. The door had been forced, where the steering wheel had been there was an amputated limb, and next to it, a spaghetti of coloured wires, like a bleeding heart. But the manuscripts reposed in the back, untouched, including My Novel. Eleanor clasped it to her breast.

'You all right now, dear? They wouldn't have any use for a novel, now, would they? Have you informed the insurance company? I'll get the garage to pick the car up for you. Better luck next time.'

The savaging of her car called to Eleanor's mind the savaging and leaving of her heart and body by Jordan Herriot, and the unrepentant attack waged by life on the project of My Novel. Jordan had telephoned twice. It had felt not unlike Eva's call – a voice from the past. But Eva's message, on which the stealing of her car had so quickly been superimposed, blotting it out, was coming through more sharply now: retreat, disguise, in order to survive.

It was August, though not particularly hot: time for the Jenkinsons' annual holiday. As money was a bit tight this year (the costs of Myra and baby George, and Uncle Hal's gift to Eleanor having been invested in fripperies such as a printer, the car, the Eden Press, and various presents for Patsy and her ulcer, which Eleanor didn't know about), the Jenkinsons took a last-minute package holiday in Crete. This entailed a small badly built apartment on a noisy hillside with an incorrectly plumbed lavatory – the Jenkinsons' chief memory of the holiday would be of holding their noses.

David had refused to give Patsy the address. 'My ulcer's playing up,' she'd warned, as usual.

'It can explode for all I care,' he retorted, unusually unkindly.

Between My Novel and My Ulcer, David Jenkinson had had enough. He'd like a bit of peace with My Family for a change.

For the duration of the holiday, Bridget was moved, resisting, to a nursing home. She was fortunately much more occupied at the moment with events in the Queen's household than her own – the man arrested in Her Majesty's bedroom, the three Germans found lurking in the Palace shrubbery believing it to be Hyde Park, and the resignation of the Queen's Police Officer following his admission of having sex with a male prostitute.

'Was it *in* the Palace, do you think?' enquired Bridget, searching the newspaper short-sightedly for clues. 'Or outside? In the shrubbery, maybe?'

Heidi was now fourteen. She was a foot taller than Eleanor and quite magnificently pretty. Nearly black hair and eyes fitted her into the south Mediterranean landscape so you wouldn't really know the difference. Early in the two weeks, she formed a friendship with two teenagers in the flat beneath – Heidi was good at forming, but also dissolving, unions of this type. As the parents of the other teenagers had rented Vespas for them, thereby facilitating trips to the nightclubs of Aghios Nikolaus of television fame, Eleanor and David must do the same for Heidi. And off Heidi went as the sun set every day, her hair streaming out behind her on the rocky hillsides, her olive skin gleaming in the same modality as the setting sun. She was off to enforce the culture of youth in a generally harmless but spectacularly deafening way in various Cretan establishments. Eleanor worried about her. This anxiety pushed all the other worries into the background. What was Heidi up to? 'Nothing, Mum, leave me alone, can't you? You're only *jealous* anyway.'

Of what? Heidi's freedom, hedged with parental constraints, to have her hearing damaged by the insistent amplified beat of what they called music? Or of what parents never themselves were allowed to do as youngsters because such escapades hadn't yet been invented? Or, in Eleanor's case, of the opportunity to leave for an hour or two the still breast-feeding baby George who, though accustomed to purées of apple and peaches and carrots and potatoes and beef and chicken and oats and semolina, and all manner of substances from tins and packets, still preferred to watch the world from the incontrovertibly rooted vantage point of a mouthful of maternal flesh?

'He's too big for that, Mum!' said Eliza (nearly thirteen). 'It'll give him the wrong idea.' Of what, Eleanor wondered. And according to whom? 'Why don't you give him a cup, like the books say?' Still the peacemaker, she'd been scouring Eleanor's baby books for useful tips. They sat George up one day and gave him boiled milk in a cup, but he doused his chin in it, screwed up his face and pretended no more knowledge of the adult human drinking mechanism than a horse. When his mother picked him up to wipe his face, he pushed up her T-shirt with the sly abandon of long practice and filled his mouth with the beloved nipple.

'You've got to wean that child,' said David, sternly. 'He's wearing you out. Don't you think you ought to take some iron pills?' He'd got so used to recommending medical therapies for women's ills that he did it without noticing.

Mrs Standman, the mother of Heidi's friends in the flat below, advised the application of bitter substances to the nipples to put George off. Eleanor's heart heaved with a dense mass of love for this child of hers, not yet the requisite nine months old, whom the world was coercing to renounce his birthright. Now Jordan's gone, why should she give up this physical connection too? She looked at George feeding peaceably and remembered Jordan rooted to the same spot. George was an emblem of her other self, as well as this one, the one which, locked in domesticity, was able to produce nothing but more of the same.

David, Heidi and Eliza dispatched her for the day by herself to Aghios Nikolaus. 'It'll do you good, Mum,' they said, which was undoubtedly true. 'We'll deal with Georgie.' Which they did, and though it was delightful to have so much attention, it was his mother (or rather her breasts) for which George looked in between all the other tidbits they offered him.

He was asleep when Eleanor came back, replenished by the purchase in Aggie of a rather fine Kelim, and by the opportunity to dream and fantasize and remember without being constantly called to task for the absent expression on her face. But happily George woke in the night and she took him into bed with her, to luxuriate in the last moments of her last lactation. George's little hands pounded her flesh like a kitten its mother's fur. Eleanor thought of Jordan in Silicon Valley, and, caught between her son and her husband with no space to call her own, was seized with lust of a sexual kind, but also a less solubly ingrained and pent-up sense of longing for that release into the paradise of the imagination which appeared constantly to elude her.

The next morning she left George and David sleeping, and the girls in their feebly shuttered room, and took Heidi's Vespa silently down the bumpy track (so no-one would hear her leaving) en route to the bar in the nearest tiny village. She fell off twice, since she'd never been on one before. The pale gold stones stuck into her, and she coughed alarmingly with the dust. She dialled the long string of numbers through to Silicon Valley watched by a group of slightly alcoholized men. She had become aware of how much Jordan meant to her and wished to tell him so. The line crackled, a Californian soprano answered, instructing her to have a good day. But no, Jordan Herriot was not there, he'd gone to New York for a few days.

Eleanor, desolated, jealous, and fed up with everything again, bumped back on the Vespa to base camp. It was the Jenkinsons' wedding anniversary, which she had forgotten, and David had a present for her, an American book called *Shakespeare's Sisters*. 'It's about women's writing,' he explained. 'It's quite good, actually. Though I've only read the introduction. I had no idea there were so many of you.'

Eliza and Heidi gave both their parents a card congratulating them on not having got divorced yet, and George got diarrhoea due to all the feasts he'd been given the day before, consequently getting his own way and needing to be put back on 100% breast milk for medical reasons.

In this manner, nothing was solved – it merely went on and on. But Eleanor, in the interstices of this time *en famille* in Crete, nonetheless had the opportunity to meditate on certain critical issues. One of which was why David Jenkinson didn't know about Jordan Herriot, though he did suspect. He didn't *know*, decided Eleanor, both because she'd been clever, and because in the life of a woman who is trying to write, this very occupation – including even succeeding at it – serves as the blindfold for diverse others. From David Jenkinson's point of view, Eleanor's obsession with My Novel had been so all-encompassing that he could easily have blamed everything on it – her abstraction stemming from the business of Janice and Michelle in the toilet in Soho, and later with Ball; her escapades with Tom Sherringham; her deviation into the affair with Jordan Herriot; the sudden need for relief with Uncle Hal in Provence. It wasn't a coincidence that this was how, for Eleanor, they had started – as experiential qualifications for a would-be novelist. If it was a bit blind of David to view them thus, the opposite line, which was one that he quite plausibly might have taken, would have been worse. He could have attributed the very seriousness of the project of My Novel to other aspects of her life, including her real or imagined sexual roving. In other words, David Jenkinson could have been under the much more chauvinist illusion that when Eleanor wrote in her notebooks she was engaging in a form of sexual conjugation.

Aside from this, he lacked the imagination to consider her capable of running a love affair in parallel with a baby, a job and the continued pursuit of My Novel. She had always been much more multi-faceted than he'd given her credit for, and he was considerably less so than she'd at first thought. (One is tempted to consider this exemplary of the general division of labour by gender, but that's the subject of another book.)

Eleanor's knowledge of David's ignorance concerning Jordan Herriot didn't mean that she herself was free from guilt. How could she be? But in a subterranean kind of way she perceived him as guilty too. Of approving her writing in such a manner that was also undermining of it. As we saw when he invited her some years ago now to consider the effect upon her family of going public with it; approval in principle, disapproval in practice. He could never have said 'don't do it', and so only allowed the prohibition 'pretend not to be doing it' to escape his lips at moments when the project threatened materialization.

Did this make Jordan Herriot a form of covert resistance for Eleanor? She was simply too nice to engage directly in rebellion. But, hang on a minute, the niceness, though believable, wasn't simple – we may indeed consider it to be a form of the Angel in the House syndrome to which Virginia Woolf, whom one wouldn't have thought would have suffered from it particularly, addressed herself so well a number of years ago. There were many Angels in Eleanor Jenkinson's house, but most of them sheltered, their wings angelically folded, inside her head.

Nonetheless, an affair such as the one with Jordan Herriot, embarked on for one set of reasons, may continue for another. Thwarted in relation to My Novel, Eleanor's creativity flourished to some extent on the deceit, delusions and general difficulty of her relationship with Jordan. It was *her* secret, *her* business, just as My Novel was, and her writing career would have been.

It was in Crete that David broke the news to Eleanor of the trip to New Zealand. He'd deferred it until January, and it might not be for a full year that he went, but go he would. Also, he'd moved its location to somewhere marginally more central – Auckland – as Cuthbert Sloane had just got the chair there. 'At least we can fly direct,' he offered lamely. He didn't say it was Eleanor's place to accompany him, but it was obvious he thought this, also that he was only half-way cognizant of the problems involved in transplanting two adolescent girls from one secondary school system to another and back again, and of tending a mother with Alzheimer's Disease from a point exactly half-way round the globe. What would Eleanor do?

Extract from:

BAD WEATHER
BY ESTHER GRAY

They say it never rains but it pours.

A great grey sheet of mist and drizzle rolled over the countryside this morning, before our eyes almost, as we prepared to have breakfast on the terrace as usual. John – or was it Frank – said, 'We'll have to have a fire tonight, don't you think?' And Frank, or was it John, or it could possibly have been Drake, said, 'It's all very well to say that, my friend, but where's the wood?'

'Got to go out and hunt it down, chaps,' I told them. 'Take your guns and shoot some, preferably dry, crackly, and sweet-smelling, that's what I say.' They went off later in their macs, trudging off into the woods like reluctant gamekeepers.

Michelle and I made some more coffee to warm our hands on while they were away. We shut all the windows and sprayed the place with insecticide, but Mr Wasp, alias Jabberwocky, was still there humming and hahaing and not even willing to entertain the thought of death throes. Then the stuff got him, coating his wings in sticky substances, and he rolled around like nobody's business on the window pane, and I took a copy of Hare and Hounds *(the house is full of them) to him and laid him to rest on the back of an amber mare, but in the process I unfortunately decapitated the window also. Michelle went out and picked it up and we stuck it back with Sellotape. We didn't consider the men would notice. They were away an awfully long time anyway, and when they came back they only had two logs apiece and their merriment was most suspicious. When the paltry fire was lit, we played Scrabble for real money, and Michelle and I had no trouble in winning a small fortune. It's an ill wind that blows nobody any good, they said, but I could think of several that did. When the sun came out later, as I knew it would, there was the telegram lying on the mat – we didn't even hear the postman. 'You read it,' I said to Drake, 'I've had enough bad news for one day.'*

TWELVE

How Many Lightbulbs?

THE RHYTHM OF THE TRAIN, bisecting the little gorges and passing busily through unmanned stations, makes Eleanor feel sleepy. She rests her head against the back of the seat.

'Tired, love?'

'Not really. It's probably the booze at lunchtime.'

'It's good to see you relaxing.' David looks at her fondly. Her short hair is coloured with gold from the late sunshine: gold and silver mingle with the light brown it used to be. She's still a very attractive woman, he thinks. Time hasn't altered the taut and economical structure of her face, save to hang a few lines on it here and there. Laughter lines under the eyes, and at the corners of her mouth. It's her hands that have aged the most. They lie now, gnarled through usage, on the lap of her green flowered dress. The wedding ring sparkles insouciantly between the flowers.

Eleanor sleeps, her head turned into the maroon fabric of the seat. As her face relaxes, the lines seem to go, her skin glows with the gloss and clarity of a peach. Then she moves suddenly, changing her position, so as to fit her back against the carriage side, inserting her body into the recesses of the seat and away from the sun.

Sun. Sunlight in Marine Parade the day Ball came down with the money. She had to shield her eyes to see him properly. 'Here you are, Mrs J, count it if you like, but you don't need to. How about a drink to celebrate?'

His roving eye had picked up the two glasses collecting dust on a shelf. 'Here's to you, Mrs J! And the novel!'

Ball had an enormous penis. Quite the biggest she'd ever seen. 'Don't worry, Mrs J.' He was very matter-of-fact about it. It was magenta in the sunlight, like a piece of polished wood. She tried to fit her mouth around it. She'd never wanted to do that before. Ball had seemed to like it. He'd closed his eyes above her and moved a little now and then, urging himself against the insides of her cheeks and down her throat. She couldn't believe what she was doing!

It'd been a long time before he'd actually screwed her. First he explored her with his fingers and his hand and his mouth. He took particular pleasure in describing for her how she looked down there: 'like a butterfly, with its wings folded back'. Each of his manoeuvres seemed to bring her close to orgasm, but then he would stop. Either it was misjudgement on his part, or he knew exactly what he was doing.

The rest of him was very thin and covered in a dark down. He put it in from behind. Lying behind her he put one hand on her breast and one between her legs and as he moved, but only a little, it was sufficient to bring her back to the edge again. He held her there for quite some time, and then suddenly he imposed on them a more urgent way of moving, speaking crudely into her ear, and in a few minutes – not more than one or two probably – she came several times with a vigorousness unknown to her before.

In January 1982 David Jenkinson flew to New Zealand via Los Angeles where he took the opportunity to attend a conference on 'Peasant Subcultures: their role in the process of resisting capitalist economic development'.

Eleanor stayed in Hove to look after Heidi, Eliza, George and Bridget, and to a lesser extent herself. Myra's dynamism swept over them from time to time when Ken made it, and in between times she put in sufficient hours to free Eleanor for (some) other pursuits. Bridget was going downhill; she had developed incontinence and the habit of appearing early in the morning with an armful of wet sheets complaining that she couldn't find Somerset, who needed to set more seriously about the business of toilet training Celia. She was found descending towards the sea by night. Her confusion was now almost absolute, and any conversation sited squarely in the here and now with her daughter or granddaughters nearly impossible.

To Eleanor it was all very trying, and emotionally fatiguing too, as she still looked at Bridget and was inclined to see the mother she would have liked to have had – or thought she would, which might have been different.

And Jordan Herriot? Abandoned again? Taking second place to Eleanor's ménage? Well, yes and no. Though the Monday to Friday sojourn with Jordan was over, due to Jordan's recall to Silicon Valley, that episode, if the truth were told, had become rather testing for both of them. Lovers' dreams of intimacy rarely take account of the nightmarish quality most dreams have. Since then, Jordan had become peripatetic again; he was presently off doing another conference centre in Sienna, and after that he would be in Rio. Between times he stayed where he could, and if he couldn't stay with Eleanor, that was only what he was used to. Absence both made the heart grow fonder, and caused what was out of sight to be out of mind. Eleanor thought of Jordan, and Jordan of Eleanor. But as time and space intervened, what was remembered was increasingly not the way it was, but rather the way each of them would have liked it to have been. Eleanor forgot Jordan's rages and complaints and refusal to do anything but live in the present. Jordan's image of Eleanor reconstituted itself as the fragile, marginal creature of the Dutch tulip fields, and the harassed housewife and mother-of-all slipped quietly away.

For Eleanor then, some things didn't thrive while others did. These included the Eden Press: in its first year it had published seven books, all of which had met with unusual acclaim. Araminta and Rowan had worked hard and deserved success. Early in 1983 they cancelled the lease on the Fulham Road office and moved to Clerkenwell, which attracted them with its down-market postcode, proximity to Sadlers' Wells (Araminta was a closet ballet freak) and acres of perfectly wonderful decrepit nineteenth-century housing. They bought a bit of this, the lower two floors to be occupied by the Eden Press, the upper two by themselves. The expansion was marked by the acquisition of extra staff. Eleanor, still on the payroll, or rather a co-MD, enquired as to whether they wished to retain her services, or had the period of her usefulness to them ended? Should she buy herself out, or whatever the phrase is? George was weaned, so that was all right. (Araminta and Rowan now of course asked rather fondly after him, and Eleanor carried a batch of renewable photos in her purse.)

And how was My Novel these days? Eleanor asked herself this from time to time.

'Well, as you know, I've taken the offending scenes out,' she answered.

'You mean those ones a third of which Tom Sherringham said you should rewrite?'

'That's correct.'

'And?'

'Well, I'm not sure I like it without.'

'Why not?'

'It's somewhat bland. It strikes me as the same as much other fiction. That may partly be because I've been reading such a lot recently – you know, with all that breast-feeding – and I've absolutely had it up to here with Fay Weldon, Margaret Drabble, Iris Murdoch, Anita Brookner, Susan Hill, Margaret Atwood, Marge Piercy, and others of lesser ilk such as Sara Maitland and someone called Barbara Trapido who seems to me to write very amusingly about absolutely nothing. I wonder, is that what I do?'

'No, of course not. Put the thought from your mind. By the way, do you only read women's fiction these days?'

'Not really. But I suppose I do tend to turn to it to see if it's got answers I haven't.'

'And has it?'

'If I said yes, then I'd never write anything again, would I? But if I said no, that'd be very arrogant of me wouldn't it?'

'Perhaps a bit more arrogance is in order, Eleanor Jenkinson. Have you considered that?'

'It has crossed my mind, I admit. It's for that reason that I've retained the non-bowdlerized version of My Novel. In fact, My Novel now exists in four distinct forms. Would you like me to tell you about them?'

'Go ahead.'

'Format number one: (these aren't in chronological, rather in accidental, order) is My Novel as it existed at the time I met Jordan Herriot. That's saved under the heading of *Stonechat*.'

'Is there any particular reason for the obscure heading?'

'All my headings are taken from the Collins *Gem Guide to British Birds*. To anticipate your next question, it seemed to me as good a source as any of suggestive titles. It's pocket-sized also, like the witch-hunting manual called *Malleus Maleficarum* which was extensively used in the Middle Ages. Stonechat, by the way, is a small bird, twelve centimetres in length, belonging to the species *Turdidae*. It's currently decreasing in numbers as stonechats die a lot whenever the weather's bad. The males make a great deal of noise and have terracotta underparts, whereas the female stonechat could easily be mistaken for another kind of bird altogether.

'Format number one of My Novel, *Stonechat*, is 100,000 words, not twelve centimetres, long. I'm quite fond of it, though not overtly so. For format number two we must go back in time – format number two is saved under the heading *Whitethroat*. This is substantially reconstructed from my notebooks as being the absolutely original version, the pre-experience, certainly pre-Tom Sherringham one, as you might say. Whitethroats, species *Sylviidae* – warblers – make a harsh scolding noise rather like irritated housewives. They skulk in nettlebeds and suchlike. Brambles, briars, etc. The species is named after the markings the male carries – specifically a pure white throat. The female will only nest in bushy messes, especially rough wasteland. I'm also fond of this one, though I suspect out of a kind of lingering fondness for the nice ordinary uncorrupted warbler I once was.

'Format number three is more recent, but not the most recent version. Called *Crossbill* on my Apple, it is a bit as it sounds: the result of a sort of mild anger at You Know Who's reaction to My Novel. A somewhat sanitized version, as I've already said. Crossbills – species *Fringillidae* – are distinguished by their possession of twisted mandibles with which they are able to desecrate larch, spruce and pine cones. However, these extras aren't always visible, as they tend to swing upside down like parrots.

'Finally we have the file named *Waxwing*. This is the one I like best, as it isn't historical but progressive. *Waxwing* takes Esther Gray out of the streets of Paris and into the future, where she no longer has the aspect of a seditious upstart, but rather of a wisewoman in the old sense of that word. Waxwings – species *Bombycillidae* – are known for feeding on scarlet berries. They are also quite fearless, flying so high that it's difficult to categorize them at all. They have a sibilant trilling call – a kind of elegant musical buzzing – which alarms of any sort will immediately transform into an insistent shrilling sound, like a stuck doorbell.'

'Have you shown *Waxwing* to David Jenkinson?'

'What a stupid question! No, of course I haven't. Consider *Waxwing* a sort of diary, rather. Though not of the confessional sort. My dislike of that word when applied to words women write has been intense ever since the day I realized it would never have been used to refer to Proust. Despite the fact that Proust's moribund self-pitying (though not self-effacing) wanderings through the past are nothing if not based on a horrid need to empty out the *poubelle* in his own soul.'

'Why don't you give *Waxwing* to the Eden Press? Forget *Stonechat*, *Whitethroat*, and *Crossbill* entirely and just go for *Waxwing*?'

'Same problem as before. What is fiction if not fact in disguise? Or fact if not the stuff of which fiction is made? Maybe I'll go to Auckland for a while. Be a don's wife, for a change.'

'Does Microsoft Inc. reach as far as New Zealand?'

'Australia only. I could commute; are you suggesting I commute? Auckland–Sydney return, please. But then Heidi's in her last year before O levels. Eliza's going to menstruate soon. At least we're out of the headlice era. For a while.'

I am tempted to say, said Eleanor Jenkinson to herself, that for God's sake, if not your own, you should get off your backside and get on with something. It doesn't much matter what it is, but this, that we're in now, is a nasty kind of stasis. Most putrefying. No-one is being edified. That's in part because everyone's in the right place. David Jenkinson is entertaining avid undergraduates and culture-starved expatriate academics in Auckland undisturbed by much in the way of domestic worries. Jordan Herriot's fixing bugs on an Italian hillside. The Jenkinson children are in Hove, and George is on cows' milk at last. Bridget's asleep in a pool of urine dreaming of the arbours of Muddenham Grange. Araminta and Rowan are womaning the Eden Press from their restored merchant's domain in St John's Hill, EC1, with an astonishingly fecund catalogue for 1984 coming off the presses (lesbian women's studies, an anthology of translated German feminist poetry, a vegan feminist cookbook, a history of women musicians, two novels called *Crab Apple*, and *As the Fish Swims or Memoirs of a Broken Bicycle* and, last and definitely least, the aforesaid autobiography by the non-pseudonymous Bea Purson.) Tom Sherringham's teaching creative writing in Saratoga Springs, where artificially oestrogenized women with shaven armpits probably twist him round their little fingers and in a number of other places. Ball is on remand and the Roller's in the garage. Janice Carew is in the nick being interrogated about her mistress-minding of the soft porn video business in Soho.

As much as Janice protested her innocence – or at least her mainly housekeeping role in the whole affair – the police considered they

231

were nailing her to the ground. For Janice looked brassy to them, and far from gullible. Her nails, her voice and her mind were sharp, her clothes hadn't come from M&S. Marlon's circumcision, indeed, had been done in a private hospital which did a lot of these, including the female type which ought to have been illegal. Marlon and his brother Eliot were at home with Janice's mum. She thought they were with Drake, but Drake had beaten a retreat, never having been much of a one to face the music.

Janice was charged with running a house of vice. There was a court case and she was found guilty and fined £500 with costs. An application for legal aid was turned down as Janice had a lot of money invested in a named bank account. Marlon and Eliot in tow, she set off to discuss some unsolved business from the past with Eleanor Jenkinson.

'Now listen to me, Mrs J,' she said, 'I helped you, didn't I? When you came to me with this whorish account of yours of life in a Spanish slum?'

'Not whorish. And Paris.'

'Yes, well, it's all the same to me, I'm sure. And there you were with this baby you didn't want, and I made you see the light over that as well, didn't I?'

'Well, I . . . '

'That's right, I did.'

Janice's self-satisfied look was ruffled only by Eliot pulling at her white linen trouser leg. 'Can we go to the seaside now, Mum, you said we could go and paddle in the sea.' (This interview was taking place in Hove.)

'What are you getting at, Janice?'

'The injustices of class,' she said.

Eleanor ignored this, not knowing what to make of it. 'It wasn't all one way. I helped you, too.'

'With the handout, you mean? But you couldn't face giving it to me direct, could you, Mrs J? That'd be too much like charity. The lady of the manor, alms to the poor, the penny'd drop then, wouldn't it? So you slipped it to poor old Ball, and he's supposed to hand it on. Which he might not have done, but he did. Yes, it didn't come amiss. But it didn't repair your sins, either. You can't pretend we're equal because of that or anything else, can you, Mrs J?'

'I didn't. I'm not.' George Henry, now a robust one-and-a-half-year-old, was completely transfixed by Marlon and Eliot, who were systematically taking all his toys and burying them in the garden. Worms, encountered in this process, and encouraged by a recent rainfall, were being bisected with what could only be described as unrestrained war cries. 'Don't you discipline your children, Janice?'

'What's discipline, Mrs J? You mean, why don't I make them behave better in this nice house of yours? Well, why should I? They haven't got a nice home of their own to misbehave in any more. So they have to misbehave in someone else's. George here will recover. He's quite enjoying it, really. Look at him, his dear little eyes are fairly popping out of his head. Handsome youth, isn't he? I expect he was reared on what my Drake would call tittie milk, wasn't he? And on organic foods of various kinds. That's another thing the lower classes can't do, isn't it?

'So, Mrs J, I'll tell you now what I really thought of Your Novel. I thought it was the most boring, self-indulgent piece of tripe I've ever read. The sex scenes were mildly titillating. I showed them to Ball, as a matter of fact (I didn't ask your permission, but then you didn't ask mine for some of the uses you've made of me), and we employed them as the basis of a rather nice small series of films that sold particularly well in Rotterdam. But the rest of My or rather Your Novel – yuk! She's an empty, spoilt middle-class girl, your heroine, whose name I forget – it must be very forgettable. All she discovers is that reality isn't nice, which is what some of us grew up knowing anyway. And who's got the resources to save herself from all that? She has. You have. Not me. Or I, is it?

'You should try life from where I've lived it, Mrs J. Then perhaps you wouldn't be possessed of such a desire to write about it.'

Marlon was now burying George under the clematis. George's straits would have been even more dire had Bridget not pruned the plant severely.

Eleanor went out to salvage her son from the worm-ridden earth. Or the injustices of class. When she came back, Janice's anger had softened and edged itself into a few tears. 'I didn't mean it, Mrs J,' she said, sniffing, 'though I did need to say it. I've been having a bad time recently, as you know. My nerves are in shreds. I keep getting these palpitations – I've got some beta blockers in my handbag. Marlon, Eliot, come here.' But they'd turned their attention to next door's cat and didn't hear her. George, whimpering, clutched his mother with gritty hands.

'Shall we take them all to the seaside, Mrs J?'

'If you like,' said Eleanor. 'But you did mean it, Janice. We're not even sisters under the skin, are we? You're material for My Novel, which is a substitute for My Life, but you'll never write one of your own, will you? You'll never use me as I've used you.'

On 21 July, Eleanor was in Clerkenwell savaging the manuscript of *Memoirs of a Broken Bicycle* (the savaging included the removal of the first half of its title). She still enjoyed such labours, though the aim nowadays was rather more constructive than it had been formerly, at Maitland & Ware, when she had used it to deflate young male writers' hopelessly overextended self-esteem. Some of them would never forgive her, which was what she'd intended.

Myra called her from Hove. 'It's your mum, Eleanor, I'm afraid to say she's had an accident. She got out again. I was reading George a story and I must have missed the click of the gate. I'm really sorry. It was a grey Talbot. The end was quick.'

After the funeral, Eleanor burnt all Bridget's bedding and took the children to New Zealand.

This was probably a mistake. Eleanor reached this conclusion fairly early on, in the aeroplane shortly after the Bahrain stop. Heidi and Eliza had made off to admire the bangles in the overheated airport concourse, and George on his reins was having a go at a pink Sony cassette recorder. He hadn't slept yet, nor would he, until shortly before Singapore, which meant he would have to be woken, an act that would put him in an even worse temper than he would have been with no sleep at all.

Heidi and Eliza were thrilled by the red sign at Singapore airport which said, 'Welcome to Singapore. Warning: Death for Drug Traffickers.' Eleanor had taken one room for all of them for the night in the Hotel Mandarin. It wasn't ready when they got there, and it wasn't the authoritative tone of her complaining voice (or her tiny figure, hardly visible above the leather-covered counter), but George's irascible screams that made the management hand over the key to an Executive instead of an Ordinary room. Heidi put the television on and Eliza buried her head in the *Straits Times*' small ads. Eleanor dropped George in the bath for a spot of water therapy. Though he slept eventually, it got worse before it got better as the fire alarm went off outside their door ('only a rehearsal, Madam'), and then a couple of tour operators phoned, inviting the Jenkinsons on a tour of the city which would take in several nightclubs. Fortunately Heidi and Eliza didn't get wind of this.

In Auckland, David was ensconced in a drab little flat near the university and a park called the Domain containing native navy blue birds, but at least there was no fire alarm in the flat (there was no kettle or heating either). David had made up his mind to save his marriage, which should have been sufficient to set off alternative alarms in Eleanor's head. 'We're only staying six weeks,' she warned. 'The girls must get back to school.'

Relax, Eleanor Jenkinson! Perhaps you have an opportunity here to sort out both your private life and My Novel? Auckland is sufficiently far away from the normal hassles and amusements – a fine place to break set, in other words.

It was the middle of the antipodean winter. Rain fell intermittently on Auckland's pleasant streets, on the gracefully courting swans of Western Springs, and on the silver beaches of the west coast. There were days of bright sunshine, too. The air smelt clean. Everyone at the university was kind. All sorts of tours were planned for the Jenkinsons: such a nice family! They were to go up to the Coromandel Peninsula, Land of the Big Boat Challenge, to Buffalo Beach Whitianga, and then to climb Mount Moehau, an area sacred to the Maoris as one of their canoe-captains was buried there – the children might like to go rockhounding – then down to Rotorua, city of boiling mud, not forgetting to take in the limestone caves of Waitomo where glow worms twinkled from the ceiling – something else for the children there – and farther still to the South Island, to Dunedin, where there were seals and penguins, and to Queenstown from where they might, if they were lucky, be able to fly up into fjordland.

One night during the first week of their holiday, Eleanor sat alone in a jacuzzi in Rotorua. David had taken George for an early supper in the Trellis Brasserie (café to him) and the girls were watching something unsuitable on the hotel video, cramming themselves with chips (crisps to you). Eleanor slipped quietly down to the sauna and jacuzzi area when no-one was looking. Air florid with the smell of methane seeped in under the jacuzzi door. She turned the dial up to its fastest speed, lay naked in its blue bubbling metallic depths, and cried with the endless struggle of it all. For her mother, Bridget, mown down by the grey Talbot in Hove, and before that by her decaying brain cells. For Jordan Herriot, loved and left with difficulty, and heard from now in the form of enveloped postcards from Mediterranean places on which he wrote of olive groves and oranges glinting on trees, and the scent of mimosa at sunset, and the hum of mosquitoes in the sapphire darkness. Where, oh where, was the bad penny that was going to turn up again? Oh Jordan! For My Novel, consigned to computer files, harassed by the ingenuity of others to defeat any other emergence from its life in Eleanor's head . . . but then the saga of My Novel was pretty boring, wasn't it?

The next day the Jenkinsons went to Waimungu Thermal Valley, where the sight of mud pools plopping away and fumes rising from steamy blue water was very jolly. They took the Valley walk through a bushland riddled with silent cicadas, admiring the chemical tessellations of the scenery: emerald water, orange-red cliffs, champagne-tinted mud. George was in good spirits and catapulted himself into the steam, against the rocks and generally everywhere he wasn't supposed to go. He pulled down his little trousers at a place called Hot Water Creek and peed in the sunlight (our hero was now at toilet training stage) and was astonished to see his pee sizzle on the stones. He repeated this exercise constantly elsewhere to see if he could obtain the same effect.

Eleanor did begin to relax. In Queenstown, she was persuaded by Heidi and Eliza to go in a helicopter up a mountain. They all sat squashed next to the pilot and thoroughly strapped in. While the girls enthused and pointed and wriggled, Eleanor sat motionless and about to throw up (this was called relaxation). They held one of her hands each. Eventually their exuberance was catching. From a patch of snow on the top of a mountain encircled with branches of tough hazel grass Eleanor thought she could see little George down the mountain peeing into the still waters of the lake ('the purest water in the world' said the guidebook referring to a time before George got here).

'Are you over it, Mum?' asked Eliza suddenly the next day as the Jenkinsons stood on the steamship HMS *Earnshaw*, which ploughed parties of mostly Japanese tourists across the lake.

'Am I over what, darling?' Eleanor watched the blue-grey mountains sliding by. She switched her eyes to Eliza's silky face, against which the sea wind whipped a side of milk-blonde hair.

'You know, Granny's death.'

'It wasn't unexpected. People must die.'

'And she was a bit of a nuisance, wasn't she?' Eliza was sounding her out.

'A bit. But so may I be to you.'

'No, you won't, Mummy! I'll always love you!' Eliza put her arms around Eleanor. She was taller already, tall and strong and confident.

But it was Heidi who said the most surprising thing. They were looking at the stars on the balcony of the girls' hotel room. Eliza was bathing George, loud splashing noises could be heard through the open doors. The stars were not the usual ones, as the Jenkinsons were upside down; Heidi knew about these things, and pointed out the Southern Cross to her mother; and how she might expect to see the Corona Australis farther to the East. Eleanor rested her arms on the balcony rail, staring out across the darkness.

'We're having a good time, aren't we, Mum?' confided Heidi.

'Yes, darling, we are.'

'As good a time as you ever had writing My Novel?'

'Well, perhaps.'

'Come on, Mum, admit it!'

Eleanor smiled, but Heidi saw. 'Why isn't it enough to *live* life, Mum, without struggling to write about it as well? Living is an achievement of its *own*.'

'Is it?'

'Look at us!' instructed her daughter. 'Weren't we worth it? Why can't *we* be your project, why do you have to produce anything else apart from us? No' – she saw Eleanor was about to speak – 'don't tell me I'll understand it all one day when I'm grown up. That's crap, and you know it. There are some things young people understand better. Listen to me, Mum. For once.'

Extract from:

LOST IN MIRRORS
BY ESTHER GRAY

The church bell struck ten. Monday morning, a wet August day. Eva went for a walk before sitting down to write a Foreword for the volume of her short stories due out in the spring: Still Life in a Field.

In Eva's garden, nesting blackbirds at the top of the old apple tree made an unholy commotion; a domestic dispute had been in train up there through most of the late spring and early summer. A couple of apples fell in consequence as Eva passed the tree. A hard, bright green, they rolled in the stubbly grass to lie with others in various stages of disintegration. I must rake the lawn, said Eva to herself, in that way people who live alone have of talking to themselves – but also to promise herself the reward of a pleasing, soothing, mindless task at the end of a day of concentrated mental labour.

The lonicera japonica she'd planted last weekend by the back wall had new shoots on it. And the blush-pink climbing rose she'd moved from a place where it had only the sky to climb to had sprung green growths. Leaves edged with traces of vermillion stood out against the old grey stone wall, into which the rose could now settle whatever attachments were necessary.

She closed the gate, and turned right. A tigerish cat from the end cottage paused in its walk round the top of the high wall to watch her balefully as she passed down the lane and in front of the farm vegetable garden. Runner beans with their marvellous orange-red flowers streaked like strips of lightning from land to sky. She took the road out of the village, away from the enclosure of clustered old stone houses and people going about their daily business, out into the open countryside.

It was a direction she'd taken many times over the past year since she'd acquired the house. Most of the time she was alone in it, though Luke visited whenever he had time – the rock band he'd helped to set up was doing well, and he didn't like taking much time away from it. She was pleased for him; he was happy. Christian found his son's choice of lifestyle more problematic, though. He thought it was because Luke hadn't found what he wanted to do. It was impossible for Christian to grasp that this was what he wanted to do. At least Belinda was settled and safe. She taught English at a girls' secondary school in Leicester, and had a daughter, Mary, from her marriage to an earnest, chess-playing physicist. Belinda brought Mary to see her grandmother sometimes, but not Joel, for Joel and Eva rubbed each other up the wrong way. These days Eva couldn't be bothered to say what people wanted to hear. She said what she thought instead. She had the reputation of being an eccentric old woman. It was a reputation she felt as comfortable with as the stone wall opposite her house revelled in the moss that grew out of and over its grainy surfaces. Made up of rumours, half-known episodes, fact and fiction knitted together, Eva's reputation was truer to the core, the kernel of Eva Summers, than any other description she could give.

Eva sees Christian regularly. He comes to have a meal once a month or so; she goes to London about as often to see her agent and him. They take short holidays together. A weekend in Vienna, or Norfolk. They're companions. Christian, instructed by Eva not to think of it as a marriage, has shifted his ideological gaze sufficiently to allow her to think the word 'wife' banished from his vocabulary. It isn't, of course, but she will never hear him speak it again, which is what matters.

Where the road divides, Eva takes neither proffered route, cutting across instead to a path between two fields. On her left is a field of cut corn, sharp as a young man's beard, utterly golden under the grey-blue rainbelly of the sky. On her right, a second field of uncut wheat sways like heavy silk in the light southerly wind. The full bodied white-gold grains strain the thin stalks, but the stalks won't break until the day of harvesting has come.

Out in the middle of the fields, Eva stands still, and concentrates on the melange of sounds and sights presenting themselves to her. From the river meadow of Church Farm fat lambs call to one another. Birds chatter; a flock of starlings cuts whirring wings through the air. A combine harvester starts up; the post van comes down the hill. Something moves in the corn, something she will never see. Ahead on the skyline an irregular range of trees, deep green like soldiers in uniform, cuts shapes from the sky. To her right, down a hollow and up and out of it again on a hill, an assembly of grey and red stone marks the next village looking across at her with a territorial air. And then, back the way she's come, the path stretches straight till it tapers out in a path of dry grass, where scarlet poppies dance in the wind at the edge of the wheat field, opening their petals and waiting for the rain.

Field and village and flower and cloud are joined in a cycle of mutual dependency. Each feeds off the other, and gives it

*life, taking what will one day be given back. To speak of their
separate identities is as false as the cuckoo's song, or as the promise
of the sunrise on a day that will be eaten up by rain. In the
interconnectedness of nature, human lives have a place most of
us have forgotten. Time weaves a different web of intricacies
which preoccupy us. Caught like spiders in this web, we see ourselves in each raindrop as in a mirror, and are confused by
what we see.*

*But each image is the same as the next. Then and now and
tomorrow are all the same; the harvested field the same as the
uncut one; the thirsty poppies the same as those that have drunk.
This Eva Summers the same as that one. Go home, Eva, and stop
thinking about who you are; time will tell its own pack of lies, and
you have, after all, written your own story.*

Eleanor Jenkinson and her children flew back to England on 3
September. David would follow in November.

Heidi and Eliza went back to school. George went to playgroup.
Eleanor went to London to see Jordan Herriot, who was temporarily
back from Silicon Valley and his other wanderings.

Jordan was golden brown all over and flushed with success as well.
'I'm going to set up my own business, Eleanor!' he told her. 'I'm
going to sell software in Sicily!'

'I wouldn't have thought there was much demand for it there,' she
remarked caustically.

'Poor old Ellie! You don't change, do you? We can't all be failures,
you know,' he said, poking her in the ribs.

They were in a delicate pink restaurant called Phood, and had just
ordered monkfish and cucumber kebabs. Jordan never ate red meat
these days.

'So what gave you the capitalist bug at last?' she enquired
suspiciously.

'Time,' he said. 'I got fed up with protesting against my background.
It wasn't interesting any more. I decided I wanted some money. I
wanted to be rich.'

'And are you?'

'Passably. Passably.' He smiled at her over the bubbles of his
Perrier water.

'Well, that's nice for you.' She was fairly choked by all this.

'I was only joking about the failures bit,' he said anxiously.

'I know.'

'Come with me to Sicily,' he invited. 'We could do desktop publishing together. We could launch *Stonechat* and *Whitethroat* and *Crossbill* and *Waxwing* under four different names.'

'It's too late,' she told him.

'I love you, Eleanor Jenkinson!'

'Love isn't enough. And I'm not a failure, Jordan. That's only what *you* think.'

THIRTEEN

Lost in Mirrors

ELEANOR HAS WOKEN UP, expecting to get off. But the train
back from Capdenac is the nonstopping variety. As they speed
through the little station which hosted them that morning,
Eleanor looks at David and David tries to avoid Eleanor's look until
finally he says, 'Sorry. It simply didn't occur to me. To ask whether
the train stopped on the way back. It stopped on the way there, so
why should the return be any different?'

'I hate you,' says Eleanor mildly. 'And I don't want to stay the night
in Brive.' The woman opposite them, fleshy in a blue-zipped dress and
quietly masticating throughout, her hand purposely lodged on a small
green suitcase, watches with interest. A marital dispute is a marital
dispute in any language. Eleanor storms off to the W.C., but this can
only be a temporary solution. David stares solidly at the landscape.
The shadows are longer now, the stone boulders menacing instead
of brave. He takes out his Michelin and looks for knives and forks
in Brive.

'There must be a train back again!'

He doesn't want to commit himself. They reach Brive at eight.
David asks: no, no train to Capdenac until 5.30 a.m. 'You bloody
idiot!' She's rooted in a pool of sunshine outside the station. The
woman from the train stands there, captivated. David takes Eleanor's
arm. He is sweating. Has he spoilt it all with his silly mistake?

'Come on, Ellie . . . '

'Don't Ellie me! I'm not having this, you know!'

'It's a mistake anyone could make.'

'Not me. I wouldn't have made it.'

'You're not as perfect as you make out.' As a matter of fact, it is
in these moments of absurd desperation, of utter infantile pointless
rage, that David Jenkinson finds his wife most perfect. In her tiny,

poised, concentrated venom, so dire a reminder of what she's never able to be the rest of the time.

'Are you going to stand there all night?'

'Well, I'm certainly not spending it with you!'

'Please Eleanor! We can find a nice hotel; I've got my credit card. You can phone George. You'd like that, wouldn't you? There may even be a shop open still, we can buy some toothbrushes. It's really not as bad as all that. We could have a nice meal . . . '

'Piss off!'

'Okay, if you like.' David knows when he's beaten, and is cross himself now. He can't be bothered with trying to pacify her any more. If she wants to be stupid and go off on her own, let her do it! He peers into the Michelin. 'I'll be at Le Manoir de Mon Ami if you want me. And if they do.'

She watches him march off towards the town. When she can't see him any more, she goes back into the station and sits down. After a while she takes out of her bag her purple notebook and begins to write:

'This is the diary of Eva Summers, a friend of mine, who walked out of my life many years ago. As I have often thought about Eva with fondness since, even for quirks such as her shopping basket on wheels and poorly controlled hearing aid, so I now find a need to construct the fabric of her life from the time she left Wimbledon, which was, I believe, on 7 September, 1968, at about 7 p.m.

'It is also the diary of Esther Gray, a woman who experienced various adventures and misadventures with men in Paris and other places, and who has written a number of volumes of autobiography, and of fiction (though it is sometimes difficult to tell the difference between the two). Esther Gray is now dead, due to a piece of deliberate male carelessness. She was a fine woman, and deserved a more complete life than she was able (enabled) to have.

'It is also the diary of one Eleanor Jenkinson, a writer, who has filled sixty-four notebooks (Ref. 141. Punched for filing), and who took half a lifetime to bring to fruition a project killed, unlike Esther Gray, many times, but whose sheer vitality kept causing it to erupt like a querulous volcano. I speak here, of course, not only of Eleanor Jenkinson's My Novel, but of Eleanor Jenkinson's My Life.

'The reason why this diary can be all of these things at the same time is straightforward: Eva, Esther, and Eleanor can all be seen as different solutions to the same problem. The problem of women, life and writing. Eva absented herself from ordinary life in order to write. Esther was never in it in the first place. Eleanor has struggled constantly with it, so much so that her only moments of success have tended to involve the assumption of one alter ego or another: the refugee or the ghost.'

Eleanor pauses in her writing at this point, as there are too many people walking past her seat. She closes her notebook and stands up. She's going to look for somewhere more peaceful. But, first, she is hungry and must do something about that.

Outside the station a sign says 'Bar Tabac Taxi Ambulance'. She crosses the forecourt and sits down. The waiter, a pretty, swift-moving youth, gives her a plastic-coated menu. Eleanor orders some *frites*, a *Croque Monsieur* and some wine. He looks a little surprised at her order, but takes it all the same. Then she purchases a packet of Gauloises, which she hasn't done for twenty-five years. The taste is wholesomely acrid, as evocative as anybody's madeleines. Eleanor blows smoke rings around herself with enormous aplomb, as though she's been doing so all her life. The scent and the fug envelop her small, evanescent figure – she's a creature living in a cloud, scudding across the sky or hovering with almost no movement at all, according to the strength and direction of the prevailing wind.

She drinks the wine, awaits the food and watches, alert and writer-like, for the sunset. The heat of the day has diminished slowly, and with it the intensity and fixed brilliance of the light. Shadows lengthen; of trees and buildings, telegraph poles and parked cars, bottles of wine and people strolling or scurrying home. The pace of life and conversation increase now that the burden of the heat has lifted. Eleanor writes, noting all this, and inscribing in the purple notebook the imagined and curiously sustaining saga of Eva Summers. At last the inflamed golden globe of the sun drops below the horizon of trees and rooftops, like the slow movement of a symphony – the Eroica perhaps, though that has the rhythm of a funeral march, and this sun, though dying for Eleanor Jenkinson now, is disappearing from view only to slip back into the sky again after an interval designed to give it a decent welcome. No death, then, but the simple reiteration of astronomical rhythms. Which, being predictable, have as much elegiacal certainty as is to be found anywhere in the galaxy.

There are church bells issuing their medieval tones across the valley, a collision of metals carried in the desiccated air, reverberating in whirlpooled echoes out of stone and rock and crag. A white cat wraps itself around Eleanor's ankles, its fur holding the heat. When she's eaten, she orders some more wine and writes in her notebook until the lights of the town are spread out below her as bright as those above: Venus, and the Milky Way, and lights that do more than twinkle, being satellites or shooting stars. Eleanor thinks about her son, George, in England, who may at this very moment be studying the heavens with his new eight-by-forty telescope.

It is by now quite late. Eleanor, sitting in the café, would be content to sit here a good deal longer, but the pretty waiter is looking at her – his other clients have left, and he'd like to turn out the lights and bolt the door for the night. She smiles at him, leaves money, recrosses the forecourt to the station. A late train has just come in, and one going to Paris and to Le Havre carrying tourist cars is preparing to leave. There are people with suitcases and rucksacks studying timetables. Should Eleanor search out Le Manoir de Mon Ami and David, which is what he expects her to do, or should she take a train herself, perhaps? Biarritz, Amsterdam, Berlin, Budapest, Pisa, Innsbruck: the destinations assemble in her mind, a seductive index of possibilities beckoning with alternative but parallel delights.

She remembers Tom Sherringham and before him David Jenkinson himself: a woman like you, with little experience of the world, now how can you really expect to write in such a way that you will be believed? But she had experience; has: experience of her place in the world. Isn't this enough? And if it is, which, now, standing here, she believes it must be, what were those adventures for – that dabbling in the semi-legal pornographic rudely sensuous domain, those faintly challenging cross-class encounters, those flimsy excursions out of her own life and into others? What was it all *for*?

I did it for My Novel, she says defensively by way of explanation to herself.

Yes, I know, says Esther Gray, in whose name it is that Eleanor Jenkinson has done nearly everything, but there are two contrasting discourses here: in one, reality is the template for fiction, while the other is the inverse of this. You believed the first, my friend, though the second is more true to my own experience, being, as you would say, myself the created one; not, perhaps, so much in your own image but in one you once or forever glimpsed in a mirror and thought it would be nice to own. But constructed images become repositories of their own power. Naming includes silences. Identities grow, and out of the chrysalis comes the butterfly with skulls on its wings. We wing our way to freedom, Eleanor Jenkinson, those of us that people like you, especially perhaps women like you, create, and as we caper across the landscape we take you with us. Assumptions of literary structure and even of pseudonymity can't contain us. Once we are gone, so are you.

Eleanor Jenkinson sits on a seat in Brive station listening to Esther Gray's didactic moralizing, and preparing Eva Summers' version in her head. As it's the height of the tourist season, the station won't close and there will be a few people about throughout the night. The white cat will come from the café and warm her feet because it's here that the cat knows she will get her early morning milk.

For a while Eleanor sleeps, but she's only slipped down a rung or two of the ladder into unconsciousness. Her mind, cushioned from deeper somnolence by this unusual habitat, is thus able to play with themes from the remote and yesterday's past, imposing each on the other like shadow puppets – an imperial elision, as richly imagined as anything conscious could be, and suggestive of shades of meaning that one supposes unlikely to be the artefacts of the conscious mind.

She is on a train. (Hardly surprising, since she sleeps at a station.) But she's on a part of a train which is unusual for being reserved for people travelling with small children, and it's fitted with collapsible seats better to accommodate them. Eventually the train reaches the terminus. Eleanor, who is with one child, sets about the task of getting herself, the child and the quite inordinately large amount of luggage she has with her, off the train. The women in the seats in front, who have a similar problem, though there are two of them, tell Eleanor not to worry, as the station master will presently come to help. When he arrives – the same large blustering blue uniformed person as Eleanor had studied yesterday at Capdenac station – he seems like a cross between a sailor and a policeman. He stands there with authority – partly, it must be admitted, due to his height, which is extended by Eleanor's own smallness and by the fact that everyone in this part of the train is still sitting down; yet mixed with the authority, the prestige of height and position, is a flamboyant, extravagant, wandering air. He takes Eleanor's child from her and holds it up in the air away from his body. The child is not one Eleanor has ever had, but is a striking assemblage of all of them, combining the wiriness of Eliza with the hair and eye colouring of George and the facial expressions of Heidi. It's naked except for a pair of navy blue knickers, the kind Eleanor had worn to school. The station master holds the child, who smiles with a slightly nervous anticipation at what may be to come, and then throws it in the air, eliciting convulsive chuckles. The action and the response are repeated. Encouraged to extend his repertoire of riotous acts, the station master then throws the child head over heels, but this time there is no answer of laughter. Eleanor takes the child from him and it places its arms around her leg, and she notes the expression on its face, a crumbling about-to-cry look, with a transformation of its previous pretty gold-haired appearance to a rather nasty menacing bright pink complexion of face and mood.

The station master is gone. Eleanor, the child and luggage are off the train, in the usual miraculous way of dreams. She feeds the child and changes it, using a towelling nappy. The child has no genitals; it is like a doll. Then she dresses it entirely in brown, and suddenly it assumes before her eyes exactly the personage of Eleanor Kendrick, aged about four, delicate, small, serious, pigtailed and above all *feminine*. It/she stands up and twirls its/her skirt around and laughs, such a silver, tinkling laugh, and seems happy. The child's hair and eyes and clothes are of exactly the same colour and texture as one another.

Eleanor wakes up startled by the image. It both discomforts and pleases her with its integration, with its transubstantiation from the liberalist persona of her own children to the firmly gendered one of her own childhood. She feels that the dream has accomplished something of profound psychic importance to her. It has pulled apart and then put together the bits of a jigsaw puzzle. Happy child, frightened child, Eleanor the child, My Novel, the child of its creator. Women, herself and two others, contending with too much luggage on the train. The pseudoliberating air of the authority figure taking children/My Novels away and giving them back apparently at will, dealing hands of luck or fate. Gender and its absence, the rough and the smooth, the raw and the cooked, the said and the unsaid, the hated blank page and the splendour of the written word. The power to transform; the power of the imagination forced by efforts of will and endurance to eject the structures which make transformation possible. Structure – marriage. David Jenkinson, her captor and her liberator. The past, and the future.

The sky is light again by the time the train to Capdenac is due. David Jenkinson walks out of the mist that hangs over the town anxiously seeking his wife. What has come over her? Her tempers are usually gone as quickly as they come – as, though he doesn't know it, this one was. But he had felt last night he had no other option but to leave her alone. To her own devices – he hopes no-one else's. And here she is, sitting with her purple notebook, a white cat asleep on the ground beside her. In the early morning haze, Eleanor's head appears encircled by a lemon diadem of light.

They go back on the train together. And then driving back to the farmhouse through the bright fields, the skins of cows and horses glinting like mirrors of a kind themselves, Eleanor says to David: 'There's a bit more of our conversation about the past we still need to have, isn't there, David?'

'Aren't you tired? Wouldn't you like to sleep first? Go to bed, we'll talk later.'

'No, make us some coffee, David, and we'll sit in the garden, the story has got to be finished. My night in Brive has helped me to think about it. I've come to a decision. I want to tell you about it.'

And so they sit. The steam from the bowls of coffee rises into the air and a light wind lifts it and carries it away from them.

Eleanor says: 'You mustn't demand to know everything, David. I don't, why should you? The basic story line is simple. I had to create my own life by writing. But I thought, and I have to say it was men who told me this, that I needed something other than my own life to do this with. The result was a certain amount of meandering. Escapades, illusions. But it wasn't the fading of love between us that caused the particular distance of which you complain. It was, rather, the fact that we came to disagree about the little matter of power. We both thought I had power. But we were wrong, for I had to find it in myself.'

'Ellie,' he says, returning her to the time before all this, in preparation for his next question, 'Ellie, why do you stay with me, why have you done? You've seemed so unhappy, to be struggling so, and I haven't been able to help you. From what you've said, there were other men who might have made it easier for you. Tell me why you stayed? You could have lived without me on your own, we could have made arrangements for the children, I wouldn't have been unreasonable. It's not what *I* would have wanted,' he adds quickly, 'but perhaps you would?'

Eleanor smiles. 'Yes, I thought I did. Sometimes. It's what happened to other women. It almost seemed the fashionable thing to do. But perhaps for that very reason to be resisted. The structures of our oppression are also those that permit us to be creative, David. By being permanently there to chafe against, they require us to dream up other options. You were my structure, David, you and the children. I used you for my own purposes. But only once I had understood how you were using me for yours. In any case,' she continues, 'a cynic would say one man's not very different from another. Passion always eventually slips over the horizon like the sun. Night falls. One is, within whatever relationship, ultimately horribly alone.'

'I have felt that,' he says quietly.

Not ignoring this, she goes on to say, 'And so there's no reason to change the arrangement. Except that its continuation depends upon your accepting *my* reality. Not me as you would like to see me, but me as I am. A person and a writer. Writing a woman's life. I published My Novel, you know, or rather you don't, because I decided to keep it a secret from you. Esther Gray wrote it in the end. She called it *Lost in Mirrors*, which is a phrase from a Christina Rossetti poem. It was quite well reviewed about six years ago. It sold 700 copies.

'By the way, the Eden Press didn't do the book, it wasn't feminist enough for them. I found another solution, though it wasn't easy. I've written another since. This one is in my name. This novel is my future which, like my past, you may find it difficult to accept. Your resistance, which was once the measure of my oppression, may henceforth be the sign of my liberation. I don't know what *you* will do, but I know what *I* will; and that is the beginning which I have managed to get to in the end.'

Extract from:

THE CAVES OF PADIRAC
BY ELEANOR JENKINSON

They pass the sign near the start of their journey home: Gouffres de Padirac 2.7 km.

Ben says: 'Would you like to go to the caves?'

Eva replies: 'Why not?'

While he queues for tickets, she looks at the souvenir shop, sheepskin waistcoats on a rail; coloured glass trinkets shelved above the usual crudely labelled pottery; on the wall some rather extraordinary clowns in gaudy satin costumes.

They take the first lift and stand about half-way down the round chasm that looks as though it's been gouged out of the earth by a giant drill. Someone looking for oil, perhaps? A covered staircase leads them to the bottom of the well. Eva thinks of peasants sheltering here through the Hundred Years War, turning natural disaster to social advantage. The metal edges of the stairs clatter, and water drips from the ragged limestone walls. She has to hold on to the rail to prevent herself from slipping. Ben, though, is striding ahead, black camera swinging against pale shirt, an image sharpened by the growing darkness around them, now they've left the top of the chasm behind and are following the trail to the underground river.

They pass a photo booth in which two women sit backs to each other reading magazines, and not even looking up as Eva and Ben pass squelchily by. It's colder now, and definitely damper. They come to some gates, an array of boats, and swarthy-looking guides in blue (the station master in a different guise?) Eva, whose knowledge of Greek mythology is vague, thinks briefly of the river Styx leading into Hades, and vaguely she remembers something about a deformed guard dog.

They're handed into a boat with about ten others. The guide's banter is too fast and too impregnated by the regional accent for Eva to understand much of it. After a few minutes, he takes his oar and the boat is pushed off. He rocks it at first (to nervous echoing shrieks from the women) across the uneven river. The water is clear, a lucid blue-green colour. Lights set at intervals on the walls are encrusted with little clumps of vegetation, the only in the whole dark dank dripping maze, spores of bracken carried by the water from its still unknown source, and fastening on to the walls beneath the lights because of the heat residing there, giving them the possibility of life. The limestone walls jut out and stretch upwards like old crenellated skin: pink and yellow and brown and green and carrying in their jagged surfaces all manner of symbols and images, like the Rorschach ink blot yielding up precisely those that live in the eye, or rather the psyche, of the beholder.

'Strange, isn't it?'

Eva nods, shivers.

'You should have brought your jersey.' Ben puts his arm round her.

They reach a landing. Another guide is to take them further. 'Vous comprenez français?' Perhaps he is able to judge from their demeanour that they don't. Ben shakes his head. 'Un peu,' says Eva. The guide's voice delivering, one supposes, more or less the same harangue for the thousandth time, occupies the sonorous spaces of the chasm. He directs them to look at various stalactites and stalagmites, monolithic obelisks which oddly remind Eva of the chocolate ice cream she ate the day before, the one that had nuts embedded in it, forming an uneven surface like this one. She reaches out and touches the wall; it's slimy and terribly cold. They are asked to look at a darkened copper bust of Monsieur Matel, lauded for his discovery of this profitable tourist attraction a century ago. The bust brings to mind for Eva, again incongruously, that of Henry Wood, founder of the London promenade concerts, in the dry symmetrical cavern of the London Royal Albert Hall.

Then the party is brought to a higher plateau containing a small azure lake, with a curved limestone dam across the middle. It sits like a jewel in this dark place, an opal ring on a giant's craggy knuckle. Eva looks into its blueness and sees nests of coins there resting clearly upon the bottom. After the others have left, she leans for a while on the rail that surrounds the lake. Ben comes and stands there with her. Together they look around and then up the cavern that blots out the sunlit world, the world of oak trees and blackberry plants and pigs, the squawking chickens, the wild cats, the silky cows with numbers in their ears; all the rich world up there, filled with colour and the shifting directions of winds, with birth and death, with crime and punishment and love and sin, is impressed on them anew by the resolutely reduced and calcified containment of this one. It's as if they're caught in the conflict between iron structure and florid experience; the one nullifying the senses, the other exhausting the same. But without the brilliant living world above, this one would excite no wonder, being merely all there is – a structure lacking the possibility of much contrasting experience. And, on the other hand, it takes this one, this elemental constriction of what can be both lived and imagined, to bring home the very creativity that attends our walking, tenuously like dinosaurs whose time has come, on the warmly shifting surface of the earth.

Fay Weldon

The Cloning of Joanna May

Joanna May thought herself unique, indivisible – until one day, to her hideous shock, she discovered herself to be five: though childless she was a mother; though an only child she was surrounded by sisters young enough to be her daughters – Jane, Julie, Gina and Alice, the clones of Joanna May.

How will they withstand the shock of first meeting? And what of the avenging Carl, Joanna's former husband and the clones' creator: will he take revenge for his wife's infidelity and destroy her sisters one by one?

In this astonishing novel, Fay Weldon weaves a web of paradox quite awesome in its cunning. Probing into the strange world of genetic engineering, *The Cloning of Joanna May* raises frightening questions about our identity as individuals – and provides some startling answers. Funny, serious, revolutionary, this is the work of a master storyteller at the height of her powers.

'Another totally original novel by the best woman writer in Britain'
Woman

'The deadly accuracy of Fay Weldon's psychology makes this bizarre tale a compulsive page-turner'
Daily Mail

'An outrageously funny novel!'
Daily Express

'A triumph of complex entertainment'
The Times

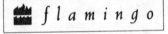

Barbara Gowdy

Falling Angels

'*Falling Angels* reads like *Little Women* on acid.' *Time Out*

Norman, Lou and Sandy are struggling through their teenage years in the shadow of a permanently drunk mother and an obsessive oaf of a father who is only bearable when occupied with the mistress of the moment. Worse, the family has a terrible secret – the drowning of a baby boy in Niagara Falls under suspicious circumstances . . .

'Set in a Canadian suburb in the sixties, this funny, touching novel is reminiscent of early Margaret Atwood, but with top-spin. Gowdy captures the mix of fear, shame and acceptance with which children regard the most lamentably deficient of parents.'
Independent on Sunday

'Barbara Gowdy has written a corker . . . the book is gripping, agonising and funny. The strength of Gowdy's narrative and the spare effectiveness of the writing make the outrageous world she describes seem coherent. This is a grim tale well told.'
Literary Review

'A chillingly effective, ultimately tragic piece of invective . . . compulsive.' *The Times*

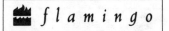

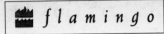

Flamingo is a quality imprint publishing both fiction and non-fiction. Below are some recent titles.

Fiction

- [ ] Life Force *Fay Weldon* £5.99
- [ ] The Kitchen God's Wife *Amy Tan* £4.99
- [ ] A Thousand Acres *Jane Smiley* £5.99
- [ ] The Quick *Agnes Rossi* £4.99
- [ ] Ordinary Decent Criminals *Lionel Shriver* £5.99
- [ ] The Cat Sanctuary *Patrick Gale* £5.99
- [ ] Dreaming in Cuban *Cristina Garcia* £5.99
- [ ] The Republic of Love *Carol Shields* £5.99
- [ ] True Believers *Joseph O'Connor* £5.99
- [ ] Bastard Out of Carolina *Dorothy Allison* £5.99

Non-fiction

- [ ] The Gates of Paradise *Alberto Manguel* £9.99
- [ ] Long Ago in France *M. F. K. Fisher* £5.99
- [ ] Ford Madox Ford *Alan Judd* £6.99
- [ ] C. S. Lewis *A. N. Wilson* £5.99
- [ ] Into the Badlands *John Williams* £5.99
- [ ] Dame Edna Everage *John Lahr* £5.99
- [ ] Number *John McLeish* £5.99
- [ ] What the Traveller Saw *Eric Newby* £5.99

You can buy Flamingo paperbacks at your local bookshop or newsagent. Or you can order them from Fontana Paperbacks, Cash Sales Department, Box 29, Douglas, Isle of Man. Please send a cheque, postal or money order (not currency) worth the purchase price plus 24p per book (maximum postage required is £3.00 for orders within the UK).

NAME (Block letters)_____

ADDRESS_____

_____

_____